Fruits of the Gods

Other books by William C. Tracy

The Dissolutionverse:
Novellas and Novelettes:
The Five Hive Plateau
Tuning the Symphony
Merchants and Maji
The Society of Two Houses
Journey to the Top of the Nether

The Dissolution Cycle:
The Seeds of Dissolution (Book I)
Facets of the Nether (Book II)
Fall of the Imperium (Book III)

Other Books:
Anthologies:
Distant Gardens
Farther Reefs
Lofty Mountains
The World of Juno

Science Fiction
The Biomass Conflux
Of Mycelium and Men
Down Among the Mushrooms
To a Fungus Unknown
The Spores of Wrath

Fruits of the Gods

William C. Tracy

Content Warning: This book contains depictions of abuse, rape, mutilation, torture, and incest.

Space Wizard Science Fantasy
Raleigh, NC
www.spacewizardsciencefantasy.com

Publisher's Note: This is a work of fiction. Names, characters, places, and incidents are a product of the author's imagination. Locales and public names are sometimes used for atmospheric purposes. Any resemblance to actual people, living or dead, or to businesses, companies, events, institutions, or locales is completely coincidental.

Cover art by MoorBooks
Editing by Heather Tracy
Book Layout © 2015 BookDesignTemplates.com

Fruits of the Gods/William C. Tracy.— 2nd ed.
ISBN 978-1-960247-15-5

Author's website: www.williamctracy.com

To all the fruit trees and bushes I've grown over the years, for keeping me happy and healthy with their produce. This is also dedicated to the deer who ate my entire garden one year. You'll find him in Chapter Four.

CONTENTS

CHAPTER ONE

Under the Malus Tree

The gods made mortals as their servants but freed them when they became troublesome to keep. When, against all odds, the mortals prospered on their own, the gods thought to bribe them with gifts to gain their worship.

It was the mistress's third miscarriage. Kisare knelt beside Bel, both sisters digging the hole to accept the little bundle. The solitary malus tree above them would take the grim fertilizer for its magical harvest.

She could feel the master's eyes on her back, and Shuma's, the guard captain. The mistress in her litter, two guards, and three slaves holding torches filled out their party. The flickering glow guttered over the little hole.

The ground resisted Kisare's chipped spade, and her breath misted as she dug. Moonlight shone on her and Bel through new leaves of the malus tree, standing alone between rows of grapevines. She brushed back long hair, bleached somewhere between silver and white, taking only a second to eye the bundle at the mistress's feet. The noble blood the child would add to the malus's harvest did nothing to offset Aricaba-Ata's frustration. The master doted on his new young wife.

Bel's spade landed with a hollow *thunk*. Curious, Kisare dug next to her sister. Something was buried here. She could see no detail in the dark but knew better than to alert their master. It might be valuable. Kisare saw Bel's eyes locked on the dark corner of the grave. Her spade stabbed underneath, prying the thing up.

Kisare knocked her sister's arm away, then dug at the opposite end of the hole. Bel took the hint and, frowning, plunged her spade in with too much force. It bounced off a rock, throwing dirt in Kisare's face. She spit out grit tasting of iron and fertilizer.

Aricaba-Ata, next to his grieving wife, pointed one finger. Torchlight highlighted the parted lock of red in his white-blond hair. Shuma stepped forward at the gesture. The freeman guard captain was a natural blond—no streaks of magical color in his tight curls. Nor was his hair bleached, as Kisare's and Bel's was.

"What was that sound? What did you hit?" Shuma towered above them, the biggest man Kisare had ever seen, rumored to be the disowned son of a neighboring noble.

"It was nothing," Kisare answered, thinking furiously.

"It was something, blond," he answered, unlimbering the whip at his side.

Kisare's back tensed, her shirt scratching against the raised scars. She had to answer. Mortal hands had buried something here. What could she get from offering up the prize? Not as much as keeping the knowledge from the master.

Bel was watching her face, spade poised. "It was a wood—"

"Root," Kisare finished for her. She pointed at her last mistake, rather than the treasure. It would give meaning to her hesitation.

"See," she said. "I nicked a root." It was visible as a glistening wet spot in the moonlight.

The master came forward and peered into the small hole. It wouldn't harm the tree in the long run, but it was still a slave's error.

Kisare kept the scream in as the whip drew a line of fire across her back.

"Keep digging," Aricaba-Ata said. "Do not injure my tree further. It is worth far more than your life, blond. I do not need added trouble." He stepped back to his wife in her litter, his umber skin blending into shadow even as her pale lily coloring reflected the moon.

Kisare put her head down and dug, her back burning. Cold air washed down her spine through a rent in her thin shirt, stark against the hot wetness. Bel followed, digging deliberately. Kisare shifted to a more comfortable position, hoping to keep her shirt from touching the bleeding wound. She didn't wish her sister to feel the whip but wondered if Aricaba-Ata would have punished Bel the same way. Her sister's gift for pruning godfruit trees excused her from all but the worst transgressions. Almost all. Kisare glanced down to Bel's incomplete left hand, resting by the grave.

They finished the hole well enough to please the master, keeping away from where the object was buried. They placed the small bundle by the guard's torchlight and filled in the dirt. Kisare took a moment to breathe—not long enough to bring Shuma's whip down, but enough to pull a ragged shawl around her shoulders. She sucked in a breath as it brushed her wounded back. Bel could look at it later. Kisare shivered into the shawl, the sweat from digging chilling her. The malus tree was past harvest, and the season was on the cusp of spring. It was the in-between time when even citrons were scarce, and everyone scrimped on godfruit.

Bel helped her to her feet, and Kisare and her sister placed the name-rail in the fence around the tree, under the master's watchful eye. There were five other name-rails already inscribed, two from the previous miscarriages, and one from Aricaba-Ata's first wife, Tiamai. The fever had taken her three years ago. Stumps of long-dead malus trees stood nearby, breaking rows of leafless grapevines with their own rotting name-rails. The grapes—normal fruit—were sold to market or made into wine.

"Girl," Aricaba-Ata directed her, "clean the birthing room before you sleep." He put an arm around his trembling wife in her litter and kissed her forehead. "Take her back," he instructed the three slaves holding the litter. The other guard left with them, leaving a torch with Shuma.

Aricaba-Ata came forward, taking a slightly wrinkled malus slice from his tunic. Kisare watched, slowly cleaning the dirt from her and Bel's spades. Aricaba-Ata pushed one red lock—magic gifted from the four gods of the seasons—behind his ear, as he popped the malus in his mouth. Kisare saw the shudder that took his body as he bit down, traces of lightning coursing down his arms, illuminating the darkness. She drank in the display.

Aricaba-Ata stepped close to the new-cut naming rail and lifted his right forefinger. Orange light bloomed in the night, a single pillar of flame. He drew a line of fire across the rail, charring in the name given his stillborn son: Aricaba-Tir. By the time he finished marking the rail, Kisare could see his jaw moving in the few last flickers of lightning as he tried to draw the last bit of juice from the godfruit's flesh. This far up in the mountains, away from the capital city of Karduniash, and near the ring of devastation the nobles called the Blasted Lands, her master would waste none of the magical juice.

Kisare spun at her sister's cough, but not fast enough. She had forgotten to clean the spade while watching.

Aricaba-Ata's backhanded swipe caught her across the face and she fell to the ground, her head bouncing. "Be on your way, girl," he huffed.

Kisare put a finger to her split lip and made the mistake of raising her eyes. This time the blow laid her flat out, darkening her vision.

She scrambled to her knees, slightly dizzy, but kept her gaze down. She probed a loose tooth with her tongue. What had he said? His blow had knocked the sense from her.

"I'll—I'll clean the birthing room now, by your leave, Master." Bel's hand gripped her sleeve, supporting. Aricaba-Ata's cold eyes were still on her, she knew.

"You can take Tashi's place filling the latrines tomorrow before your other duties, to remind you not to get ideas above your place."

She bolted, Bel close behind. The blood in her mouth and on her back were worth the secret buried under the malus tree.

* * *

"It was hollow," Bel said, holding the wheelbarrow near, but not too near, as Kisare shoveled dirt into a pit of still steaming filth.

Kisare had cleaned the birthing room and washed out all the bloody rags and sheets. The thought of the buried treasure kept her going, then, since it was already close to dawn, she had started on the latrines. If she didn't finish it early, one of the other slaves would complain, and Shuma would be out with his whip. She plotted how best to finish her chores, slotting each one in the fastest order. The larger moon—Shir-Gal, the great light—poked its head out from a stand of nearby trees.

"We have to go back," Bel said, then draped an arm across her nose and mouth.

Kisare threw another shovelful of dirt. She had a cloth wrapped around her head, but the stench still came through. "Keep your voice down," she hissed, then regretted having to breathe. She gagged but controlled her stomach. It almost made her forget about the open sore on her back and the loose tooth. When she could speak again, she said, "We'll get back there, but not now. What do you think they would do if they found us near the malus tree with no guards?" She flipped dirt into the hole, watching the yawning man eye them from the porch of the house. Slaves were almost never unobserved. The smell was getting fainter the more dirt she piled on the mess. The grass would be very green here.

"What if someone else finds it? There could be a slave's freedom in that box."

Kisare rolled her eyes at her sister's words. If Bel would only take a moment to plan, she would see how unlikely it was anyone would go back to the grave. But Bel got away with more than Kisare ever could. Her sister's cheeks were pleasantly round compared to Kisare's thin face, her waist smaller, her complexion a nice, dark chestnut. Kisare's skin was the color of sand and burned in the height of summer. It had freckled her skin. No wonder everyone thought Bel was the younger of them, though she was a good five years older.

The guard was nearly asleep, but it still paid to be careful. Even other slaves could not be trusted. "No purpose wondering what it might be until we get there," Kisare told her. "Soon, we'll go back to the grape arbor under night's cover and see what's buried under the tree. You've waited twenty-three years for something like this. You can wait a little longer."

"We could imagine," Bel mused, absently stroking her long hair. Like all slaves, their hair was bleached once a week, whether or not they were naturally blond. Even if a slave had only a few strands of magical color, it was death to eat godfruit.

"Imagine what? Treasure? As like to find a wagon waiting to carry you off to Karduniash." Kisare snorted. "You wish for that. I'll take a day without work for each one that comes true. Go get me another barrow of dirt. We've still got to repair the toolshed, mend the shears, and till the fields today."

Bel turned the barrow, then stopped. "Promise me we will dig that box up," she said.

Kisare watched her sister. She was as serious as Kisare had seen her; her face almost pained. "Do you think it could really help us?"

Bel gestured to Kisare's split lip. "Anything is better than this."

CHAPTER TWO

A View of the House

Dumzi, the trickster, put his guile in the morus.
Our minds gain unearthly powers to serve us.
Geshtna's passions are always intense.
Her prunae increase all five of the senses.
Kigal can call all the elements to her.
The malae juice gives them out to the user.
Enta, old man winter, hard as leather.
His citrons make our bodies fitter, stronger, deadlier.
Children's Rhyme

"Tree girl!"

Belili's clippers slipped, cutting the branch just below a promising bud. She felt her lips purse but smoothed her face before turning.

"Yes, Tashi?" She thought the edge was out of her voice, but Tashi grinned all the same.

"The mistress needs more soaking salts for her feet. And the chamber pot is full."

"Isn't that your job?" Kisa stood from weeding another peach tree. Belili would have smiled at her sister's fierce protectiveness at another time.

"I do what that mistress tells me," Tashi said, shrugging her thin shoulders. "I don't question my betters. Might wanna get to it—the mistress has been pissing a storm since she dropped her babe all cold. Probably drinking too much."

Tashi sauntered away, and Belili watched her shirt's fabric, tight against her hips in all the right places. Tashi's work had been hers, when the old mistress was around. Belili *had* cleaned the chamber pot. Not that the old mistress smelled like roses, but Belili didn't foist it off on others, and she certainly didn't use her flimsy clothes to attract attention.

Tashi turned, and Belili barely averted her eyes before she was caught staring. "Oh yeah. Your sister can start on the bed linens. I have an important errand to run for the mistress."

"I *know* that's her job," Kisa muttered, "because it used to be *my* job. I'm supposed to be cutting firewood."

"Look." Belili broke into her sister's muttering.

"What?"

Belili pointed at a bulge under Tashi's linen shirt, visible as she turned away.

"I don't see anything."

"She has something under her shirt," Belili said. It was obvious if you paid attention. "Errand for her mistress indeed. I bet she's stolen something from the house again. She has her arm cocked to hide it."

"We can't do anything about it. Come on," Kisa said. "Don't want to keep the swamp princess waiting."

One of the other slaves said they ate frogs where Ubala, the new mistress, came from. No wonder her chamber pot smelled so bad.

"There you are," came the mistress's high soprano as they entered her rooms. She was wedged into a chair, pillows mounded around her and a glass of wine close at hand. Her normally pasty face was red and puffy, her lock of dark, magical brown in otherwise white-blond hair pinned to prominence. She had a book nearby, and Belili burned to see what it was. The old mistress used to read to them exciting stories of lands far away and long ago.

"Tashi said you two were lazy, but I tried to give you the benefit of doubt. I see she was right." Ubala made a shooing motion. "Get on with your duties. I must not strain my nerves. Neither of you have lost a child, after all."

Belili kept her face neutral. It had been two weeks, but the mistress was still incapacitated from her miscarriage. A slave in that condition was expected to work the fields the next day. This woman had no excuse.

Kisa pulled Belili back. She had stepped closer to Ubala's chair. Her thoughts went to the thing buried under the malus tree again. Was it valuable? She had never owned anything. The master of Aricaba orchard even lent her clothes.

"We'll be done in no time, Mistress," Kisa said beside her, still pulling. Belili relaxed and followed. The mistress snorted, muttering something under her breath.

They worked quickly, the jobs still familiar after three years outside the house. Kisa was gathering the last of the linens when she froze, her pale freckled face tight. Belili, attuned to her, stiffened. She glanced a question.

Her sister raised one finger to her lips, pointing with the other hand to the sitting room, where Ubala had pried herself out of the chair and was puttering around. Her voice was just audible.

"I'll be a fruit weevil if I can remember where I put it. I know I had a slice or two on this table. Maybe in the other—"

Belili scooped up the dirty chamber pot and walked out of the house with Kisa, soiled linens under her arm, moving no faster than they needed.

"She was looking for malus slices," Kisa hissed at her outside, and Belili nodded back.

"I know what she was doing. No wonder Tashi gave us those jobs." Her hands shook, and she put the pot down before she spilled it.

"What do you think Tashi's doing with them?" Kisa asked.

"Selling them or trading for a big favor, I guess," Belili told her. "She wouldn't dare eat them. We need to put distance between us and the house."

Kisa handed her the balled-up laundry and picked up the chamber pot. "I'll throw this out if you take the linens to the laundry. They'll get done soon enough for Mistress Swamp Princess."

Belili frowned, looking away from her sister. The master's nearest neighbor and cousin, Enti-Ilzi, was heading right for her, a big smile on his face. When had he arrived? She tried to listen, to be aware when other nobles came to the orchard. Especially him. She'd been distracted by Tashi's deception.

Ilzi's large lock of jet black was pushed back over his ear, his shoulder-length blond hair greasy as usual, framing his copper-skinned face. Kisa noticed him moments after Belili, and stepped half in front of her—a habit she had picked up after they lost the protection of the house and old Mistress Tiamai. Though Kisa could dissuade other slaves, and even the guards, nobles were to be obeyed at all times.

"We can trade," Kisa said, and handed off the chamber pot. Belili held it like a shield.

As Ilzi got closer, the smile on his broad face grew strained, eyes squinting at the smell. But he kept coming. Belili stood motionless, Kisa beside her. Ilzi had a new slave—a strong-looking woman who was hunched behind him, wringing her hands. Belili's heart went out to her.

She was pretty, startlingly so, though perhaps her nose was a little too big. Still, she would be striking if she was properly washed. Ilzi was never good at caring for his slaves. He ran through them at an alarming rate.

"Good afternoon, my dear," Ilzi said, his voice condescending as usual. "That is a powerfully unpleasant task to give to a beauty such as you." He reached into the little pouch at his side that most nobles carried. He drew out a small malus slice and raised it to his lips. "Let me help you." He bit down, then shivered as little bands of lightning wrapped his arms.

As he did so, Belili felt the liquid in the chamber pot swirl and move, as if it wanted to escape. The metal handle grew cold in her hand, and she looked down to see the filth inside frozen, the smell dissipating. Her gaze rose to Ilzi's lock of black in his otherwise blond hair.

"Much better. Now, give that to your little sister. I am to meet with Ata, and I wish to have an attractive face around." He gestured backward, turning his high cheekbones to catch the afternoon light. "This new girl is not yet performing her duties adequately. Perhaps you can teach her your superior skills."

Belili hesitated only a moment before giving the chamber pot to Kisa, who had the linens bundled under one arm, her eyes wide. Belili only gave her a slight nod. She didn't dare even look at the new slave. Ilzi was as jealous as he was vain. Was it strange to envy her younger sister's plain looks and hard manner? Kisa's dedication to whatever task was set in front of her had grooved lines into her face—a barrier to advances the other female slaves dealt with.

Belili walked stiffly, aware of Enti-Ilzi's hand guiding her around the orchard's main house. They found Aricaba-Ata near the citron tree, one leg propped up on a stump of an old oak. A switch dangled from one hand. His swarthy face was calm, relaxed, as he observed an older blond tied naked over a log, barely conscious and shivering.

"What has this one done?" Enti-Ilzi said in greeting. Mulagun's bleached hair had been chopped off short. Belili and Kisa both warned him against his yearly escape attempt, but their warnings had done nothing, as usual. The older man was one of the strongest slaves in the orchard, kind to Kisa and Belili where some others were not.

Aricaba-Ata sighed, heaving himself to his feet. "I am surrounded by those trying to undermine me, my friend." His eyes passed over Belili, but he said nothing about Ilzi keeping her from her work. "This one tries to run away every year, though he knows I cannot afford a new slave with such strength as his." He walked around the bound man, tapping him with the switch every so often as he spoke. "The trouble is, my hounds take until evening to track him down, wasting me a day of his production." The master brought the switch down on Mulagun's raw and bleeding back, and the slave grunted. Belili winced inwardly but kept the emotion inside.

"You and I are destined for greater things, Cousin," the master continued. Ilzi nodded sagely at this. "I sought to make a good match with Tiamai, and we were happy enough, but her family never fully paid her dowry. Then when she died—"

"You will get the recognition you deserve one day, Ata," Ilzi broke in. "Surely Ubala brings more contacts from near the capital. She can introduce you to other nobles down south."

"From one originating so close to Karduniash, one would think she would know better society," the master answered. "I was promised status, yes, and I was also promised children." Now Aricaba-Ata glanced at Belili, frowning. "She can tell you how well Ubala is performing on that front." Belili shrank in on herself, trying to stay far out of the noble's conversation.

"I heard of the recent sadness," Ilzi said. "My condolences. But next time—"

The master cut his cousin off with a slap of the switch on Mulagun's back. The slave groaned. "What next time? Tiamai was childless, and now Ubala has had three miscarriages. I blame our many times removed ancestor, for deciding to make his fortune so near the Blasted Lands. Chasing after some ancient legend of power." He snorted. "Cursed lands, more likely. Your godfruit harvest is as limited as mine, save for our malae. At least they, of the four, grow well at these altitudes."

Ilzi rubbed his neck with his free hand. His other, still on Belili's shoulder, tightened. "I get by, Ata," he protested.

"Yes, and you have no wife, no children, only ten blonds, and two guards." The master tilted his head to look behind Ilzi at the new slave. "And this new plaything. Did you wear out the last one already?" He sliced the air with the switch. "No matter. Look at the mouths I have to feed. Yet some decide to run away, rather than thank me for the sustenance I provide them." He brought the switch down with a *smack* and Belili jumped despite herself.

"It's not entirely my fault I'm not married," Ilzi said, heat rising in his voice. He let Belili go to reach back and grab the new slave by one arm, jerking her forward. "She will not even—"

Aricaba-Ata cut him off. "No. I will not discuss this again. Look to the capital if you wish a real wife. Stop chasing fruit filled with worms. Karduniash has plenty of untethered noblewomen, though it seems many are but spoiled adolescents."

"They will not even look at me," Ilzi whined. "What must a man do to be appreciated? If you would only let your—"

But Aricaba-Ata stopped him again before he had even finished his motion toward Belili. "That is not a topic I will entertain. You know this."

Ilzi frowned, and the woman tensed as his fingers made white marks in her arm, her face tightening in pain. Belili rubbed the stump of her little finger nervously. She would do almost anything to get away from this conversation and take the poor woman with her. She twitched as the master addressed her directly.

"Girl, pour that over his back." He pointed at a bucket with his switch. Belili went to it, glad to be out of Ilzi's reach, then drew back, nose wrinkling at the smell of vinegar.

"Come now, I have little time to waste." Aricaba-Ata tapped the switch into his left hand, and Belili's eyes followed it as it rose and fell. She hefted the bucket—rice vinegar from the year before.

"All over now, quickly."

The stream of pale liquid splashed across Mulagun's back, and he twisted in his bonds, screaming. Belili turned away, but met Ilzi's new slave's eyes. They were as haunted as Belili felt, and she looked away again, only to see her sister approaching from the laundry house. Kisa recoiled, and a wave of equal parts embarrassment and anger washed through Belili.

Aricaba-Ata lazily dragged the switch across Mulagun's back as the bound slave's scream died. "You know I can't afford another blond right now."

"Yes, sir." Belili could barely hear the man's hoarse mumble.

"You think you can steal from me by running away."

"No, sir."

"You will work at one and a fourth quota for every task this year. If you make enough for me to buy another slave, I will bring you down to quota next year. If you do not..." The master tapped his switch again on the slave's glistening back. Mulagun convulsed and sobbed. "Might be I can save money in meat for my hounds."

He swung around to Belili, who stood still, refusing to step away from him. She braced for a blow.

The master didn't bother. "Cut him down. He has work today. As do you and your sister." His glance took in Kisa, Ilzi, and his slave. "Leave them be, Ilzi. Surely you have enough to do with your new play toy."

Kisa came to Belili's side, a knife in one hand, and severed the ropes cutting into the bound slave's wrists and ankles. Belili tried to dab the wounds on his back with a cloth, but Mulagun moaned with every touch.

"If I had stood up to him, I'd have another loose tooth," Kisa muttered to her. "Lucky the master needs his prize pruner in working order." She turned back to Mulagun. "Up now. Get his pants, over there." Belili obeyed, silent. Kisa was right. She got away with more insubordination than the rest of the slaves. She wondered if one day Aricaba-Ata would tire of it.

Together they got Mulagun up and moving, just in time to see the mistress come out of the orchard house, rushing toward Aricaba-Ata. She was pointing to Belili and Kisa.

"She's figured it out," Belili said. Indeed, Aricaba-Ata was striding over, wide and swarthy. His coat tails floated behind him. Kisa took a small step back.

"Come with me," the master told them. "My wife has brought a troubling matter to my attention. She has misplaced three slices of malus. She implicated you two, but I wish to be fair." His eyes were hard on them. "I know your characters, after all."

Belili and her sister followed the master, Ilzi and Ubala behind them. Belili itched to turn and run, but the guards would bring her down in a moment.

Shuma appeared at the master's signal, then departed toward the fields.

By the time they got to the central yard, where Aricaba-Ata usually gave his speeches, the guards were bringing the rest of the blonds in from working. The freemen carried manacles with them and were armed.

When they were all gathered, the master repeated what he had told Belili and Kisa, hands on hips. There were gasps from the blonds, and even one from a guard in back. They all knew the penalty for stealing godfruit. Even the master's claim he didn't have enough to purchase new slaves wouldn't stop him. Some rules were always enforced.

"She has brought her suspicions to my awareness." His eyes glanced across Belili, flicked down to her left hand. Nearly always enforced. She tensed but kept her face calm. Kisa's mouth was pinched like a month-gone citron, shriveled and puckered.

"Search them," Aricaba-Ata commanded. "I want those malus slices found."

* * *

When all the slaves had put their clothes back on, the godfruit was still missing. The afternoon was getting dark, and the master paced in front of his gathered slaves, freemen, wife, and Ilzi. His new slave crouched behind him, and Belili wished she could comfort her—or maybe be comforted by her, depending on how this went.

"You have already lost me this afternoon's production. To bring this matter to a conclusion, and drive home the situation, none of you will eat tonight. You will be chained together so you may discuss the matter among yourselves, confined to your cabins." Aricaba-Ata's eyes raked over his slaves. "I do not wish to execute the wrong blond. By tomorrow morning, I want the perpetrator's name, or my men will flay the information from you." He looked over his assembled workers. "The first one who does give me the correct information gets a day off." Ata nodded to Shuma and the guards. "Lock them in."

The manacles, connected to one another by lengths of iron chain, clanked and rang as the guards fastened them to wrists and feet. They put males in one group and females in another.

"He was supposed to kill you and be done with it, tree girl," Tashi hissed, coming close. Belili was afraid that might still be the case. Ubala could convince her husband, given enough time. She loved Tashi far too much and the vicious blond had a smooth tongue.

"You're dead," Kisa hissed back. "We know you did it. Bel's the master's best pruner. He won't sacrifice her even for his new mistress's whims."

"What about you?" Tashi asked. "I don't see him giving you any long looks. I don't think he's nearly as hard for you as for your pretty little sister here."

Kisa's face fell. Belili knew she should stay quiet but couldn't. "I'm the big sister, and the master knows I won't do any pruning without Kisa. Once morning comes, and he's calmed down, we'll tell him everything. It'll be nice to have a day off." She glanced at the guard coming up behind Tashi.

"Not if I tell him firs—" Tashi halted as one of the guards pulled her backward.

"In line. Hold your hands out." Belili caught a glimpse of Tashi's pinched face as the guard threaded a chain through her manacles. They connected Tashi to the other women, then Kisa next, a head taller than both of them, then Belili on the end. They were herded into the slaves' houses, a stout oak plank locked across the brick entrance to keep them in. There would be no rest this night.

Their beds in the female slaves' house were not ever comfortable, but now it was impossible for anyone to take a seat. The chains between the manacles were too short, so they ended up cramped together in the middle of the floor.

There were only nine women. The Aricaba orchard was not large, especially compared to the holdings Belili had heard of down south, near the capital, Karduniash. In a way, it was fortunate that Aricaba-Ata had fewer resources. A larger orchard owner might have killed a few slaves at random to incite the others to talk.

"Who was it?" called Anu, the eldest, from the other side of their chained circle. She had been the midwife at both Kisa and Belili's births but could pull in a bigger harvest than any other slave, male or female. Slaves normally didn't live to her age, and Anu wasn't known for being soft.

She waited, and when no one spoke, she snorted, eyebrows drawing down over her wide face. "Someone's going to die before tomorrow's out, and it ain't gonna be me."

Finally, Kisa tried to put her hands on her hips, but the manacles stopped her with a clank. "Tashi was in the house with the mistress. She took them."

Anu nodded. "The same house you got kicked out of? I'm watching her, but you're not so holy as you think."

"I was out of the house when it happened," Tashi said, and pointed. "The mistress called those two in to carry out her dirty linen and chamber pot. They probably did it then."

Now Anu turned her glare to Belili and Kisa.

"How would you know that's when it happened, unless you knew when the malus slices were taken?" Kisa leaned toward Tashi, ankle manacle clanking. "We saw you."

"I've been working in the house for three years. Why would I risk my life now?" Tashi shot back. She turned one rounded hip, showing off the finer clothes she wore. There was muttering from the other women. None of them liked Tashi, but Belili and her sister weren't popular either, for having held the same position.

"As Anu said, it's about not getting caught," Belili said. "For all we know, you've been stealing godfruit for years."

"Yes, at least we didn't get kicked out over getting caught like a boll weevil in a nut," Kisa said, and opened her mouth for more, but Anu threw both hands as wide as they could go, making her chains ring and clash together. The muttering silenced.

"Enough. I ain't knowin' which of you three did it, but it was one of you."

"Then let me settle it," Tashi said, pulling a little set of bent metal rods from somewhere.

Belili looked over the woman's clothing. "How did you get those past the search?"

"You learn tricks, coming from a real city, tree girl," Tashi said. She shuffled closer, drawing Kisa along. Tashi reached for the lock on the end of the chain tying them together. Belili thought about resisting, then looked to Anu to see what she would do.

Anu shrugged, watching Tashi pick the lock, but she also gestured to the slave women, who shuffled closer to the door, pulling the chain tight.

"You're just going to let the three of us go free?" Kisa said. The lock made a *snick* and Tashi exclaimed in triumph.

Belili shook her manacles, threading the chain through the constraints on her wrists and ankles. Kisa followed, though Tashi was waving at her to go faster. Belili watched the other women near the door.

"Now what's your plan, little one?" Anu asked. In answer, Tashi crossed to the oak plank chained across the doorway. She reached an arm through the crack between the plank and the brick doorway to grab the lock hanging outside.

"With this unlocked, I'll be free to sneak away. I told you I'd handle this. You slaves can figure out who you're going to give up for a hanging." The other lock clicked open. Tashi was surprisingly adept at lockpicking. She stood, gesturing with her tools. "I can...heh...open doors for all of you. Just say it was one of them and get your day off." She threw a finger out toward Belili.

Anu chuckled, an unpleasant sound. "Tempting, but things work different out in the country, city girl." Another blond produced a shorter chain. "Thank you, Muna." Two more removed Tashi's hands from the plank, ignoring her shrieks.

"What is this?" the girl cried. "Let me go! I'll tell the mistress and she'll have you all whipped."

The other women brought Tashi—holding her arms so she couldn't scratch them—close to Belili and her sister. Kisa was pale and silent. Tashi continued to wail and shriek.

Belili let Anu insert the chain back through her manacles. "Nothing personal, girl," Anu said over Tashi's insults. "I'm sure Tashi is guilty of some idiocy, and that ain't good for long life in a blond. But I also don't want the mistress stringing us up over turning in her favorite little wench. Better to look like a fight between enemies." She looked in Belili's eyes. "Try to bring the slices back. It'll be better for all of us."

Kisa moved away, but the other women surrounded them, and Belili's breathing quickened.

Anu threaded the chain first through Belili's manacles, then Kisa's, and then Tashi's. There was a smack of flesh against flesh, and Anu grunted, then caught Tashi's arms.

"None of that," Anu said. "I'll be taking those picks of yours. They'll be mighty useful when one of us learns them."

There was a bleat of indignation from Tashi, and Belili watched her shaking sister, willing Kisa not to do anything. She had less practice than Belili.

Anu pushed them outside and pulled the oak plank back in place behind them.

Belili looked at Tashi, whose eyes were wild. Kisa shivered in the cold.

"Who's first?" Tashi asked, her feet set wide.

Kisa moved toward Tashi, but Belili held her back. "She's baiting you."

"I know she is," Kisa growled. "So I'm going to beat her senseless." She pulled free of Belili's grasp and lurched forward, but Belili saw the knife glint in the moonlight. It sliced out, and only a last-second twist saved her sister's throat from getting cut. The knife slashed across her shoulder instead and Kisa fell back with a cry.

Tashi moved back as far as the chains allowed, and Belili followed, forcing Kisa along with her. Her sister's hand was over her left shoulder, blood seeping through her fingers, and she kept her eyes on the shine of the knife.

Tashi walked backward, eyes flicking between Belili and her sister. They were near the slave's toolshed, which was filled with broken and worn-out equipment. "You two never got used to being rejected by the new mistress, did you? Saplings."

"How did you hide the slices from the guards?" Belili asked, more to keep the woman talking. She used the time to judge distances.

"Flash the boys a little tit and you can get away with almost anything. Let them feel you up and they won't even notice your clothes have hidden pockets. When I sell these slices, I'll almost have enough to buy my freedom. You two aren't going to stop me."

She darted forward in one lithe movement, knife flashing. Belili pushed her sister out of the way and sharp pain bit into in her thigh. She growled and twisted, clapping a hand over the knife wound. Her fingers hit the hilt of the knife, still embedded. She shuddered, jerked it out, and flung it away.

Tashi's hands followed the arc of the weapon, but Kisa tugged the chain and Tashi stumbled forward, her fingertips just missing it. Something white, glistening in the moonlight, tumbled out of one linen sleeve.

"Malus," Belili said shortly, and dove for the evidence that would prove them right. Tashi and Kisa dropped at the same time, hands and heads banging together as they reached. Something gouged at Belili's breast, and she shoved and reached blindly. A smooth and slippery surface tingled with magic against her fingertips. Kisa growled beside her, whether in pain or anger or both, she couldn't tell.

A long fingernail raked her cheek, but Belili kept reaching. It was just...out...of...

She grasped and straightened away from the nails and clinging hands. Tashi and Kisa came up with her, Tashi with murder in her eyes.

Belili looked at the magical slice of godfruit in her hand, then up to Tashi. The wet surface tingled against her fingers like a tiny lightning strike. The instant stretched out to a short infinity. Back to the slice, then back to Tashi.

Belili popped it into her mouth.

"No!" came from both women, but Belili bit down, teeth crunching against bits of dirt.

Juice like liquid fire filled her mouth, igniting her tongue. Her head jerked back. She had never tasted a malus before. It was almost certain death to taste the source of the nobles' power. She didn't care.

It tasted wonderful.

"What have you done?" Tashi wailed. "They'll kill me for sure!" Kisa was gaping at her.

Belili couldn't talk, holding the juice in her mouth. That was what the nobles did. Magic flowed through her, but she hadn't thought this through.

She stepped close to Tashi, pushed her to the ground, and followed her down. As Tashi's head hit, dirt climbed toward her face. Belili watched little rocks bounce uphill, surprised at first, but then certain in her power. The magic was not what she expected. Loose dry grit filled Tashi's nostrils, and Tashi breathed in reflexively, choking.

The juice in Belili's mouth was losing its flavor, breaking down. She concentrated, and the dirt moved faster, filling Tashi's mouth, nose, ears, and eyes. Tashi tried to scream, but the sound was smothered to a tiny wail.

Belili was surprised to see her knuckles white against the girl's shoulders. The dirt was moving slower now, weighing Tashi's head down even as she choked. Her struggles weakened.

Belili's teeth ground against the pulp of the godfruit, prying the last bits of magical juice from it. The dirt was slowing, making a pile on Tashi's head, her features nearly hidden. Belili raised her hands, watching the chain between them. She could *see* little bits making up the iron and told it to move. It did, flowing away from the center of a link.

With a short yell, Belili pulled the weakened chain apart, the metal shrieking in protest and snapping.

She swallowed. Was there more juice? She chewed, and the barest dribble of juice touched her tongue. Not enough to tell the dirt to move. She swallowed again.

Kisa's voice, close behind, intruded on her, sounding hoarse. Had she been yelling?

"She's dead, Bel. She's dead. Get up. You have to get up."

Belili rose to her feet, looking down at Tashi. Ata wouldn't be happy. She scraped her left thumb across the stump of her little finger. Not again.

CHAPTER THREE

Flight

Dumzi, the young god of spring, was the first to bless the trees, choosing a morus to carry his power of the mind. Where before there had been the white and red mulberries, now they wilted and died, leaving only the magical, dark purple one to propagate.

"You killed her," Kisare whispered. She shivered in the sudden cold. Bel seemed in a daze, and Kisare reached out to get her attention. Pain spiked through the slash on her shoulder, but she ignored it.

Bel didn't answer but pulled at Tashi's shirt sleeve. Two more malus slices rolled out. She reached for them, but Kisare caught her hand.

"No. Not these too. You can't eat them." Kisare refused to think about what that meant. Not yet. Her eyes went to Bel's white-blond hair. Her sister looked back, almost uncomprehending, then shook her head.

"No. You're right." Bel's voice was harsh, though it had been Kisare who had yelled. "What do we do?"

Kisare picked up the other two malus slices, shivering a little as the magical godfruit tingled against her skin, then laid them on Tashi's chest, not looking at the mound of dirt covering her head. The slices were still wet, though Ubala had cut them hours ago. Bel had *eaten* one. Used magic. Her head spun.

"We must tell Anu what happened. We won after she attacked us. Say Tashi only had two slices. She'll believe us. We don't say anything about the one you..."

Bel watched her. "Why?"

"Why what?"

"Why go back?"

Kisare tsked. "What are you talking about?"

"Killing another slave, especially the swamp princess's pretty? Do you want to be hung up by your feet and flogged? Maybe the master will pour vinegar on you like he—I—did to Mulagun."

Kisare shivered at the memory. "We did what he wanted," she answered in a small voice. "He wanted to find the one who stole the malus slices." She knew the flaw in her logic.

"Aricaba-Ata won't like us taking matters into our own hands, despite what Anu says," Bel told her. "We might be faking it. Tricky blonds."

Kisare's mouth went dry. Punishment on punishment, any way they turned.

"Let's run away. Right now."

Kisare laughed, a gasp in the cold, dark night. "We're still chained to..." She inhaled as Bel held up the dangling ends of her chain. "How did you? No, never mind." Kisare shook her head. She needed to think, to plan.

"Even if we leave now, and I'm not saying we should, the master will have his dogs after us faster than you can think." The idea of being free pulled at her—how could it not—but so much could go wrong. If they stayed, they would be punished, but they would survive. Tashi was the one who stole, and they could prove it, or at least Tashi couldn't talk back anymore. Run and the master would be much less lenient.

"What if we have money to pay for our freedom?" Bel said. Kisare's head snapped up from where she studied the ground.

"Tashi's savings?"

Bel scoffed. "We'll never find that in time. We can take the malus slices—"

Kisare cut her off. "No. They'll try even harder to catch us if we take the slices."

Bel shook her head. "Fine. Then we know about another treasure: under the malus tree."

Kisare had almost forgotten about that. It seemed so long ago. "That box could hold nothing," she hissed, flicking another glance to the slaves' house.

"Or be full of jewels," Bel answered, just as quiet. "More than Tashi could save up in a lifetime. Why else bury it underneath a malus tree?" She paused, brow furrowed. "If you won't let me take the slices, let's make a wager. We go to the grape arbor. We still have time before Anu and the others come looking. If there's nothing valuable in the box, I'll come back with you and tell Anu all about it. We'll get our punishment and if we live, I'll promise to follow your lead forevermore."

Kisare snorted. That was hardly even a promise. "And elseways? What if there is treasure or coin in there?"

"Elseways," Bel repeated, then paused again. Her eyes were worried, catching stray light in the darkness. "Elseways we leave tonight and never look back."

Kisare shook her head. "We're going to wind up dead."

One murdered slave, two stolen malus slices, a broken chain, and suspicions of the mistress. Slaves died for much less. She threaded one end of the chain from her manacles. "Help me carry her into the toolshed. Then if the others come out, they'll think we moved farther off to argue."

"You mean, to kill each other," Bel muttered.

Kisare winced. There were no torches or lanterns wandering the property. The guards usually drew lots for nighttime sentry duty over the slaves, but they were probably slacking off, as the master had all their charges chained up.

They hefted Tashi's slight body, Kisare taking the legs. The dirt trailed off as they lifted her, and Kisare tried not to stare at the blank dusty eyes, the lips, open and caked with soil. They put her in a corner with the oldest tools, covering Tashi with bags of manure, and laying broken planks on top. Hopefully it would be a while before she was found. Kisare placed the two slices on a workbench. When they found Tashi, they would find the malus slices, know it was an accident.

"Come on," Bel hissed. "Anu won't wait forever."

"Hold a moment." Kisare rooted through the bits and pieces piled in the shed. The master and the guards threw broken things in here, letting the slaves make their own tools. When had she seen the old lantern? She had left it at the time, intending to come back later in the year when the days grew shorter.

"Aha." Kisare bent, pushing aside the split shaft of a wagon. The lantern was underneath, one metal side bent in so far it would be hard to carry. She sniffed, catching the faint aroma of oil. There was barely enough left to light the path to the grape arbor.

"Flint and steel, over by the door." Kisare heard Bel scuffle while she pried the lantern door open. She found an empty feed sack and folded it over itself, judging the fabric's thickness.

Bel handed her the flint and steel. "What's that for?"

"Hiding the light. Now we're ready," Kisare told her sister. "If I let you plan anything, we'd be caught before we started." She took an old, rusted spade as they left the tool shed.

They moved from shadow to shadow, Bel limping from the wounds in her thigh. Her coloring blended better with the shadows, though there was no mistaking her bleached hair. Kisare was sure her pasty skin reflected every bit of light. Her shoulder was already stiffening up in the cold, but that also meant it bled less. She'd had worse and still worked the fields. They watched for guards, but no lights appeared. Kisare kept the lantern folded in the feed bag with the flint and steel, so neither of them would clink together. They walked in silence, and Kisare offered thanks to Enta and Dumzi, gods of winter and spring, for the nearly dark moons that hid them. As they passed nearest the orchard house, she could hear music and laughter. Most of the guards were warm in the house, and if they were lucky, the ones supposed to be outside were napping. Kisare pulled her arms in close, trying to keep heat in her thin shirt.

They stole through the rows of grapes, buds just appearing on thin stalks. In the near darkness, Kisare heard Bel snap off an offending twig.

"No time for your pruning," Kisare muttered to her, but her sister only shrugged. Bel's vines and trees were works of art. The master was lucky he had her to keep his trees fruiting at maximum capacity.

Soon they were at the malus tree near the center of the grapes, passing a stump with its rotting naming rails. She thought of Tashi, still in the shadow of a barn. The girl would soon be laid under this malus tree, or maybe the citron. It hadn't had a new body in a year, though the malus was the master's favorite. If they weren't careful, she and her sister would be fertilizer too.

Kisare struck the flint and steel together, trying to direct the sparks toward the little pool of oil left in the lantern. On the eighth strike, one caught, and light flared.

"Quick, wrap it around the lantern." She held it in the air and Bel wrapped the fabric around it. The light died away to the barest glow, just enough to work by.

She leaned close and sniffed the newest rail. There was still a hint of char, even two weeks later. Both sisters went to their knees, Bel grunting in pain, Kisare doing most of the work with her spade. She was used to working while injured, but it would have taken twice as long if the dirt had not been disturbed.

They made as little sound as possible during their grim work, and soon uncovered the little bundle. Bel lifted it and set it to the side by the pile of dirt. The worms had started their task, and Kisare hoped Kigal would not curse them for desecrating the grave. They were in enough trouble already.

"It's here," Bel whispered. Kisare forced through the hard earth with the spade. Even if the air was warmer than last time they were here, the ground still held winter's chill.

Kisare knocked a knuckle on the box and heard a hollow sound. "We need to work around this way," she said, carefully excavating under a root.

Bel looked up, and Kisare froze, listening. "Someone?" she mouthed. Her sister didn't answer, eyes scanning over her head. Kisare scooted the lantern between her knees, hiding the light with her body.

Finally, Bel shook her head. "Must have been an animal." Kisare tried to keep away images of Tashi's dead eyes staring at them. She straightened, moved the lantern back, and looked over her shoulder. There was no light nearby, but she could see far off lanterns, near the orchard house, moving around. They didn't have long before someone found them.

They extricated the box a few minutes later.

"Finally," Bel said, standing painfully, her dirt-stained treasure tucked under one arm.

"Now where are you going?" Kisare asked. She tucked the fabric tighter around the lantern, already guttering and dim. Fool woman would get them both killed.

Bel looked down at the pile of dirt and little wrapped bundle. "Can I not even open it?"

"Not yet. Help me fill this in. We can't leave the spade lying around or someone will notice. We'll have to bury it with the body."

Bel's mouth pursed, and she took a step away, box clutched to her chest.

"Do you want to lose another finger? Maybe the whole hand?" Kisare watched her sister. "Even if the box holds nothing, and we put the spade back in the shed, someone might realize it was used tonight."

Bel flexed her left hand, hiding the maimed finger.

"Fine," Bel pouted, setting the box down. She helped Kisare move the bundle back in the grave, on top of the spade, then piled the dirt on top. It was fresh enough it was hard to tell the site had been disturbed a second time. Kisare stood, brushing away dust and dirt. She only had the one set of clothes. She realized she was calculating how to hide their deed when they went back to the slave's house. *When* they went back, not *if*.

Her sister picked up the wooden box again. Kisare could see bands of metal around it in the dimming light, and an old, rusted lock on the front. It must be something important. Why bury it out here?

"Remember our wager," Bel said, as if it were possible to forget. Kisare swallowed. One blond had already died, connected to this box. Would there be more?

Bel tapped nervously at the box, the *tok* echoing far too loudly in the night's stillness.

"Do you really want to be a runaway blond?" Kisare asked her sister. Bel's face was pale, but she nodded, slowly.

"We could end up like *him*." There was no need to name names. Mulagun would never meet his new daily work quota until he healed from his punishment.

Finally, Bel spoke, but too quietly. Kisare caught a glint of a tear on her sister's face.

"What?"

"I still think we should go."

Kisare shook her head, but inside, a tiny bloom of hope took hold. "Give it here," she said, and snatched it before Bel could protest. She grabbed a stone from the ground and swung it against the sturdy box. Her shoulder twinged in pain, but she ignored it. With a satisfying crunch, the lock dropped to the ground. She handed the box back.

"Well, go on," she gestured impatiently. "It's your discovery. Open it up."

Bel was staring at her in a way she had never seen. Kisare didn't have time for it.

"Go on. We either need to get back to the orchard soon, get our stories ready, and treat these cuts, or we need to be as far away as possible from here by morning. Either way, there's no time to stand around." She lifted the lantern up, loosening the fabric just enough to illuminate the box. Light reflected off the metal bands.

As if in a daze, Bel opened the top of the box.

"What...?" Her brow furrowed, and she twisted the box for Kisare to see.

Inside was nothing but dirt.

Kisare took the box back, cradling the lantern in the crook of an arm. The box was small, only a hand and a half long, less than that across, and shallow enough she could hold it on one palm. Four metal bands of either copper or brass held the wood slats together, one with a scratch across it where she had smashed it with the stone. The hasp was intact, if a little bent. It was strangely warm.

She plunged a finger into the dirt and swirled it around. If Bel was the expert at pruning, Kisare's expertise was in growing. The trees she tended gave better godfruit the next year, not that anyone noticed. This dirt was like no other she had felt. It was smooth and so black it was hard to see even with the lantern. She raised a pinch, rubbing between her fingers, then smelt it. A scent of old leaves, and minerals, and the paths of worms in the ground, with just a hint of telltale copper. This was *good* dirt.

"I...I guess we can go back now," Bel said, her voice tinged with disappointment. "It's just dirt."

Kisare stuck her finger back in the box. "This is the best dirt I've ever seen. I wouldn't be surprised if a noble—a powerful one—died to fertilize this dirt."

"No matter who died for it, you want to run from the orchard with a box of dirt?" Bel asked. "I was hoping for money—enough to buy our freedom, or passage somewhere. Even I'm not crazy enough to think dirt is equal to the price of a slave." She looked back to the orchard. "Come on, Kisa. Throw it away. My thigh hurts and you're bleeding again. Maybe Anu can patch us up. If she stands for us tomorrow, maybe the master will let us off like Mulagun for killing Tashi."

Kisare didn't even look at her shoulder. She could feel the renewed warmth. Her finger came up against a resistance underneath the top layer of dirt.

"Wait," she said. "There's something else in here." She felt around, pushing the dirt aside. "There's a seed."

Bel only looked confused, now. "One seed?"

Kisare plucked the little kernel from the box and held it up, trying to look at it in the weak light from the lantern. It was small, so it was hard to see. Was it a malus or citron pip?

As she held the little thing, it began to glow. Not brightly, but in the darkness of the grove it was enough to illuminate the box. She didn't think the seeds the master saved after eating godfruit did that, but she had rarely been close to one. She looked to her sister.

"Bel, what if this is a magical seed? One for a godfruit tree? We could have our own magic."

"Why hasn't it grown?" Bel asked, but her eyes were on the seed. "Even I know it should have sprouted by now. Surely some water's gotten to it over the years."

"There's no mold on it either," Kisare answered, holding the glowing pip close to one eye. "It's not even dried out, and it's certainly alive. The nobles don't let blonds plant the godfruit trees. I've only ever gotten a citron sprout to care for." The other magical trees in the orchard were older than she was. "I always wondered if it was more than keeping slaves from stealing them." She looked up, pressing the seed back into the dirt and closing the lid. The glow dimmed and went out as she did, though the heat of the box seemed to increase. "What if there are special ways to make magical trees sprout? Bel, this box could make us a fortune, and free us too. It's nothing if not valuable."

Her sister's mouth worked. "All this? Over one seed? I don't care if it was glowing. You, the most practical person I know, will run away with me tonight, risking life and safety in the process?"

Kisare shrugged. The little light of hope in her chest was growing stronger. The glowing seed caught in her mind. Could it be something even more valuable than a godfruit tree? "We're already at risk. I don't think the master will be as gentle as you expect. You're his favorite. You don't know how easy it is to get whipped. Now, are we going, or not? We only have a few hours until dawn."

"I'm ready. I've been ready," Bel said. Her voice grew more confident as she went on. "Give me the box. Which way out?" Kisare gave her the little box of earth and Bel tucked it tightly under her arm.

"Does it matter?" Kisare answered. "As long it's away from the orchard. This side leads into the mountains." She reached a finger up, tracing the heights blocking part of the night sky. "When the master goes down to the city, he goes through a pass there." Maybe in a city, they could find someone to help them. She had heard of slaves buying their freedom in the capital. If it could happen in Karduniash, maybe it could happen out here, near the Blasted Lands.

Bel nodded. "Then we go that way."

As they moved through the rows of vines, Kisare thought of all the things that could go wrong, all the people who could catch them. What were the chances the seed was really magical, and not some sick joke to trap slaves? If they only had a plan, she would feel better.

She heard something crunch and both she and Bel whipped around. Nothing moved in the dark.

"An animal again?" Kisare asked, but Bel only shook her head. They moved faster.

Soon, she could see the edge of the arbor, where no tree or bush grew until the edge of sight. No place for slaves to hide from guards' eyes. Kisare crouched between two vines and put the lantern down. The light was almost gone, its leftover oil used up. "We'll have to run for it. I haven't seen any guards out here, or any lights. Do you think it's safe?" She thought of the sound behind them. They had no plan ready if someone followed them.

Her sister shook her head. "Probably not. Still better to run. Come on." She gripped the box with her elbow and sprang up with a grunt. Kisare had seen Tashi's knife wound in Bel's leg. It would need to be cleaned, and soon.

She tried to follow, but something caught at her shirt, and she rocked back.

Before she could cry out, a large and hairy arm hooked around her neck and dragged her to the ground of the grape arbor. She clawed at the arm, struggling to breathe. He must have followed their light and left his own. If they hadn't run off at a moment's notice, she would have—

"Two runaways. How did you get out of your chains?" the man said, his voice gruff. Kisare recognized the voice but couldn't place him. "Guess getting the short straw tonight is liable to get me some bounty pay after all. Aricaba-Ata won't like you two getting away."

Kisare thrashed in his grip, but the guard didn't seem to notice. Bel took one step forward, letting the box fall from her hand to the ground with a dull thud. Fortunately, the lid stayed closed. Was it strange she noticed that one detail?

"Let her go, Zima," Bel said. Her voice wavered in the darkness. "Take me instead."

"Tempting, but I don't think so." Kisare felt cold sharp metal at her cheek. "If you like your sister as much as I think, you won't run. She may be plain, but I can add to those freckles, real quick." He trailed the knife down Kisare's cheek for emphasis. As the knife parted her skin, Kisare stopped clawing his arm, praying he didn't do anything worse. Blood dripped from her chin to her chest, hot in the cold night air.

Bel said nothing.

Come on, Bel. Do something crazy. Something he doesn't expect. It's what you're good at.

"Come on now, darling," Zima said to Bel, his arm just loose enough to let Kisare gasp air in. "Maybe you and I can have some more fun before we go back. You're good for it, aren't you? I'd even let your sister here join in, though she's not such a beauty. I won't even tell Aricaba-Ata you were trying to escape. Out for a stroll, right?"

Bel pulled something from her sleeve and shoved it in her mouth. Her head tilted back, and sparks of lightning lit the night. *She took a slice of malus!* Kisare should have checked the workbench again when they left the toolshed. Her sister had given up the argument too easily. But then—

"What—?" Zima's arm loosened on Kisare's neck, the knife falling away from her cheek. Bel's hands were out in front of her as if she was pulling something.

The earth moved beneath Kisare's feet, and she fell forward. Zima fell the other direction, somehow, away from her. She saw Bel scoop something from the ground and pass her. There was a *clop* and a gasp. When she looked back, Zima was limp.

"Get up. Get up," Bel told her. Her throat was raw, and she still gasped for air. Bel pulled her to her feet roughly, dropping the rock in her hand.

"You...took another...slice," Kisare gasped, feeling her throat with one hand. She winced, moving her injured shoulder.

Bel left her and picked up a grape arbor stake, knocked over in the scuffle. The little lantern was lying on its side, still emitting a faint light. Kisare saw Bel point the sharp metal end at Zima's throat. "I left the last one. I promise. It's enough to incriminate Tashi."

"Tashi's dead," Kisare panted. "You killed her."

"Zima's next. He knows who we are, and where we were."

"I would appreciate it if you left him alive," another voice interrupted. Bel jerked the stake's point up. Enti-Ilzi sauntered out of the grape arbor, into the dim light of the lantern.

"How did you—" Bel began, but Enti-Ilzi cut her off with a gesture.

"I'm not here to take you back." The man raised something to his nose and Kisare caught the scent of citron. "In fact, I want to help."

"Why would you help us?" Kisare was instantly on guard. Nobles didn't help slaves.

"I've seen your sister's demonstration. I knew there was a reason I liked her. Not only is she strong, but she also has noble blood. If Ata does not realize it, perhaps someone else might." The noble watched them, his streak of black standing out against his white-blond hair, even in the low light. "Plus, Ligish—my new companion—seems to think it will endear you to me. She has a good mind, that one. If you two escape, Ata will be in even more debt this time next year. He will have no children from the unlucky Ubala—not if I have any say."

What did Enti-Ilzi do to Ubala? Kisare recited a quick prayer for Ligish—Enti-Ilzi's unlucky new slave. They rarely lasted long, but it was good—and unusual—of her to help them.

"If my cousin has no heirs soon," Enti-Ilzi continued, "he will be forced to choose among his kin to take over the orchard in the event of his death. I have no wife, and no heirs. Few nobles live out here. A noble wife is not the only—"

"Never!" Bel spit at the man's feet. Kisare stared at her.

"Bel, listen to what—"

"I won't. Never."

Kisare was about to argue more, but Enti-Ilzi made a lazy wave of the hand not holding the slice of citron. "It does not matter. Leave for a while. It will only help me. You will be back, sooner or later. Blonds do not fare well by themselves, away from the guiding hand of the noble class."

He stepped closer, and both Kisare and Belili stepped back. "Do not worry. I mean no harm. You know what those of the black hair can do with the citron?" Slowly, he raised the slice of godfruit to his lips and took it into his mouth. He bit down, shuddered, and Kisare saw the now-familiar lightning dance on his skin.

"Healing," Enti-Ilzi said through the juice held in his mouth. "Come closer." He gestured to Kisare. She thought about resisting, but before she could move away, he was there, laying a hand on her shoulder. Warmth passed through it, and Kisare sighed in relief. The pain and tearing were not gone, but it was better.

"I cannot heal you both completely. I do not have enough citron for that," he said through his teeth. "But I can make it easier for you to escape." He moved to Bel, but she moved back, disgust on her face in the waning light from the lantern.

"He's telling the truth," Kisare told her. "He's helping us."

"He's helping himself, as always," Bel answered. "Healing isn't the only thing he can do with a citron." She stopped, though, and let Enti-Ilzi lay a gentle hand on her leg. She grimaced as he half-healed the stab wound in her thigh, but Kisare could tell Bel's pain was less. What had she meant about the citron?

"Now go, quick as you can," Enti-Ilzi told them. "Lose your master some profits for a time. I cannot keep Ata from chasing you, but perhaps I can misdirect him a little longer."

Kisare left the lantern. The oil was nearly gone. There was enough light to see Bel scoop up the box as she turned away. Even though he was helping them, Kisare couldn't trust the man, not with her sister's reaction. She hoped he hadn't seen the box—no telling what he would say to the master.

She and Bel ran from the orchard.

CHAPTER FOUR

One Flower

Hot-tempered Geshtna, the summer goddess, chose next. Not to be outdone by her younger brother, she chose the prunus as her symbolic tree, bestowing the power of her senses. All other cherry trees burned to ash.

They crossed the flat grass at an easy pace, Belili still limping, despite Ilzi's aid. No one called after them, though her back twitched as she imagined the greasy man watching. As she ran, her tongue searched her mouth for particles of malus. Now she wished she *had* taken the third slice from Tashi. Her only comfort was imagining Ligish—she whispered the name, rolling it in her mouth—persuading Ilzi to let them free. Her face rose in Belili's mind, urging her to freedom.

Scrubby bushes enveloped them on the other side of the open ground. They ran on. There were boulders here too, rolled down from the mountains. The town where the master sold his produce was through the pass and down the mountain. Past more towns and cities, somewhere far down south, was Karduniash, the capital. There the royal pair, the Dyad, ruled over all other nobles.

They ran for perhaps an hour, darting from rock to rock, watching their footing. Belili stumbled often over unseen roots and stones, but they couldn't stop, even with Ilzi's help. She ground her teeth. She wasn't surprised he would turn on his cousin. Now she knew for certain why Aricaba-Ata had such terrible luck with his children.

Kisa scuffled and slowed, and Belili passed her at a run before stopping, gasping, her thighs wobbling with pain, especially the right one where Tashi stabbed her. The moons were only slivers above them.

"Did you know how the malus slices would affect you?"

"You're not stupid," Belili answered, angry both for her sister's need to ask, and for her own ignorance.

"You have magical color in your hair." Kisa's outline raised a hand, pointing. "Did you know?"

Belili sighed. They were going to do this now. She wanted to be covering ground.

"Obviously, I have a little brown somewhere in my blond." Brown like the swamp princess herself—the master's new wife—brown hair let her control the earth when tasting the juice of a malus. She tried to remember what else Ubala did when she ate a citron, or a prunus, or a morus.

"Did you know?" Kisa repeated, still not moving.

"I...may have suspected." Belili looked away. Kisa never knew their mother. She had been a vibrant woman, strong and handsome. A favorite of the nobles. "We should keep moving," Belili said again. She rubbed her thumb over the stump of her little finger, squeezing the box tightly under her other arm. It seemed warm in the cold night.

Kisa shook her head. "Fine. We'll talk about this later. We'll have to get off this road soon."

Belili suppressed a sigh of relief her sister didn't press further. "The mountains are harder to navigate, and we'll move slowly. Can't we stay on the road?"

"We could. It would be faster, but the master's dogs will track us anywhere," her sister answered. She pointed up the slope. "There's meltwater flowing downhill this time of year and we must go cross-country to find it. No matter what Enti-Ilzi does, come morning we must be invisible, through streams and into the wilds." Bel saw her look around at the gray slabs of mountain surrounding them in the pre-morning darkness and pick a direction seemingly at random. "There. That's a game path. It will lead past a stream." Belili had no idea how she could tell in the dark. Kisa strode to the side of the road, then scrambled onto the rocky slope, littered with scrubby plants.

The next few hours were an agony of stumbling and climbing, ever upward, through briars and stinging nettles, following what Kisa said was a path, but then Kisa always looked in control. By the time her sister was six, she was telling Belili what to do. Their little bit of education under old Mistress Tiamai only meant she was more confident when she did it.

"Another game path crosses here," Kisa said, pointing to a patch of trampled grass, almost visible in the early dawn. Belili couldn't make anything of it. They turned on the new path. "Hopefully something else is using this path and will throw off the scent. Hopefully, it will lead to a stream."

Then maybe a short rest. Belili's thigh was a mass of fire, and there was a long scrape down the left side of her face from Tashi's nails. Ilzi hadn't healed that, or the rest of her cuts and bruises. She could feel them stiffening up.

"Do you think they'll be after us yet?" she asked the shadow in front of her.

"Probably," Kisa said. "Anu might not have found Tashi, but I'm sure Zima is up. We can only hope Enti-Ilzi leads the master to search the orchard first. Maybe he'll tell them some caravanner stole us away."

Belili snorted. Hardly likely. She would have said something, but a flash of white caught her eye. "Deer." She pointed a finger. A small herd was about fifty paces away.

Kisa crouched down instantly, pulling Belili down with her. "They might be headed for water." Kisa followed the herd. Belili shivered. She had kept warm in the cool night by climbing across the hard mountain terrain, but their simple clothes—all they owned—would not hold off a late freeze, especially now they were higher up. In the true winter, the master handed out extra coats to the slaves when the weather stayed below freezing. He took them back as soon as it was warm enough, as he had done a few weeks ago. No sense wasting cloth on blonds.

"Come on." Kisa moved ahead, getting closer to the herd. Belili shook her head and followed her sister, resettling the precious box. It was definitely warmer than the surrounding air.

They crept along at a distance, keeping close to the ground for several minutes. Belili was getting nervous. "We're moving slowly," she finally whispered. "They can make good time on the road."

"They probably are," her sister answered, "but if we can shake off our scent in water—" She cut off as something whizzed through the air. Belili flattened to the ground, visions of hunting nobles filling her mind, until she felt Kisa's touch.

"Look."

One of the deer, an eight-point, was stumbling, something sticking from its neck. The rest of the herd scattered. Belili frowned until she realized it was an arrow. Who would be shooting at the deer, instead of two runaway blonds?

Kisa stiffened as a form emerged from a rock cluster, following the dying deer. It was hard to tell in the early light, but Belili thought the figure had long hair, all of one dark shade, not the light shade of a natural blond. Magical hair.

"Is that a noble?" she asked. Kisa shook her head, holding a finger up for silence. She sank below a boulder, rolled here from some ancient landslide, and pulled Belili down next to her.

"The hair," Kisa told her.

"I'm looking at the hair," Belili answered. The sun was rising, and she could see more detail every moment. "I've seen nobles with red, black, brown, and silver in their hair, but this looks almost...purple. Who has *purple* hair?" It was nearly all that color, too. He was a powerful magic user—more than Ata or Ilzi. This figure's hair had only a few strands of white blond near the temples and ears.

"I think the caravanners do," Kisa said. "They travel all around, but I had no idea any were this close to the orchards."

"Not that we're world travelers," Belili said. "I've never been off the orchard."

"If you came hunting, you'd hear the stories the male blonds tell."

Belili gave an involuntary shiver at that. Surrounded by vicious slaves and randy guards, killing everything they saw. Not her thing. Tashi's face and too-tight clothing flashed through her mind, but she firmly pushed it away for Ligish's proud nose and handsome face. Yes, Ligish was a far nicer thought.

While they talked, the purple-haired person approached the deer, fallen near where it was shot. He was dressed in rough leather pants and shirt with a bow and quiver slung on his back. A bound, almost cylindrical goatee hung beneath his chin. He knelt by the deer, running hands over it, plucking the arrow from its neck. He took something from a pouch at his belt, then held it up, head bowed, as if offering it to the corpse.

It was a slice of citron.

Belili exchanged glances with Kisa as the man ate the slice. They could just see the shock of light around his body in the morning sun as he threw his head back. Belili remembered the feeling vividly. He held the arrow up and let a drop of the deer's blood fall. Then he held a hand over where the drop landed, still chewing the citron pulp.

"What is he doing?" Belili whispered.

"I don't know," her sister answered. "I've seen the master use a citron to pull a stake out of the ground even Mulagun had trouble with.

He gets stronger, but he has red hair. Enti-Ilzi...healed us." She shivered. "But I don't know what magic a citron would give one with purple hair."

Belili squinted. "There's something under his hand," she said.

Gradually Belili made out a single stalk of green, which opened beneath the man's palm into a light-colored flower.

"I haven't seen that before," Kisa said.

The man stood, hoisting the deer over his shoulders and around the bow and quiver. As he turned to leave, he called out, "The flower was my offering to the rest of the herd, since you are wondering. A sacrifice of magic for their sacrifice of protection. You can come out now. You make enough noise to rouse the dead." His accent differed slightly from the aristocracy of the orchards, with rounder vowels, but more cultured than how the slaves spoke.

Belili felt Kisa stiffen beside her. What was she afraid of? If the man knew they were there the whole time, then he wasn't trying to capture them. It was better than what the nobles would do to them.

She stood up, box held tight.

"Can you help us?" she asked.

"What are you doing?" Kisa hissed. Belili waved a hand to quiet her. She stared at the purple-haired man; the deer slung over his shoulders. If he wasn't a noble, then maybe he could help them hide. He watched them, his head cocked to one side.

"You are servants of the fourcolors?"

"The who?" Belili hadn't heard the term.

"The ones who newly plant this land, down to the south."

"You mean the nobles?" She had never heard them called "new." The master had a book in which, she was told, he had written of generations of ancestors, all living in the same orchard. "We were slaves, not servants. They owned us."

The man gave her a long look.

"Oh, get up, Kisa," Belili whispered. Kisa rose to her feet.

"You say the fourcolors own you. Are you owned by them?"

"That's the same thing," Kisa called out. Nothing like a contradiction to give her sister her tongue back.

The man walked closer. His eyes were deep brown and penetrating. He was much taller than her, and a couple of hand widths taller than Kisa. "It is not. The fourcolors can say they own you. It is only true if you agree you are owned by them. Did you give them permission to do this thing?"

Belili looked at her sister, who shrugged. "No."

"Then you are not slaves." The man turned and walked toward a shelf of rock sticking out of the mountainside. "You are free to do what you want."

Belili could see her sister struggling with the idea. Belili had no problem grasping it; it was the reason she was missing most of her little finger. "They would not let us leave, so we escaped." With a little help.

"Then you were prisoners," the man answered over his shoulder. "You bring the fourcolors upon us."

"Won't you help us?" Belili called after the man. He kept walking. She pulled at Kisa's hand.

The man was not walking fast, burdened with the deer, and they soon caught up. The deep purple of his hair was like a mane around his head. From what she could see, much of it was braided in little pieces, the length of a finger. He had strands of white blond mixed in, and more in his beard, but mostly, the color was pure. If all that color was real, then he was...powerful. She had never seen a noble with a full head of non-blond hair.

"You could answer her," Kisa said.

"You do not seem to need help," the man answered. "You were prisoners. Now you are free. What help do you need?"

"The ones who owned—held us prisoner—are coming after us," Kisa said.

"Then run fast."

Belli held in a snort of laughter as Kisa's hands clenched by her sides. The man seemed not to notice. It was time to intervene before Kisa beat the man over the head with his deer.

"Can we move faster—" Belili started as a howl split the air.

"He's coming," Kisa said. "But the hounds still sound a ways off—"

Another howl sounded, this one longer and closer. The man was almost jogging, and she and Kisa ran beside his long legs. Their flight was not like Mulagun's yearly escape. Belili had no illusions that their punishment would be quick, or lenient, even for Aricaba-Ata's best pruner and favored slave. Whatever Ilzi promised had not been enough, or more likely, he had done nothing. She rubbed her pinky stub.

"Through here," the man said, ducking into a natural arch of rock. Belili followed close behind with her sister. On the other side was a sharp slope, with a trickle of water.

"They'll find you if they find us," Kisa panted as they ran through the trickle, quickly becoming a stream. Trees rose up on both sides. The man didn't answer. Determined was one thing, but was Kisa trying to anger him?

They splashed through the stream as a second voice joined the hound behind them. "I have no wish to be found at the moment," the man said. "Stay in the middle of the stream." He sounded calm, and Belili hoped he hadn't taken offense at Kisa. They had to escape Aricaba-Ata and his hounds.

They ran downhill for several minutes, the rocky terrain dropping in altitude as the trees grew taller. Cold water splashed around them. Her leg still felt as if it might fail. She and Kisa panted, but the man, with the deer and his weapon bouncing on his shoulders and his hair flying around his head, breathed steadily, in through his nose and out his mouth. The deer's antlers clacked against the fiber sheath of the quiver.

All at once the ground dropped again and the stream became a creek. The purple-haired man waded into the middle of the creek, and Belili followed him, giving up on keeping her pale linen pants dry. The water came up to her thighs, and she sighed as the cold bathed the half-healed knife wound. She held the little box high in one hand, above her splashes. Kisa was falling behind, struggling through the water, and she was holding her shoulder. Belili could see blood through her fingers. It must have opened again while they were running. Belili wondered if Ilzi used more of the citron on her than on her sister.

"Along here for a little longer," the man said, forcing his way through the creek. The deer's head bobbed on his shoulder, giving Belili a reproachful, glassy-eyed stare. "Those dogs will be at the source of the water by now." The howls did sound closer. Belili's heart raced, and not because of the exertion. "They will be confused."

They waded through the creek for several minutes, while Belili traded looks with her sister. They were moving too slowly.

"What do we do?" Kisa asked. "They'll catch us. We obviously took the stream. If you dropped that animal, we would move quicker."

In answer, the man stopped, turning to them, and Belili became aware of a pungent wet leather smell, both from the man's dress and, she thought, from the deer. He was breathing heavier. "We go to my caravan." He eyed them. "With the deer."

"Thank you," Belili said, before Kisa could say anything else.

"The water will throw off the beasts. As for their masters who might think further ahead..." He walked to one bank, lifted the deer's carcass from around his neck, then gently set it down on the ground, its head lolling, antlers digging gouges in the soft earth. Belili and Kisa followed him. He fumbled in a pouch at his belt with one hand, the other still resting on the deer's chest. Half of a small malus came from the pouch, a little crushed from their flight, but Belili watched it hungrily. The man glanced at their surroundings, gauging.

"This will take precious time. Stay close and be ready to leave. We must hope they do not gain too much ground."

"What are you—" Kisa started, but Belili shook her head, shivering in the cold of the water flowing past her legs. The days had not warmed enough to make wading through a mountain stream in any way comfortable.

The man took a large bite of the malus, shuddering as the juice took him. He raised his other hand from the deer, pulling something filmy and gray as he did. He cast it at the ground, where the gray mass distilled into the shape of a deer, antlers ready and sharp. The same resentful eyes stared at Belili.

He spit malus pulp into the creek and Belili and Kisa gasped. To waste godfruit was unheard of. He hadn't even gotten all the juice from the pulp.

The man took another large bite of the malus, shivering and chewing furiously. He dipped his hand into the creek. A filmy shroud followed his hand, dividing into little silver forms. The water grew even colder around Belili's legs, and she inhaled at tiny pricks of teeth. They did not quite break the skin.

Again, the man spit out malus pulp, and this time bit the core in half, shoving both parts in his mouth. He shuddered and drew a hand through the air. Sparrows, flies, mosquitoes, and even a lone hawk formed from mist, swooping and buzzing around their heads. Belili could see through them, but she felt wind from their wings.

The man spit one more time, wasting the precious seeds in the creek. "Guard this crossing," he instructed the spirits of the beasts, and made for the other bank. The sisters followed him, Belili glad to be away from the nibbles of the spirit fish.

"When our old master used a malus, he could control fire," Belili said. "His new wife can control earth. But what—"

"Five elements, for five hair colors," their guide told her. "Fire, earth, water, air, and spirit. These are the gifts of Kigal through the malus."

"You're not chewing anymore. How are these...spirits still here? How long will they last?" Kisa asked. Belili watched the group of hazy animals, fluttering above and stamping the bank.

"Long enough to dissuade our pursuers," the man said shortly. Another howl sounded in the distance, very close. Belili noted the use of "our" instead of "your."

"Then hurry," Kisa said. "Should we run ahead on our own? What do you think, Bel?" She walked back across to where the deer and its ghost patrolled the far bank. She was massaging her hand, casting sharp glances whenever a hound called. The man ignored their exchange, picking through a patch of bramble.

Belili glared after her sister. "I think our best chances are here," she called. Kisa turned at the far bank, her hands on her hips.

"I don't want to wind up like Mulagun," Kisa began. "I don't..." Belili looked where she did.

The purple-haired man had produced half of a citron, already peeled. He bit deep into its center, trembling with the burst of juice. Some ran down into his beard. His eyes rolled back momentarily, and Belili wondered if he would faint, ingesting so much magic at once. Instead, he bent, holding his hand over the bramble. As with the primrose, the bramble thickened and grew, and he followed, mouth working. He crouched, drawing it across the creek as it lengthened and bifurcated. In moments, the mass of vines was the height of a man, twisted and sharp. It was between them and their pursuers.

Howls shattered the air, and Belili could see shapes by the creek, pushing through the underbrush. Dogs were barking and men yelling.

The man ignored it all, guiding the vine toward the bank with the deer and bird sentries. Jagged thorns as long as Belili's fingers popped out along its length, and she and Kisa hurried behind its protection.

Kisa flinched as a massive hound burst through the brush, but Belili saw the deer's ghost lower its head and charge. The man raised his hand from the bramble to the deer, and as the ghost splashed through the creek, it grew larger as well, towering over the dog. Aricaba-Ata's hound swerved to avoid it, but an antler grazed its side. The dog howled, turning away. An angry red streak marred its flank, the hair around it crisping as if burned.

A guard came through next, whipping another dog forward. A silvery hawk's shade dove for him, growing big as an eagle. He dropped the whip, stumbling into a massive bramble. Belili almost winced. Aricaba-Ata would never have been able to do something like this.

The man scooped up his deer, throwing it back over his shoulders, and started running. Kisa was close behind.

Belili followed them up the slope of the bank, her thigh tugging painfully. Behind them she heard Aricaba-Ata's distinctive voice, yelling.

"Stop them! Get those dogs moving again!" His voice turned to a yell of pain, and she stopped long enough to see a giant sparrow pecking at her former master, his arms raised to ward it off.

Belili ran after her sister.

CHAPTER FIVE

The Asha-Urmana

Kigal, she of the great earth and harvest, added her bounty third, choosing the noble malus to bear her elemental strength. Though there had been many varieties of apple before, the others crumbled to dust like old leaves.

Kisare jogged after the man through woods shaded with morning sun. Shadows dappled his broad back under the dead thing on his shoulders. Was it somehow more dead now its spirit was guarding the creek behind them? Yells of the hounds followed them, but they were getting farther away, for the moment. No telling how long those spirits would last.

She watched Bel's shorter, curvier figure as they half-ran. Her sister was favoring her right leg but was able to keep up. She was also more relaxed around this caravanner than she had been around the nobles since Mistress Tiamai died. Kisare was not as calm. Wouldn't this man blame his use of the godfruit on them? That payback was measured in months, if not in deaths. But wasn't she a free woman now?

"What's your name, anyhow?" she said to the man's back. They were moving fast, but not fast enough to take her breath away. Her shoulder tugged with every step, and Tashi's nail marks burned a trail of pain down her right arm.

"Ishkun-Dim-Hbelu." He didn't even stop his long-legged stride. She had to jog to keep up.

"Three names? Don't most nobles only have two?" Kisare asked. Bel was shooting her quieting looks—as if she needed quieting.

"Those are not all of my names," the man answered.

"Then I suppose you're some sort of high noble of your people. Imagine one of our nobles going out to hunt for breakfast." She barked a laugh.

"You may call me Hbelu, if that is more satisfactory."

"I am Belili, and this is my sister Kisare," Bel said quietly.

Kisare glared at her, but it was too late to take that information back. "How do you know our language? Did one of you learn it from a noble and pass it on?"

He grunted a laugh. "Hardly. We taught the fourcolors our language when they could not communicate with each other. They took our words and put them to their own use."

"You know these 'fourcolors' have lived here for hundreds of years, don't you?" Kisare tried not to pant. She would not let this Hbelu leave them behind.

"As they have 'owned' the blond peoples for hundreds of years?" Hbelu's voice was scornful, his back still to them.

"Not all blonds are prisoners," Bel told him. "Some earn their freedom and work for the nobles. Some in Karduniash even own businesses."

"You think you can do the same, with whatever is in that little box."

"What do you know of that?" Kisare said, sharper than she intended. The man—Hbelu—finally stopped and turned to look at them—at her. His features were sharp, sun-browned, though lighter than Bel's, and his lips were nicely full. Even his bound goatee had purple in it, though the larger part was white-blond. All in all, he was not unattractive. Kisare pushed the thought aside.

"There are few reasons prisoners of the fourcolors would attempt to free themselves. They are too comfortable in their current place."

"Comfortable!" Kisare bristled. "Do you know how many times I've been whipped, kicked, and beaten for no reason?" She flung a hand at Bel. "The nobles act like we're their playthings. Bel's little finger—" Her sister laid a hand on her back, and she subsided, fuming.

Hbelu nodded once. "Yet you escaped now, when you found this prize." His eyes flicked to the box, under Bel's arm, then back to Kisare's face.

"It's not important. Just our things," Bel said. At least she made some effort to defend their position.

"Slaves and prisoners have no property," Hbelu countered. "I am not so ignorant." His eyes went to the box again. "Unless I miss my guess, possessions are not kept in boxes glowing with inner power and engraved with the names of all four gods of nature."

Bel started, looking to her prize. Kisare frowned. "There are metal bands on the wood, but nothing etched on them." It wasn't glowing now, though it had been warm.

"Then you do not know. I saw them clearly when I took the juice of the malus."

Kisare exchanged glances with Bel. The seed was obviously important, but when each godfruit had multiple seeds, why single one out?

She jumped as a trio of howls broke the air. A flight of quail broke from the oak above them, squawking in flight.

"We must not stay here," Hbelu said, his voice now urgent. He turned away, the deer's legs swinging in a circle, and strode forward.

"Those aren't from behind us. They're off to the side," Bel said. She limped a few steps, looking back the way they came. "The master must've sent two teams after us. Ilzi." She whispered the last word.

"Then the creek will not stop them," Hbelu sighed. He took half a malus out of his bag, balancing the deer with his other hand. "You two must be worth your weight in godfruit to him." Before Kisare could object, he took a large bite with a shiver, squatting to the ground. He put the rest of the godfruit back in his pouch.

"Hey! We didn't ask you to use a malus!" Kisare shook her head as Bel tried to calm her. She knew the value Aricaba-Ata and the other nobles put on godfruit. Why was this man wasting so much on them?

Hbelu wasn't listening to her. He held one hand over the ground, as if searching, crab-walking a few steps here or there. Then he made a grabbing motion and stood up.

As he rose, a gray mist stuck to his hand. The film resolved into a partially decomposed man, his rotted head at an angle. Another ghost, spectral as the animals at the creek.

Kisare made a sound of disgust and stepped back, though Bel watched Hbelu work with interest.

Another baying cry broke the silence.

"We need to go, quickly," Kisare said. She dug her fingernails into her palms. Hbelu gave her a look and she closed her mouth.

The rotting ghost stood, head lolling, in front of Hbelu. Its clothes hung in tatters, and a putrid gash went from one ear to the other side of its pelvis, almost cleaving its neck. Its hair, though gray and translucent as its body, was bound in a similar style to Hbelu's.

Hbelu swallowed malus pulp and spoke. "Follow and confuse our trail as long as you are bound. Move our footprints. Make new ones. Divert our scent. Direct our pursuers away from my people's camp."

The corpse nodded its head, reaching up with one hand to keep it from falling to one side. It bent to wipe at the ground with translucent fingers and shuffled away.

"Come," Hbelu said, and strode off. Kisare hurried after, torn between escaping her old master and looking eager to obey Hbelu's commands.

They walked in silence, listening to an occasional bark or howl in the morning air. They were moving upward, a gentle slope on either side of them, the ground held together by tree roots.

Then a bark sounded sharp, to their left, and Hbelu's hand went to his pouch, hovering. "I suppose neither of you can use godfruit?"

"I can try—" Bel started, but Kisare overrode her.

"How would we know?" She deliberately snatched a stout stick from the ground. It was solid enough to keep a guard away.

As the barks and grunts of dogs and men got closer, they positioned themselves at the top of a slope where a rockslide had long ago cleaved a natural path from lower terrain to higher. On either side, the rocks were much steeper. It was as good a place as any to meet attackers.

Kisare left Bel with Hbelu and took her place in front. Bel hadn't found a suitable weapon yet, for all the good Kisare's stick could do. Still, it would be hard for a man to climb up while she was swinging for his head.

She heard the thrash of paws through the underbrush, and growls from the dogs the master kept chained and hungry. She looked back to see Hbelu crouched down again, citron in one hand, the other held splayed over the ground. Kisare shook her head. One could eat godfruit all day long, but a good stout stick could knock the juice right out of a noble's mouth.

The first dark head broke through the brush, chain clanking around the dog's neck. Kisare saw glistening white teeth bearing down and swung the stick, shutting her eyes. She felt a shock through the wood and was rewarded with a yelp of pain. Close behind the dog came Zima, a bandage around his head. Where was Bel? She should be beside Kisare, swinging a branch.

Zima looked furious, the dog shaking its head. Then the guard's expression turned to surprise. Something tickled Kisare's leg and she jumped to the side with a screech. A trail of ants, each as long as her foot, scuttled past her leg, whiskery antennae matched to the tail of the

ant in front of them. Kisare hopped away, hoping the bugs wouldn't
mistake her for a meal. They headed straight for the surprised guard
and his dog. Another pair of guard and hound broke through behind
them but stopped at the sight. The ants climbed over the dog, pinching
with wicked-looking horns at their mouths, and the dog convulsed.

Zima batted at the bugs around his legs. "Get them off!" he cried,
dropping the leash. The other guard went to help him and Kisare
backed up the slope.

Something rumbled beneath her feet, and she caught at a tree for
balance. An earthquake?

Rocks and loose rubble tossed down the sides of the slope and back
toward the pair of guards.

"Up here, quick!" Hbelu shouted. She scrambled up the slope as a
rumble sounded behind her, then there was a sound like a pile of logs
falling over, and she went to her hands and knees. When she looked
around, the way was sheared in two and they were separated from their
pursuers by a sharp spike of rock. Not that Zima and the other guard
were in a position to care. Both were on the ground, furiously battling
the giant insects swarming around them. The dogs charged back and
forth, worrying small forms with their teeth. As she watched, the bugs
shrank.

A hand pulled her up. "Come on, Kisa," Bel said. "We need to move."
Kisare looked at her sister, then at Hbelu. The earthquake. What had
she done? She got to her feet and they ran, Hbelu's broad shoulders still
supporting the load of the deer. It stank of death, and from its dunking
in the stream. They jogged until the yelps of the dogs and cries of the
men fell behind them.

"It will take time to find another path up that slope," Hbelu said,
slowing his pace. "We should be safe for the moment, and my caravan is
not far."

"Then could you tell us more about the box?" Bel asked.

Hbelu shook his shaggy head. "Not I, though I know it is unique."

"What about the marks of the gods?" Bel pushed.

"With few exceptions, the only other things so marked are the
godfruit trees." He studied the little wooden box under her arm.
"Normally I would not interfere between the fourcolors and their
prisoners. It has caused too much strife in the past." His face was
pensive, but his eyes assessed Kisare. "However, this box is clearly

blessed by the gods. It was found now, when so many of us find the gods silent." Kisare's thoughts went to the glow of the seed when she touched it. "This will go far toward convincing my people their path is true. One of the elders of my caravan may know more. This way."

Hbelu was unhesitating in his choice of path through the mature woods, despite the lack of trail markers. It was several hours after dawn when they emerged into a large space—several times bigger than the master's entire orchard—carved out of the center of the woods. Here and there trees shadowed buildings, but mostly the land was given to a small village. Purple-haired men and women with varying amounts of the magical color wandered between buildings of wood and stone. Many wore their hair in little braids, like Hbelu. The construction was finer than the master's house, and the boards on the upper portions of the dwellings were coated with a clear varnish that kept the original glow of the wood. The stone at the base looked like polished marble, and Kisare wondered where they quarried it. The stone at the Aricaba orchard was gray and drab granite. This marble fit together so tightly she could see no crack between the blocks. The streets were similarly made of flat fitted stones. A lone dog barked as they passed, and a child ran to claim it.

"I thought they traveled. I didn't know caravanners had cities," Bel whispered.

Hbelu must have heard her. "The fourcolors call us 'caravanners' because they see the way most of my kind lives now. They purposefully forget the Asha-Urmana settled here first and taught them many of their building techniques. My people's nomadic lifestyle is protection more than choice." There was a heat in his words, which Kisare for once identified with. She had never seen any Asha-Urmana at the Aricaba orchard, yet here was a whole village of them, a day's travel away. It was nearer than the market where the master sold his produce. Why didn't he sell to these people, or buy from them? If nothing else, he could learn from their building style.

The inhabitants of the caravan watched them openly and with interest, but stayed back. Several ducked their heads or waved to Hbelu, who returned the gesture, walking by a row of houses with displays of crafted goods. One family, mother and father standing with a girl and a younger boy, were talking with an older man who had several scrolls tucked under his arm. As Kisare passed, the man unfurled a length of parchment dotted with cartographic signs. She recognized them from one of the maps Aricaba-Ata kept in his house. The family's daughter was eagerly pointing out places and trails on the map. It covered an area extending from the mountains and the edges of the Blasted Lands, down to the southern coast, past Karduniash. Kisare craned her neck to see the map. Maybe she could come back later.

Aside from the family and a handful of others out on errands, there were few people around compared to the number of buildings. Hbelu saw her looking and explained.

"Most are working the fields, getting them ready for the spring planting. You will meet more of my caravan tonight."

"You call it a caravan when it doesn't move?" Bel asked.

"Most of them do," Hbelu answered, with a slight smile.

A tall boy ran up to their guide, his eyes darting to Kisare and Bel every few seconds. His hair was in braids, but he only had a small lock of purple, near his temple. "Welcome back," he said. "May I take your load, Ishkun-Dim-Hbelu?"

Hbelu swung the deer carcass around, rolling his shoulders. "Of course, Urha. Please take this to Ahiva so he can butcher it." The boy trundled off, staggering under the deer.

Bel pointed into the village. What could only be a well was dug into the ground, but rather than a winch and pulley, there was a strange contraption made of wooden scoops, grown together end to end, dipping down into the well, and dumping water into a basin as they moved in a loop. A length of pounded bark drew water off into the village.

On one side of the well, a bulky creature of shining silver walked in a housing, turning the chain of scoops and a grinding wheel attached to the other side of the mechanism. Kisare squinted at the silver thing—a large bear, like the spirits she had seen at the creek. Kisare pursed her lips. "I see you aren't above captivity," she said, gesturing at the water system and the grinder.

Hbelu glanced where she pointed, then shook his head. "The bruin had a natural death in the forest nearby. One of our elders spoke to her spirit, finding she had a desire to relive the strength of her youth. She has agreed to work the mill for another month as needed, after which she will return to the beyond. We will then find another volunteer."

"Oh." Kisare felt her face burn. "What if no spirits want to work for you?"

There was the merest beat before he answered. Had she finally broken through his stoic resolve? "Then we will work it ourselves. The cost in malae is high to keep her here, but while they are in season, the extra production from the mill is worth it."

Kisare tried to think of an answer to his logic as they progressed farther into the village, but the expenditure of the past day drew on her. She stifled a yawn. They had not slept the night before.

"I will give you some time to rest from your flight. You will be safe with the caravan until you wake. Then we can discover more about the box you carry."

Kisare forced her mouth shut. What if they had not had the box? Would he have left them for Aricaba-Ata and his dogs to find?

"Thank you for your kindness," Bel said in the silence. Hbelu inclined his head.

A group of purple-haired youths ran up, gravitating to Hbelu, though they watched Kisare and her sister. One little girl sidled forward, head down, to touch her hand, her tanned skin a contrast against Kisare's much paler hand. She smiled despite herself. From the children's conversation, Hbelu had been gone since the day before, tracking the herd of deer. The others in the village were eager to see him again, and Kisare wondered what they saw in the laconic man. After a brief exchange, he ruffled one boy's braided hair, and sent the boys and girls ahead to prepare a place for Kisare and Bel.

Hbelu led them on a brief tour, pointing out residents' houses, the butcher where the deer was being prepared, the smithy, and even a small clockmaker's shop. Kisare lingered at the last one, drawn by the intricate gears and linkages. The clockmaker, a stooped older man, and one of the elders, also made moving toys for children. As she watched the tiny mechanisms, Kisare could almost see how they worked. She would have to come back to talk to the man.

Through the town, Hbelu joked with children, asked various adult Asha-Urmana how their days went, acting as if he knew everyone. Kisare kept her eyes peeled for anything suspicious these people did. Hbelu was interested in the box, even without knowing about the seed. She had a hard time believing anyone was so generous. He must want something from them.

Soon, they wound up near a stone ziggurat dominating the center of the buildings—the only one without wooden construction. To the right corner of the building was an elder citron tree, a few of the magical godfruit still on its branches, even this far into spring. On the left corner was a tall morus, leaves starting to bud.

"You may rest this afternoon in here," Hbelu gestured at the opening to the building. "You must be tired after your escape from imprisonment."

The ziggurat had no door and as they passed through, Kisare saw the blocks that made the walls were surprisingly thin. A firepit occupied the center of the single room inside, but it was unlit. Any gloom was chased away by openings on the walls above their heads, bouncing late morning sun on polished marble blocks until it lit every corner. There was a set of stairs in two corners, leading to a higher level. The opposing corners had stairs leading down.

"If this is acceptable?" Hbelu indicated a pile of wool blankets, obviously placed there for them, and Kisare nodded. They were better than anything she had ever slept on. "There are clothes, simple, but clean, and a basin to wash in along that wall. Remove the plugs above it and you will have water. Thanks to the bruin." He raised one side of his mouth in a sardonic smile.

He moved through the open door, pointing out a thick cloth to cover the opening. "Rest well. I will ask the elders to speak with us this evening and we will investigate the origins of the box you found."

Kisare immediately crossed the distance and pulled the cloth down. It would not keep others from hearing what they said. They would have to whisper.

Bel was already kneeling to adjust the blankets. "It's quite warm in here," she said without inflection. "I doubt we'll need many blankets, even on the stone."

Kisare stalked back to her sister. "Getting comfortable?"

"I am. I'm about to fall over." She tucked the box by the blankets, near enough to reach while sleeping.

Kisare knelt down next to her. "It can't be safe to stay here."

Bel finally looked straight at her. "The nobles never treated me so well in all my life, not even the old mistress."

Kisare's mouth worked. She hadn't expected such a direct statement from her sister. "We...we know nothing about them."

"Yet you stayed eighteen years under Aricaba-Ata's yoke and only fled when I insisted yesterday."

"It was the first real chance we got to be free." Kisare crossed her arms.

"You almost didn't take it," Bel answered. "Have they put us in chains? Have they beaten us? Does anyone look at us like *property*?"

Once again, no sound came from Kisare's mouth.

"Hbelu showed kindness to two blond *slaves*." Bel's voice rose, and Kisare's eyebrows lifted. She hadn't heard her sister's voice so forceful. "For once, I feel as if I don't have to watch my every move. You create discord where there is none. *Why?*"

"I'm not..." Bel's stare made her stop that sentence. "I don't know," she mumbled. "I'm afraid. I've never not been a slave. I've never been free. Hbelu keeps talking about the box. Should we not suspect them at all? He might try to take it."

"He could have taken it at any time," Bel said. "He didn't. Did you notice his hair?" Kisare, looking inward, glanced up at the sudden change in questioning.

"It's purple. What of it?"

"He has more purple hair than anyone else here. He must be one of the most powerful magic-users around."

"You're saying he's important."

"That's how it works with the nobles." Bel picked up a blanket and held it under Kisare's nose. "Do you suppose the caravan has a special building set aside for visitors, with blankets ready?"

Kisare looked at the blankets in a new light. It was her sister's ability to see patterns, so useful in pruning.

"You're saying this is...is his—"

"His home, made of stone between houses of wood, set in the center of the village, surrounded by one of each godfruit tree. I assume his bed is upstairs."

"He's their leader? Their prince?" Kisare frowned. She assumed his three names were an Asha-Urmana tradition. *More than three*, he had said. She shook her head. "He doesn't *act* like a leader. I suppose you're the expert on magic now you're high and mighty like them."

Bel's face slipped from frustrated to angry.

"Three times you've used godfruit. You have brown in your hair. The dirt moved under your hands. Like *her*." Kisare didn't name the master's new wife. "You made the earthquake that saved us from Zima and the dogs, didn't you? I used a stick like a slave."

"You're jealous." Bel spoke quietly, but all her attention was on Kisare. It was...disconcerting.

"I've never needed magic before, and I don't need it now."

"You might have it whether you like it or not," Bel answered, still kneeling, hands on hips. "You haven't tasted godfruit. Maybe our mother had brown in her hair."

"Or maybe your father did and mine didn't," Kisare rebutted. "Whoever our fathers were—you've always said Mother didn't tell you."

"It doesn't matter," Bel said, suddenly dismissive.

"Of course it doesn't matter. That's what I said." Kisare moved blankets around, though they were already in place.

Bel passed a hand across her face and went to the marble basin on the wall. She briefly investigated the small plugs above the basin, then twisted one out. Water flowed freely, and she replaced the plug. She pulled the other and Kisare heard her grunt with surprise as water flowed over her hand.

"What is it?" She was willing to let it go if Bel was.

"It's warm."

Kisare joined her, anger fading. Sure enough, one plug gave cool clear water. The other produced water as warm as if sitting in the sun for hours. "The bark pipe system," she said, her eyes far away, visualizing the network of curled wood. "It must have a basin to warm the water. The Aricaba orchard didn't have this."

They washed their faces and cleaned their cuts and scrapes. It had been weeks since she'd had a bath. There were bandages available too.

They hung their ragged clothes up to dry, still wet from their trek through the creek. They'd be stiff later. Kisare didn't feel completely safe undressed in this strange place, but the clean clothes were soft, made of some fabric she didn't recognize. They both slipped on the simple white shirts and pants, and she joined Bel beneath the blankets, curled together, the box near at hand.

* * *

Kisare jolted awake at knocking, ready to defend herself from the guards' whips. Where was she? Her eyes widened, taking in the slant of afternoon sunlight, bouncing across polished surfaces. Memories flooded back, as did the pain in her shoulder.

Hbelu's house. Palace?

The knock came again, and Bel grunted beside her. "Not weeding again."

"No more weeding, unless it's your own godfruit tree," Kisare told her, and Bel's eyes fluttered open.

"Oh—what time...?" Bel straggled out of the blankets, grunting with pain as she put weight on her thigh. She had taken most of the covers, as usual, but Kisare didn't mind. It was warmer than outside, even with no fire going. How was the ziggurat heated? Maybe the water pipes were routed through the walls—

The knock sounded one more time. "We're coming," Kisare called. Her colorless dress was nearly dry, though wrinkled. She tried to smooth it out, then gave up. She would not be seen as a lazy slave by these people, especially by their rescuer. Better to keep their new clothes, whatever they were. She tried to find a reflection in one of the polished marble blocks scattered around the structure, beating her long bleached hair into submission. Bel was calmly raking a hand through hers. Her sister's dark chestnut complexion hid the bags under her eyes. Kisare was sure she looked the worse of the pair. Her freckles stood out more when she was tired.

They emerged into the late afternoon sunlight, Bel's box under her arm, to face Hbelu. He had traded his wet clothes for clean, stitched leather ones. Behind him were a cadre of elderly men and women. Kisare recognized the clockmaker among them. All had large locks of purple, though much was streaked with white, and none of them wore braids. They were dressed like Hbelu, even the elderly women wearing workable leggings. Hbelu's hair was combed and oiled, the little braids reworked. Kisare barely restrained a hand from flying to the mass of tangles on her head.

"If you are rested, we might discuss your god-marked box, and your future plans," Hbelu said, standing perfectly erect. The shadow of the citron tree fell across the doorway.

Kisare frowned at him. Always the box was front and center. She was a free woman now and wasn't sure she wanted them to know her plans. She opened her mouth to argue, but Bel got there first.

"Of course. Are these your caravan's elders?"

"They are the wisest among us and visit often with other caravans to trade knowledge and craft. Follow." Hbelu held out an arm.

Kisare followed silently, Bel limping beside her. They walked around the circumference of the marble ziggurat. It was in the center of the settlement, and past the morus tree, on the other side of the entrance from the citron, was a strong and symmetric prunus. Kisare could see the branches of a malus poking out from the fourth corner.

They left the ziggurat and traveled across the village, past buildings with varnished wood on top and polished marble beneath. Soon they entered an open pavilion, plank floored, shaded by a lattice wood pergola. A blooming honeysuckle vine grew up one side and over the top, filling the air with its sweet fragrance. Chairs for more than twice their number, made from trained vines, were set in a circle around the circumference.

Hbelu and the elders took their seats, pulling the ones they chose into a smaller circle. Kisare met her sister's eyes, both still standing. She deliberately chose a chair before she was given permission, a muscle in her back tightening at the memory of whips. Kisare held her chin high, jaw clenched, and sat in the smaller circle occupied by the Asha-Urmana. Bel followed, clutching the box, wincing as her wounded leg bent. The chairs were comfortable, as if they had been grown to the shape of a body with the help of a citron.

Two old men and four old women made up the elders. Hbelu was much younger than the others, though none of the elders looked frail. One woman, whose shoulders were even wider than Anu's, spoke first. "Not often do fourcolors enter Asha-Urmana caravans. We have helped their blond prisoners in the past, but rarely."

"From the Aricaba orchard?" Bel asked before Kisare could. Their neighbors were a good two days' travel.

One of the men crossed his hands on his small paunch and nodded. "Before your birth. More have arrived from the other direction." He waved a hand to his left. It could have been the correct direction. After their rush through the forest, Kisare had no idea.

"Are they still with your caravan?" Then she realized *all* she saw here had at least a small lock of purple. She had seen no blonds. What happened to those with no magic?

Another woman shook her head at this. Her voice was creaky and soft, and she had a small satchel filled with blocky shapes resting by her chair. "All those who come to the Asha-Urmana seeking shelter eventually move on, in our caravan and others. They leave us, eager to try for their fortune as free men and women. They have a need to flee from this life."

"Do your own leave too? The ones born with no purple?" *If this is so much better than slavery, what makes the blonds run away?*

There was a quick exchange of glances. Hbelu answered them. "There are none born to the Asha-Urmana without some small blessing of the gods. We do not mix with the fourcolors, or they would quickly absorb our culture into their own. Their fate would be the same if they had kept their faith and followed the paths their progenitors chose."

"Progenitors?" Bel looked confused. Kisare was sure her face showed the same thing.

"Do your captors not speak of these things to you?" another woman asked.

"The old mistress taught us how the gods made the nobles, and then the blonds to serve them. She did not say much about the...the Asha-Urmana"—she stumbled over the name—"except they were nomads—caravanners."

"Yet those they call 'caravanners' have better plumbing than the Aricaba orchard," Bel noted. Kisare raised an eyebrow, but also stifled a smile.

The other male elder—the clockmaker—snorted. Where the first was prone to extra fat, he was birdlike, in both movements and build. "Then they did not teach you that those of the white-blond hair were the first creation of the gods. They should be respected as firstborn but pitied as they have no magic of their own." Kisare traded another look with her sister. No, Mistress Tiamai didn't tell them that.

"The fourcolors broke their original oaths made to the gods both to protect the blonds and to keep their own magic strong. When they came to us as refugees, we helped them start anew, freely and without judgment. Little did we know they would not return the favor. Instead, they stole cities and trees from us, twisted our teachings and made war, and pushed us to roam the land." The little clockmaker spoke quickly, gesturing in agitation. "Now most of them have little to no magic. Some of their children are as blond as the ones they were meant to protect." He eyed them for a moment. "No offense to you."

"They bleach our hair this color," Bel said, "so we can't tell if we have any magic."

The third woman spoke up. Her hair had more remaining purple than the others, pulled back in a sharp bun. "Though we have cause to be angry, we have stayed out of fourcolor business ever since our people last fought the soldiers of Karduniash. They may have lost much of their magic, but they are strong in the arts of war."

"When was this?" Kisare had not heard tidings of war. Even if the nobles tried to keep it from the slaves, something so big would be common knowledge.

The woman waved a hand. "It was when my grandmother's grandmother was but a child." She held Kisare's eyes. "It is the reason we rarely let their prisoners into our caravans."

"Yet it would be wrong to say we have no business with them," Hbelu interjected. It had the sound of an old argument. "Even if we do not war, we fight with the fourcolors. Ahiyaba was the last one captured, from our caravan, twelve years ago."

The first woman spoke up again, setting her wide shoulders. "We have you to thank for stopping them since then, Ishkun-Dim-Hbelu." She locked eyes with Kisare, and then with Bel. "This was soon after our Hbelu became the leader of our caravan. He rejected the traditional wandering ways of our people, forcing us to build a permanent settlement. With a village, we could fortify and resist attempts by the fourcolors to kill or capture our people. Our godfruit trees flourished, giving us more power. Yet the only place free to settle, and far enough from the fourcolors' influence, was in this little corner of our former domain, close to the borders of the Blasted Lands." The woman spread her hands, taking in their mountainous location.

"The time will come when all Asha-Urmana are free to settle where they want," Hbelu said.

"I hope that is the case," the female elder with the bag said. "But we should come to business. We hear Ishkun-Dim-Hbelu has a special interest in you and your box."

Kisare's eyes flicked to the younger man amid the elders and caught a slight reddening of his cheeks. He *had* become a lot friendlier after seeing the box, and whatever the malus told him about it. Then she understood and looked to her sister. Even with a nasty scrape down the side of her face, she was beautiful.

The nobles and guards paid less attention to her homely face and slender build, thank all the gods, though she had fended off her own share of wandering hands. Bel's grip tightened on the box, and Kisare narrowed her eyes at Hbelu.

Hbelu was steadfastly looking at the box. "It held a great interest from the start, gods-marked as it is," he said, a little too fast. "I knew it would greatly interest the elders of my caravan. Perhaps it could be a tool against the reign of the fourcolors." Kisare spared him a tight smile.

The clockmaker popped up from his seat, as if his legs could not stay bent a moment longer. He stepped across the pavilion to Bel, through the dappled afternoon light coming through the curtain of honeysuckle. His leather boots made little sound on the wood planks.

"May I?" He held a hand out for the box, and Bel sat back a little. She glanced at Kisare, uncertain. There was nothing they could do to resist them, but as Bel pointed out, the Asha-Urmana could have taken their prize from them at any point. It was more than the master had ever done for them, all in one afternoon. She imagined a future where she had her own godfruit trees.

Bel gripped the box, frowning. Kisare nodded toward the skinny elder, patiently waiting with his hand out. His other hand scrabbled in a felt pouch at his side and produced a curious device from his pocket, carved or maybe grown from wood. It was like a tiny carnival mask for just the eyes, pieces of glass fixed in place of the eyeholes. He set the device over his nose and the legs over his large ears. He looked up and Kisare jumped at his oversized eyes. Had they been that big before?

With a small sigh, Bel handed him the banded wooden box.

"I am Anagmeshu-Ea. You have seen my shop, where I tinker with clocks and other intricate mechanisms. I am also familiar with those few artifacts we know were blessed by the gods." He made humming noises at the box, fingering the edges, and careful not to turn it upside-down, as if he already knew what was inside.

Finally, the elder produced a small slice of malus. He popped it into his mouth with a shiver, eyes rolling back, lightning dancing down his body, then directed his gaze back to the metal bands.

"Yes, here." He pointed a bony finger above the nick in the metal where Kisare had bashed the box with the stone. "And here, and here." His finger touched things Kisare couldn't see, one on each of the four bands. He turned the box around. "Then repeated on the back. This box has indeed been marked by the gods, all four of them." He looked up again. "Shall we see what could be so precious?"

Kisare tensed as he opened the lid. The pavilion was quiet, except for birdsong above them and far-off speech from other Asha-Urmana. She forced herself to relax. If they took the box, she and Bel would steal it back. They had their own godfruit trees here. They couldn't be interested in one more—

"A seed," Anagmeshu-Ea said, swishing a finger around in the black dirt in the box. "Most curious."

Kisare hadn't had another chance to see inside, what with their escape. She stood, ignoring the pain in her shoulder. Brushing hair back from her eyes, she leaned over the little elder—no noble would ever have let her do that without a backhand to her face—staring at what he pulled to the top of the dirt. One small seed, unfamiliar to her.

The elder still chewed the pulp of the malus slice as he stared at the tiny thing. "This also has the marks of the gods on it, as all godfruit tree seeds do. It glistens to my eyes. Oh my, that *is* unusual."

"It glows to our eyes as well. What kind of seed is it?" Hbelu asked. The seed was glowing faintly as the elder held it, hard to see in the late afternoon, but brighter than when Kisare had picked it up in the orchard.

Though the sunlight was fading, Kisare could see Hbelu's hands gripping the edges of his woven chair. So, this was not what usually happened with a godfruit seed. She had been right to suspect this box held something more. Hbelu met her eyes for a moment, then looked away. She and Anagmeshu-Ea shook their heads at the same time. It was not a malus pip, or citron seed.

"I do not recognize it," the elder said.

"I might," said the woman with the soft and creaky voice. They all looked at her, but she was already digging through her satchel. With a cry, she pulled out an ancient bound book, the cover worn away to a threadbare tatter.

"What do you know, Ku-Baba?" Hbelu asked.

"A single seed, a god-marked box, lost near the edge of the Blasted Lands." She turned pages carefully. "Yes, there is a record here, though old and incomplete." She settled the book in her lap. "Let me tell you of the fifth godfruit."

CHAPTER SIX

Old Stories, Old Threats

Blustery old Enta, winter god, chose last. He had some respect for the frail beings who resisted his frozen bite and added the magic of his cold body to the citron, the only fruit to produce in his time of the year. Though he spared lemons and limes, all other oranges froze solid, melting to nothing in the spring.

Ku-Baba cleared her throat, glancing between Belili and her sister. Kisa still hovered over the box as if she wanted to snatch it from the elder.

"This dates from the creation of the godfruit trees, back when the gods still walked among us. Much wisdom was passed between the caravans' elders over the years, but the oldest stories, from before the fourcolors displaced us, are recorded in these." She hefted the book in her lap, then ran a finger across the page in front of her. Belili had a sudden urge to sit by her side, as with Mistress Tiamai when she was young.

"'Unlike the morus, prunus, malus, and citron, the gods fashioned the last godfruit, the fifth godfruit, in secret,'" Ku-Baba read. "'They harbored anger at the refugees. Only I, Darice-Ili-Aya, Princess of the Asha-Urmana, was told the secret of the fifth godfruit.'" Ku-Baba cleared her throat again, running her finger down the page.

"'The fifth godfruit was meant to balance the gods' domain after the Blasted Lands were created. To show their submission, all five hair colors gifted with magic must bring the godfruit to life together. However, the other four colors come to us as refugees, ragged things, incapable of further wrong, as they are incapable of solidarity between themselves. The Asha-Urmana have since deemed the fifth godfruit unnecessary.'"

"This princess was obviously mistaken," Kisa said into the silence. "I assume she meant the nobles." The little elder beside her blinked through his magnifying lenses.

"Yes, on both accounts," Ku-Baba said.

"Is there any other record?" Hbelu asked. "Why was this fifth godfruit not used before?"

"There is no further record," Ku-Baba said with a shrug. "Though there are dissenting and less accurate accounts. The four gods chose the original godfruit trees after they were fully mature, fruit hanging from their boughs. The fifth godfruit, once deemed unnecessary, was lost. No one knew in what form it existed. Others over the years have looked for a grown tree, to no avail. The story is treated as all but myth these days." She closed the book and placed it back in her satchel.

"What does the fifth godfruit do?" Belili asked.

"That is the question," Ku-Baba said, leaning her slight form back in her chair. "Some think the new godfruit will bring prophetic wisdom to tell right from wrong, or new and strange magic to change the land, or maybe nothing at all. But all think it will reverse the advantage the fourcolors have over the Asha-Urmana. Dumzi, Geshtna, Kigal, and Enta no longer speak to us, so we cannot know for certain."

"Won't the nobles also have this new godfruit?" The nobles already had absolute dominion over the blonds. Belili had her own set of scars on her back, though not as many as her sister. Her invisible scars were more numerous.

"Then we must keep it away from them," Kisa said. Belili raised her eyebrows. "With the power this seed could give us, we could remove the tyranny of the nobles! It could be the chance to free us—free all slaves."

"It will not be so simple," Hbelu said in his deep voice. He gazed at Kisa, who glared back. "Yes, my people ruled this land before the fourcolors came, but over a thousand years ago. We have fought them before, and the fourcolors are powerful."

"We can fight," Kisa said. "If the blonds join you, then you will have a better chance." She was staring back at the prince, and Belili's eyes flicked between them. So, they had found something to agree on.

"Yes. It is time for the Asha-Urmana to stop hiding in the hills and valleys of our own land," Hbelu said. He spared a look for the elders. Anagmeshu-Ea was still clutching the box and returned to his seat. Belili watched how he curled around it, but he seemed interested only in observing the glowing seed, not in its worth. "With the fifth godfruit, we can take back what we lost."

"If we hadn't found the box, and risked our life to escape our imprisonment, the fifth godfruit would still be a myth to you," Belili reminded them. "We deserve some compensation for it." Since she was no longer a *prisoner*.

"What of the godfruit I used to enable your escape? Does that not count as some payment for your discovery?" Hbelu shifted his legs in his chair, hands gripping the sides. Ku-Baba bent toward the female elder with the wide shoulders, whispering and gesturing.

Kisa thumped her hands on the arms of her woven chair. "The treasure is ours. After all, what of the blonds—those without magic? They have a stake in this too. You've suffered much less at the hands of the nobles than us." What a change from Kisa gaping at the prince spitting out barely chewed malus.

Hbelu looked to Kisa. "What price would you set on this inheritance of the Asha-Urmana? The seed's existence could reunite the caravans. Together, they can overturn the fourcolors' rule. I would consider all debts repaid, and you both great friends of the Asha-Urmana, if you gave the box to us freely."

Kisa was already shaking her head. "So, *you* can overturn their rule? What about the blonds? I will not give you our only possession. We have a stake in this too, and I like the idea of getting back at the nobles."

"The prisoners have no society of their own," the prince countered. "Would they not get in the way?"

Belili saw Kisa bristle. "No society? Only because the nobles beat it from us. You are free, though you sit here on your hands."

If Kisa had been this brazen back in the orchard, Belili would have been an only child. She cut in before the argument could get worse. "We ran from the orchard in the hope of starting a new life. If we instead risk our lives to fight the nobles, we should have control of what we contribute."

"I must agree with the sisters," said Anagmeshu-Ea, still clutching the box in one hand, the seed in the other. "Such a treasure has no price." The other male elder and Ku-Baba nodded in agreement.

"Exactly," Kisa said. "So some of you can see sense."

Hbelu didn't answer, pulling at his beard. Then, "What if you *and* the box stayed here with us? You can work for our caravan, helping to plant and tend our crops, and maintain our equipment. You, and the blonds, if we can recruit any, can add your strength when we fight."

Belili narrowed her eyes. The man wanted her sister here not only to fight, if she was any judge. Kisa was too worked up to see it.

"As free women," Kisa said.

"Only if we own what we tend and grow," Belili added. She did not want to work *for* anyone.

Several of the elders spoke heatedly, until Hbelu silenced them with a wave. "In no way do I mean servitude. We do *not* own slaves, unlike the fourcolors. You would stay with our caravan, have the use of a house, and eat meals with the rest of us. We gain the magic of the fifth godfruit, whatever it is." Hbelu stared back at Kisa.

"Ishkun-Dim-Hbelu, have you forgotten the path of the Asha-Urmana, the way we keep our magic from the fourcolors?" the wide-shouldered woman asked.

"I have not, Muze-Shi," Hbelu answered. "I remember you also questioned my decision to settle here rather than wandering."

"What does she mean?" Kisa asked.

There was another exchange of glances. Finally, Ku-Baba sighed. "The fourcolors try to dominate all magic in the land, grasping for ours as well. Before the Blasted Lands and the refugees, the gods warned that ambition for magical power would lead only to loss. If we bred only for range of magical coloring, our power would instead dilute. We would end up no better than the blonds, with no magic."

"The nobles did this," Belili said. Four colors. The Asha-Urmana epithet made sense.

"All Asha-Urmana have some purple hair," Muze-Shi said, gesturing to her own partially white hair. "It fades as we age, but per individual, we have more magic than the fourcolors."

"You don't let any non-Asha-Urmana stay with you," Kisa said.

"It removes ambition for different gifts of the gods, yes," Muze-Shi said. Belili saw the woman was also watching Hbelu.

"The nobles have many who can use different kinds of magic," Belili said. "Surely it's worth the sacrifice in power to have more choice? I've even heard of some using more than one magic. Is that why they defeated you when you fought?"

"Each generation of their children will lose more magic," Anagmeshu-Ea said. "Eventually, the Asha-Urmana will be the only ones with useable magic, and we will take back our rightful place."

"That's many years away," Belili said, "and we have the fifth godfruit now."

"Which is why I have invited them to stay," Hbelu said to the elders. Belili watched his eyes. His glance went most often to Kisa.

"They cannot stay!" Muze-Shi insisted.

"If we go, we take our box with us," Kisa said.

"Muze-Shi, this seed is the chance I have spoken of for years." Hbelu stood and paced in front of his chair. The sun was going down, and shadow and light played over the prince of the Asha-Urmana's face as he passed under the slats of the pergola. The slight glow of the seed was brighter now, as Anagmeshu-Ea peered at it.

"With it, we have a piece of our history, to unite the caravans and start the process of rebuilding our society, whether in this place, or another." Hbelu gestured at the village surrounding them. "The sisters must stay, along with their box. If we took it, we would be no better than the fourcolors. Are there any other objections?" He stared down the elders. Even if they didn't agree, no one else questioned him.

Belili cleared her throat. "What about Aricaba-Ata? He will come for us, eventually."

"I assume he will. In a matter of days, most likely." Hbelu turned his gaze on her, and Belili stared back coolly. "The nobles have many times forced us farther and farther away from the best growing lands. We owe them no favors."

"So, we will protect these runaway slaves from their former master?" Muze-Shi asked. "At the risk of our village?"

"We will," Hbelu said. "The sisters will be part of our caravan."

Kisa looked to Belili, then her eyes flicked back to Hbelu. When they returned, Belili nodded to her.

"We agree," Kisa told Hbelu.

"Anagmeshu-Ea will keep the box for further study of the magical seed," Hbelu told them. The elder looked up, almost guiltily, from where he studied the inlaid metal of the box. He finally placed the seed back in the dirt, and the glow faded. Belili held her tongue. They were not taking it from her.

Ku-Baba was already rising, and so Kisa and Belili rose too, Belili wincing at her stiff leg.

"There is an empty house you may stay in," Hbelu said. "The owner was a widower who recently departed for the beyond. It was kept empty for a new couple to inhabit."

Belili and her sister had a quick supper under the gaze of the elders in the area the caravan took its meals. In the light of pitch torches, they ate greens and fruit, and the meat of the deer Hbelu killed that morning. Hbelu served Kisa a cut, and her sister accepted it with a rare smile. Belili watched the prince through the rest of the meal, grateful, but wary.

Afterward Ku-Baba directed them to the empty house, giving them extra blankets and a beeswax candle. It was dark, and Belili was tired and stiff from their chase, not to mention the fight with the guard and Tashi. Her nap during the day had helped little.

"We will find you work clothes tomorrow," the old woman told them. "You will need to work to pay us back for them."

"Huh," Kisa grunted, crossing her arms at the elder's retreating back.

"We are using their resources," Belili said. "It's fair we pay for them. The cost is small compared to the price for the box. We've upset their society already."

"Not so much, I'd wager," Kisa answered. "Surely other blonds have stayed here for a few nights before." Belili wasn't sure, remembering Muze-Shi's glower.

They found two crafted wooden beds in the house, which was constructed much as the others. Kisa looked to her in the flickering of the lit candle. They had never spent a night apart since Kisa was born, in or out of the master's house.

"The nights are warming, and there is a stout door," Kisa said.

"Of course," Belili answered her, spreading blankets over the straw-stuffed mattress of a bed. "I'm sure we'll be more comfortable with a whole bed each. See how kind the Asha-Urmana are?"

Kisa harrumphed but spread her blankets and climbed under them. "At least I don't have to watch out for your cold feet."

"Or me for your bony elbows," Belili answered. The old jest fell short tonight. She blew out the candle. "Goodnight."

"Goodnight."

It was several hours later when Belili felt Kisa climb in bed with her.

The next day, they engaged in hard, but fair, work around the village. Anagmeshu-Ea was holed up in his clockmaking workshop with a steady supply of malae, trying to glean more information about the box and its glowing seed.

The Asha-Urmana found Belili's skill in pruning, as it was time to clear the final deadwood before spring fully took hold. Kisa was engaged in planting new crops, but found a skill of her own: tinkering with the caravan's mechanical devices. She corrected the spin of a windmill by wedging a weighty stone in the crossbar of one of the sails. The Aricaba orchard ran on slaves rather than mechanics, and Kisa had never had a chance before to examine mechanical contraptions. It was good to see her sister's pragmatism put to more use than calculating the day's quota.

Belili kept an eye out for errant hands or eyes, but even without Kisa beside her, the caravan's inhabitants were kind and generous, if a little distant. Despite her natural suspicion, Belili's guard began to drop. She even tried out a smile for one of the more handsome women of the caravan, but Ligish's strong nose and fearful eyes kept intruding on her thoughts.

"Sumul the miller thanked me for my work today," Kisa told her as they got ready for bed that night, again making separate beds. She sounded confused, yet almost happy.

"Then it was a good day?"

"I suppose so," Kisa said. "I worked as hard as any day in the orchard, but there were no guards breathing down my back. No whips cracking the air."

"How long do you think we can stay here?" Belili asked.

"I don't know," Kisa said. "Hbelu hasn't said anything about fighting back. Still, most of the people here seemed happy to help an outsider. I wonder how many other...prisoners they've seen?"

That night, Belili awoke with a strangled grunt from a dream where Tashi ate the other malus slice and fought back, pushing cold dirt down Belili's throat. It was chilly, so she decided to keep her sister company. Kisa was probably cold, after all, and they should see which bed was more comfortable.

The next day was weeding and planting seeds, and most of the village helped. Belili's wounds were healing well—the one in her thigh only hindered her when getting up and down. They were treated no differently, and even given the same break in the middle of the day for a large lunch of winter nuts, meats, and roots, prepared in a stew. They gravitated to an empty table at the edge of the dining area, but Hbelu, still wiping dirt from his hands, showed them to a seat at one of the nearer tables. He pulled a chair out for Kisa. Belili watched him until he sat down with the elders. He had made no untoward moves, but Belili vowed to keep her little sister in sight at all times.

They sat next to a family with several adorable children, one with nearly as much purple as Hbelu. The father watched them as carefully as she watched Hbelu, until Kisa made faces at the youngest, and soon they were all laughing with her.

That night, Belili, tired from the day's work, fell asleep as soon as her head touched the small blanket she used as a pillow. There may have been dreams of Tashi again, or of the guard, but she didn't wake from them. In the morning, she shared a look with Kisa, from their separate beds. It was the first time they had slept apart.

There was sadness in Kisa's eyes, but also pride. "You were right, Bel," she said. "They do treat us well here. For the first time, I feel...safe." Kisa looked confused at her own words, then shook her head.

"We're planting again today," she said. "Arala and Dari want us to help in their field. It's near the woods on the edge of the village, a fresh field, so they'll need us to work with them to turn the ground." Their new clothes, leather pants and shirts, were hanging in the corner of the room. The thick material resisted dirt stains.

"I think Dari might have a little crush on you," Belili told her. "She thinks you a hero, for having run away from the nobles." Kisa smiled but shook her head again. Yes, this new freedom was good, for both of them.

The morning was weeding, tilling, and planting. The Asha-Urmana kept similar crops to the Aricaba orchard. This early in the season they were planting peppers, greens, early gourds, and many types of beans and peas. Belili was familiar with planting, but Kisa had always taken the lead there. She even had a few tips for Arala and Dari, the mother and daughter who had taken a liking to Belili's sister. Kisa gestured at a line of seeds with her hoe, explaining something to Dari, who shyly clutched a pail of water. It was good to see Kisa's hard edges softening.

Belili started as a horn echoed across the fields.

"What was that?" She shaded her eyes from the morning sun, looking around. The forest was thicker on this side.

"Fourcolors," the matronly Arala said beside her, hands on pudgy knees. She had a large font of purple hair in the front, and she swept it away from her eyes. Her cheerful face had taken on a dark hue. "Never any good."

One of the village's scouts, a teenage boy, approached them from the forest edge. His eyes were wide, his hands stiff by his sides. He panted, and only after she noticed this did Belili see who was behind him. The boy was tall, and almost obscured the reason for his slow and painful walk.

"Ilzi," Belili hissed. "Stop hiding behind that boy."

Her former master's cousin emerged from behind the purple-haired teenager, holding something in one cheek. His black lock was almost blue in the morning sun. He kept one hand on the boy's shoulder, as if in a friendly gesture. Belili remembered that touch all too well. He must have citron juice in his mouth. A way to heal. A way to hurt.

"Calm, Bel," Ilzi said, his voice dry. "I've only slowed the boy down, given him a touch of that tightness older men feel in their heart. I could have killed the caravanner, but I am merciful."

Kisa and Dari came up behind her. Arala's face was tight and furious, but she said nothing. Kisa was the one to step forward. "You let us go," she said. "Why come after us now?"

"You were supposed to lose him profits for a few days, then come back when I found you, to show Ata how much he needs my influence in the orchard. Instead, you took up with these"—he sneered— "caravanners. I am merely correcting the situation."

Ilzi had said Ligish gave him that idea. Belili kept her head still, deliberately not looking for Ilzi's new slave—new prisoner—trailing behind him. He wouldn't bring her here, of course. She was being silly. She hoped Ligish hadn't been beaten hard.

"How will you do that?" Kisa asked. "There are four of us and one of you. We could call the guards in the village to take you down." Belili shook her head. She knew what the man would do and wished Kisa didn't have to learn of it. It would be a rude awakening. Ilzi was a twisty one.

"I think they are all busy at the moment, likely with Ata and his guards and dogs. I thought I might do a little reconnaissance, and here

I find our prizes, tending fields like they used to. Is it really any different if you do so here or at Ata's orchard?"

"You—!" Kisa moved forward, her hoe raised in both hands.

"Stop!" Belili told her, but it was too late. The boy gurgled, and dropped to one knee, Ilzi's hand still on his shoulder. Kisa slowed, confused.

"I still have enough juice of the citron to kill him," Ilzi said. "And probably a few more of you. Think carefully."

Kisa's hoe drooped, and Belili hung her head. She should have told her sister what Ilzi was capable of.

"But you healed us," Kisa said. Her voice was small.

"What is healing but changing the body to its owner's benefit? The change need not be beneficial." The boy moaned, one hand clutching at his chest.

"Stop it," Belili said. "Heal him and...I'll come with you."

"No!" Kisa cried, but Ilzi was lifting the boy to his feet, his pasty face regaining its usual tanned color.

"I accept," he said, and Belili went to him. The boy stumbled to Dari and Arala, who hugged him close. Ilzi placed his hand on her shoulder, as he had with the teenager, then produced another slice of citron. At least it was better than the mental intrusion Ilzi could summon with a morus.

Another horn echoed through the village.

"I suggest we attend the summons," Ilzi said, pulling her backward toward the forest. She stumbled back, her thigh wound pulling. "Ata will see I've already completed half of his objective for him, and maybe he will finally show favor at my choice of companions. Those city women have nothing on strong mountain stock."

CHAPTER SEVEN

New Strength

The gods had chosen their magical fruits, but their blond-haired servants lacked the ability to unlock the power of the godfruit, and the four gods' effort was wasted. The magic contained therein needed a catalyst to work.

"Your former captor is here," Hbelu told Kisare when she reached the entrance to the village. "The spirit I summoned delayed their arrival by a few days, but now the fourcolor is—" he broke off. "Where is your sister?"

"Taken," Kisare said. "My mast—former master has a cousin who lives near his orchard. Enti-Ilzi. He has some design on my sister, and she only went with him in trade for the life of one of your sentries." She tried not to put too much emphasis on the last two words. It had been Bel's choice. She dug her fingertips into the palms of her hands around the hoe, encrusted dirt grinding.

Hbelu's face darkened. "I promised you shelter. We will get your sister back."

Kisare felt a stab of relief and gratitude at the prince's words. She hesitated, then touched his arm, drew back. "Thank you," she said. "Where is Aricaba-Ata?"

"My sentries have orders to let him through," Hbelu answered. His eyes landed briefly on her hand, then returned to her face. "I want to speak to this fourcolor who invades my land, who lets his kin threaten boys and abduct women from underneath my nose."

The path where Kisare and her sister had followed Hbelu into the village was ahead of them, trees to either side. There were shouts, and the whine and bark of hounds. Kisare clenched the hoe and saw Hbelu reach a hand into the pouch by his side. He must have godfruit. Other Asha-Urmana trickled in from the fields and watched from between the houses. Kisare wondered how many of the villagers could fight or use godfruit aggressively. She hoped there were enough to stop Aricaba-Ata and his guard.

A group of men and women, all with purple locks, burst from the forest. There were maybe ten, a few covering the rest as they retreated, spears pointed toward the woods. Behind them, hounds crashed through, her former master holding chains leashing the barking dogs with one hand, the other spreading a fan of fire in front of him matching the red in his hair. The last few Asha-Urmana guards, several with singed leathers, fell back to the village, leaving Aricaba-Ata alone. He was chewing a malus, the rest still clutched in his hand. Five of his blond guards trailed behind him, but Enti-Ilzi was not with them. Kisare hoped Bel was fighting him.

"Where are they?" Aricaba-Ata roared through the godfruit in his mouth. A dog sent up a whine that split the air. "Where is my property?"

Kisare gasped at the man's face and arms. Long leather sleeves covered his forearms, though the bottoms were shredded. Through the holes, she could see streaks of red, which continued to the tips of his fingers. His face was a mass of red welts, bites, and scrapes, some still oozing whitish pus. Kisare smiled viciously at the results of Hbelu's trap at the creek.

"There is no property here," Hbelu called back in a loud voice. "Only free people." Kisare noticed the elders now stood behind him, stony faced. Anagmeshu-Ea adjusted the lenses over his eyes, but all six of the older Asha-Urmana held godfruit.

Her former master's expression clenched with fury, and he took a step forward, tugging the chains that held his hounds—nasty black beasts with foam-flecked jaws. Many of the blonds in the orchard carried scars from bite marks.

"I see one slave here. Where is the other, my best pruner? If you do not give them back, I am owed one tenth part of my store of blonds. I can take it from your flesh instead." He jerked a dog forward. It snapped at the line of Asha-Urmana guards, who stepped back. Kisare saw a flash of orange from Ku-Baba, whose head jerked in shock. Vines under the dog's feet spiraled upward, tangling it. The beast gave a plaintive whine and tugged its legs, trying to retreat. The other dogs stopped growling and took positions behind their owner.

Aricaba-Ata's face grew even darker than usual at the display, and he threw a thick finger out at the dog. "What right do you purple-haired caravanners have to steal my labor?"

He transferred the rest of the malus to his free hand. Aricaba-Ata did not have nearly as much color in his hair as Hbelu, but Kisare knew what her former master could do when angry. She had seen the burn marks and broken limbs on slaves who disobeyed him.

"The women are under my protection." Hbelu said. Kisare watched Aricaba-Ata's eyes rove over the prince's hair, taking in his greater potential of magic. Did he know what abilities the godfruits gave those with purple hair? Not well, considering his surprise at the vines trapping his struggling dog.

"I thank you for finding them," Aricaba-Ata said, "but they are my property, and expensive to replace. Return them." He made a gesture and his own guards moved closer, brandishing swords and clubs. They had even more welts and scratches than their employer.

In response, the Asha-Urmana sentries tightened together. Each held a spear and a rectangular shield. They placed them end to end, making a wall against attack.

"You will not break into my village," Hbelu called. "I have greater numbers than you, and more of mine can use godfruit."

Bushes rustled at the edge of the forest, and all eyes turned that way, Aricaba-Ata leaning to one side to keep both the Asha-Urmana and this new threat in his vision.

Bel emerged from the tree line, followed by Enti-Ilzi. He pushed Kisare's sister close to his cousin, obviously enjoying the attention. "I believe I may adjust the balance of this negotiation," he said into the silence.

Aricaba-Ata boomed a laugh. "Good work, Ilzi. Where blunt force does not work, a little persuasion might."

Kisare locked eyes with Bel, who gave a minute nod. She was unharmed, for the moment. Kisare needed to find a way to get her back.

"Then would now be a good time to recognize the benefit I have given you?" Enti-Ilzi said, tugging Bel closer. "Perhaps in marital compensation?"

"Gods take you, man," Aricaba-Ata shot back. "Save it for later! Help me."

"Fine. I will remind you of this when you are enjoying the benefits of your blond's labor."

Hbelu's face reddened as the two nobles spoke. "You will not take these women back," he said to the fighting nobles. "They are my responsibility now, and I will not let them leave my sight."

Kisare was suddenly aware of a heat in her own face. The hoe's shaft dug into the bones of her hands, and she loosened her grip. Three men with magic were discussing her and her sister like sides of meat.

"A slave stole slices of malus from my wife," Aricaba-Ata said. "Tashi, my wife's best slave, is dead. I will have justice done. My orchard barely makes a profit, and if I lose any more blonds, none of them will have any place to live. Do you see my problem?"

"I do," replied Hbelu. "You treat these people so badly they wish to run away. You also do not take a good account of how your godfruit is used."

Aricaba-Ata took a step forward, his face darkening with rage, then glanced at his dog. It was still biting the tendrils trapping its legs.

"I only want my blonds back," he said, softer. "Tashi has been punished, whatever her part." Kisare pushed down an image of Bel crouching over Tashi, dirt clogging Tashi's mouth. "These two I will reprimand, but lightly. Then they will continue to work to earn me profit from my godfruit trees." Kisare noticed he didn't specify the punishment.

"I do not see how your society functions." Hbelu shook his head. "How much longer until it topples?"

The Asha-Urmana sentries held their shields and spears at the ready, while Shuma and the other guards watched for obvious openings in the greater number. It was a standstill, with the blonds caught between as always. Bel strained under Enti-Ilzi's hand, the citron threatening disease.

Bel rolled her eyes up at her captor's face, then down to his pouch, then looked straight at her. Kisare's eyes widened. There was no way the nobles could keep juice so long in their mouth while they talked. Enti-Ilzi was bluffing.

Her former master shook an impotent fist. "They are *my* property. They owe me." He glared at Bel. "Twenty-three years I have clothed and fed this girl, and few less for her sister. You shall not lose me my best pruner." No mention of Kisare's talents in planting and tending. Well, was she a prisoner, or a free woman? Now was the time to act.

"How much have you paid her for her services?" Hbelu asked.

Aricaba-Ata scoffed. "She should be grateful to have a roof and shelter. What does a blond know of economy, trade—"

Kisare walked forward, holding the hoe loosely at her side, as if she had forgotten about it. She heard Hbelu grunt in surprise behind her. He should have let her speak for herself.

Her former master stopped in mid-sentence and stared at her as if she was crazy. Maybe she was. She kept her course steady.

"You make a good case," she said, still walking. The two nobles were about twenty paces away. "I'm tempted to come back. After all, I have no idea how to bargain for myself, or how to deal with these people."

"That...is correct." Aricaba-Ata looked suspicious.

"If I went back to the orchard, you'd be lenient, wouldn't you, Master? You'd provide for me?"

"Of course." The noble straightened. Five paces maybe. She took another few steps.

"Then there's only one thing I need to do."

"What is that?" Aricaba-Ata asked.

In answer, Kisare rammed the hoe upward. After years of weeding with the tool, she had good aim. The blow took Enti-Ilzi in the nose and she felt something crunch. Her second strike popped the pouch of godfruit off Aricaba-Ata's belt even as he grabbed for it. She struck again, swinging the hoe overhand at Aricaba-Ata's face, but the large man caught the hoe and tore it away from her, then reached for his sword.

Kisare backed up. "Run!" she shouted and reached for Bel's hand. Her sister struggled forward, then stopped, as Enti-Ilzi threw an arm tight around her neck. He leaned back, biceps and forearm straining. His other hand held his nose, blood running freely, while Bel gasped in his grip. Her face was going red. The noble's knees were bent, and he only stayed upright by the weight he put on Bel's neck.

"Go. Box," her sister gasped. Her former master had his sword free, and Kisare threw one more apologetic look before running back to the Asha-Urmana village.

All six elders behind Hbelu had malae to mouths, and Kisare heard the crack of teeth biting into crisp godfruit. From the ground at their feet rose the ghostly forms of past Asha-Urmana, their hair a pallid shade of purple. The shades stalked forward, pushing back the nobles and their guards. The hounds skittered away in fear.

"Call them off!" yelled Aricaba-Ata. Kisare only saw her sister, struggling backward, hands clawing at Enti-Ilzi's arm. They would kill her. Best pruner or not, a slave wouldn't survive in the middle of a fight.

Shuma stopped his retreat, growling, and tried to spear a ghost on his sword. The spirit only looked down at the sharp metal passing through her body and grinned at him. She reached out with a pale hand and stroked Shuma's face. The large bodyguard shouted and clapped a hand to his cheek, a red welt growing underneath.

"No more harm to my people or the blond dies!" Aricaba-Ata drew a citron from his pouch and put a section in his mouth, then tossed the rest to Enti-Ilzi, whose hand left his nose long enough to catch the godfruit.

"Fight him, Bel!" Kisare called. Maybe her sister could free herself while the noble healed.

The ghosts made a circle around the guards and the dogs, blocking off the nobles from the village. Kisare's heart sped as she saw the Asha-Urmana pressing the attack, despite the threat to her sister.

She ran for Hbelu, but he was already moving toward the nobles. He took a peeled citron from his pouch and bit deeply into it. She had never seen so much godfruit used at one time.

"Stop!" she cried, but he paid no attention. Kisare turned to the elders and repeated her cry, but they didn't hear her, or didn't care. Only Anagmeshu-Ea's eyes flicked to her. They were all staring at their ghosts.

When she turned back to Hbelu, he was facing Aricaba-Ata, already passed through the ghosts' line. She realized the prince towered over her former master. Hbelu's leather clothes stretched to their limits to cover him, making him look like a man wearing boy's garments.

But Aricaba-Ata had already bitten into his own citron. She could see the juice running into his fingers. Hbelu swept into Aricaba-Ata with a roar, his voice deeper than usual. Aricaba-Ata resisted the charge. Kisare had seen him rip a tree from the ground with the strength the citron gave those with red hair. Little stabs of lightning trailed down the two magic users' arms and legs, and Kisare stepped back, wincing as the two crashed together with a smack. They were like two slabs of rock, one twice as tall as normal, the other with strength to raise boulders above his head. Hbelu slowly pushed the noble away, large hands clasped on arms.

Enti-Ilzi was steady again, wiping blood from his face with one hand, his nose straight once more. His arm was still around Bel's neck, and her face was going pale. She struggled weakly for a moment longer and went limp. The noble guided her to the ground, then drew his sword. He grasped in his pouch with his other bloody hand and produced a slice of malus.

The Asha-Urmana sentries stalked toward him. Enti-Ilzi saw this and bit down, standing over Bel's unconscious body. As the sentries came close, Enti-Ilzi's sword grew a band of frost, then ice, white contrasting with the black lock of his hair. The ice lengthened, and he whipped it forward into the nearest sentry. A wicked shard of ice flew toward him, stabbing into his leg. The sentry stumbled backward. Enti-Ilzi followed with several more slashes of his sword, each dislodging a spike of ice at a sentry. Kisare ran toward him, but Enti-Ilzi stood his ground, his sword wavering in Kisare's direction.

The ghosts were closing behind Hbelu as he pressed Aricaba-Ata into the woods. Aricaba-Ata's strength would fail before Hbelu's increased size, if they ate the same amount of godfruit. Hbelu by far had more magically colored hair.

Kisare wavered between the two groups, scanning for another weapon. How could she help against the tidal forces fighting here? She was a blond. She had no magic.

With a roar, Hbelu pushed Aricaba-Ata to one side. He tripped backward, his magic used up, and went sprawling. Hbelu began to shrink.

Enti-Ilzi took that moment to swing his sword in a large arc, as if cutting stalks of wheat. The ice from his sword liquefied and flew through the ghosts, splitting their forms. The ghosts dissolved in mist, and Kisare heard gasps from the elders. How much did their power decrease with their white hair? The ghost Hbelu raised had lasted for several days. Enti-Ilzi bent and scooped Bel up, holding her in both arms. His sword dangled from one hand, dangerously close to Bel's thigh.

Hbelu made a spiral motion to the elders, and the drifting mist condensed again into human forms. The nobles were backing into the forest, Shuma and the other guards taking position in front of them. The right side of the captain of the guard's face was a mass of swollen red, as if a bee had stung him.

Kisare found her feet moving, until she was in front of the swirling mist, anger rising. Hbelu still had to rescue her, like a useless *slave*.

"Leave us alone!" she shouted. "Bel and I owe you nothing. We are no longer your prisoners. We are *free women*."

Aricaba-Ata only laughed.

"Free women? Little blond, you hardly know what to do off the orchard. You have yourself a caravanner stud here, but he will use you worse than I. Come back with me and your sister and I shall let you go with a flogging. I am reasonable."

He *was* being reasonable, for him. The worst part was, some part of her was tempted. Enti-Ilzi had Bel, and he could have her beaten, or take her for his orchard, or even force her to marry him. The box and the fifth godfruit meant she could help free *all* slaves, not just her sister. She just wanted to go back to the slave's house, back to her chores. Take her punishment and let Aricaba-Ata provide for her. Be with her sister. She glanced to where Enti-Ilzi held Bel, draped in his arms.

She stepped back, shaking her head. No. The box was a sign that the world did not need to be this way, and if she was free, she could free Bel again.

Aricaba-Ata laughed again. "Just like a blond. You will die in a week without me."

A wordless anger filled her. *I am a free woman!*

Hbelu, now his normal size, stood where the ghosts were reforming. Even the prince was careful not to touch the spirits.

"Let us speak calmly," he told them, with a side glance at Kisare, his expression apologetic. "Surely there is a way—"

Her former master stopped laughing. "No. We are beyond reason. I will return with an army to destroy you."

"You would have to *return* to gather that army," Hbelu breathed. "My scouts will hunt you. If I have my way, there will be no killing today."

Aricaba-Ata's face was cloudy. "And if I do *not* have my way, there will be at least one dead slave."

"He'll do it," Kisare told Hbelu. "He's killed blonds for less." She could only let her sister go if there was a chance to free her later. Otherwise, she would go with them. Hbelu's face was set. "Please," she continued, "let them go for now. They have *Bel*."

Hbelu's jaw worked. "I have given my word to protect these two women, and that I will. Too long have we stayed away from the fourcolors, letting you live in cities we once owned. That changes today. The fourcolors will see battle again."

Aricaba-Ata gave a short laugh. "You do not speak for all of your caravanners," he said. "What of the rumors the Dyad has their own purple-hair?" The orchard owner waved a hand at Hbelu's locks.

Kisare saw Hbelu pause. She knew little of the Dyad, the ruling pair in Karduniash, save they were powerful magicians.

"No Asha-Urmana would let themselves be held by the nobles," Hbelu said. "That does not affect our arrangement here."

"Think what you will," Aricaba-Ata said. "The Dyad will take your caravanner power."

"Go," Hbelu commanded.

"Come, Cousin," Aricaba-Ata said. "We have messages for the capital." They faded into the woods, a guard helping Enti-Ilzi carry Bel. One of her arms bounced as they walked.

The reformed ghosts melted back into the ground as Hbelu rounded on the assembled townsfolk. "The elders and I must convene," he called. "Those who have jobs, tend to them. I will let everyone know when we come to a decision."

The others made their way back into the village, though the scouts faded into the trees at a gesture from their prince.

A hand caught her arm and she whirled to Hbelu. "What now?" she said, her anxiety pouring out. "Back to planting your crops? Let Bel be enslaved again?"

Hbelu's grip did not waver. "This was a long time in coming." Kisare glanced up to his frowning, bearded face. "My scouts will follow them from a safe distance. For now, your advice is needed. With the treasure you brought us, my people have more power than in a long time— enough to fight the fourcolors."

"So we go after them?" The sooner her sister was safe, the better.

Hbelu only shook his head. "Not yet. They will be ready, and I fear your sister may not survive a second encounter like today. I promise we will rescue her soon. They will travel slowly. The juice of the citron will not heal the injuries given by spirits."

"Then I will advise," Kisare said, reaching for the calm Hbelu somehow managed. Trying to be *free*. Her mind screamed to run after Bel, attack the nobles on her own, but that would achieve nothing.

The elders gathered around, and Hbelu addressed them. "Our people shall move again. Too long we have been sedentary and separated. Now the fourcolors know the location of our village."

"You mean to gather our nation again," Ku-Baba said in her soft and creaky voice.

"I do, and to take back our cities," Hbelu said. "With the help of the sisters' box."

"What of the godfruit trees?" This was Anagmeshu-Ea, his lenses making his eyes look large. "We have only just started the summer crops. Shall we leave them to die?"

Hbelu shook his head. "No, but time is of the essence. Pressing now, there is a chance for surprise, if the other caravans join us. Along the way we will release Belili from the fourcolors' influence."

Muze-Shi squared her broad shoulders. She had the least purple of all the elders, but a commanding presence. "This does not answer our concerns. The fourcolors will be back before we can depart. Will you leave our village without its best soldiers, off to convince our brethren to return? The next time, the slave master will have troops from Karduniash."

"We will not stay here, Muze-Shi," Hbelu told her. "Those who remain will uproot our village, gather seeds, dig up the godfruit trees, and disassemble buildings. We will go back to a caravan, our trees in pots and our houses as wagons." There was a collective sigh from the elders. Kisare wondered when they would get back to Bel.

"Even though you led us to settle here," Ku-Baba said, "to keep better communion with the gods?"

"What has that done for us in the last twelve years?" Hbelu said, his voice rising. "The gods no longer answer prayers of the Asha-Urmana." The elders were silent. The old mistress had told Kisare and Bel stories of long ago, when Dumzi, Geshtna, Kigal, and Enta walked among mortals.

"Why now?" Kisare asked. "With so many Asha-Urmana, all of whom can use magic, you could fend off an army. Why move this village?" She ached to be after her sister, but she also knew an extra day of planning could make the difference between Bel surviving, or not.

"The box," Anagmeshu-Ea answered.

"The box, and its seed, is the key to it," Hbelu said. "Finally found near the Blasted Lands, where no godfruit grows—a sign at last from the gods that we will reclaim our cities from the fourcolors." The prince's eyes were intense on her, and Kisare swallowed, feeling the beginnings of a blush.

"If they sent us and the box, why was Bel captured? Why hasn't the seed sprouted on its own?" She kept her head high.

"Ku-Baba's story suggests we need all five hair colors," Anagmeshu-Ea said. "Since the normal methods did not work—"

"What!" Kisare shouted. Her gratitude vanished. "You tried to make the seed grow without my...our...permission?"

The little elder ducked his head, but Hbelu showed no signs of embarrassment. "Trees take time to grow. Even if we had activated the seed, it would be years before it could give fruit. We must be in place before that time to force the fourcolors out."

Kisare bit her tongue. She would have argued, but she was worried about her sister. Besides, the man was right, though she hated to admit it.

"How do you grow a magic seed, anyway?" she asked, trying to keep anger from her voice. "Aricaba-Ata never showed the slaves."

Muze-Shi raised her head at the words. "They did not tell you?" She grunted. "Fourcolors. The way to make a magical seed grow is simple. It only requires a touch from one with magic in their hair, and a sprinkle of juice from that kind of godfruit. Obviously, this did not work for the fifth godfruit. It only glows when someone touches it."

Kisare frowned. That was...simple. No wonder the nobles hid it from their prisoners. Bel could make a godfruit tree grow. They could make a living outside the orchard, once Kisare got her back.

"To get back to the point," Ku-Baba said, frowning, "the seed did not sprout, since we do not have all five magic colors."

"How much magic does it require?" Kisare asked.

Hbelu nodded at her. "If this will really bring all creation back in balance, it is likely the gods did not mean this as a simple task. It must require a great concentration of magical ability."

"So, we couldn't capture the first nobles we see and force them to touch the seeds," Kisare said.

Hbelu inclined his head. "Unlikely. Such mighty people would be at the center of power."

"The Dyad," Kisare said. They were the most powerful magicians among the nobles. "That's why you want to go to Karduniash."

"If we already must be within the walls of the capital, we can retake it." Hbelu swept out his hands. "The scouts are following the nobles. Once they return with the fourcolors' location and direction, we will go after them. There can be no chance of failure."

Failure meant Bel's death. "Rescue happens *first*, before all this about overthrowing the nobles. Both Bel and I will see this to the end."

Hbelu met her eyes for a long moment, then nodded. "I promise we will free your sister first," he said. A couple of the elders made dismissive motions, but Kisare watched their leader. He had kept his word so far. His people would follow him. If he could rescue Bel, then she would have proof of his intentions. Maybe that would keep the blighted butterfly from fluttering in her stomach whenever he looked at her.

"Fine," she said. "Why do you need to move your village?" She had to ask the piercing questions, now that Bel wasn't here.

"When we retake the capital, I plan to have my people there, not spread out for the fourcolors to capture as they see fit," Hbelu said. "The Blasted Lands are too far away. All the Asha-Urmana should have the chance to return to the way we used to live."

"After rescuing my sister, uprooting the village, and uniting all the Asha-Urmana, we're supposed to sneak into the palace of Karduniash and force the rulers of the people that enslaved us to activate this seed?" Kisare asked.

"We shall," Hbelu answered. "Between them, the Dyad have the other four hair colors—all but that of the Asha-Urmana," Hbelu said, running fingers down his bound goatee. "We have kept our power from them for all these years. That is why you will take me along as a captured 'caravanner.'" His face twisted at the word. "You will arrive as foreign nobles from the Blasted Lands, hair dyed with streaks of color. Both of you. You will offer them the box as a gift, a token from fourcolors who survived in their original lands, bowing to Karduniash's might."

Ku-Baba and several other elders protested over each other, but Hbelu held up a hand and they quieted, save for grumbling.

"Then when all five magical hair colors have activated the seed, we will use the fifth godfruit's power to unite my people and overthrow the Dyad."

"But first, my sister," Kisare said.

CHAPTER EIGHT

Prisoners and Freedom

Shamed by their failure, the gods conferred. They decided to create five pairs of mortals with great power, each with a different shade of hair, activating a different portion of magic in each godfruit. These men and women would protect and lead the blonds.

Hbelu ordered a feast for breakfast, to let his people celebrate after fighting the fourcolors the day before. It would also placate them before he revealed their return to the transitory life of the other caravans. He did not relish that speech. If only the mori were ripe, such persuasion would be easier, but that was a month and a half away.

Further discussion with the elders the previous night had been...involved. At least Kisare had gone to her bed before the real shouting started. If the elders wanted him to lead, they had to listen to him. However, if they believed their leaders still heard the wishes of the gods, they were mistaken. With all his heart, he yearned to hear the true orders of Dumzi, Geshtna, Kigal, and Enta. He desperately hoped the treasure was a sign.

He found Kisare in line at a table of fresh fruit. Her movements with her left arm were still tight. Her shoulder must pain her even after the days she'd spent with them. She spun when he touched her back, eyes tight. He could tell she had not slept well.

"You still agree to accompany me to the capital?" he asked.

"That's a stupid question," she answered. "I've been up all night thinking about Bel, and the first thing you ask me is about the nobles? Do you still *agree* to get her back?" Kisare arched a blond eyebrow at him.

Hbelu speared a fried dumpling filled with sweet potato—his favorite—to give him time to push down his immediate response. He did not appreciate having his words thrown in his face. Yet the woman had a point. "I do."

When he looked up, Kisare was staring at him. "And the elders?"

Hbelu sighed. He had thought Belili the perceptive one, but Kisare continued to surprise him. "They finally agreed, grumbling as usual. One would think they would listen to the one they chose to lead."

That got her attention. "You weren't born to this position?" She sounded surprised. "The nobles quarrel all the time over their ancestry—who has more right to rule."

Hbelu shook his head. "The elders choose one of age, with the greatest amount of purple in his or her hair. Out of all the caravans, the most powerful of all the leaders is the prince or princess of the Asha-Urmana. So, it is not my fault a simple hunter was chosen this way. The little girl Nin will likely be leader after me." The girl was only two or three years old now.

"I've seen her." Kisare frowned, absently running a hand through her hair. It was clean and framed her pale face well. With skin such as hers, it was easy to see the little freckles that added to her striking features.

Hbelu cocked his head at her. "You are thinking of your sister's magic?"

Kisare's head shot back up, her eyes wide. "What do you know of that?"

"I was next to her when we evaded Aricaba-Ata in the forest," he said. "She used one of my malus slices to—"

"The earthquake." Kisare clapped her free hand to her mouth. "Of course you know." She met his eyes. "It's a secret. Don't tell anyone." Her eyes darted, as if someone would overhear—or care.

"It may be a secret now, but once her bleached hair grows out, all will know your sister has a lock of brown." His eyes went to Kisare's bleached color. "You might even have something yourself."

Kisare looked as if he had stabbed her. He wondered if the possibility of having magic had occurred to her. It was quite common, from what he knew of the fourcolor's slaves. They interbred so much with the blonds, there was almost no difference between the two.

Finally, Kisare relaxed. "Hmpf. I have work to do with Arala in the fields. The more I put in now, the faster we can leave. When will you have information on Aricaba-Ata and Enti-Ilzi?" Her mouth was turned down in a frown, but her eyes took in his whole face as she spoke.

"Soon," Hbelu promised. "I cannot promise it will be today, but my scouts should have their intelligence by tomorrow. We will leave soon after."

* * *

That day, there was no word, and Hbelu spent the hours assigning duties and planning the village's destruction with the elders. He tried to freeze memories of the village hard at work. Twelve years in this location, meant to replace the majesty of Karduniash. He had given it all up for a chance to take back their true home.

The second day, in midafternoon, Hbelu walked along the outskirts of his village, a malus in his hand, short knife in the other. One slice of the godfruit was missing, and the spirit of a badger walked beside him, snuffling in the remains of leaves fallen the previous year. She would scent any incursions his remaining scouts missed, though he doubted the fourcolors were anywhere near. New leaves already grew on many of the oaks and poplars. It was pretty, but meant more cover for an enemy traveling through the woods.

Hbelu's sentries must have journeyed farther than usual for none of them to return the first day. He hoped it was only that. Surely the fourcolors would not detect the scouts, not with Nidintu and Zikar leading them. Likely this red-hair Aricaba-Ata was planning something, possibly with his aide, Enti-Ilzi of the black. With the malae and citrons at the end of their season, there was not as much of a threat from their troops as in summer. Fortunately, boiling or preserving the juice of godfruit destroyed the magic, or the fourcolors could be even more of a danger.

The younger Asha-Urmana were excited at the news they would travel as their fellows did, but many of the older members of the caravan grumbled at the memory of following the line of mountains near the Blasted Lands. Hbelu himself had distinct memories of hunting the lands farther to the south and east in his late teens, and for the first few years after he was made the leader of this caravan, before he made the choice to settle. Was it a mistake, or a sign from the gods the world was ready for another change? If he could leave this world with the Asha-Urmana in control of their destinies, he would be satisfied.

The she-badger snuffled loudly and Hbelu looked up, tensing. Nidintu stepped from between two budding chestnut trees. He felt something in his shoulders unknot.

"You have information on the fourcolors?" Hbelu asked.

The tall, lean woman nodded sharply. "The slavers made a straight line from our village. We expected them to turn to nearby orchards, but they did not. We think they are following on their threats to alert the capital. I have been alive long enough to be wary of them." The scar that puckered one cheek was proof of her past interactions.

Nidintu resettled a knife in its sheath at her belt. She carried all she needed with her on scouting trips, preferring to live off the land as she moved, and preferring the scouts under her to do the same. There were several spears, a bow and quiver, and a sack slung across her back. The tight braids in her hair kept it from getting too oily as she traveled. "We thought they would drop the slave girl off at the Aricaba or Enti orchards, but they did not. She travels with the black-hair, bound." The scout watched him for a moment. "Do you wish us to catch up to them again?"

"No," Hbelu told her. "We will leave tomorrow, if we can, with you and Zikar. We will take Belili back from them." He heard the she-badger's mental request to continue hunting while she had a form, and he granted it. The spirit animal waddled off.

"The other slave is coming too?" Nidintu folded her arms. "She will slow us down."

"The former *prisoner*," Hbelu lightly stressed the word, "is coming with us, for a very good reason. Once both sisters are free, they will impersonate fourcolors when we encounter their cities."

Nidintu snorted. "Be careful your eyes do not wander too far toward the blond. She may not be pretty, but I know you prefer initiative to features. Muze-Shi would burst a vessel if there were any little Asha-Urmana with freckles and a streak of red or brown."

Hbelu fought down a comment on Nidintu's own habits. "I will take care of myself, and I will thank you to keep your opinions to yourself." Hbelu preferred the Asha-Urmana of his caravan to speak their minds. Otherwise, how would he know what they felt? Still, he would not have her spreading such words around. Not of him and Kisare, or even of the cold, calculating Belili. "Scout the edges of the village until I call for you."

Nidintu faded into the forest with a smirk, and Hbelu turned for the village's center, whistling for the she-badger to continue her hunting. Her form would last until the magic faded. He was glad the fourcolors were moving away, but concerned with where they were going. If any troops *were* to attack them here, they would come in numbers, and with variety. Aricaba-Ata's straight path worried him. To come back with a force of nobles would sorely test them.

Red-hairs like Ata were most often soldiers, with direct abilities. In the dry winter when only malae and citrons were available, their strength and control of fire was devastating in numbers. Brown-hairs, like Belili, scouted and provided up-to-date intelligence, phasing through obstacles. If Belili had any chance to steal a godfruit from her captors, she might meet them halfway and solve many of their problems. Black-hairs were prized for their healing ability, of course, and silvers, like browns, were often spies on the battlefield, and in the fourcolors' rivalry with each other.

The variety of the fourcolors' gifts meant the Asha-Urmana were pressed into their nomadic lifestyle. The gifts of the purple hair tended to philosophy and stability rather than fighting. Hbelu sighed. Conflict was coming. He must understand the wishes of the gods, and steer the struggle's flow, if any Asha-Urmana were to survive.

* * *

Hbelu met Kisare that evening with Nidintu and Zikar, his best fighter. Where the scout was hard wiry muscle and little fat, her hair tied back in many braids, Zikar was built like a stone wall, his hair, unusually, cropped to a frizz of light blond and purple. Both had a few locks of magic in their hair, but not enough to earn them a place as elders when older.

"Who are they?" Kisare asked, pointing out the two.

"Nidintu," Hbelu said, gesturing to her, "and Zikar. They will accompany us when we leave for the capital, Karduniash. Your former captor is traveling in that direction already, with your sister. We think Enti-Ilzi enforces his claim on her."

Kisare sneered at that. "They'll never let us be free." Then she squinted at Nidintu. "Why have I not seen them before?" Hbelu heard Zikar sigh.

"Both Zikar and I saw you when we held back the fourcolor's guards," Nidintu said. "Since then, I have been following the orchard owners and the other slave."

Hbelu thought Kisare might lunge for the scout. It would be a quick fight. "You mean my sister. We are free women. We escaped our imprisonment."

"Did he tell you that?" Hbelu's scout jerked her head toward him.

Kisare reddened, and Hbelu broke in, directing his question to Zikar. "How long will the journey to the capital take?" Kisare was trying to find her own way, but still unsure of her place. She reminded Hbelu of himself, younger. He would have to talk with her later.

"A month," Zikar replied, "keeping to the forests, and away from fourcolors."

Hbelu nodded. "Along the way, we will meet up with the other caravans to share news of what we have found."

Zikar crossed his arms. "Then I would plan for longer." The warrior never spoke much, and gave no other explanation, but Hbelu trusted his instinct. Neither Nidintu nor Zikar were the friendliest of his people, but they were also the best scouts, trackers, and pathfinders in the caravan. If they could not escort them to Karduniash safely, no one could.

"We leave tomorrow," Hbelu told them, then looked to Kisare. "Will you be ready?"

"Yes." Kisare was still eyeing his scout. Nidintu was always ready to travel.

"Pack light," Zikar said, then turned away.

* * *

In the morning before they left, Hbelu tracked down Anagmeshu-Ea. He was overseeing a crowd of villagers transplanting the caravan's godfruit trees from around the ziggurat. His elder was not only the clockmaker, but also knew best how to care for godfruit trees. Maybe in the future, Belili and Kisare could help too. Kisare's natural talent in nurturing plants was easy to see.

Hbelu shook the thought off. When the caravan became like the others, there would be no room for outsiders. It was for the best that Hbelu would travel with the sisters to the fourcolor's capital. It would remove any of the elder's worry that the sisters would mix with the Asha-Urmana. Kisare's face, framed by her long blond hair, rose in his mind's eye, but he pushed it away. She was a complex woman. Especially now, they could not afford to weaken the magic of their people. However, to go against the other four magics by themselves was foolhardy. They would need the support of the few free blonds and of the prisoners of the fourcolors. Kisare—both sisters—could help with that.

Anagmeshu-Ea was observing a group of Asha-Urmana digging around the prunus tree. Once it was free of the earth, it would travel in a massive wooden planter, waiting nearby. The long, low coach it sat on, pulled by twelve oxen, was the largest of the moving buildings the caravans used. It was always well-guarded to protect the godfruit trees.

"Will the prunus and morus still produce?" Hbelu asked the elder.

Anagmeshu-Ea wiped sweat from his forehead despite the cool air, leaving a smudge of black dirt. They had been working since before dawn. "If we use the rest of our citrons to stabilize them in the planters, I hope so. We can encourage new root growth, where they are damaged. Both trees have buds, and the prunus is just flowering." He pointed to a few branches with delicate, light pink flowers. "The girl Belili pruned them admirably before she was captured. She has true talent there, and I think it will help their chances. The godfruit are more resilient than normal trees, so I pray it will be enough to save their harvest this year. If not, we will be defenseless should the fourcolors attack."

"Not defenseless," Hbelu said. "We have those trained to fight."

"That is twenty percent of our number," the elder protested. "Forty percent if one counts everyone who knows how to swing a club or thrust with a spear without hurting themselves." He held up a hand to stop Hbelu from arguing. "Yes, everyone will fight should we come to it, but I do not wish to needlessly sacrifice our tradespeople for the fourcolors' bloodthirst."

"We will not, my friend," Hbelu said. Sometimes the birdlike elder got too excited, thinking of all possible outcomes. It came from tinkering with gears and contraptions so much. "If my plan works, we will draw the eye of the fourcolors when we gather the caravans together. I want to be almost to Karduniash before they try to stop us."

Anagmeshu-Ea shook his head. "I hope you are sure of this, Ishkun-Dim-Hbelu. You leave your caravan without a leader, and your people without a prince. You travel in a small group, two of which will be blonds. The other elders and I are not happy with this course of action."

"I know this. It is why the wise elders advise the impulsive younger leaders. Sometimes, caution is not the best course of action. The fifth godfruit is found. If Ku-Baba's stories are true, then we must seize this opportunity to take back our land."

"As you say," the little elder answered, but he pursed his thin mouth until it nearly disappeared. Then his head jerked to one side, watching Urha as the boy tried to hold the prunus while men dug under its roots. "Careful there," he called, then turned back to Hbelu. "Stay safe on your travels." He hurried off.

Hbelu watched as several of the older workers—ones who had been alive when the caravan used to travel—passed around slices of citron. Magic did not affect godfruit trees strongly. Hbelu hoped it would be enough to keep them from dropping their flowers. The caravan would need all the godfruit it could get to prepare for the upcoming battle.

CHAPTER NINE

Firelight Truths

Those two mortals with locks red as blood and dark, narrow features went north. The couple with straight brown hair and wide faces chose their path to the west. The pair with silver curls and pale freckled skin went south to find their fortune, while the man and woman of the jet-black tresses and high cheekbones went to the east, certain their destiny lay there.

"That's the last of it." Arala put her hands on wide hips, staring at the pile of cotton sheets and towels.

Kisare put a last fold of cloth on the pile. Early morning light shone through the east-facing bedroom window. She would leave soon with Hbelu and the scouts, but not with things so untidy here, even if the building would become one of the moving homes the Asha-Urmana used. It was the house she had shared with Bel. Even though they had spent less than a week in this village, it felt like a home.

Kisare looked to her pack near the doorway. The top barely closed. Ever since Bel was captured, Kisare had been ready to go, but getting all their new possessions to fit in the pack was impossible. They now had several sets of leather clothes, warm blankets, and a few trinkets and hairbrushes. She had to carry her and Bel's things, and the box.

"Come dear, she will be well." Arala must have seen her staring at the pack. "Ishkun-Dim-Hbelu will get your sister back. He is the best leader in many a year, young as he is." The matronly woman was a comfort. Her daughter Dari was only a few years younger than Kisare, and Arala had helped them move in and get comfortable in their home. She crossed to Kisare's side of the bed and raised a hand, reaching.

"They did bleach your hair. I did not believe it when you first arrived." Kisare felt a gentle touch stir the hair near the top of her head. Like the old mistress used to do. She stared forward, thinking of Bel, feeling her throat tighten.

"Well, soon all will see your true color," Arala said.

Kisare made a quick mental calculation. "It's been a few weeks since my hair was last bleached." She felt a stab of anticipation, Hbelu's words from the day before coming back.

You might even have something yourself.

As if the thought was a summons to the gods, Arala's hand paused. "What is this?"

"What is what?" Kisare tensed, her nostalgia forgotten.

"Come, come." Arala sounded excited now, pulling Kisare's hand. She led her to a pile of small objects, a silvered reflecting glass on top. The intricate relief of a prunus tree on the back was carved into the wood of the frame. Kisare thought the wood might even be from an old godfruit tree, perhaps a mori. It was much bigger and clearer than anything the nobles had, and one of Arala's prized possessions.

While she waited, Arala positioned the glass, turning Kisare's head with the other hand, humming and chuckling to herself.

"What is it? Let me look." Kisare struggled in Arala's firm grip. Amused, the woman handed her the hand mirror.

Kisare held it above her head, watching out of the corner of one eye, trying clumsily to position it, moving the wrong direction until she concentrated. She dragged a finger through her roots, trying to find what Arala had. Under her bleached hair, there was a brighter, natural, white-blond. Finally, she pulled up a lock near the top of her head, and there they were: a small clump of strands, all exactly the same color. The color of magic.

Silver.

"Arala, I have it too," she breathed. "Silver. What does it do?" Not brown, like Bel. There were few around the Aricaba orchard with silver hair, and Aricaba-Ata controlled the godfruit with an iron fist. Would she dare ask Hbelu for a slice of godfruit?

In response, Arala hummed, then sang, a light lullaby:

"Dumzi the trickster put his guile in the morus. Our minds gain unearthly powers to serve us.

"Geshtna's passions are always intense. Her prunae increase all five of the senses.

"Kigal can call all the elements to her. The malus's juice gives them out to the user.

"Enta, old man winter, hard as leather. His citrons make our bodies fitter, stronger, deadlier."

A memory flashed through Kisare's thoughts—a snippet of Tiamai singing the same song to her and Bel when they were both very young.

Aricaba-Ata had come in when the old mistress was singing. It was the only time she had seen him lift a hand to her.

"But what do the godfruits *do?*" she asked Arala.

"We sing this to our children," the woman answered. "It tells of the gifts of the gods, but to truly learn them you must see and understand each one. Ask Ishkun-Dim-Hbelu, as you travel. He is much more knowledgeable of the gifts."

Kisare felt her gut tumble at the suggestion. Why didn't she want the Hbelu to find out? "This means Bel and I aren't blond. We have magic. How many slaves do?"

Arala only shrugged. "This is why we do not think the fourcolors are fit to rule. What separates a slave and a fourcolor?"

Kisare stared at the older woman. Slaves were ignorant. Slaves couldn't read. Slaves didn't know about magic. How much of their existence depended on the nobles keeping them ignorant?

"I don't know," she answered. "Though I know Aricaba-Ata has no claim on me. Not anymore."

* * *

Later that day, Kisare followed behind Hbelu, Nidintu, and Zikar. For now, they made a trail through thigh-high grasses. The morning's revelation lent a spring to Kisare's step, though that lagged as they walked, hour after hour.

They were lower in altitude than the orchard, but it was rockier here, boulders showing their heads above the sea of grass. They had left the forest around the Asha-Urmana's village from the opposite direction to where they entered it. Now, there were miles and miles of openness. Zikar said they were passing nearer the Blasted Lands, avoiding the nobles' roads. The sun blazed down, only starting to gain its spring strength.

Kisare regarded Nidintu. The lean scout had a bundle of spears strapped to her back, along with her supplies. She was lightly equipped, but everything she carried was used; a pan for cooking, a bundled tent, a small bag of necessities, a few knives, and a small pouch, probably holding slices of godfruit. She carried a sharp-looking knife which she used to mark their passage or cut through tangles of grasses and bushy vines.

She and Zikar looked nothing alike, yet were similar in intent. The thickset warrior seemed to look everywhere at once, his saber held loosely but at the ready, though Kisare couldn't imagine anything sneaking up on them in the middle of nowhere. She wondered how far it was to the nearest orchard. Did anyone live in the Blasted Lands? She had only heard the words as a prohibition and knew nothing about them. She imagined some boundary beyond where the grass died and the dirt was hard and lifeless, but there was nothing, as far as she could see.

Hbelu was behind his two scouts, moving with his heavy pack as if it were stuffed with feathers. She saw the outline of his nose and beard as he turned his head. He'd taken the greater share of the provisions, and he held the main supply of godfruit, carefully wrapped to preserve them for as long as possible.

Kisare readjusted her pack away from her healing shoulder. Had a week of freedom softened her so much? A guard would have whipped her for lagging, in the orchard. Now, they had only walked a few miles, and she was already thinking of taking a break and putting down her weight. She rolled her shoulders and took larger steps. It wasn't even noon.

Zikar said they would intercept the nobles in a few days. Would her sister be able to steal a piece of godfruit? Maybe if she and Enti-Ilzi... Kisare cut off that thought. She just wanted her sister back, to share with her how they could make their lives anew now they both had magic.

Kisare burned to hold a piece of godfruit, but the mori weren't ripe yet, and it would be even longer before the prunae were. Hbelu had the last of the old malae and citrons in his pack.

She had the malus figured out. The goddess Kigal gave the malus the power of the elements: fire, earth, water, air, and spirit. Red hair— Aricaba-Ata—could control fire. Bel—and Ubala—could control earth. Bel had demonstrated that with Tashi. Kisare had seen how Enti-Ilzi threw water and ice from his sword during the fight, and Hbelu and the elders could talk to the ghosts of dead creatures. That meant Kisare, with silver, could control air.

Tonight, when they camped, she could ask to taste a malus. She realized she was staring at Hbelu's pack and moved her gaze across the grass. Would they laugh at her? No one let a slave taste godfruit. Hbelu didn't see them as slaves, but Nidintu and Zikar still did.

As the sun set, they camped near a stream. They were at a gentle spot in the mountain ranges surrounding Aricaba-Ata's orchard, many miles behind them. Nidintu chose a spot near an outcrop of boulders with trees for firewood. Kisare almost went to get an armful, on instinct, but stopped herself. What would the Asha-Urmana think? Just like a slave to expect to serve the others around her. No, she would make her own spot to rest. If they asked her, she would *help* gather wood, *help* cook, but she would not be their—

"I will find us some tinder to start a fire." Hbelu interrupted her thoughts. "Nidintu is a fair cook, whenever Zikar gets back." The warrior had absented himself, hunting for small game to go with the vegetables they had packed. "We will move fast in the next few days to get out of territory owned by the fourcolors. You need your rest. I am sure you are not used to traveling for an entire day."

Kisare popped up from the blanket she had spread on the grass. How dare he! Mocking her like a noble.

"I can cook," she growled. "The old mistress loved my cooking. I'll do it." She went to their cooking supplies, selecting what she would need.

Later, with grudging help from Nidintu, who looked as if she would rather have eaten their meat unseasoned, they had a stew of rabbit and vegetables. It was quite good, if Kisare said so herself. They ate in relative silence around the little fire. The moons were not high in the sky yet, and there was little light. The two scouts seemed content not to say anything. Hbelu's face was half shadowed by flickering flames, but Kisare could still see his eyes stray between her face and her pack. It held the box, carefully wrapped and equipped with a new lock—a gift from Anagmeshu-Ea—to keep it from spilling out its precious contents.

As the silence stretched, Kisare had an urge to ask for a piece of godfruit—just something to find out how her magic worked. She clenched her teeth. Why was she afraid of asking? What did she think Hbelu would do?

She steeled her nerve. "You said you knew the gifts of the godfruit." Arala's advice from that morning rang in her head.

"I do," Hbelu said. "Five hair colors and four godfruits. It is not so long a list to memorize."

"Have you seen them all firsthand?" Kisare asked, before she could scare herself into silence. She wanted to tell the prince about her silver hair, but it wasn't the time yet.

"I...have not," Hbelu admitted. "Though I have seen many. All the abilities of the Asha-Urmana, of course. Encounters with fourcolors are rare but happen. The abilities are seasonal, coming as the godfruit ripens, though we have tales that our ancestors in Karduniash could make trees bear godfruit year-round. The autumn and winter godfruit, the malus and citron, are direct and powerful. Kigal and Enta gave us these to offset their harsher seasons. The spring and summer godfruits, the morus and prunus, are subtler, affecting the mind more than the body." He paused, firelit face turned to Kisare. Even Nidintu was paying attention, though Zikar was a shadow, watching out over the grass.

Then the warrior chimed in unexpectedly. His deep voice was hard to hear, against the night noises of roosting birds and chirping insects. "When the fourcolors attacked, it was the first time I had fought against the power of black hair using the malus. The fourcolor was surprisingly inventive with such a thing as water." He fell silent, and Kisare was about to speak when he continued. "I will never forget a clash with two fourcolors, a red-hair and a black-hair, in the high summer, eight years ago." She saw his outline shudder. "My body and thoughts turned against me—I was helpless. If she hadn't killed one and knocked the other out"—he jerked a thumb toward Nidintu—"I would be one of the ghostly sentinels you saw."

Kisare waited again, but it seemed he was finished. She swallowed, flattening her hands on her legs to keep them from shaking. They were calmly discussing the noble's magic, forbidden to every slave.

"I was...wondering what abilities the citron gives those with brown hair and silver hair." Kisare's voice wavered. "I've seen the others," she added quickly.

Hbelu nodded. "So you have. I have not seen the citron's effect on those with brown hair directly, but I am told it lets the taster's body be affected either more or less by the world around him."

"Meaning what?"

"In the extreme, the power to walk through walls, or resist swords and knives with bare skin," Hbelu said.

Kisare's eyes widened. Good thing it was dark. "What about silver hair?" she said, trying to sound natural.

"That I have seen, and it is extraordinary. The taster gains a remarkable sense of timing and balance. A silver-hair eating a citron could dodge though a hail of arrows, or balance on a spearpoint. Of course, the more hair color the user has, the stronger the effect will be."

Kisare frowned. So, Bel got the power to shrug off a whipping and hers was only to dance on needlepoint? Just like back in the orchard. Bel got all the special treatment.

"Perhaps we will be able to practice on our journey," Hbelu said.

"What do you mean?" Kisare tried to keep surprise from her tone.

"I would like to see the effects of a citron on brown hair," he answered, "once we have your sister back."

Kisare breathed out.

"If Belili has color in her hair, you might as well."

It was the same thing he'd said to her after Bel was taken. Did he suspect? He had helped her, ever since they met. Why couldn't she trust him?

Kisare stood up suddenly, making Nidintu jerk and reach for a spear. "Well, I'm going to bed," she said. She stretched her arms, trying to coax out a yawn.

Nidintu grunted a laugh. "Scared you might have magic, slave girl?"

Kisare's mouth worked, but she said nothing. Hbelu's face was dark, though she heard him sigh. Zikar hadn't moved, his back to them like a man-shaped tree.

Awkwardly, Kisare went to her blanket, spread out on the ground. She arranged it, then lay down in silence.

Nidintu was right, she was a slave girl, scared of her own ability. An escaped slave couldn't trust anyone, especially not if she had magic. But the Asha-Urmana village had stood up to Aricaba-Ata, using she didn't know how many pieces of godfruit.

Kisare took a long time to fall asleep, until Shir-Gal, the large moon, was high in the sky. She longed to taste godfruit. Could it be so simple as asking?

* * *

They packed the camp in silence the next morning and headed out after a breakfast of fruit and bread. Kisare wondered if she had asked too much.

The land sloped downward, becoming lusher the farther they went. The second day, more trees dotted the landscape, not just the pines and short deciduous trees around Aricaba-Ata's orchard and the Asha-Urmana village. These were large trees, wider around at the base than she and Bel together could reach. They followed a stream for a while, winding downhill. She wondered if there were any old homes, retaken by the forest. Or might there be godfruit trees around, planted by some traveling noble?

"We should dye your and your sister's hair, when we retrieve her," Hbelu said as walked. Kisare bristled.

"I've had enough of dyeing my hair for a lifetime." She tugged at a bleached lock. "This identifies me as a slave. I can't wait for it to grow out."

Except my silver will be obvious to him then, and everyone else.

"That is precisely why we should dye your hair," Hbelu answered with his infuriating calm. "If you bear the purple hair of the Asha-Urmana, even if you are a little too pale, we will only look like five caravanners traveling to the fourcolors." His mouth twisted in that little sneer at the word "caravanners."

"I thought the elders made it clear we were not accepting former slaves into our caravan," Nidintu said, and Kisare ground her molars together.

"That is enough, Nidintu." Hbelu did not ignore this jibe. His voice was a low growl. "You know as well as any the point is to hide the sisters, not make them Asha-Urmana."

"There is much effort devoted to these two," Nidintu countered. "Zikar agrees with me." Kisare looked to the stern man, who made no indication whether he agreed or not.

"There are more factors in play than you know," Hbelu said. He stood tall, taller than both the scouts. "If you think I lead poorly, feel free to leave."

After a long silence, Nidintu looked away from her prince, and Kisare realized the two scouts did not know about the fifth godfruit. Hbelu had kept information from the rest of the caravan, yet she and Bel knew.

Kisare hardly paid attention to the landscape for the next while, lost in thoughts of Bel, until she dabbed at her forehead and found her fingers wet with sweat. She loosened the leather vest the Asha-Urmana had given her, letting the cotton shirt underneath breathe. She had seen the fluffy plant it was made from around the caravan's village but didn't think much of it before getting the shirt. It was a weed around the Aricaba orchard. All those seeds and gristle in it—how could anyone do anything with it? But the inventive Asha-Urmana had a hand-cranked machine that spun the plant fiber into usable strands. She had worked with the village smith to repair the blades on a free-standing mill. She missed all the curious machinery the Asha-Urmana owned. Everything the nobles owned was made by hand—slave's hands. The mechanisms of the purple-haired people were so much more interesting.

"We should start looking for a campsite," Nidintu called from in front. The day had lengthened into afternoon and evening, the land transitioning into a forest again. "Preferably near a river."

An hour later, they made camp next to a river Nidintu had located. From the way the water flowed, it was deeper than it appeared. Kisare kept silent, volunteering by action to cook again. Hbelu went for firewood with Nidintu and Zikar stalked away with a spear and a bow to hunt.

She thought of Bel again while she worked. Aricaba-Ata was steering them down into the lowlands, where there were more nobles and they held greater power. Hbelu said her former master and Enti-Ilzi were running to the capital to gather troops. Bel shouldn't be a part of that. She had no idea what Ilzi was doing to her, and she was cooking vegetables.

Hbelu and Nidintu came back before Zikar. There was an undercurrent between them, as if Hbelu acted more a prince and Nidintu a subject.

A few minutes later Zikar stalked into the camp, holding a brace of rabbits, though his face did not reflect his success.

"What happened?" Hbelu must have seen the same indications Kisare did.

"There are signs around us that should not be there." The warrior slapped the rabbits down on the ground by the campfire and began dressing them. Kisare looked away from the dead black eyes.

"What kind of signs?" Nidintu had one of her spears in her hand, but Zikar shook his head.

"Uncertain. We should be half a day out from the fourcolors in front of us." Kisare brightened at the news that Bel was close. "But these signs are older, and others were too fresh. It makes little sense, or my tracking abilities are not what they once were."

Nidintu hefted the spear. "I will take a look. Save me some supper." Zikar grunted in response. Kisare watched Nidintu disappear into the forest, feeling suddenly exposed. She gripped the knife she had been using to chop vegetables.

A few minutes later, Zikar stood up from the dressed and cooking rabbits and stalked away. "Something is wrong. I will patrol until the food is ready."

Then Kisare was left with Hbelu. The two stared at each other for a moment, until Kisare drew her eyes back to the fire and the rabbits. She put the knife down.

"I...ah...heard a rhyme from Arala, back at the village," she began uncertainly. Anything to break this tension. Her stomach felt like it was trying to climb out of her mouth. She didn't know if she could eat anything tonight. "It didn't help me figure out what the godfruits could do. Did you learn what you know from that rhyme?"

Kisare was surprised to hear Hbelu chuckle. "No—I have long memorized the entire list of the gods' gifts. Though I know the rhyme. We teach it to our children, much as we taught it to the fourcolors, back when they first arrived in our land as refugees."

"You taught—" His ancestors, obviously, but Kisare wondered if Tiamai had any idea her lullaby had come to her through "caravanners." "Can you give me a better answer than the rhyme?"

"Certainly," Hbelu answered. He came closer, though she noticed his eyes scanned the encroaching darkness seeping through the overhead branches. "The abilities of the prunus are simple. Sight, hearing, taste, smell, and touch, one for each hair color. The morus gives red-hairs the ability to move objects with the mind, and brown-hairs the ability to move themselves without actually moving. It may be the most powerful of the godfruits, offset by a shorter bearing season." He was close to her now, and Kisare kept her attention on the rabbits roasting on the campfire. "I wager you could memorize the gifts easily. You have a good head for numbers and mechanisms. You set out to achieve what you want."

Kisare looked up. Was that a *compliment* from the mighty prince?

"I...I kept the planting schedule, back in the orchard." Why did she feel bad when hearing others say good things about her?

Hbelu paused, as if thinking of how to phrase something important. "We, the Asha-Urmana, I mean, do not allow others to join us, as you know. To keep the fourcolors from assimilating us and our culture. To keep our magical strength."

He stopped, and Kisare waited for him to make his point.

"I would welcome you to our caravan, if I could," he finally said, and something in Kisare relaxed, like a muscle she had held tense so long she didn't know she was doing it any longer.

"I have magic in my hair," she said. The words popped out of her mouth, and one of her hands came up of its own accord, as if she could catch the words before they got to him.

Hbelu only nodded. "I guessed that might be so."

Their eyes met, then jerked away at a crash from the forest. Hbelu ran to his pack, with his godfruit. Kisare looked for her own pack, where the box was packed near the bottom.

"What was that?"

"Nothing good."

A light bloomed in the forest, not far, like a campfire raging out of control. The clang of metal on metal reached her.

"The signs Zikar saw," Kisare said, and Hbelu nodded. "The nobles laid a trap."

"I believe you are correct." Hbelu fumbled with the ties on his pack, drawing out a malus and a citron, both a little bruised from riding in his pack. He began peeling the citron.

Zikar stumbled into the clearing, backing away. His sword was in front of him, parrying.

Aricaba-Ata followed, his umber face aglow with light from his flaming sword. He batted the warrior's blade away, and Zikar hissed as the heat singed him.

"The tracks," Zikar called. "The fourcolors sent a decoy group ahead." He swung but did not move Aricaba-Ata's blade quite enough. The glowing edge scraped along his leather armor, leaving a smoking trail.

Kisare froze, watching as six soldiers followed her old master out of the woods. They were men and women she didn't recognize, better dressed and armed than the guards in the orchard. Aricaba-Ata had been busy in the few days since they took Bel.

Where was Bel? And Enti-Ilzi, for that matter.

Hbelu reacted far faster than she could, rushing forward, trying to reach a weapon and eat a slice of citron. He got to neither before the soldiers surrounded him, grabbing his arms.

Zikar was still backpedaling, Aricaba-Ata following him with large, strong strokes of his fiery blade. It cast ghoulish shadows on the trees as it moved through the twilight air. He might have had citron juice as well as malus in his mouth, for each strike pushed Zikar's blade far outside his guard.

Kisare finally found her feet, taking a single step forward before her old master grunted and struck. Kisare gasped as the tip of his blade, still alight, stuck through Zikar's back.

The warrior collapsed when Aricaba-Ata pulled his blade free.

Hbelu struggled against his captors, but now Aricaba-Ata was free, he had little chance. What could she do? She scooped up a branch from the fire, hoping she could hit or maybe distract with it. Where was Nidintu?

"Do not attempt it." Aricaba-Ata snapped a finger in her direction and the flame at the end of her branch flared. She dropped it and the fire went out. Stupid to even try. She was worthless, and now she would be caught again.

Hbelu must have eaten some portion of the citron he held. With a cry, he pushed the circle of soldiers back a step, a head taller than usual.

"Kisare—escape!"

Something flew at her, and she caught it on instinct. It was a peeled citron, half a slice torn from it. Juice oozed from the wounded flesh, tingling where it touched her skin. She stared at it, her mind blank.

Balance. That was what the citron would do for her. Trembling, she tore the rest of the mangled slice free and put it in her mouth.

She shook as the power of the juice hit her, barely managing to hold on to the godfruit. Kisare felt the world slow around her, her reactions heightening.

She forced one foot forward, then the other. There was no noise as she walked.

"Keep her here," she heard Aricaba-Ata shout. "Kill her if you must."

Something else flew toward her with a hiss and she pivoted. The spear brushed past her, and she completed a full turn, continuing forward with no loss of momentum. The taste of the citron faded, and power with it. She had used some of the magic and wasn't sure how much was left. Kisare ate another piece, her eyes rolling up. Lightning flowed through her, and down her arms and legs.

Four of the soldiers still held Hbelu, back to his normal height. The other two and Aricaba-Ata came at her.

Kisare kept her distance from them constant, walking as easily backward as forward. She could *feel* the ground beneath her. Her feet avoided rocks and sticks almost by themselves.

Zikar stood up, a bloody hole in his chest.

No, not Zikar. His shade. His body was still on the ground, a spread of red growing beneath it.

The ghost moved toward the soldiers and Aricaba-Ata, and they faltered. Kisare looked to Hbelu, but he was held fast. He hadn't raised the warrior.

"Kisare! *Go!*" The last word was muffled as the soldiers bore Hbelu to the ground.

Kisare ran into the woods, the ground flying beneath her. No branches touched her, no roots or vines tripped her.

"There was another caravanner with them. She's controlling the ghost. Find her!" Aricaba-Ata bellowed from the clearing.

Kisare ran, panicked, until she rebounded off another soldier.

As the electric tingle of the citron receded, she realized where she was. Bel, with manacles on ankles and wrists, standing with her head down. Held by Enti-Ilzi. His new slave, Ligish, was similarly bound next to her. Four more soldiers. She recognized two of these—Shuma and Iral.

"Catch her!" Enti-Ilzi shouted, and Bel lifted her head, seeing Kisare for the first time. Her sister's eyes widened. Kisare put another piece of citron into her mouth, shaking at the magic flowing through her, the lightning flowing down her body. All four guards moved to her, Shuma's bulk in the lead. Kisare threaded through them as if they were marble pillars.

The last, Iral, reached for her, as if in slow motion. Instead, she caught his arm, spinning out of his way, exactly poised on one foot. As she pulled, she found new knowledge. The instant her momentum broke the line of his balance, Iral was as good as down. Kisare completed her turn, twisting Iral's arm with a wet *crack* and sending him flying into a tree trunk.

Enti-Ilzi was in front of her, holding Bel, who had one hand out to Ligish. The juice was losing its power already, but Kisare was ready with the next slice. She didn't know whether she was moving faster, or she could just think faster, but Enti-Ilzi's arm rose in slow motion to put a citron slice in his mouth. His hand left Bel as he did so, but Kisare knew which half of his power would be in effect when it landed again. Healing and hurting, two sides of the coin. She could have taken the slice from him, but she had a better idea.

Kisare stepped past them, turning and scooping her sister from under the noble's arm. Hand raised to mouth, teeth biting with a *pop* into the godfruit. Three soldiers, running back to her. Hand falling again as she scooped Bel forward, manacles clinking, twisting again. Her sister gasped at the sudden movement.

Her other hand, remains of her peeled citron sill grasped in it, hooked a soldier's arm. With herself as the land in the middle, the others as the two moons above, Kisare rotated, bringing Bel away from Ilzi and putting the soldier in her place.

Enti-Ilzi's hand fell, but on his soldier's shoulder, not Bel's. The man lurched.

The juice was losing its flavor fast, but Kisare jerked Bel back through the other two soldiers. The manacles on her sister's ankles impeded her motion but were long enough for her to take quick steps, and they were going the right direction. The soldiers weren't. She heard a gurgle behind her and looked back to see the one she had put under Enti-Ilzi's hand clutching his chest, falling. That would have been Bel, incapacitated until the black-hair could heal her later.

She tore the rest of the citron in half as they ran, pushing it at Bel. "Take a slice and get out of those manacles."

Kisare knew when Bel had found the power of the citron as her limping steps stopped for a moment. Kisare almost tripped. Her own power was waning.

Then Bel's arm grew strange, almost squishy, like Kisare could have pulled her own hand through Bel's.

There was a click of metal, and Kisare saw Bel's wrists and ankles free, manacles fallen through her to the ground. The last twilight rays of the sun almost shone through her sister.

"Thank you," Bel said. "But I have to go back for Ligish."

Kisare shook her head, pulling her sister along. "There's no time and not enough godfruit. Keep running. We're not out of this yet."

The magic of the citron dwindled quickly, and Kisare felt as if her limbs were made of wood, after the freedom the juice gave her. She wanted another slice, but she had to save it. To save Hbelu.

They burst into the clearing's campfire light. Zikar's ghost was still there, but faded and misty. Out of the original six guards, three held Hbelu down, another was fastening manacles to his wrists, and the others battled the shade. Aricaba-Ata's sword glowed dull red, and he used it to poke at Zikar's ghost, keeping it at arm's reach.

Hbelu saw them first and shook his head. "Stay away," he called.

Aricaba-Ata dispersed Zikar's shade with another swipe from his sword. The mist remained, but thin, beginning to drift apart. He and his soldiers came forward.

"I see Ilzi was as useful as always," he growled.

"I can get the packs," Bel whispered to her. "I think I can fade through the guards with a citron. Then maybe there will be time to—"

Kisare cut her off. "No time. Hbelu first." They both knew there wouldn't be another chance with Hbelu captured like that. She wondered how hard this would have been had her old master trusted his soldiers with godfruit. She could see a stripe of brown peeking from one woman's helmet, but as men and women in that uncertain category—not slaves, but not nobles, they were not offered that privilege.

"You get the one on the far side," Kisare answered, nodding to Hbelu's pack holding the rest of the godfruit. It wouldn't do to let the nobles have it. "I'll get mine. Then we rescue Hbelu."

"I don't think that's—" Bel started, but Kisare didn't listen. She prayed to the gods that Bel followed her lead and used another slice of citron. Only one left. She tried to ignore the shock of the juice filling her mouth.

Kisare twisted through the soldiers, feeling the heat of Aricaba-Ata's sword as it passed within a hand's width of her body. Her steps were light, her body a leaf in the wind. Bel ran directly through a soldier barring her path, one hand snaking out to grab the pack.

Kisare retrieved her own, feeling the weight of the box at the bottom, swinging it around to rest on her back. The weight would have pulled on her, but with the juice of the citron, she counterbalanced without thinking.

While they got the packs, Aricaba-Ata shouted directions. Now all six guards stood between them and Hbelu. Kisare looked down at her hand, slick with electric juice, holding one citron slice. Not enough to rescue Hbelu and escape. Certainly not enough to get back to Enti-Ilzi and his new slave. No time to get a new godfruit from Bel's pack. She could tell her sister made the same calculation as her mouth hardened into a line.

"Go!" Hbelu shouted from behind the wall of soldiers. "You cannot rescue me." He was right—Enti-Ilzi would be coming any moment with more soldiers. She and Bel had their backs to the river, trapped, Hbelu captured.

"You are more important, now," came Hbelu's voice. The soldiers advanced. "Convince the others. Spread word among the prisoners of the nobles as you speak to the Asha-Urmana."

Aricaba-Ata nodded sharply, and a soldier smashed Hbelu in the head with her sword hilt. The prince slumped.

"Yes, run, little slaves," Aricaba-Ata said. "I have something worth far more than both of you combined, and Karduniash's soldiers will burn the caravanners' village to the ground. See how far you get as escaped slaves, no matter what piddling color you have in your hair. It will not be enough."

"The river," Bel said quietly. "It's the only way."

Kisare nodded, reluctantly. She had her sister back, but she longed to continue her conversation with Hbelu. How far would he have gone against the elders' wishes? Would he have truly brought her into his caravan?

She turned, and as she did, eyes caught hers, high in a tree to her right. Nidintu was up there, with a malus in her hand. It was she who had raised Zikar. Kisare could tell, even from this distance, there were tears in her eyes. Nidintu would take care of Hbelu, and maybe even Ligish, and Kisare would continue their interrupted conversation soon.

Bel had one slice of citron left as well. "Meet me on the other side," Kisare told her, and put the last slice in her mouth. She judged her distance, took one step, and then ran forward. When she hit the bank of the river she didn't stop. She felt her sister behind her, making much more noise.

As the magic of the godfruit flowed into Kisare, sparking down her arms and legs, she stepped out quickly on the surface of the water, skipping from ripple to ripple, so exquisitely balanced, she didn't even break the surface.

Kisare ran to freedom on top of the water.

CHAPTER TEN

Dyed Locks

Allaru-Urma and Sumuel-Asha, the woman and man of the braided purple hair, stayed where they were created. They learned from the gods and traded with the blonds, eager to discover all they could about the world.

Belili ran *through* the water. Her body was insubstantial, as if she ran on a cloud. She could have sunk into the riverbed if she wished, though she didn't know how long the citron slice would last.

The shouts of Aricaba-Ata's soldiers behind her had cut off abruptly when the river's surface passed over her head. Belili desperately kept those memories away. Ilzi. The past few days had been a nightmare of chains and cold nights, tempered only by comfort from Ligish. She had listened to Belili in the middle of the night, when the nobles were asleep, and they were chained together to a tree. Ligish had shared that she had not been born into slavery like Belili, but had been sold to Ilzi to repay some debt. There was more to it, but Ligish didn't elaborate and Belili didn't push her.

Then, when she saw Kisa flying along like a graceful dancer, she had thought it was a dream—no, a hallucination. But it had been real. Kisa had magic too, and she gave Belili godfruit. But they hadn't saved Ligish, and now it was too late.

She had to keep going. Belili kept the ground solid in her mind and told herself the water was like air. She could feel its temperature on her skin as she ran—the chill from the mountain tops in early spring—but none of the wetness. The stream was not hard to cross, though it was deep and wide. At the bottom, black mud hid creatures from the sunlight.

As the ground rose up on the far side, her skin grew wet, and the ground more solid. The citron juice's flavor was fading. Just a little longer. A little more...

Her head pushed through the muddy brown of the river and Belili drew in a gasp, swallowing the rest of the citron and not a little river water. She grasped at the slick riverbank, overgrown with weeds and cat's tails. A hand found hers in the darkness and drew her from the water.

"You made it," Kisa said.

Belili gasped for breath, coughed, gasped again. "Thank you."

Kisa drew her into a hug. Belili hugged her back fiercely, getting mud and water all over Kisa's leather jacket and cotton shirt. Her thigh was still tight from Tashi's knife, even with Ilzi's partial healing. She shivered at the memory of his hands on her, Ligish doing her best to draw him away.

"Come on," she said. "The soldiers have bows and I don't want to get shot. They might still be able to see us."

Kisa resisted when Belili tugged at her. "Hbelu."

Belili shook her head. Ligish wasn't the only one they'd left behind. "We can't help them right now, and if we get caught, we won't be able to help them later."

They ran farther into the woods, keeping each other close in the twilight. Belili was hopelessly lost as soon as they entered the tree canopy. She prayed Aricaba-Ata and the others wouldn't be able to cross the deep river anytime soon.

Soon, Kisa signaled a halt, blowing her cheeks out and supporting herself, hands on knees.

"Will they be after us, do you think?" She must have been thinking along the same lines as Belili.

"Unless Ilzi and Aricaba-Ata want to swim after us themselves, I don't think so. Ilzi could control the water with a malus, but I doubt he could carry many soldiers with him, without using a lot of godfruit. They don't have that much left."

"They wouldn't do such menial work in front of the soldiers," Kisa agreed. "Besides, he has Hbelu instead of two escaped slaves. Enti-Ilzi might come sneaking over after us, though. He could freeze himself a path across the river."

Bel agreed, though she privately wondered if Aricaba-Ata would try to take Ligish away from Ilzi in recompense. Would that be worse or better for her?

"So what do we do?" Kisa asked.

Kill Ilzi. The thought flashed through Belili's mind. She had the power. Belili hefted the pack she carried. It had got a dunking in the river, but the canvas bag was oiled and tied tight. They would have to dry out the godfruit to make sure it didn't rot. It was the only thing that had kept her back as a slave—no access to the magical godfruit. She rubbed the stump of her little finger. No more punishments. No more chains.

"Bel?"

Belili focused on Kisa. "We can't go back, not right now," she said, trying not to let her face show her feelings. It didn't work this time. "In the morning, though, I'm going to bury them all." She gripped the pack. She could, with enough malae. Ilzi would sink beneath the ground, screaming.

"No, Bel," Kisa said, then flinched back from her stare. Belili blinked and looked away. "We can't take them all, not alone."

"We can think of a way," Belili said. "Sneak back across—"

"No, Bel!" Kisa grabbed her arms and Belili jerked back. Kisa frowned but kept on. "We need to rescue Hbelu, *and* Ligish—I can't imagine what they'll do to them—but the two of us can't overpower the nobles and their guards."

Belili set the pack down and rubbed her wrists together, if only to prove the cold metal was gone. "Then if we aren't going to kill Ilzi, we need to get far away. As long as we have the box." She stared at her sister. "You do have the—"

"Of course I have the box." Kisa patted the bottom of her pack.

Stupid question. If Kisa was on her deathbed, she would know where everything was. Belili tried to slow her breathing, to think rationally. "Then do what Hbelu told us. Go to the other caravans, tell them about the box. Tell other slaves they might have magic, like us. Free them from the nobles. Then come back."

"How?" Kisa waved her hands around in a circle. "I don't know where we are. I *know* you don't." She hiked Hbelu's pack up on her back. "We can't find the other caravans, even if we wanted to."

"Can we find the capital? Make our new lives in Karduniash?" Belili looked up into the night sky, trying to even out her breathing. Shir-Gal and Nana-Ru were both up, the moons giving some light. As if she could tell from them which direction was which. That was Kisa's purview. She realized her sister hadn't said anything, and looked back down, blinking the light away to see through the dark forest.

"Kisa?"

Kisa bit her lip. "I...I think we should find out where they're going, follow them."

Belili raised her eyebrows in surprise. "Now? I thought we couldn't take the nobles? We have the box. We have godfruit." She shrugged her shoulders, hefting her pack. "We can go anywhere, do anything." *We can find Ilzi and make sure he doesn't hurt anyone else.*

Kisa was silent before saying, "Hbelu had purple dye in his pack. He wanted us to pose as traveling Asha-Urmana with them." She screwed her face up and words came pouring out. "Now Zikar's *dead* and Hbelu's captured, and Nidintu—well, who knows. And the mas— Aricaba-Ata said he would burn the caravan's village, but they're tearing the village down so they can travel like the others. And. Um."

Belili shook her head over the new names. Zikar must have been that big Asha-Urmana ghost fighting the soldiers. Kisa had been busy the last few days. She was so serious sometimes even Belili forgot Kisa was the younger sister. She frowned as something registered.

"The Asha-Urmana are tearing down their village?"

"Yes, to turn it into moving carts. They'll be disorganized, and the soldiers will kill them. We have to warn them. Maybe we can find Nidintu. She'll help us." Kisa ran out of breath.

Belili sighed, feeling tension leave her—only a little. They wouldn't get anywhere tonight. She thought of Arala and her daughter Dari. The two had been friendly, as had many of the other Asha-Urmana.

"We'll have to sleep sometime. Better now than later." Belili finally spared a glance for her sister's hair, and the secret it hid. "Aricaba-Ata and his guards will be busy with Hbelu tonight." Maybe she could find Ilzi alone, and—

Kisa saw her looking and glanced upward. "Oh yes, and I have magic in my hair. Silver. I might have told Hbelu."

Belili raised her eyebrows at that. Kisa *had* been busy while she was captured.

They found a stand of bushes under an oak tree and burrowed into them, displacing a family of quail who chattered as they flew to a nearby low tree. Belili tried to get the worst of the river mud off her clothes before Kisa gave her a new set from her pack.

"I'll keep watch first," Kisa told her. "I'll wake you in a little while." She opened Belili's pack and drew out the godfruit to dry, putting cloth over the top to keep away the worst of the insects.

Belili nodded. "We'll figure it out tomorrow." She curled up on the ground, sleeping blanket pulled tight around her. When Kisa tried to sleep next to her, Belili turned over, her back to her sister. She was cold, but she couldn't bring herself to touch Kisa, not yet.

* * *

The next morning Kisa insisted on taking a full inventory of the packs. Belili wanted to start immediately, but she reluctantly unpacked. Besides the all-important box, Kisa's pack held another change of clothes, a few cooking utensils, and some bread, cheese, and dried meats.

Hbelu's pack, the one Belili had carried, was much more interesting. Besides a larger store of food, a pot and a water canteen, another shirt, a strange cylinder, and a vial of dye, it held all the godfruit for the group, which Kisa had unpacked the night before. Belili was surprised he had taken so much with him. There were ten withered malae and nine citrons, which Kisa had made sure dried off.

"That must be a good part of what's left from the last harvest," Kisa said, hands on hips. "I don't want to waste them."

"Is there enough citron to follow the nobles unseen?" Belili asked. "You won't make any noise, and I can hide in the trees." Maybe pick off a noble or two.

"Or we could give them to slaves to see if they have magic in their hair," Kisa said.

"That's assuming we can find slaves not under heavy guard, who won't turn us in for an extra portion of food," Belili countered.

"We don't even know how to use the godfruit, not really. I still haven't tasted a malus." Kisa stared at the godfruit hungrily.

"With silver, that means you can control..."

"Air," Kisa finished. A strange look passed over her face, and she advanced. "Can I see it? Your lock?" She reached out a hand, and Belili took a step back.

"No. Not...not now." Belili tried to keep what she was feeling from her face. Ligish had helped her through the worst, while they were manacled and defenseless.

"You love it when I play with your hair." Kisa watched her. "Are you all right? What—"

Belili shook her head. "We should get moving. No telling when the nobles will decide they want their slaves back. I'm surprised we didn't wake up in chains."

Kisa nodded slowly, still watching. "What about practicing with godfruit?"

"We can use the godfruit if we need to defend ourselves," Belili said. "Now we need to go."

"We can't learn everything the first time we do it," Kisa answered. "At least I can't."

Belili ignored the jibe and put the packs back together, handling the cylinder from Hbelu's pack, remembering where she had seen one before. "Then we'll practice, but not now. Can we please wait until we have a few days travel between us and Aricaba-Ata? I want to be far away from here. We need to get ahead if we want to warn the caravans." How could she both want to run as far away as she could and to storm back and tear Ilzi to pieces at the same time?

They made their way back to the river, Kisa following some trail that was lost to Belili. She couldn't have found the river again, much less the place where they crossed. If Kisa could retrace their steps, then the nobles and their soldiers could have tracked them. Why didn't they?

"Can you see?" Kisa asked. The river was not so wide they couldn't see across, but it was hard to make out detail. From here, the camp looked deserted.

"One moment," Belili told her, and brought out the cylinder. She uncapped it and held it to her eye. The far bank of the river jumped into view, as she'd suspected. She moved the tube around, scanning.

"What is that, anyway?" Belili could almost hear Kisa craning her neck. Wordlessly, she passed it over. She had seen what she needed. The nobles and their soldiers had moved on, taking Ligish and Hbelu with them.

Kisa's cry of wonder made Belili smile. "How did you know what this did?"

"Ilzi has one." Belili's smile faded. She didn't know where the noble got it. Aricaba-Ata didn't have one. Maybe the slimy man killed an Asha-Urmana. She didn't think the nobles could make one. "So, are we following them, or going our own way?" She couldn't tell which one she wanted more.

Kisa took the looking glass away from her eye. "Don't we owe it to Hbelu to see where he's going? We can send others to rescue him."

Belili sighed. Kisa nodded and put the glass back to her eye.

"I'll have to get back to the camp and see which way they headed." The river was still flowing heavily from the meltwater. No way could they cross it without using more godfruit.

Then Kisa gasped, and Belili looked where she pointed the glass. There was a figure on the opposite shore. One of the nobles? No—she could make out dark purple hair.

"It's Nidintu," said Kisa. "She's gesturing—" She took the glass away again and looked downstream. "Come on." She started walking, and Belili followed.

"I didn't hear much," Belili volunteered, "but Aricaba-Ata talked of traveling to Karduniash. That's south."

"Downstream." Kisa nodded. "So, they're still going the same direction?"

"Seems like it."

Kisa sighted every few minutes across the river with the glass, which she had taken control of, as usual. Whatever she saw drew her on. A few times Belili saw a figure, presumably Nidintu.

They traveled for a few hours before finding a natural ford in the river. By the time they stopped, her thigh was starting to ache, and Kisa was rolling her shoulder to loosen it. Here, Belili could see the other woman clearly, waving them across.

The water was only thigh-deep, still shockingly cold, and they hefted their packs to keep them from getting wet. Belili looked back at their path. Was the detour enough to keep Ilzi from sending soldiers after her? Not likely. Maybe Aricaba-Ata had something to do with it. She hoped the angular Asha-Urmana could tell them.

Nidintu had spears strapped to her back and had a knife at her belt, but that was all. Did she travel light, or had the woman lost her pack? She had a puckered scar on one cheek, but was otherwise well built, with lean, tight muscles, different from Ligish's curves. The Asha-Urmana saw Belili staring at her and gave her a slight nod of greeting but addressed Kisa.

"I see the fourcolors did not recapture you in the night, no matter how reckless you were in escaping. Showing your magic means the slavers will kill you now, rather than capture you. Slaves who have had a taste of magic are tainted. Surely you know that?"

"I...no...I..."

Belili was impressed. She would have to learn this woman's tricks to render her sister speechless. "I think you may be mistaken about our former master," she said. And about Ilzi. "Do you know where the nobles went?"

Nidintu regarded her a moment, then gave her another nod. "The fourcolor, his lackey, and his soldiers are traveling south. Toward the middle of fourcolor lands. Likely they will gather more troops to them with their prize."

Kisa finally found her tongue. "We have to warn the caravan about Aricaba-Ata. He's going to come back with soldiers from the capital."

The other woman waved a negating hand. "I have spoken with Ishkun-Dim-Hbelu already, though I was not able to free him. He has other plans, so despite my feelings to the contrary, and with Zikar dead, I will go back to the caravan to warn them. The fourcolor will not return soon, but soldiers may. You two will follow him. I can show you the way."

"You snuck into a guarded noble's camp to speak with Hbelu?" Belili asked. "You have proof Aricaba-Ata is taking Hbelu to Karduniash? Do you know why?" She resisted asking if Nidintu had seen Ligish. If Ilzi had done something to her, Belili didn't want to know.

"I do not." Nidintu glared as if it was their fault. "I do know you have to free our prince. He thinks the box you carry is worth something to the Asha-Urmana, and who am I to argue with him?" Her expression spoke otherwise. "You must free him before they arrive. He must be able to speak with the other caravans."

"How are we supposed to do that?" Kisa asked.

"No idea." Nidintu shrugged. "Nor do I know how my people will throw off the yoke of the fourcolors we have struggled under for so many centuries. Yet this is the will of our prince." She glanced between their packs. "You have the godfruit?"

Kisa looked put off by the sudden change in topic. Slowly, Belili nodded.

"You will need them. I will take a citron and a malus with me on the trip back to the caravan." Belili swung the pack around and the woman picked one of each and put them in a pouch at her belt. She hated to lose the precious magic, but if Nidintu said she needed godfruit, Belili doubted she was joking.

"Any other questions before I go?"

"How do we follow the nobles?" Belili looked around. The forest around them was all the same to her.

Nidintu speared Kisa with a glance. "She's a fair tracker when she puts her mind to it. You can follow a gods-cursed lot of noisy men, yes?"

Reluctantly, Kisa agreed that she could.

"Anything else?"

"I may be passable at tracking, but how do we find the other caravans to tell them about Hbelu?" Kisa asked.

"We will send word. They will find you." Nidintu spared them a glance over her shoulder. "Your task is to save our prince. Our people are depending on you, so try not to mess it up." She turned and faded into the woods.

* * *

They followed—or rather Kisa followed—Aricaba-Ata's trail for the next two days, through a vast and airy forest. Their wounds were healing, but slowly. The scrape down the side of Belili's face was nearly closed, as were the gouges from Tashi's nails on her upper arm. Her thigh still pained her, though that was not the only reason her walking was stilted. Kisa's shoulder was obviously hurting, but she said nothing about it.

They talked of dyeing their hair but decided to wait. They were not likely to run into anyone except the ones they were tracking, and neither wanted to take the time. Besides, they could be mistaken for natural blonds from a distance, rather than bleached blond slaves.

The trees here were much bigger than at the orchard, and Belili surveyed their canopies as they walked, picking out weak branches she would trim to make each tree a work of art. If she were the custodian of this forest, it could be a sanctuary, a garden fit for the Dyad themselves. Sprays of light fell through openings between leaves, illuminating patches of ground holding new spring growth.

Once they even passed a prunus tree, just budding, and Belili had to stop to break off a few branches, creating a scaffold to make the budding tree produce larger, juicier prunae in the year to come. The property must have been an old farm or cottage, far from the trade routes between rich lowlands and poorer mountain orchards. Kisa pointed out a mound of leaves and bushes she said was an old house, and Belili took her word for it. It was pure luck the tree was growing so well. The stump of the old tree was readily apparent. It had blown down in some storm, and the new tree grew not ten feet away. Had some noble or Asha-Urmana passed by here years ago, to give the magic spark the seed needed to grow?

They left the old house behind. It was fortunate they were far enough away from the main roads. Two slaves—with roots showing in their bleached hair—would be picked up by any group of nobles or servants passing too close.

Belili saw nothing of where the company had passed, but Kisa would search the ground and bushes by the side of the deer path they followed, and pronounce they were going the right way.

She had to admit her sister was correct when they found the remains of a camp on the second day. Kisa said there were more than a dozen men and women, pointing out patches where the loamy ground had been disturbed. She even pointed out which traces were Hbelu's and Ligish's. They had slept not an hour's walk from this site. They might have seen Aricaba-Ata's fire if the trees didn't block so much of the sky.

"We have to walk faster," Kisa said, as they left the camp. She snacked on a piece of dried jerky as she walked. "They're ahead, but not far. I'm sure Hbelu is putting up as much resistance as he can to slow them down." She stopped and turned back to Belili. "You don't think they would kill him, do you? They must be taking him to the capital for some reason. Nidintu didn't say why."

Kisa had mentioned Hbelu several times in the last few days, wondering how he was. Belili gathered something had happened between them as they traveled together. Kisa hadn't asked about Ligish, but then Belili hadn't mentioned her much either. It was better that way. She had to accept she was unlikely to see Ligish again.

"What do we do when we catch up?" Belili asked. "We can't fight twelve armed men, two of them nobles."

"I've been thinking. Maybe we…can use the godfruit." Kisa crossed her arms.

Belili sighed. "Even I know that isn't a plan. You've eaten a citron once. Aricaba-Ata and Ilzi have been eating them since they were children."

"We need to practice," Kisa said, sullen. She started walking again.

"You want to taste godfruit again."

"Don't you?" Kisa kept her face turned away so Belili couldn't see her expression.

"Of course, but we have to ration it. Otherwise, we'll eat through all we have."

Kisa whirled on her. "You've had a malus. Is it like the citron? Does the magic feel different?" Belili blinked at her sister. Kisa's words were fast, tinged with need.

Maybe one slice wouldn't hurt—she felt that hunger too, if not so intensely. There were still ten malae. It was long after their harvest, but the magical godfruit always lasted longer than the mundane counterparts.

"We should be walking," Belili said, but put her pack on the ground and felt for the smallest malae. She drew a knife from one of her pockets and cut a small slice. The godfruit was a little dry, but still had good juice, and she was careful to keep any from spilling. She handed Kisa the slice.

"You first. I want to see you control the winds." Kisa nodded and accepted the slice. Belili waited until Kisa's hand was halfway to her mouth. "At least more than you do with your snoring."

Kisa glared at her, then bit off half the slice. She stopped, shaking slightly, little strikes of lightning running down her arms and legs.

"What does it feel like?" Belili asked softly,

Kisa held a hand up. "I can feel it, all around me, like a blanket." She spun, and Belili felt the breeze she generated. "I can push the air where I want it." She waved a hand forward and the leaves rustled above them. Belili's cheeks cooled in the moving air. Then Kisa snapped her fingers, and something snatched all the leaves from a branch.

"This can cut through any fire Aricaba-Ata throws." She snapped again, and another branch rustled, but most of the leaves stayed. "The juice is almost gone. Three or maybe four good strikes per half a slice of malus." Kisa's eyes were far away, calculating, as always. "Although a fresh godfruit would have more juice."

Belili wondered if they had enough magical color in their hair to challenge Aricaba-Ata and Ilzi, even without their guards. Their former master had two large locks of red. Belili's hair—well, there wasn't as much color.

She held out a hand. "My turn." Kisa handed over the rest of the slice, watching as it traded hands.

Belili put it in her mouth, shivering as the juice released from the pulp. She nearly couldn't taste the godfruit itself, so overpowering was the magic of the juice. She wondered what citrons and malae would taste like if they were normal fruit like peaches or pears.

She held as much juice as she could in her mouth and stretched a hand glowing with electric energy over the forest path. Kisa's talk about weapons had given her an idea. She felt the earth beneath her, stretching into the bones of the land. There were sharp rocks down there, and harder metals. She gathered the pieces mentally, as the juice lost its flavor. Then she gestured sharply, and a thin spear of rock and dirt sprang out of the road.

Kisa stepped back, eyes wide. "Can you do that again?"

Belili shook her head. "Just once." There was barely any flavor left. She pressed down through the air and the spear crumbled into a pile. "That's all I have." She swallowed the malus pulp.

"If we surprise them, it *could* work," Kisa said, though her face was pinched with concern. "We'll have to aim for the nobles first, then take out the guards."

"I'll take Ilzi," Belili said immediately. "You can have Aricaba-Ata."

Kisa nodded. "The faster we catch up, the faster we can free Hbelu."

They slept in the forest again that night. Kisa said they were gaining on the others, though Belili couldn't see it. Despite walking all day, she took time to fall asleep. She imagined spearing Ilzi on a shaft of rock. It wouldn't remove any of the times he had cornered her on the Aricaba orchard. It wouldn't erase the bruises and the sickness. It wouldn't reverse the days she had spent with him while captured, when she and Ligish couldn't distract him. But it would help.

The next day she was ready to go before Kisa. Early in the morning, the game path they followed intersected a larger road, winding through the forest.

"Anyone who sees us will know what we are," Belili said, flipping a blond strand of hair. "Do you think it's time for the dye now?"

"In a bit," Kisa answered her. "We can move faster on the road, and I don't want to waste any more time. Do you want to get your hands on Enti-Ilzi or not?"

Belili remained silent. Hopefully they could get off the path if they encountered anyone.

They said little, walking fast along the path. It might have been the same road leading down from the Aricaba orchard. The morning passed, and after a quick meal of jerky and dried fruit, they continued on.

Soon after, they came across another house, this one with a carefully tended yard in front. It was still inhabited.

"Now we should get off the road," Kisa said, and Belili wondered if they should have stopped to dye their hair, despite the time it would take. They moved to the woods on the side opposite the house.

"Are those for nobles?" Belili asked, pointing at a second brick building, visible in the distance. It was bigger than Aricaba-Ata's house in the orchard.

"Well, they can't be slaves' houses," Kisa answered, pulling her into the forest beside the path. "Do you think guards or servants could afford something so big?"

They made their way behind another dwelling, creeping through the woods. A woman was out in the yard, tending to a garden. She didn't look like a noble, but she didn't look like a slave either. The trees were trimmed back, and their cover was sparse, so the two faded farther into the forest. It was easy to see the beginnings of a village. The houses were all two stories, and brick, with little gardens. Every fourth or fifth house had a godfruit tree. One had a prunus, in full bloom. This one wasn't a deserted godfruit tree in the middle of the forest but was well tended and fertilized—as the grave rails around it testified. Belili regarded the branches doubtfully from the cover of the trees. The pruning job was adequate, but she could have done better.

A cart pulled by an ox trudged the way they had come. The man driving it was worn and old, but his hair was not the dull blond of bleach. It was the natural white-blond of those with no magic. There might even have been a few strands of red in it. A man and woman walked the other way, carrying baskets.

"Where are we?" Belili asked. They couldn't be at Karduniash already, but where else would so many—freemen? Freewomen? Servants?—be crammed together? Kisa only shook her head.

"Somewhere Aricaba-Ata wants to go."

The houses grew larger and closer the farther they went, and they crept slower and slower, hoping no one saw them. They might be able to pass without notice for a while, but natural blond hair had a shine to it theirs could never replicate. In fact, there were slaves here too, and she could see the difference in their hair as they carted goods and hurried on errands. Sometimes they were under the watchful eyes of a guard, but just as often, they weren't.

They cut back into the woods, away from the houses and the road, until they were forced to stop at a border in the forest, where the woods had been cut back in a wide swath. Across from them was a stone wall three times as tall as Belili.

"Do you think they went in there?" she asked Kisa.

Kisa nodded, swallowing. "It's the only logical place. We'll follow them in." She turned back to Belili, eyes searching her face and hair. "Get out Hbelu's dye. We'll go in as Asha-Urmana."

CHAPTER ELEVEN

Brittle Chains

When the gods made their new servants, they did not know the magic they imbued the mortals with was impermanent. The gods do not have children as we do, and magic is not inherent to mortals as it is to gods. The children of the five pairs of mortals had less magic than their parents, as did each generation after.

Ishkun-Dim-Hbelu awoke, his head pounding. He attempted to feel the lump, but manacles binding his hands, visible in the glow from the campfire, hindered his action. He rattled the chains and settled for a sour expression.

"He is awake," said a soldier, looming over him, and the fourcolors turned from their conversation, dark shapes contemplating the river the sisters had crossed—the only thing that had gone right. Hbelu glanced to the side, saw Zikar's body lying still, a dark puddle reflecting firelight. No sign of Nidintu—she must not have been captured after letting Zikar's spirit fight one last time.

While the higher ranking fourcolor came toward him, Hbelu glanced around the camp. Of ten soldiers, all but two were men, and two looked like orchard guards, not professionals. Five guarded him while the others fixed up the camp. Two fourcolor nobles, both with godfruit, he assumed. They would not share any with their guards. It was the way of these people, to handicap their own assets to look stronger.

"Where have they gone?" the large umber-skinned man asked. Ata. He was a red-hair, with a temper to match the fire he favored.

Hbelu shook his head. "You heard what I told them. Did I give them specific directions? You know as much as I."

Ata growled and lifted a hand, but visibly restrained himself from hitting Hbelu. Interesting. Then they knew his value and did not want him harmed. Yet.

"No worry. I shall find them soon enough. The girls will be hopelessly lost in these woods. The only question is whether to terminate my workers now they have tasted godfruit. I could not afford to lose the income until your capture. Now, the prestige I will gain in the capital may make this all worthwhile. The Dyad will pay handsomely for a captive caravanner and a way to finally bring your people to heel." The fourcolor turned away, heading for the black-hair who was contemplating the river.

Perhaps the sisters could contact a caravan. Hbelu spread his legs as far as they would go in the manacles, judging his ability. It was enough.

He rolled back into the soldier behind him, knocking him off his feet, then used the momentum to rock forward, levering to a crouch. He let the weight of the chains around his hands reach to their extent, catching another of the soldiers across the cheek. The man collapsed in a heap, and Hbelu spun, whipping the chain around. It slapped across the arm of a woman reaching for her sword, knocking her hand away. Hbelu took a hopping step, tumbling forward and kicking his feet over his head. The force of his legs came down on yet another guard, crumpling him to the ground.

Before Hbelu could get up, the two remaining soldiers had grabbed the length of chain binding his wrists and ankles, jerking him to his feet, holding his arms by his sides so he couldn't move.

Ata had not yet made it to the river, and Hbelu let a small smile come to his face as the fourcolor spun back.

"Ilzi, come here," he called. The oily fourcolor had one hand in a pouch by his side. Behind him hunched another blond female prisoner, chains on her hands and feet, trying to hide the strength Hbelu could see beneath the grime coating her.

Good to know where one store of godfruit is. And another potential ally.

When both fourcolors were standing before him, Hbelu addressed them. "I do not think you have enough guards to keep both me and the sisters restrained. Please, though, try to follow them across the river. Should you take five of your soldiers? Four? Six?"

Hbelu could see a muscle bulging in Ata's cheek, reflecting the campfire flame. "We'll find an easier way across the stream downriver," the man decided. "The slaves will get nowhere in this darkness."

"Ata," Ilzi spit through clenched teeth. "I am promised Bel, and now that girl frees her sister and whisks her away in front of your soldiers. What good are they? They are supposed to be trained better than your orchard guards. At least I am left one servant, or I would be reduced to living like the guards."

"We will get her back. Later." Ata was not watching his fellow. His eyes fixed on Hbelu.

"Then when? When they are on the other side of Karduniash, or away into the Blasted Lands?" Ilzi flung a hand behind him, encompassing the whole world.

"Not now," Ata growled, turning to look at Ilzi. "Whose money is paying for the soldiers?" Hbelu watched both fourcolors, noting the frictions between them. There were many to choose from. As he watched, the woman behind Ilzi raised her eyes momentarily and stared back at him. Even that one look told Hbelu she was anything but a cowed slave. He had to speak with her.

"The money is only yours because our great-grandfather doted on your grandfather instead of mine. Otherwise, I might be the one with the large orchard."

"But still with no wife," Ata countered.

"Then let me go find her—"

"*Not now.*" Ata's voice was a whipcrack. "This caravanner will take too many of our resources. I do not wish to waste more godfruit on two slaves. We only have that which is with us, or which we can buy, in this dearth between seasons."

Ilzi stalked away, grumbling, the woman following him like a shadow. Hbelu thought of the elders after a long day of determining the next year's crop schedule. Especially Muze-Shi, when Ku-Baba got on her last nerve.

The soldiers secured his chains tighter, one woman leaning in to whisper in his ear. "We will remember how well you struggle, caravanner." She pulled the chains between his wrists until they nearly touched, then locked them.

He watched the three he had taken to the ground. Fourcolors could hold a grudge for a long time. Better to save his next escape attempt for later, perhaps with Ilzi's prisoner's help. Ligish, Belili had said her name was. More important was that the sisters were not captured again. He had seen the look Kisa gave Ata. She must be free to develop as a person, not as a captive. Her sister must be free for different reasons. He had no wish to see the mistrust he saw in her sharpened into cruelty, but it would be, if she was in the fourcolor's care much longer.

It was not long before the soldiers, better trained than the orchard guards—maybe from one of the northernmost fourcolor towns—settled the camp again. They made the fire larger, appropriated Zikar's brace of rabbits for the next breakfast, and set a tent for Ata and Ilzi where Ligish served them both. Hbelu and the soldiers slept as best they could in the still brisk air. Hbelu did not mind, save for the chains.

It was several hours later, when Shir-Gal and Nana-Ru were both high in the sky and the soldiers dozing, that Nidintu touched his shoulder, her other hand on his forearm to keep his chains from rattling. Hbelu resisted the urge to move his leg, which had fallen asleep.

His best scout raised all ten fingers, making circling motions around the camp. Hbelu nodded, and lifted two fingers and half a third, pointing to the tent. He opened his other hand in a bursting motion.

Ten soldiers, around the camp, and two magic users in the tent with the prisoner.

Nidintu mimed a question to him, touching the lock of the manacles. He shook his head. It would make too much noise to open them now, surrounded by guards. Nor should she try to free Ligish yet.

Next, she touched her lip with a finger and closed her teeth in a mock bite. Did he want a piece of godfruit. If she thought she could get one—and Hbelu trusted her evaluation—then he surely did. The scout raised her eyes to the moons above, pointing to one, and then the other. Hbelu nodded to Shir-Gal, Enta's great orb, pale yellow, the great citron of the sky. Nana-Ru, his younger sister, embodied the goddess Kigal and the malus. Raising and communicating with spirits was helpful, but he had no way to know if a powerful creature had perished nearby. He could not fight the fourcolors with a host of ghostly moles and wrens.

Nidintu left his side, making no sound as she crept through the sleeping soldiers. She hugged the ground, careful not to make a silhouette. Half the guards were on watch around the perimeter, periodically passing through the camp. Nidintu's progress was agonizingly slow, freezing every time a sentry moved. Finally, her head and shoulders disappeared into the tent. Hbelu saw Ligish shift out of her way from where she had been sleeping on the ground in front of the tent, providing a clearer path.

While she worked, Hbelu stared back at the moons. In this time of transition, the moons were properly the realm of no god. In the high summer, Dumzi would trick old Enti, masking one half of Shir-Gal with his dark mori as the moon waned. Then Geshtna would take the ownership of Nana-Ru from her sister, when the other moon's rusty glow turned from malus to prunus red.

Soon the scout crept back, slow as the moons overhead. Five of the soldiers were asleep, and Hbelu dared not move for fear his chains would clink together. Halfway there, one soldier snorted and rolled over, and Nidintu flattened herself. Minutes passed before she crept forward again. It seemed another age until she reached him.

She tucked a half-slice of citron, wrapped in oilcloth, into an interior pocket of his vest. The soldiers had removed his godfruit when they captured him, but would not think to check again, when he had been in their guard the whole time.

They made plans without speaking. Two fingers walking, a touch at temple and to white shirt. The sisters. A gesture at the river, at the camp. More gestures, back the way they came, and a motion of turning wheels.

Finally, Nidintu gripped his shoulder, hard, then silently rose to her feet. She would contact Kisa and Bel, telling them to follow Hbelu without coming too close. If he and Ilzi's prisoner could not escape, they must free the two of them. For now, he would gain information on the nobles' intentions.

Meanwhile, Nidintu would travel back to the caravan, alerting the elders to hurry. By the time they reached Karduniash, the rest of the caravans would surround the capital. Once there, the rest was up to the gods and the seed the sisters found.

He fell into a dreamless sleep.

* * *

The soldier he had knocked over woke him with a rough boot to the middle. Hbelu took his time getting to his feet, requesting water, food. He got some of the first, brought by Ligish, but none of the second. They would have to feed him eventually.

"You are well?" he asked Ligish in an undertone as she handed him a skin of water. The guards were busy for the moment, packing the camp.

"Well enough, with Ilzi as enraged as he is at losing Bel." Her voice was low and husky for a woman. She wore manacles clasped around her wrists and ankles, but without chains attached. Free for now to serve Ilzi, but easy to restrain.

"You have become close with her?" At Ligish's quick nod he continued. "That is good. Belili needs more friends. I plan to give them more time to escape."

A guard wandered within earshot and Ligish ducked her head, whisking the water skin away.

They traveled slowly, as a large troop of soldiers would. They kept to the pace of the slowest, and Hbelu made sure that was him. Every second let the sisters solidify their plans, let Nidintu find them.

It was late morning when they reached a ford in the river. Ilzi ventured across halfway, testing the depth of the water. "Cousin, here is our chance," he said to the red-haired fourcolor. "I can take a few of the soldiers and capture the girls. They cannot have made it far. I would be back in a few hours."

"What of their newfound magic?" Ata grumbled. "More likely I will have to fish you out from whatever hole they toss you in."

Ilzi put hands on hips. "I am not so unskilled. The two used godfruit but once. I doubt they have any idea what they can do. They may have a few strands of color at most, not enough to challenge a true nobleman."

Ata was silent long enough that Hbelu began to fidget. He would have to use the half slice of citron soon, before it dried out, but he was hoping to wait a little longer.

"You know not what they are capable of. If you are so insistent Belili will be a match for you, do not underestimate her ability." Ata glared at his cousin.

Hbelu saw the black-hair rub at a small mark on his arm. A scar? "I do not underestimate her. Four men and a noble can take on two slave girls."

"And leave me six men to tend to him *and* your new slave?" Ata stuck a finger out in Hbelu's direction. Such caution. He had scared them the night before.

"Surely you can handle one *caravanner*, oh noble Cousin," Ilzi scoffed. "My new companion knows her place. After all, you are the one with money to hire soldiers from the local militia. Even if you lose him, you have enough land to produce a good store of godfruit to sell. Not to mention peaches, grapes, and yams. I would think you have plenty of *resources* to hold on to one purple-haired nomad."

"Do not bring your lack of success and ambition into this, Ilzi," Ata countered, a growl rising in his words. "Not every one of your failures is my fault."

"Enough of them are," Ilzi snapped. "Let me have this one thing. Bel will make a good breeding wife, once I take that wild streak from her. You can have the sister for the orchards."

"You could find a better, more noble wife in Karduniash."

"Not one I've had such time to mold," Ilzi said. "Look at your troubles with Ubala."

"That is not—" Ata clutched his hands, knuckles whitening. "That is not the issue we are discussing."

"Is it not? I thought we were talking of my future *wife*, slipping away?"

Hbelu judged this was the correct time to intervene. "Just think, his children can take over your orchard, should you die childless, rather than letting a stranger take over." He looked to the red-hair.

Ata's face colored, and a soldier cuffed Hbelu. He staggered, but knew his guess at Ilzi's interference with Ata's children was accurate, considering what the sisters had told him. He caught Ligish's quick smile.

"You stay out of this," Ata said, and turned his back to Hbelu. To Ilzi, he said, "You can see the risk here. Think of the reward in bringing the prince of these people to court." He spread his hands as if the meaning was clear. "If we hurry, we will be in time for the Prunus Festival and the Dyad's Naming Day. They have wanted the caravanner's magic for years."

"The capital is far away," Ilzi said, "and the Dyad are capricious. If we do get there in time, will this one caravanner offset our rustic lineage? Is it comparable to the production of regaining one of your workers?"

"It should be two workers," Ata grumbled, but Hbelu could see he was wavering. Letting the girls run free would sting his pride, no matter how tempting a prize Hbelu was. He clutched the citron half-slice inside his leather vest. Ligish's eyes followed his subtle movement, though none of the guards saw.

"We need all the advantages we can grab, Cousin," Ilzi pleaded. "We mountain nobles must work together. Do not let the lowland nobles wipe our names and lineages away."

Ata shook his head, but Hbelu saw the resignation. One-handed, he unwrapped the citron and brought it to his mouth with a rattle of chains. He caught Ligish's eyes widening, as she took a step away from Ilzi.

"What was that?" a soldier asked, grabbing for his manacles. Hbelu jerked his arms out of reach and bit down.

The rush of the godfruit was small—it was old and dried out. But lightning strikes ran down his arms and legs, skittering over the metal of the manacles. Hbelu felt limbs stretch, muscles grow. The soldiers shrank to chest level, then to his navel.

"Where did he get godfruit?" Ata was grasping at his pouch. Ilzi was unsheathing his sword.

With a roar, Hbelu threw the circle of soldiers back like children, snapping the chain binding his wrists together. The manacles bit into his enlarged wrists, drawing blood. They twisted, but the metal did not break. He kicked one leg out, nearly as long as a man, buckling the links in the chain and pushing a soldier away to tumble head over boots.

"Get him!"

"This side! Circle around to the side! Watch out for—"

Hbelu swung the ends of the chains like whips, waiting for Ligish, unnoticed, to draw away from the group. He was not trying to kill, which would set the fourcolors and the soldiers against him. They might forget Ata's idea to bring him whole to the Dyad. However, a few broken ribs and some cuts would not be amiss.

By the time the juice of the citron ran out and Hbelu shrunk to his normal size, six of the soldiers were groaning on the ground, including the two he had pegged as Ata's orchard guards. Enough to keep them occupied, but not so much they injured him greatly. This was not an escape attempt, but a persuasion.

After everything, they had to bind his hands with rope, as they had no replacement manacles.

"Now do you see?" Ata asked his cousin, standing over Hbelu, who was kneeling on the ground, five soldiers around him while the others tended their wounds. "What if you were gone with half my men? This tricky caravanner might have escaped and our fortunes would be reversed."

"Not all of them." Ilzi tucked his lock of black hair behind an ear, wiping at a gash in his cheek that had appeared during the altercation.

He raised his hands at Ata's indignant look. "Yes, Cousin, I understand." He waited until Ata had turned back to regard Hbelu. "Though should they not be considered *our* men?"

"Surround Ilzi." Ata bellowed, eyes hot with rage. Ata's guards and eight of the soldiers leapt to do as he bid. Two were slower than the others, and the circle did not include Ligish. Hbelu hid a smile. It seemed Ilzi had some of his own resources.

"Does this answer your question, *Cousin*?" Ata locked eyes with the smaller black-hair.

Ilzi bowed his head. "Most certainly, Cousin."

"We head to Neharda," Ata commanded, and the soldiers returned to their tasks. "If we cross paths with my workers, then we will take them back, but until then the priority is this caravanner. Is that clear to everyone?"

There was a chorus of agreements.

* * *

They kept a much tighter watch on Hbelu after that. Ata ordered him stripped and searched for more godfruit. He had none, though they picked through his finger-length braids and felt in the seams of his clothes. Hbelu could see the glint of steel in the red-hair's eye when his soldiers found nothing. Even then, the man did not punish him, though he did not discipline his soldiers from their rough service in re-binding his hands and getting him dressed. Hbelu's traveling leathers grew new rips and tears from their treatment.

Ilzi grew restrained, but Hbelu saw new bruises on Ligish's upper arms. He wished he could reassure her, just for a moment, but Ilzi had kept her close the past day. Hbelu kept an eye on both fourcolors, but he especially made sure he could see the pale black-hair at all times. That one was too clever for his own good. Oddly, he was reminded of Belili, and could see why the man regarded her as an acceptable match. Were Belili willing, and Ilzi not so unctuous, they would make a pair to rival most of the fourcolors Hbelu had met. He could see them worming their way into the channels of power, in the southern lands.

Thankfully, Ata was a contrast. The big man commanded respect from all the soldiers. One was whipped for sleeping on watch, though how Ata knew of it, Hbelu could not say. Perhaps his household guards kept a watch on the hired soldiers. The orchard owner saw attempts on his absolute control of the party as a threat, and Ilzi wisely kept from suggesting alternate courses of action once it was clear they would not search for the sisters.

The second day from the ford, they angled to the west for a time and Hbelu watched the trees. Ligish fetched for the fourcolors, and sometimes for the guards. She passed by enough times for them to exchange a few words in whispers, giving him information she'd gleaned from listening while Ata and Ilzi planned.

He had not been this way in many years but remembered the area. If they were heading where he thought from Ligish's information, then there might be a chance yet. Later that day, they intersected the trading road that ran between the mountains and the plains, and the fourcolors stopped to plan.

"Neharda is your destination?" Ilzi ventured, confirming Hbelu's guess. He had phrased any challenge in the last few days as a careful question.

"It is, though I have my misgivings," Ata answered. He fingered the whip he kept coiled at his side. "It is the closest city for many leagues, and we need supplies. Plus, I hope to gather more nobles to my cause."

Hbelu knew of Neharda, and the caravan that claimed the lands nearby during the year. Mushezibti-Lila's caravan was the richest of them and had almost as much influence with the Asha-Urmana as his. It would be good to see them again, though he knew Ata would avoid them if he had the choice.

"I have not been there before," Ilzi said. "Do they truly let their property run free and talk back to nobles?"

Ata nodded. "A lax practice, and I know for a fact they have many runaways. More, the place is a haven for escaping slaves. You'd best watch that one." He nodded toward Ligish. "The city's position far from the capital means corruption runs deep. Most nobles do not even treat their lineage with the respect it deserves, associating with servants and merchants and traders of little magic."

"Barbaric," Ilzi agreed. "I hope Shuma and Iral get no ideas above their station. There is only so much backtalk I will accept, even from freemen. You understand that, girl?" He clasped Ligish's wrist and twisted so she cried out.

"I understand." Hbelu could barely hear the woman's whisper.

Ata only grunted at Ilzi's suggestion, but Hbelu watched the black-haired fourcolor. Could he use the man's dissent to his advantage?

The nobles began walking along the road and a soldier poked him in the back with the handle of a whip. Hbelu walked at his shuffling pace, his legs jerking as they met the bounds of the ropes hobbling him. He was not trying to be the slowest this time. He was sure the fourcolors would find a new set of bindings for him in Neharda, but this place also seemed the best to get word to another caravan.

As they traveled, freemen and women on the road moved out of their way. Hbelu watched for any sign of his people. They would be rare, but he knew they traded to the fourcolors. He began to plan.

CHAPTER TWELVE

Neharda

All five pairs of magical mortals prospered, increasing in number until there were five civilizations to rival that of the blonds. The godfruits gave them great power. These mighty mortals pleased the gods more than their blond children, and the four argued and feuded over who was worthier of their creation's worship.

"This looks black, not purple." Kisare held the vial of dye up to the late morning light.

"I'm sure Hbelu knew what he was doing," Bel said. "Do you think the part we don't dye will pass for true blond?"

Their roots definitely showed now, though the contrast with the bleached rest of their hair was difficult to see unless one was close.

Kisare considered. "It will have to pass, unless we dye all of our hair purple, which would be more suspicious."

It took longer than she would have liked, and she could feel Hbelu getting farther away. The frustrating man had saved her too many times. She had to save him, if only to continue their interrupted conversation. He thought enough of her to invite her into his caravan past the objections of his elders.

He was also the only way they could talk to the other caravans. Nidintu *said* the caravans would find them, but how could the woman know? She would have to walk back to the village before the message even got out. They would be too far ahead.

"Shall we try the city?" Bel asked. She ran her fingers down a length of dyed hair, trying to get a look at it. They had several large locks of purple, enough to show they were Asha-Urmana, but not enough for others to gawk at the amount of color. Kisare had patterned the dyed areas after less powerful villagers from Hbelu's caravan, over the ears, a little in the front, and sections in back. Both her and Bel's hair was long, though usually tied up and out of the way.

Kisare gestured for her sister to lead the way.

"Through here," Bel said, pointing to an alley between two houses, backing up to the edge of the woods. Both houses had high peaked roofs and timbered beams surrounded by whitewashed plaster.

"It'll have to do." Kisare looked both ways. There were a few people in the street, dressed in cotton shirts like the Asha-Urmana gave them, though these were in blues and greens and reds. Where theirs were simple, most inhabitants had decorative stitching or extra buttons. She tried to look casual as they exited into the main street. Some watched them, but not all.

"They must trade with the Asha-Urmana to get those clothes," Kisare whispered, and Bel nodded agreement. Aricaba-Ata hadn't known how to effectively remove the burs in the plant's fiber. Almost every piece of clothing here, from shirts, to jackets, to pants and skirts, was made from the soft fiber, rather than the wool that was the norm in the orchard.

The street intersected with the wall they found in the woods, but here, there was a gate in the high wall of the city. Two armored men, both sporting locks of magical color in their white-blond hair—one brown and one silver—stood at either side. They had spears, and round pouches at their waists that must hold godfruit.

"What business do you have in Neharda, caravanners?" asked the one with the silver lock. He didn't quite sneer as he looked them both up and down.

"Selling clothes and other fabrics," Kisare said, drawing his attention back to her. She tried to affect the same light accent Hbelu had. She must have gotten close.

"Well, if you get bored, she can come back and see me tonight," Silver-hair said. "I'd be willing to buy some of her clothes myself." He gestured at Bel and the other guard laughed at his joke. "Move along."

Kisare seethed, forcing herself to smile and walk through the gate. Bel had her head down, but her hands clenched. Once they were past, Kisare let out a heavy breath. "Men! Are they all like that? I thought it would be different now we're—" She glanced around. Probably not the best place to advertise they were escaped slaves.

"It's not different," Bel growled. "If I could wipe the sneer from his face—" Kisare reached one hand out to touch her sister's arm, but Bel pulled back again. She had been angry, distant, since Kisare rescued her. Was it only that they had not been able to rescue Ligish, or had Ilzi done something else to her?

"Let's find him," Bel said, watching the many brick houses surrounding them, and Kisare didn't know whether she meant Hbelu, or Ilzi. "They probably stopped at an inn."

"How do we find one?" Kisare asked. She tried not to stare like the bumpkin she was. She had never seen so many houses so close together—as if they were trying to crowd each other out. Contrasting styles and stories battled, and the dirt streets were muddy and slippery. "It's not like I can follow their tracks here." Where the Asha-Urmana village had an aura of cooperation, this town—Neharda—was at once frantic and slovenly. Barely anyone spared them a glance.

Bel waved a hand forward. "Somewhere along the main street."

They passed buildings with signs advertising in both words and pictures. There was an apothecary with a bundle of dried herbs and a tailor's shop with a pair of scissors crossed with a needle and thread.

"There," Bel said. It was a larger building with three stories, in the most popular whitewashed stucco. The sign had a bed and a steaming pot of stew on it.

Kisare looked down the street. There was another building, made all of brick, with a boar's head and a mug of beer. Another, at the edge of her sight range, with a dancing woman and a full plate of food. That one had a circular second floor with a domed roof. "Which one?" Bel followed her glance and frowned.

"We could try all of them."

"How suspicious would that be, for Asha-Urmana to go into each tavern and look for Aricaba-Ata? I doubt he has Hbelu tied up with him. Shuma and Iral probably have him hidden somewhere."

"Not at all, if we're selling wares." Bel tugged at her pack. Her face was pinched, and Kisare knew she was still thinking of the gate guards.

"Maybe we can get a drink and a meal too, though I don't know with what money. We should get off the streets before anyone else—"

A hand fell on her shoulder.

"There you are! I have a knot to polish with you two, leaving like that. Caravanners!"

Kisare whirled under the hand, reaching behind her for her pack with the godfruit. Bel had her mouth open in surprise.

An old woman, pale, wrinkled and with white hair, waggled a gnarled finger at them. She held a basket of vegetables like a mace, out to one side, as if ready to hit them. Kisare had never seen anyone with completely white hair before—not even the elders.

"Leaving like that, before you finished, *and* before getting paid!" She turned to a passerby, gesticulating with her free hand. "I try to be nice to caravanners and see what it gets me!" The other pedestrian, a corpulent man in a red cotton vest, shook his head and kept walking.

"Now, come back to my house, and we will finish this. Those shirts don't grow on trees, and you need to get the rest of my measurements." She grabbed for Kisare's arm, but Kisare jerked back, glaring. She'd expected to be called out for a slave, but not confused for some Asha-Urmana who hadn't followed up on a deal.

"I think you're mistaken," she said. She looked to Bel for support, but her sister was staring at the woman, eyes slightly squinted.

"Don't tell me what I know," the woman snapped back. "I expect you think you can leave without finishing a contract, just because it pleases you! You think the Dyad's laws don't apply to your kind."

"Maybe we should go with her, Kisa," Bel said. Kisare turned an incredulous look her way.

"Yes, listen to her," the woman said. "The faster we get this straightened out, the faster I get my new clothes." She made another grab for Kisare's arm, and this time caught her. Bel, insanely, joined the woman, taking Kisare's other arm.

"We'll figure this out when we're not in the middle of the street," Bel hissed to her. More people were looking their way.

Kisare let herself be pulled along. She didn't want to attract attention either. The old woman certainly wasn't a guard and didn't have the muscle to hold them back from leaving, should they choose so.

The woman made a steady stream of complaints, dragging Kisare through muddy cross streets and around a square with kiosks selling wares and vegetables. Bel kept up, one hand on Kisare's other arm, not quite hard enough to hurt her injured shoulder.

They came to rest by a little house butted up against the city wall. Like the other buildings, it had white stucco surrounding dark brown wooden beams. It was only one story, but had an arched entryway over a stout wooden door.

"In here, quickly," the woman said, and her voice was no longer the complaining old lady. She fumbled with the door, producing a large iron key from somewhere in her layers of clothes, then pushed the sisters inside.

"Now, will you tell me what's going on?" Kisare said when the door banged shut. She tried not to sound petulant. They were in a comfy looking sitting room, with two chairs piled with pillows, and a hearth laid with tinder. A doorway led to a kitchen, but Kisare could see a mattress through the door. The house only had two rooms—one more than the slave quarters at the Aricaba orchard.

"Who are you?" Bel asked, and Kisare flicked her a glare for the extra question. They needed answers, not confusion. The old woman's eyes moved back and forth between them.

"I can keep you from being killed as runaway slaves," she said. Kisare stiffened and saw Bel's face slide into expressionlessness.

"Your hair isn't actually white," Bel whispered.

Now the woman paused. "Astute." What had Bel seen? The woman stood straighter and it seemed she wasn't as old as Kisare had thought. Some of the wrinkle lines around her eyes and mouth were paint.

"Who are you?" she said, then realized it was the same thing Bel asked. She frowned, daring her sister to make a comment. Bel held her tongue.

"I am Gemeti," the woman said. "And no, my hair is not all white, or not yet. As for your first question," she turned to Kisare, "I help slaves looking for a...better life."

"Why do you think we're slaves?" Kisare asked. She brought a hand to her dyed hair. "We have items to sell, we have purple hair, and we come from the forest outside. Why shouldn't you think we're Asha-Urmana?" She spared a glance to see Bel's reaction, but her sister was impassive.

The woman stumped around her and her sister. Though she wasn't as old as she appeared, she wasn't young, either.

Gemeti ticked off a point on one gnarled digit. "First, you are too light." She poked a finger at Kisare's pale, freckled, cheek. "And you are too dark." This at Bel. "Wrong bone structure. I doubt you have been around many of their people, but where the nobles come in all shapes and sizes, the Asha-Urmana all look similar, wherever they are." Kisare frowned. True, the members of Hbelu's caravan shared similarities in their features, but she assumed it was because many in the town were related. Were *all* Asha-Urmana like that?

"The Asha-Urmana will give you some fluff about protecting their magic," Gemeti continued, "but whatever the reason, they do not mix outside their caravans." She paced around them, marking another finger. "Second, you have the wrong walk. Asha-Urmana, to a person, are arrogant. They walk like they own everything."

"I can believe that," Kisare mumbled, thinking of Hbelu, Nidintu, Zikar, and even Arala and her daughter.

"Don't interrupt," Gemeti snapped. "Third, you do not carry items for trade openly, as Asha-Urmana would. They never set up stalls in the market, but wander the town, and if they sell nothing, they leave without regret. Fourth, your hair." Gemeti flipped one of Bel's free locks of hair, and her sister flinched. Bel was much jumpier lately. "Asha-Urmana travel with their hair in braids, to prevent it from getting in the way."

Kisare blinked. Hbelu's long hair had braids, as had Nidintu's, though Zikar had worn his too short. Most of the village wore braids, but again, she assumed it was the style of that caravan.

"How do you know so much about the Asha-Urmana?" she asked.

"Why are you telling us?" Bel countered.

Gemeti pointed one finger at Bel. "Your sister gets to the heart of things."

"How do you know we're sisters?" Kisare would not let the woman get away without explaining her little mysteries.

"That one's pretty easy, Kisa," Bel said, and Gemeti croaked a laugh.

"So many questions." The woman stopped pacing, pushed a chair forward, and arranged the cushions. "Come, come, have a seat. Tell me your names and introduce yourselves. Would you like something to eat or drink?"

"We're in a hurry," Kisare said. She stopped before she said anything more. This crazy old lady didn't need any more information.

Bel straightened, and Kisare realized she had been hunched over ever since they escaped Aricaba-Ata. Her sister took a deep breath, as if coming to a decision.

"My name is Belili, and this is my sister, Kisare."

The woman only nodded. "You are welcome in my house. Chasing after the noble who came to town with the captive Asha-Urmana, if I guess correctly," Gemeti said, placing a finger beside her nose. "Keep your eyes in your face. It is not hard to speculate. The noble—a country bumpkin with more arrogance than sense—paraded in here yesterday like he was bringing a nameday gift to the Dyad. Well, maybe he is. But you will get nowhere near him soon. He has surrounded himself with the good-for-nothing sons of the town, going on about his brave capture of an Asha-Urmana leader. Hmpf." Gemeti rolled her eyes. "As if that will do anything but keep the other caravans away from Neharda for months. We will have no new fine clothes but what we make ourselves, mark my words. Now have a seat." There was a command in the woman's voice this time.

Kisare and Bel put their packs against the wall and sat in the offered chairs. Gemeti shuffled into her kitchen, her many layers rustling around her. There were skirts, underskirts, and petticoats. She had at least three cotton shirts Kisare could see, underneath the jacket, vest, and wool scarf. They disguised the woman's figure.

She leaned close to Bel, in the other chair. "How soon can we get out of here?" she asked.

Bel shrugged. "Gemeti might be able to help us, and we need help. If we stay, we might catch up to Aricaba-Ata and Ilzi sooner."

"I don't trust her," Kisare said. The woman disguised her appearance. How trustworthy could she be?

"She took us in, even though we pretended to be Asha-Urmana," Bel said. Kisare glared. She was fairly sure her sister couldn't read her thoughts. "She knows a lot about them," Bel continued. "Even if we can't get close to Hbelu, she might introduce us to the local caravan. We need this." Kisare realized her sister's eyes were not just intent, they were frightened. "I need something stable. Gemeti reminds me of Mother, a little."

Kisare was about to answer—she had no memories of their mother—when the woman came shuffling back in, dragging another chair. She disappeared into the kitchen again and returned with a wooden tray holding three mugs and a bowl of candied fruits and nuts.

"Eat, drink, and we shall talk," Gemeti said. She set the tray down on a table and groaned her way down into the third chair, then passed mugs out. Kisare sniffed at hers, and found a savory roasted smell, with a hint of bitterness.

"What is this?" she asked. Bel took a small sip, and her eyes went wide.

"You have never tasted roast kaba?" Gemeti eyed them. "Well, that confirms you come from the outskirts of civilization, does it not? Escaped from that nobling who came in yesterday, did you?"

"His name is Aricaba-Ata," Bel said. Kisare drew her eyebrows down, but it was probably too late to hide anything else from this woman. She seemed to know half their history.

"The other slimy wretch with him is Enti-Ilzi," Kisare supplied, not looking at her sister. "They caught us as we traveled south with the Asha-Urmana he captured."

"Ishkun-Dim-Hbelu," Bel mumbled into her drink. So, they really weren't keeping anything back, were they?

Gemeti sat forward at that, her mouth open. "*That* is Ishkun-Dim-Hbelu? Oh dearies, this is much worse than I thought. He is from a stationary caravan, far up in the mountains. Is that correct?"

Bel nodded, but Kisare was incredulous. "Wait. How do you know Hbelu?"

"He is only the leader of the entire Asha-Urmana nation in exile," Gemeti said. "Surely he told you that much. Why else do you think he was traveling to speak to the other caravans?"

"He may have mentioned something about it," Kisare said.

"He told us," Bel corrected her.

"If you know so much about the Asha-Urmana, can you explain why Karduniash is so important to him? He seemed obsessed with it, even before..." Kisare did not finish her thought. She was sure even Gemeti couldn't know about the box.

The woman's eyes narrowed, but she didn't comment on Kisare's dissembling. "The nobles ignore the Asha-Urmana, even as they buy products they cannot make. I have worked with the caravan near this city for over thirty years, helping escaped slaves. Neharda is perhaps the one city in the entire realm of the Dyad willing to turn a blind eye to slaves moving to freedom." She plucked at a multi-colored cotton vest. "You will not see clothes of this make except in the capital, where they have enough money to import it from here."

"But why—" Gemeti held up a hand to stop Kisare's question.

"Quiet, child. I'll get to your question." Kisare held her silence, fuming inside.

"Did you know the Asha-Urmana used to live in Karduniash?" Kisare cocked her head in interest. "Or so the Asha-Urmana say, in any case. Whatever happened, it was centuries ago, and the nobles banded together to drive them out. It is why they refer to the nobles as 'fourcolors.'"

"So, he wants to take back the capital," Kisare said. An impossible task.

Bel sat forward. "You haven't told me this part, Kisa."

Kisare shrugged, both to not give away too much to the perceptive old woman, and because she hadn't thought of it while they traveled.

Gemeti sat back in her chair, positioning a pillow behind her. "This is something I never thought to see. Ishkun-Dim-Hbelu is one of the greatest Asha-Urmana leaders in over two hundred years, if his reputation is to be believed. If anyone could do it, he could." Then her brows drew down. "Though why now, of all times?"

Kisare exchanged a look with Bel. Neither of them would say anything about the fifth godfruit.

"I see." Gemeti watched their exchange. She clapped her hands and pulled herself to her feet. "If that is the case, you two must follow him."

"Don't you mean rescue him?" Kisare asked. She fought down a pang of panic at the thought of Hbelu being in iron manacles for so long.

"Your noble is already taking him to the capital," Gemeti said, hands held wide. "Presumably he will give the prince to the Dyad. They have lusted for control of the Asha-Urmana's magic for years. Maybe your noble thinks he will earn a place at court. Whatever the reason, Ishkun-Dim-Hbelu will be in the perfect place to lead his rebellion against the Dyad."

"Except he's held captive," Bel put in. She was still sipping her kaba. Kisare had taken a few swallows of the drink but deemed it too rich.

"Yes, yes." Gemeti was pacing back and forth now. "Which is why you two need to become nobles."

"Nobles?" Kisare came to her feet. "How do you propose to do that, if you can pick us out as slaves so easily?"

"Minor nobles," Gemeti amended, eyeing them. "From even farther out than wherever you came from. Maybe even from the Blasted Lands. Such exotic locations are all the rage at court, so I hear."

"So you hear?" Where did this woman get her information?

"Yes," Gemeti continued, still pacing. One hand rubbed her mouth. "If the prince wants the other caravans, you must rouse them to movement along the way. I can help with that, but we must make sure Ishkun-Dim-Hbelu gets to the capital in good health and ready to lead his people in rebellion."

"We?" Kisare was getting lost in the myriad plans, but that word stood out.

Gemeti stopped pacing. "I would not miss something like this for all the godfruit in the world," she said, eyes shining.

"So, not only have you pulled us away from following Hbelu, you'll now tag along with us and slow us down. You might even get us caught." Kisare crossed her arms and frowned at the old woman. Gemeti gave her a level stare, and Kisare wilted.

"Girl, if I don't go along with you, the only part of the capital you will see is the inside of the prisons, then the gallows. You think you can learn to pass as a noble in an hour or a day? I will be by your side, coaching your every action all the way to the city. I have watched nobles compete for nigh on fifty years and have passed slaves to the Asha-Urmana for thirty. I have seen enough to get by."

Kisare shot another glance at Bel, who for once had an eyebrow cocked. "While we're parading as nobles, what's to keep Aricaba-Ata from torturing Hbelu?" Kisare wasn't about to let rescuing him go until she was convinced.

"They won't kill him," Bel said.

"Correct," Gemeti said. "He is much too valuable. The Dyad would trade many things for the Asha-Urmana's magic."

"Won't the Asha-Urmana choose a new leader when they learn there's little chance of rescuing Hbelu?"

"They could," Gemeti answered. "But they will not. Ishkun-Dim-Hbelu is well loved by the caravans. Besides, there is something coming, though I know not what. The caravan near here has been restless the past week. Some word came through recently, but they will not tell me the news."

So, they did have some way to pass word quickly. Was this Nidintu's work?

Then she noticed Bel was digging at *her* pack, still sitting against the wall. Kisare was too far away to stop her.

"What are you doing?" she said. "Don't tell me you're going to show—"

Bel turned around, the box clasped in her hands. Kisare groaned.

"This is what the Asha-Urmana have been talking about," Bel said. "A gift from the gods. Ishkun-Dim-Hbelu thinks it may change the balance between the nobles, the slaves, and the Asha-Urmana."

CHAPTER THIRTEEN

Moving On

During years of strife, the gods favored one civilization, then another. Over time, Dumzi and Geshtna, the gods of spring and summer, became particularly enamored of the red-haired and brown-haired peoples.

Belili couldn't say for sure why she picked up the box—it seemed faintly warm again, as if the seed inside knew when it was near someone with magic. Was it to spite the nobles? Or was it because Gemeti reminded her of her mother, a strong, no-nonsense woman? Their mother had died at Kisa's birth, so her sister couldn't see this woman like she did—the furtive trek through the city, the disguise she wore to divert the nobles' attention.

Gemeti lived at the edge of the city, in a house barely bigger than a slave's quarters. She obviously had connections with Karduniash, and with the Asha-Urmana. Had she started as Belili and her sister had? Maybe sold into and escaped slavery? Regardless, if the fifth godfruit brought an end to the abuse of the nobles, Belili would do anything to make that happen.

The woman stood gaping like a fish as Belili brought the box forward. "We found it on the Aricaba orchard, buried under the malus tree." She pried it open to show off the rich black dirt. Kisa winced, but Belili ignored her. "It has one magical seed in it, but the elders of Hbelu's caravan couldn't tell—"

She would have said more, but Kisa flapped her hands, cutting her off. "Enough. Anything else is just stories. We don't need to bother her with them."

"Does your former master know about this?" Gemeti asked.

"No," Kisa said. "We want to keep it that way."

"Kisa rescued me from them," Belili added, shivering, "but Hbelu traded himself to let us go free." She tried to think of some way to say what Ligish had done for her, but there was too much to form into words.

The woman's eyes widened again. "Sacrificing his freedom for slaves?" She waved a gnarled hand at Kisa's open mouth. "Former slaves. What do you have over him?"

"The seed is our discovery and our property," Kisa said. Belili could tell she had given up on keeping things back. "His people think the seed will help them, so he bargained with us. When they took Bel, he promised he would rescue her before he united his people."

"I see," Gemeti said, but the woman's eyes shifted from Belili to Kisa. She probably guessed there was something between Kisa and the prince, as Belili had. It may have been what saved them from the Asha-Urmana taking the box. In any case, they had to stay free, and Gemeti was another path to that end.

"Can you help us?" Belili said. "Can you really make us into nobles?"

Gemeti had her composure back. She nodded. "I can, but not in Neharda. You will be far too conspicuous. We must leave for the caravan. There are some there who help slaves, instead of simply letting them pass through. We will transform you."

"Good. Then let's go." Kisa went to her pack and pulled it over her shoulder.

"Not today," Gemeti objected. "I am old, and it will take until past nightfall to get to the caravan." She cocked a hand on the small of her back, hidden under the multiple layers she was wearing, made of cotton, wool and other fibers. Belili reassessed how long it would take to get to Karduniash.

Kisa pursed her lips. "Then tomorrow? I don't want to be too far away from Hbelu." She saw Belili looking at her and added, "He might give away information about us or the box."

Belili shook her head. At least it would also put her nearer Ligish.

* * *

They stayed the night with Gemeti, on an extra mattress Belili suspected slaves used when being smuggled from their nobles. As they settled for bed, they heard Gemeti shuffling about, moving things from one place to another and cursing quietly.

The next morning, there was an empty feeling about the house, with little things cleaned up or moved. There was a third large pack by the two they'd brought. The woman proved to be a decent cook, and despite protestations of being old and slow, she was ready to leave early in the morning, after a hearty breakfast of porridge and bread. Belili took the time to stretch her leg out. It was getting better, but still pained her. She noticed Kisa rolling her shoulder.

They made three stops on the way out, Gemeti tapping at the doors of other houses and talking with the owners in a hushed voice. Several times, Belili saw something change hands.

This early, there were few people out in the town. Almost all were true blonds, whitish hair reflecting the sun. A few had strands of magical color. Belili had never seen so many in one place. In the orchard, some true blonds might be slaves, but offspring of nobles with no appreciable magic became guards.

As they neared the gates of Neharda, Belili could see bleached-blond slaves carrying produce or bags, passing by the sentries at the wall. There were nobles near, but no guards following the slaves. No whips of any kind. She expected the slaves to make a break at any moment, but they didn't. In fact, they were talking amongst themselves. One gate sentry leered at a young woman carrying a basket of turnips. Belili almost growled as the woman blew a kiss back.

She never wanted to be like that. Animals.

They had surprisingly little trouble. Gemeti hobbled through the gate without a glance at them. Kisa, of course, panicked, trying to draw her vest up around her head. Belili took her arm, as if they were taking a stroll for the morning.

"Don't do that," she whispered. "You'll get us taken in."

"Would you rather they saw two blonds with dyed hair?" Kisa hissed back. She must have over-applied Gemeti's warnings, as usual.

"They don't," Belili answered. "They see two Asha-Urmana with a woman known to travel to their caravan. Watch Gemeti." She pointed forward, where the old woman waved a bony arm at a guard young enough that spots still covered his face. She passed a small loaf of bread to him, saying something Belili couldn't catch.

"Why did she do that?" Kisa asked, clutching at Belili's arm.

"Probably because she knows him and made him a loaf yesterday. Didn't you see them in the kitchen? She's been here most of her life. Maybe it's her nephew or someone who once helped her."

Kisa continued to stare around her as if every person might carry a set of chains. Belili pulled Kisa through the gate and out of the city.

Once in the country, Kisa relaxed, though she darted nervous glances around. For all Gemeti's complaints, she walked nearly as fast as the sisters, and they stopped for a lunch of bread, cheese, and dried fruit when the sun was overhead.

They didn't speak much during the morning besides small talk. Now they were farther from the city and the threat of the nobles, Belili was curious.

"Do the caravans have names?" she asked.

Gemeti chewed a mouthful of bread. "Not such that I know. They will refer to another caravan by the leader's name, but they regard themselves as one spread-out nation. They have none of the petty bickering as between rival nobles over titles and money." She pulled off another hunk of bread and placed a slice of cheese on it. "This caravan's leader is Mushezibti-Lila. She's led the caravan to become one of the richer ones from trading with nobles, not that they do much with the money. They are largely self-sufficient." She took a large bite of the bread.

"Then why do they trade?" Kisa asked. "What do they gain?"

Gemeti cocked a finger at her. "It keeps the nobles happy and idle. For all the Dyad want to assume the Asha-Urmana's power, the nobles do not realize they depend on their technology. I wonder if we could have peace if both sides gave up their arrogance and cooperated."

They continued walking into the afternoon, under the canopy of the forest surrounding Neharda, following a path bearing signs of wagon ruts. Even though Belili had rested her thigh at lunch, it was sending a jolt through her with every step.

Belili hoped they would get to the caravan before long. If the Asha-Urmana farmed cotton for cloth, they must have space to do it. For that matter, she remembered Hbelu telling them the other caravans were nomadic. How did they grow the little plant? She asked Gemeti as much, in part to take her mind off her leg.

"Oh, it grows wild all over." The old woman waved a hand encompassing the forest. "You'll see when we get out from under the trees. The Asha-Urmana plant new seeds and pick the previous crop as they travel from camp to camp. Children are set the task as a chore."

"Do you know where they are now?" Kisa asked.

"Hmm. Generally," Gemeti answered. "They will find us before we find them." Kisa didn't seem happy with that answer, peering around as they walked.

The trees thinned and gave way to plains, dotted with shrubby green plants, some bearing the distinctive explosion of soft white fiber. They were mixed in with meadow weeds. Belili could see where a swath was devoid of the fiber.

"They came through here recently." Gemeti pointed at the picked plants. "Likely they settled down not far away for the night. Let us hope they are near. I do not wish to sleep on the ground if I can help it."

"You will not need to, kind mother," came a voice behind them. Belili turned with her sister to find an Asha-Urmana. The front section of his hair was purple, but only in parts. The rear was white-blond. He had less color than many Belili had seen.

"Who are you?" Kisa asked him.

"Kinel," the man—boy, really—answered. "I will lead you to the caravan." He eyed the two of them for a moment. "You are escaped prisoners of the fourcolors?"

"How did you—"

Belili interrupted her sister. "Yes. We came through the caravan of Ishkun-Dim-Hbelu. Our former master captured him."

The boy's eyes widened, and Belili saw the telltale indicators. Dusky olive skin, high nose, sturdy frame. He could have been Hbelu's cousin. Gemeti was right—the Asha-Urmana looked far more similar to each other than the nobles or even the blonds.

"You are those prisoners!" The boy turned. "Quickly. Follow me. I will bring you to Mushezibti-Lila."

* * *

Mushezibti-Lila's caravan was a long clump of wagons, stretching across the plain. At first Belili thought they were stopped, but then she saw the hooves of the great oxen lift and fall. Each wagon had two beasts. The caravan was moving, but so slowly it was no trouble to catch up on foot. They passed two low vehicles bearing the caravan's godfruit trees. Six oxen pulled each cart—long, low, platforms set on sixteen wheels apiece. On both carts, two godfruit trees sat in large wood boxes, deep rich dirt overflowing the top. The trees were small, but well trimmed. The caravan would never grow as much godfruit as if the trees were planted in solid ground. The malus and citron on the first cart were bare of any godfruit. The morus and prunus were on the next cart, the morus bearing little clumps of white-green berries, on the edge of bursting into ripeness. They would turn to red and black within a few days. The prunus had immature godfruit. It was nearing that time of year where magic was abundant.

Belili's heart sped at the prospect of two new trees in season. She craved the taste of magic, and glanced to Kisa's pack, holding the elderly malae and citrons. They wouldn't last much longer, despite their magic.

Kinel led them along the line of wagons, waving to other Asha-Urmana walking beside the carts. The caravanners eyed them, but none approached, as in Hbelu's village. Belili saw children ranging out, picking the white puffs of cotton.

This caravan was smaller than Hbelu's, though there were a hundred wagons or more. Near the head, Kinel drew them to a wagon hung with brightly colored orange and yellow cotton fabric, decorating the wooden framework of the traveling structure. It was bigger than the others, drawn by four oxen rather than the usual two. The number of oxen—more untethered beasts were herded behind the caravan—told of the wealth of these Asha-Urmana.

"Mushezibti-Lila and the elders are in here," Kinel told them. "They have been expecting you."

"How did they know?" Kisa whispered to her as the boy climbed up the steps of the moving wagon. Belili shrugged in response.

"Maybe Gemeti sent word ahead. Maybe Hbelu did. Maybe they saw us walking. Does it matter?"

"Of course it does," Kisa said. "We should know how they're watching us."

Belili only rolled her eyes. Gemeti climbed up, grunting at catching the slow-moving steps, and Belili followed.

The inside of the wagon was oddly large, even though it held four elders and the woman Belili assumed was Mushezibti-Lila. She was older, with nearly as much purple as Hbelu, and a few strands of white. She sat cross-legged on the floor, back straight. The wagon had wood sides and a rounded roof, high enough that only the tallest would have to duck. The walls were bright yellow, making the room seem larger.

Shelves ran around the top of the wagon, holding books and papers kept in place with leather straps.

"You are welcome here, Gemeti," the leader addressed their guide. "I see you bring us prisoners of the fourcolors. Have you news of Ishkun-Dim-Hbelu?"

"I do not, but they do," Gemeti answered, gesturing toward Belili and her sister. "They will be happy to tell you."

"Good," Mushezibti-Lila said. Her mouth drew down a little. "After they give us news, I will provide them a space in the bathing wagon."

"Are we that dirty?" Kisa asked. Belili knew that wasn't it but didn't know what had caused the leader agitation.

"No, child." Mushezibti-Lila gestured to their heads. "We are uncomfortable with others pretending to belong to our people."

"Hbelu told us—" Kisa started, but Gemeti broke in, casting a warning glare.

"I am planning on making these two into minor nobles for their travel into Karduniash. They will need to wash the dye out anyway."

Mushezibti-Lila nodded. "Then sit and tell us of Ishkun-Dim-Hbelu."

* * *

It was very late in the day when they finished telling the elders of everything since they had found the box buried under the malus tree. Kisa even took the seed out to show its glow when touched. They were served a meal while they talked—roast field vegetables and thick bread with butter and honey. Kinel, who seemed to be an errand boy, showed them to an empty wagon near the end of the line.

"We will stay here tonight and for the next few days." Gemeti puttered around the little wagon, tidying.

"Are we supposed to sleep in here?" Kisa asked. Belili watched her little sister. She was paler than normal.

"Unless you plan to run alongside while you doze," Gemeti said.

"They move all the time? Don't the oxen get tired?" Kisa asked. She put a hand on a wall as the cabin rocked.

"I believe they change out oxen every day. The caravan pauses occasionally to rest but is in motion while they move to a new location."

"Oh." Kisa didn't look well.

"I'm sure we'll get used to it," Belili assured her. "Let's find the bathing wagon, and then we'll have a restful sleep." Belili found the protection of the Asha-Urmana strangely comforting. The only thing better would be if Ligish were here to...

Belili pushed the thought away. She would likely never see her again and she had to deal with that.

The bathing wagon was filled with water. The sides were low, with an inward facing lip to keep the liquid from sloshing out. Kisa left her clothes hanging on the sides of the wagon and climbed in, looking around nervously. Belili kept hers on—she could change into her spare set in the wagon. She would not be naked out in the open. Not any time soon. Kisa gave her an odd look when she eased into the water, fully clothed, but said nothing. The water was warm for this early in the year, and it soothed her aching thigh. Kisa sighed as her shoulders submerged.

None of the Asha-Urmana joined them. Gemeti had made some excuse about tidying up their cabin. Belili hadn't yet seen the woman without a voluminous amount of clothes. She must be permanently overheated.

A wooden structure surrounded the bath, and Kisa studied it as they bathed. Belili half-listened as her sister rambled on about angled panes of reflective metal attached to the structure. Evidently, they caught the sunlight to heat the water. Elegant, like the mechanisms in Hbelu's village.

The purple dye came out easier than Belili expected, leaving them with bleached hair again, except for the roots, which showed a further few days of white. She pulled her long hair back as they left the water, carefully covering the section with her magical color. No sense advertising anything. Her sister wouldn't understand if she saw. Kisa left her hair down as she gathered her clothes. Belili could see the roots of the silver lock near the top of her head. Once again, they were marked. If any noble saw them, they would know what they were. It would take months to be able to hide as freewomen, without cutting away most of the length.

* * *

The next day Belili blinked awake to the trundling of the wagon. It had lulled her to sleep the night before, as had the soft cushions of the bed. She moved her legs—feeling tightness in the right one—against the smoothness of the fabric. Cotton, like everything else this caravan made.

Kisa stared at her from across the cabin. Gemeti's bed was wrinkled, but the old woman wasn't there. With all three beds pulled down from the ceiling, there wasn't much room to move. The beds were stored above their heads during the day.

"How can you sleep with this thing moving all over the place?" her sister asked. "I think those oxen hit every stone and root on purpose."

Kisa's eyes were red and puffy. Had she slept at all last night? Belili was about to ask when the door banged open, wedging against Kisa's bed. Her sister winced at the noise.

"Finally awake? There is food to break your fast in the meal wagon." Gemeti bustled in as Belili yawned and stretched. Gemeti frowned at Kisa. "Looks like you would do well to have something to eat. And maybe a mug of kaba to wake you up."

Kisa wrinkled her nose at the suggestion, but rose from her bed and folded her sheets. Belili had slept in the dry clothes she changed into yesterday. A mug of the rich nutty drink sounded fabulous. If only she had known about it when working in the orchard, not that she would have gotten any.

Gemeti fluttered her hands at Kisa. "Go on, get something to eat. You look like death. I'll pack up the beds. We'll begin when you get back."

Belili left her bed as it was. She didn't need to be told twice. That Kisa left her bed in its half-made state with minimal grumbling spoke volumes about how she felt.

The meals in the caravan were like the ones with Hbelu, with everyone helping, and general chaos. Most walked while eating, or picked a seat on the edge of a wagon if they had too much to hold. A few boys and girls even rode the oxen, a pottery plate balanced in one hand. No one welcomed them to join in, but no one protested either. Belili felt eyes on her, interested, but not hostile. They had seen other runaway slaves.

Belili felt much better after a full meal and a mug of the divine kaba. She even got Kisa to try a few sips along with her porridge, and she looked more awake, or at least her grumbling was less.

The floor of their wagon was clean when they got back, the beds winched to the inside of the roof by an intricate pulley system. There was a musty smell. Likely the wagon hadn't been used in a while.

Gemeti had changed her clothes while they were out, but she still wore so many skirts and shifts there was no telling where her body ended and the clothes began.

She was standing over their packs as they climbed in the wagon. She pulled a malus from Belili's pack, and Kisa stiffened.

"Hm. This will go bad soon," Gemeti remarked, peering at the malus. "Godfruit lasts longer than normal fruit, but even malae and citrons have their limit. We must use them this week while traveling."

Kisa bristled, leaning forward against the sway of the wagon, and Belili settled back against a wall, letting her sister take the argument. Hopefully it would take Kisa's mind off the motion.

"What right do you have to go through our packs?" Kisa started. "We can't use the godfruit for games. Those might be the last malae and citrons of the year."

Gemeti calmly regarded them. "Spoken like a true slave."

Kisa stepped forward, but Belili caught her arm. "Listen to her."

Gemeti had years of experience. "If you will pass yourselves off as nobles, you must know how they think, how they reason. You must do things as they would." She tossed the old malus in one hand. "It is a worse sin to let godfruit rot than to waste it in a display of power. The latter can be used for your own means." She put the malus back and picked up a citron, peeling off the rind.

"Put that down!" Kisa pulled out of Belili's grip. "Now it'll go bad even faster."

"It will not." Gemeti peeled the skin away. The spicy scent of citron oil filled the cabin. She picked out two pieces and popped them together into her mouth, eyes closing as a tremor ran through her.

"Stop!" Kisa stepped forward, raising a hand, but Gemeti caught it, chewing the slice of godfruit. Little veins of lightning raced down her arm, jumping through her sleeve. Kisa gave a cry, and Belili pushed off the wall. Knocking sense into her little sister was one thing, but hurting her...

Kisa's cry turned into a grunt of relief, and she sagged. As Gemeti released her hand, Kisa reached up to finger her shoulder where Tashi had stabbed her. The wound had been well on its way to healing, but as Kisa pulled her shirt back, Belili saw only smooth skin. Kisa's eyes were no longer red, either.

"You have black," Belili accused Gemeti. Ilzi's greasy hair flashed through her mind. The healing power of the citron could harm as easily.

Gemeti swallowed, shivering. "Only a slave is surprised someone has magical color. You must assume everyone you meet can use magic, even slaves." She peered into Belili's face.

Control. Always control. Belili made her face relax.

"Better, but you must remove that reaction entirely. Give me your hand."

As Belili held out a hand to the woman, Gemeti ate another two slices of citron. Lightning crackled and as Gemeti touched her, the lingering pain in her thigh, the deeper hurt in her belly, and a hundred other bruises and scrapes washed away like a bucket of water thrown over a dirty shovel. Belili sighed in relief.

"Thank you," she said.

"Do not thank me," Gemeti answered. "Take it as deserved. From now, I will act as your servant, or paid freewoman."

Belili blinked at the words but felt herself stand a little straighter.

"Better. We may turn you into a noble yet."

The Gilded Rose

Kigal and Enta, embodiments of autumn and winter, favored the black- and silver-haired civilizations. Even today, some competitions pair the red and brown against the black and silver, traditions left over from before the gods stopped speaking to us.

The walls of Neharda rose in front of Hbelu. They were nearly as tall as those of Karduniash. Though the original stone was stuccoed over, he could see evidence of the original Asha-Urmana handiwork. It was all that remained of the original city.

Their group of fourteen arrived to little fanfare, late in the third day after his capture. Hbelu hoped the sisters found Nidintu. He hadn't seen her since and assumed she had returned to the village. The sisters must be behind their group, somewhere.

The guard he had bowled over the first day prodded him, not gently, to keep moving. They passed through the gates, where the men on either side spared little attention, spending their time watching Ligish and the other female bleached blond prisoners passing by.

The inhabitants cast looks at them, but did not intervene, though he was bound at hands and feet. With his braided purple hair, it was obvious who he was. Yet men and women in clean and brightly colored cotton clothes made by his people paid him no mind. Twice he attempted to catch someone's eye. They traded with his people, yet they would stand idly by while he was paraded through the streets?

Aricaba-Ata led their party to a well-kept inn, not far into the city. No one stopped them. The sign proclaimed it the Dancing Waitress, featuring the profile of a buxom young woman balancing a steaming plate of food on her generous chest. The second floor was circular, under a domed roof looming over the street.

"We will stay here while we gather supplies and soldiers," Ata told the others. "Make sure he doesn't escape. There is godfruit here, and no telling what the caravanner is capable of." The mori were just turning, and the city was still in that time of year where godfruit was exorbitantly expensive. His only option would be what the fourcolor carried, not that he needed it any longer. He had made his point and let the sisters escape.

They were on the second floor, in a large room meant to house traveling groups. It was laid out almost like a soldier's barracks, though with richer furnishings. Hbelu noted the cotton sheets, the small mirror bought from one of the caravans. Ata and Ilzi had their own rooms, of course. The guards deposited him on the bed, hands and feet bound together, then dispersed to the common room save two set to watch him.

Ata left for a time, as did Ilzi, though only after the black-hair made sure his cousin was out of sight. One of the hired guards and Iral, from Ata's orchard, went with him, while two of the other guards stayed in the room. The younger fourcolor had some agenda, and Hbelu did not like it. Ata was cruel, but direct. Ilzi was hard to read. Hbelu had watched the two fourcolors, finding cracks in their relationship to exploit. Ilzi obviously resented Ata, and Hbelu was sure he was bribing Ata's guards.

Would he be better in Ata's hands, or Ilzi's? The best alternative was to escape, but not too soon. The sisters had to contact the caravans and spread the word of the fifth godfruit. The farther Belili got from the venomous black-haired man, the better. Among the Asha-Urmana, forced attentions were dealt with directly. The offending party, male or female, was stripped of enough resources to care for the victim, then moved to another caravan.

The door to the room creaked open and Ligish slipped in, away from Ilzi for once. She turned to one of the guards, her hands finding his arm.

"I can watch the caravanner for a few minutes. Surely you and your friend are as parched as those who got to relax in the common room?"

The guard smiled down at her. "You could always accompany me down there, blond."

Ligish giggled, pawing at his arm again. "And I would *love* to. But Enti-Ilzi said I should *entertain* the caravanner." She dropped her voice to a stage whisper, though Hbelu could still clearly hear her. "Maybe he'll give away more with a little kindness. Worth a try? I'll be sure to put a good word in for you with the master."

The guard nodded to his fellow over her head. "Give 'em ten minutes. We can watch the door while enjoying some drinks. Everyone else got to get some ale after that gods-cursed march through the forest."

Ligish crossed quickly to the bed the moment the guards shut the door. "We have a few minutes. Ilzi is out on an errand. Please tell me you have a way to escape these vile nobles."

Her voice was low and intense, and Hbelu stared at her. This was not the same face she'd shown during their journey. Was this what Belili had seen?

"You seem more knowledgeable of the fourcolors' ways than the sisters," he said, leaning forward in his bonds. There was only so much he could move, on the bed. She watched him squirm, but didn't offer to loosen the knots.

"That's because I'm not a bumpkin like these country nobles," Ligish sneered. "Ilzi coerced me into serving him through threatening my little sister, but my parents were both shadows, servants of nobles in the court of Karduniash. Get me a morus and I'll escape and bring you along." She gestured to her bleached hair. "I think Ilzi's already forgotten about my silver."

Hbelu smiled. There were probably a few of the spring fruits ripe already, certainly a few to be had in Neharda. It was a perfect place for Ligish to escape as well, with its lax view toward those the fourcolors imprisoned.

"I plan to make it difficult for Ata and Ilzi to gather any other nobles to them. Those who live here regard Asha-Urmana with more respect than in other places. With any luck, the townsfolk will force them to free me. If not, we will find godfruit. Worry not."

Ligish stared at him for a long moment, her face unreadable.

"How long has it been since you've been to the capital?"

"More than a dozen years, why?"

"You won't find the nobles there as easy to lead around as these two," she jerked a thumb toward the door. "Best to escape here. I can lend you my services as a shadow."

Hbelu discussed plans with her for a few moments more before Ligish cocked her head. "Time to go." She was back at the door before he could object, her posture changing back to the mousey woman he'd seen on Ilzi's arm.

"He's all yours again, boys," she trilled into the hallway, slinking around the partly open door. "You just have to know the right *motions...*"

Hbelu heard the guards laugh at some gesture she made as he sat back, thinking on what they'd discussed. It could work.

Ilzi returned before Ata, well into a pint of ale in a large glass mug. "Switch out," he commanded to the two guards watching Hbelu. They obediently left, likely happy to get an extra drink in the common room. Neither mentioned Ligish's visit.

Iral and the hired guard, a woman whose name Hbelu had not yet learned, entered the suite when they left. They took up stations by the door while Ilzi collapsed into a stuffed chair by a window, grumbling about the blonds clogging up the common room.

Hbelu observed the fourcolor and his guards, twisting in his bonds on the bed. These were different guards than those who had been slow to surround the black-hair in the forest. Others on Ilzi's side?

"You know why I hate them?" Ilzi asked into the silence. He swirled his drink, and Hbelu could see the ale was cut with malus mash, likely left over from juicing. Particles swirled through the drink. The glass frosted under Ilzi's fingertips and one flash of lightning crawled up his fingers. There was enough magic left in the pulp for a buzz. Hbelu's village used the same process, on feast nights. It seemed he would have more than one interesting discussion today.

"They are everywhere. They outnumber nobles five to one. They work until they die." Ilzi swirled his mug again, looking out the window. Their rooms overlooked the street. They must have been expensive, but Hbelu did not think Ata was a wealthy orchard owner.

"They choose to be enslaved," Ilzi continued. Hbelu did not seem required to answer, so he kept his place on the bed, ropes restraining his hands and feet. He could have wiggled off if he wanted, but not before the guards got to him. "If they did not want this situation, why allow us to bleach their hair? To chain them up? Our magic makes us naturally superior."

He turned to look at Hbelu. The fourcolor had obviously consumed several other drinks already. Yet his gaze did not waver. "Even the ones with magic, like my Bel, will stay slaves, unless a noble elevates them. Why not band together? Take us out of power?"

"You keep the blonds and those with little color as prisoners because you have lost the path to the gods. This was not their original intent," Hbelu said.

Ilzi scoffed, and took another sip of his drink. "Your gods, maybe. They have not been seen in centuries, if those old stories are even true." His eyes roved over Hbelu's face, his hair. "Maybe your seclusion has merit. All the caravanners in your little town had much color in their hair." He gestured, nearly slopping his drink. "How do you keep them in line? Get them to avoid the nobles?" He lowered his voice. "I could offer a significant amount of compensation for the chance to make a child with purple and black hair." He gestured again. "Something to rival what we plan to give to the Dyad."

"This is not a new proposal." Hbelu kept from rolling his eyes. "We keep our magic apart from you, or you would steal it as you have everything else." He pushed thoughts of Kisare from him. He had already told her he would welcome her into his caravan, though none of the elders would allow it without a fight. "I do not think Ata would appreciate you changing his plans."

"Ata does not know all," Ilzi spat, his face screwing up. Hbelu glanced to the guards at the door, facing forward, gazes blank. Definitely in the man's pay. "He thinks he is ambitious, but he is limited. He will receive whatever reward your capture grants and go back to the Blasted Lands to farm for the rest of his life." Ilzi shook his head. "No, I think I shall stay in Karduniash when we get there. The opportunities—"

"What of your own orchard?"

Ilzi waved a hand. "Let Ata take it. He is skilled at that kind of work." He tapped his temple. "No, I can think of a dozen ways to live with much less effort in the capital. With Bel by my side, we would make a pair to rival many noble families..." He trailed off.

A wash of revulsion went through Hbelu, then immediate guilt. *I mock his offer, yet I wish Kisare to join me, against the rules of my people. It is not the same by any means, and I believe she wishes the same, but—* He pushed the thought away.

"Do you agree with what Ata has fated for me? Perhaps together we could—"

There were heavy boots in the hallway outside. Hbelu knew that step, as did Ilzi. They both looked to the door. Ata's large form burst through, metal clanking in his hands, two guards following him.

"I see you have been busy, Cousin," he said to Ilzi. The black-hair scowled into his drink. "I at least have acquired a new set of restraints for the caravanner—difficult to find in this town—and a few interested noblemen and women. We will have quite a following by the time we bring him to Karduniash." Ata gestured with the manacles to Hbelu, then thrust them at a guard. "Get those ropes off him and these on."

Finally, he seemed to recognize the atmosphere in the room, Hbelu and Ilzi's positions in relation to each other. "What were you two discussing?"

Ilzi levered himself to his feet, holding his glass like a precious sculpture. "Nothing as usual, dear Cousin," he answered. "Complaining about the number of blonds who do not know their place." Neither Iral nor the woman said anything, and Hbelu held his tongue. "I think I shall get some rest." Ilzi staggered to the door, and his guards followed. Hbelu watched them go as Ata's guards untied the knots on his ropes.

* * *

The next day, Ata roused them early. Ilzi was slow to get ready, obviously feeling his drink from the night before.

"Come Cousin," Hbelu heard Ata boom, through the thin wall. "Slovenly behavior is no excuse. We come as beggars to this town, but I plan to leave as kings."

They got out of the inn by mid-morning. Ata led them in a line, his guards after him, Hbelu rattling in his chains in the middle, and Ilzi yawning at the end with Ligish making certain he kept up. They'd exchanged only one glance this morning, but now Hbelu saw the steel hiding behind her subservient expression. The guards watched Hbelu with eagle's eyes, familiar now with his tricks. When he smiled back, one man flinched.

The streets held locals walking to their businesses and speaking in small groups. Hbelu attracted notice, seeing fourcolors turn to each other and whisper.

"They see our skill and fortune in capturing an Asha-Urmana," Ata called back. Hbelu held his head high, back straight. The people of

Neharda were familiar with freemen and women. Their blonds were kept on a long leash and seemed happy, for all they were regarded as property. Those inhabitants of this city watched their passage, their conversations dying as Ata's line passed a file of bleached-blond men and women.

"Yes, I am Asha-Urmana," he called out. Several people looked away. "Your trinkets and fine fabrics come from our caravans."

"Someone shut him up," Ata called. One of his guards punched him in the side.

Hbelu winced at the pain, but kept on. More passersby were looking. "What do you think the caravans will do when they hear this fourcolor has me prisoner?"

An elderly blond—a freeman—with a heavy beard started toward them. "Most of my stock comes from the caravanners." He arrowed in on Ata, who nodded to his largest guard, the one called Shuma. "Sir, why do you have this man—"

He folded over as Shuma's fist took him in the gut.

"It is time caravanners were shown their place," Ata called. The line of bleached prisoners put their heads down. No one else came to Hbelu's defense.

It was just before noon when Ata found a common house he deemed appropriate for their group. Hbelu's new manacles chafed his wrists and ankles, and he wished he had an orange slice, though seeing the unwillingness of the townspeople to help tempered his wish.

There were a few here this early, and Ata claimed a table for them, ordering drinks and a midday meal.

"No, you shall stand," he told Hbelu as he made to sit. "You shall be the mascot of our triumph. Stand here, where your chains are evident."

Hbelu considered the man, wondering if his shackles had enough slack to reach his neck. Ata could not taste his godfruit in time. But no. If he would bring down the fourcolor's rule, he had to know them intimately. How their politics worked, why they fought each other, what it took to bring them together. He turned his back on Ata, spreading his hands as wide as they would go in their chains.

"Come, see the Asha-Urmana," Hbelu called out to the common room. He had to bring enough attention to himself so that Ligish could find a morus. Or maybe the townspeople would find their spines. Heads poked up from their tables. "The mighty Aricaba-Ata has bound one man using only twelve of his own. Come, see his triumph."

He stumbled as Ata pulled him backward. "Sit then, caravanner," the man growled. "I will announce our presence." He tried to push Hbelu down on the bench, but Hbelu locked his knees.

"You trade with the Asha-Urmana for your clothes," he called. "Do you think the local caravan will sell you fine garments when you let one of theirs be treated so?"

At a gesture from Ata, his soldiers caught Hbelu and forced him down, but by now, other patrons were leaving, and the innkeeper, a tall and wide woman who looked as if she might eat a few of Ata's soldiers for a snack, was striding toward them. Out of the corner of his eye, he saw Ligish slip behind the bar.

"Help me, Cousin," Ata said, struggling with his men to keep Hbelu from popping back up.

"See the love between the fourcolors and the people who welcomed them to their cities," Hbelu said into the gap. A soldier punched him in the jaw and he fell back into the table, sloshing drinks.

"You seem to have things in hand," Ilzi called from the other end of the table.

"Out, out! All of you!" The innkeeper was in front of them, hands on wide hips. Her hair was a natural white-blond, but for one or two red hairs in her short-cropped cut. "I will not have this in my place of business. If you wish to annoy the Asha-Urmana, do it elsewhere." She pulled Iral away from Hbelu, who was rubbing his jaw.

"Is that how you speak to your betters, blond?" Ata asked. "I will have my lunch before I leave, and no trouble from you."

"You'll have the town watch me drag you to the prisons," the woman said. She looked to Ata's red hair, then to his hand, creeping to his pouch. "What? Will you burn my business down now? Or tear holes in the walls?"

Ata's hand moved away from his pouch and Hbelu smiled. He might have less trouble than he thought breaking the fourcolor's rule.

"Come Ilzi," Ata said over the din of the innkeeper arguing with his soldiers. "I can tell who is a friend of the nobles and who is traitorous to the rule of the Dyad."

"The Dyad have never come to my inn," the innkeeper told Ata's back. "They have no sway here."

Hbelu let the soldiers lead him by his manacles, not fighting, but not helping. Ligish gave a minute shake of her head as they exited. Ilzi watched him as they filed down the street.

* * *

Hbelu made a similar scene in each common room. Most were run by blonds, a few with tiny locks of color in their hair. None wished to anger the Asha-Urmana, and Ata's face became darker and darker with fury. Hbelu relaxed as noon turned into afternoon, letting the soldiers use up their energy to get him to the next destination rather than wasting his own. The punches and kicks were worth it to see the faces of the men and women turn as dark as their employer's. His actions would not be tolerated forever, but he intended to make the most of it until Ata grew smarter. Ligish, however, was having no luck stealing a morus, or any godfruit for that matter. Though Neharda was more lenient than many other towns, the inhabitants didn't leave godfruit out where any prisoner might try it.

Ilzi helped in pulling Hbelu to the next common room only enough to count. Several times, he motioned to one guard or another in a code Hbelu didn't understand. Most often, he kept Ligish close enough she didn't have time to slip away.

It was near evening when they collapsed at a table in The Gilded Rose, a rich looking inn with a rich looking innkeeper who prominently displayed the few strands of brown in his otherwise unremarkable blond. His waitresses were all bleached-blond prisoners, studded collars around their necks.

"This is more appropriate," Ata said as they entered. There were a few fourcolor nobles at other tables, their clothing rich dyed cotton. Several diced in a corner, and others were talking in front of the fireplace.

"Please, welcome to the Gilded Rose," the innkeeper told Ata, gravitating to him as a dog to his master. His heeled boots thumped on the wooden floor planks. "I am Abisare, proprietor, and eager to serve. You can chain your slaves"—he cut off, twisting his hands together—"oh my, a caravanner. Well, that is new." Abisare looked lost for a moment, then gestured to the long table before the hearth. "I am certain your peers would be enraptured to hear stories of how you captured such a fearsome warrior. I will attend to your men and get you my finest ale." Abisare set off at a near run, cuffing one of the collared blonds to get him more mugs for drink.

"Finally, one common room in this gods-blighted town with an owner who treats nobility with respect due their station." Several of the seated fourcolors laughed at his comment. Encouraged, Ata took a seat among them, recounting Hbelu's capture. The tables had small iron rings, and a miserable blond was chained through one, cutting his jailer's meat.

"This will do nicely to cut down on that arrogance," Ilzi whispered next to him, opening the lock on Hbelu's manacles with a clink of metal. Hbelu jerked with surprise. He had not heard the black-hair approach.

Ilzi threaded the chain through the ring on the table, connecting it to the chain that bound Ligish. "I have seen how you undermine my cousin's plan. I may not have all the same objectives, but I do have some. I will be watching." He spared a glance for Ligish. "Both of you." The lock closed again with a *snap*.

Hbelu could barely move his legs. There was no bench or chair to sit on. The table was just low enough, and his manacle chain just short enough, that he could not straighten while chained to the table. He shared a dark glance with Ligish, who was hunched over the table, trying to avoid Ilzi's attention.

He listened while Ata recounted their attack on the village—a small group of caravanner huts—and how they took one of his escaped slaves back. Ilzi in turn told how they had tracked and outsmarted the caravanners who wished to ambush them, instead taking them by surprise.

"Yet your own slave showed herself to have magic," Hbelu put in. "She not only freed her sister, but they both escaped."

"You let your slave talk to you in that manner?" a fourcolor called, and Ata gestured to Shuma, who backhanded Hbelu across the face.

"Yes, my slaves escaped, but at the cost of a much bigger prize—the caravanner you see before you, regarded as nobility among his people. Two rebellious slaves are hardly worth the trade." Ata forced a great laugh, and the others laughed with him.

"That is why I need your help, my friends," Ata continued. "We are bound for the capital, and recruiting soldiers and nobles. This caravanner thinks he can bring all the roving bands together." He stood, and necks craned upward.

"The caravanners could be an annoyance, if united. Instead, we will give the Dyad what they want—power over the caravanner's magic. Make your wagers, my friends, on how long it will take to break and civilize them. Come see for yourself. What do you say?"

Excited murmurings erupted from the table, and from the corner dicing table. The clinks and tumblings of dice had ceased several minutes ago. Hbelu bent forward so his chained hands could rub his jaw. It would be bruised tomorrow, adding to his collection of injuries.

"We will achieve nothing here," he barely heard Ligish whisper from behind him.

"I put five to one against the caravanners uniting their bands," one fourcolor with a splash of silver said. She sat with two prisoners behind her, one waiting with a wine bottle.

"A good start," Ilzi said. "I'll bet on that myself."

Shouts of wagers and odds crossed the room. The more Hbelu interfered in the fourcolor's affairs in this place, the worse his situation would grow.

"Forty to one the caravanners make it through the capital's walls!"

"I'll take that bet." A heavy fourcolor with a narrow band of red thumped one meaty hand on the table.

"Fifty to one we can wipe them out entirely." Hbelu watched the speaker, an older fourcolor, his hair turning white around a streak of black.

"Who wants to put together a hunting party?" There were cries of encouragement.

"We have not gone caravanner hunting in years. I remember when I was young—"

"What about our clothes and bedsheets?" someone called. The noise in the room dampened.

"You have plenty, Danos," another called back. "It will not hurt you to wear the same shirt two days in a row. We only need take slaves as the enterprising Aricaba-Ata has done."

There was a cheer from several around the table, men and women alike.

Hbelu's elation from earlier deflated. The fourcolors already thought little of his people. Those in the larger cities were often lazy, content to let others be as long as they were served. But with Ata's provocation, they would make the Asha-Urmana supply them by force instead of trade. If only he had a few days to speak with those of the nearest caravan.

Money from wagers was trading hands. Ilzi, for once moving with alacrity, took up offered coins and signed letters of intent. He unchained Ligish from the table, so she could help him carry and organize the wagers. She bore the taunts and wandering hands of the other fourcolors with stoic meekness.

The fourcolor nobility who imprisoned the blonds and forced the Asha-Urmana to live in remote areas was a small percentage of the fourcolor empire. Even so, Hbelu had misjudged them. The fourcolor nobility simply did not mix with those they regarded as beneath them. If he was to convince the caravans to unite and overthrow the Dyad, he must move faster than he thought. Could the fifth godfruit even correct this imbalance, as the gods promised?

As the fourcolors called for more drink, their boasts and plans got more outrageous, the demise of Asha-Urmana culture all but certain. Only when the call came for godfruit did Hbelu perk up again, watching bowls of newly-ripe morus passed around. He found Ligish's eyes, across the room. She was busy serving Ilzi yet another ale spiked with malus pulp, but she was ready.

Annoying the fourcolors would not work. Mushezibti-Lila's caravan was close. He hoped Ligish could get a message to them as they'd discussed. He stood, knees bent and cramping, jaw aching. He felt a loose tooth with his tongue, and hoped the sisters were doing better than he.

"You fruit weevils!" he roared. "Rotten cores, all of you!" The chains were strong, but the table was only wood, and old at that. He struck the table with a length of chain as hard as he could considering his cramped posture.

The boisterous room quieted, all eyes turned to him.

"I am a prince of the Asha-Urmana, and you dare to make plans against my people as I sit here? Why not challenge me directly, you weak-willed bunch of badger droppings?"

Several fourcolors laughed weakly at his threats, but he had shocked even Ata into gaping at him with his outburst. The only one moving was Ligish, creeping soundlessly behind Ilzi, toward a bowl of mori.

He pounded the table again with the chains. The prisoners were staring now as well. The obsequious innkeeper was wringing his hands, though he dared not come closer. "Well? Come, try me or give me a drink instead! Your minds are as liquid as your excrement, I'd wager."

He felt the ring loosen from the table. A few more strikes and he would be free.

"Stop that caravanner!" one of the fourcolors shouted, and the stillness broke. Hbelu pounded at the table in a vain hope he might free himself. As the first fist struck his jaw, he saw Ligish lift something to her mouth and disappear. At least one of them would escape.

"You see why we must teach the caravanners the consequences of their egoism?" Ata yelled. "It's far past time to hunt them down."

Hbelu defended as best he could, but the drunken mass of fourcolors surrounding him felt little pain, and were riled up by their boasting and drinking. As blackness descended, he saw the door to the inn open and close by itself.

CHAPTER FIFTEEN

Noble Blood

Those of purple hair stayed out of the fighting, living in the center of the other civilizations. They followed the old ways, worshiping all four gods, who loved them in return. During the war, the purple-haired people worked with the blonds and with refugees from the other civilizations, teaching them advanced farming, construction, and mechanics.

"What if I don't want to be a noble?" Kisare grumbled at Gemeti. She caught a handhold on the wall as the cabin swayed. How *did* these people live with this horrible weaving? It would make anyone sick.

The old woman put her hands on her hips, holding the rest of the citron. "You will be a noble if you want to see Ishkun-Dim-Hbelu again."

"Won't the Asha-Urmana rescue him? They have the numbers."

Gemeti sighed. "Probably, but that decision is Mushezibti-Lila's. Either way, he will arrive in Karduniash. Of all Ishkun-Dim-Hbelu's calls for his people to act, his imprisonment by your Aricaba-Ata seems to have inspired the other Asha-Urmana the most."

"He's not *my* Aricaba-Ata," Kisare said. "If that's the only way he'll get these people to move, it's little wonder they lost the capital to the nobles." She stumbled and caught her balance.

"Do you want to see him again or not?" Gemeti held out the citron to Kisare. "Practice. You will use up half of your godfruit by the day's end, between the two of you. While you do, I will show you a noble's manners."

The rest of the day was an agony of practice and punishment. Kisare almost wished she was working in the fields at the Aricaba orchard. Almost. Gemeti stuffed their heads with numbers and facts about how the nobles lived. She had to hope Bel was picking up enough to remind her of some parts, though that was hoping for prunae in winter.

Most of their lessons were outside. Even if they had to stop for a time to practice or for Gemeti to drive home a point, it was easy to catch up to the caravan.

Between lessons on politics and noble houses, they ate citrons and malus.

"Good, now step *into* the ground," Gemeti called to Bel, who passed halfway into the ground, looking anxious for once, little splashes of lightning zipping up and down her arms and legs.

"Hold yourself there as long as possible," their instructor called. "Use all the juice of the citron, until you barely have enough left to climb out."

Kisare wrung her hands until Bel pulled her solidifying body from the earth, swallowing. Gemeti gave Bel another slice. "Now, make your body harder. Your sister and I will test you by throwing rocks at you."

Kisare would have protested, but Bel shook her head.

"Do it, Kisa," she said. "I have to learn how to use godfruit. I won't be caught off guard the next time. It's your turn next."

So Kisare threw rocks, which bounced off her sister's iron skin.

"Next, take this malus slice and the citron slice," Gemeti ordered. Bel obediently took them. "Go bury yourself in the dirt with the citron and dig yourself out with the malus."

"That's crazy," Kisare protested. "What if she can't move enough dirt?"

"Then she will learn her lesson," Gemeti answered. "That is not for you to judge. Take these." She handed Kisare another slice of citron and malus. "Get to the top ridge of a wagon, using only your feet—no hands—with the balance from the citron and control of air from the malus."

Kisare gaped but took the sticky godfruit.

"Do not waste the juice."

Kisare cupped the slices by instinct, glaring at her tutor, then put both slices in her mouth at once, and bit down. Magic flooded her, and her eyes rolled back. Her hand twitched. Lightning tickled, running down her arms.

There was so much juice, blending in her mouth. She had to keep her lips closed not to spill any. The world slowed, and she could sense the air, knowing how it moved around her.

Kisare leaped lightly to a fallen tree, then kicked up to a magnolia behind it and balanced on a low branch. She tucked her hands in the back of her pants, chewing the godfruit and resisting the urge to grasp a limb.

The caravans rumbled by slowly, time passing at a crawl. Kisare found the perfect angle, sensing a slight breeze at her back.

Now! She catapulted from the low tree branch, one foot touching a leaf, another on the horn of an ox. The wind pushed her hard, pressing her forward. One more step, balanced on the yoke tying the oxen to the wagon, then another to the footboard, the door handle, a touch on the front lantern casing, and she was up.

The juice in her mouth was losing its flavor, and Kisare chewed the pulp. One of her feet was on the ridge of the wagon, the other lifted in the air like a weathervane. How had she thought the wagon's sway was a problem? It was natural, a timed variation of movement and seconds. Kisare pirouetted, writing her name in the air currents.

As the juice faded, Kisare realized she also had to get down.

She wobbled on the ridge, balance faltering, then went to all fours. She swallowed tasteless pulp.

"A good lesson," Gemeti called up to her. "Always have enough juice left to get out of whatever situation you put yourself in." Kisare would have shot a reply, but she was too concerned with not falling and breaking her neck.

* * *

The citrons lasted for two days, the malae for three. Kisare grew accustomed to the balance given by the citrons and the control of air given by the malus. Gemeti separated them while training so they could work on their different abilities. She was nearly as strict as a guard.

The fourth day, Kisare awoke with a massive headache. *A slice of godfruit should make that go away...* She winced as she remembered the malae and citrons were gone. This would not be a good day. She and Bel were both short with each other, snapping over little things.

"Now you know the dangers of consuming too much godfruit over too little time," Gemeti told them. Kisare only snarled back.

They barely spoke with the members of the caravan, as Gemeti had them busy except for meals. Those were in the meal wagon with everyone else, though they could have been spirits the Asha-Urmana raised, for all they were noticed. Only the children stole furtive glances. The caravan differed from Hbelu's people. They did not farm, as they traveled most of the time. There was at least one wagon dedicated to refining the cotton they picked as they traveled, and occasionally Kisare would see a completed shirt or pair of pants trade hands. Try as she might, she was not allowed to see the machinery they used.

She saw none of the Asha-Urmana use godfruit, either, so they must have used their winter crop, waiting on the prunae and mori. Every day she watched the trees, as did Bel, for the first ripe godfruits of the year—the mori.

As they traveled from Neharda, Kisare's thoughts drifted to Hbelu. She had been too busy to think of him for the past few days, though he was surely suffering, under Aricaba-Ata's control.

"Have you received any word of Hbelu?" she asked Gemeti before breakfast one morning.

"He is still in Neharda, though the Asha-Urmana report Aricaba-Ata is readying for travel. They have gathered quite a few of the ne'er-do-wells of the city to them. The scouts are keeping an eye on the prince to ensure he is not too mistreated."

"Will they rescue him if he is?"

Gemeti waggled a hand. "I do not know. The caravan elders do not want to show their hand too early."

"Do we get a say in any of this, as bearers of the fifth godfruit seed?" Bel asked.

Gemeti regarded them both, eyebrows drawn down. "I am uncertain what treatment you received in Ishkun-Dim-Hbelu's village, but the elders are not prone to sharing their councils with escaped slaves."

Kisare opened her mouth.

"And I will not ask them."

When they were not stuffing their heads with knowledge, Kisare watched the landscape evolve. It had been several days of constant travel, and as they moved south, the sun got hotter, and the air felt like it was holding a pool's worth of water. Even when not working, Kisare's clothes were drenched with sweat while walking.

The trees changed too. Some species here had wide glossy leaves, and there was fruit—the non-magic kind—in abundance. The pears were ripening, and she saw pomegranates and fruits Gemeti called "mangos" and "guava," which gave fruit more than once in a year.

On the eighth day, Gemeti produced vials of dye. Kisare had grown more accustomed to the wagon's sway but had to leave occasionally to get her composure back.

"Today we will color your hair. If you are to be nobles, even distant ones, you must show your power openly." She glanced at Bel. "No hiding your coloring beneath the rest of your hair."

Kisare noticed it too. Bel always tied her hair back, letting the bleached mass of it cover the new roots. Kisare let hers fall as it would. There was little reason to fasten her long hair in a complex knot— Gemeti's training often ended with Kisare as sweaty as a day out in the orchard.

"I will accentuate your locks as the nobles do, and make sure the rest does not look like a slave's." Gemeti shook one of the dye containers.

"The nobles really dye their hair?" Kisare asked.

Gemeti barked a laugh, echoing off the wood walls of the cabin. "Many nobles have little more color in their hair than you. Why do you think they defend their titles with such vehemence? The Asha-Urmana, as insular as they are, have much more power."

She held up a set of colored vials. "Now, which color do you prefer?" She looked at Kisare. "Silver, I assume?"

"What else?" Kisare asked. If she dyed her hair the wrong color, that farce would only last until she was forced to prove herself to a noble.

"For you?" Gemeti turned to Bel. "Just brown? Can I interest you in a spot of black? Or maybe red?"

Bel shook her head, looking more off her guard than Kisare had ever seen. The training must be getting to her. "Just brown," Bel confirmed.

Gemeti was a decent hairdresser, overlaying the bleach with another dye, coloring the hair shining white-blond. The dye was bitter and pungent, but no worse than their weekly bleaching. She extended the silver lock in Kisare's hair down its length—past the small of her back— and made it wider.

On Bel, whose hair was just as long, Gemeti brought out the streak of brown in the same way. After a moment's contemplation, she arranged Bel's hair so the lock hung on the left, opposite Kisare's.

"Now," Gemeti said, stepping back a pace and regarding the sisters, "a new style, I think."

"What?" Kisare started at the same time Bel spoke.

"Cut our hair?"

"Of course." The woman produced a set of scissors. "I will not have my handiwork worn in a rat's nest. Now, outside, both of you. I do not want to sleep in a pile of hair."

"But my hair!" Kisare protested. It had never been cut, save hacking off the tangled ends. It was the one thing the guards didn't touch. Slaves all wore their hair long, and it was the only thing that was totally hers.

"Must we?" Bel's voice was shaky.

"You look like slaves," Gemeti said. "It was how I marked you in Neharda." She crossed her arms, scissors poking out from underneath one elbow. "If you won't be reasonable, I might as well stop teaching you. I'll leave you to make your own way in Karduniash. Without more training, the first soldiers you see will probably capture and enslave you."

Kisare raised her chin. She would not be called out like a child. "Well, if it's the only way—"

"It is. Out with you." Gemeti pushed her from the wagon, crowding her to climb down the moving steps. Bel followed, silent and pale.

Kisare was adult enough to admit she might have struggled more than necessary, and even Bel's reassurance didn't ring true. When Kisare dried away all her tears, she had to admit the new look was striking. Gemeti had a small piece of silvered glass, courtesy of the Asha-Urmana, much clearer than the looking glasses of the nobles.

Kisare's hair was only chin length now, save for the lock of silver. That section, on the right side, Gemeti had left long, draped down over her shoulder. Kisare was the first to admit she had never been called pretty, but her new haircut softened the angles of her face. Even her freckles didn't stand out so much.

Bel's haircut only enhanced her beauty, of course. She hadn't cried, though she shook. Gemeti left both sides shoulder length, again letting the swath of brown hang longer than the rest. It curled around Bel's face, making her cheeks even rounder.

"There," Gemeti pronounced. "A nobler pair of sisters I have not seen in many years, and styles worthy of the capital. Once we get you better clothes and a little paint for your faces, you will have half the population of Karduniash falling over you." She leaned in closer. "And I'm not just talking about the men." She laughed at Kisare's expression, but Bel looked thoughtful. "The capital is a lot different from a mountain orchard."

* * *

Five days later, the train of wagons stopped at a prairie used as a camping ground. They had traveled south from the forest and Neharda, away from the Aricaba orchard in the mountains. Those were only distant shadows now, and the canopy of the forest was long gone. The occasional mango or guava tree dotted the landscape. They were surrounded by open grassland, cotton and wild vegetables growing near. Kisare suspected the caravan seeded the ground to welcome them in the spring. Wild lettuce, kale, onions, and root vegetables grew nearby, attracting rabbits and deer. The Asha-Urmana set traps as soon as their wagons were tied down. They herded the scores of oxen to a corral on the edge of the camp, to be used for milk and meat. The caravan even brought the godfruit trees down from their carts, carefully placing them in a circle around the wagon belonging to Mushezibti-Lila, as was done with Hbelu's house. The mori were plumping and turning from green, to red, to a deep purple.

They helped with making the campsite secure, and it occupied their time for two days after the caravan stopped. Gemeti hadn't let them wash their hair, even though Kisare's was filled with dust and wood shavings from sawing new posts for the cattle pen.

"I will not have you washing away the dye I put in there. Took me long enough the first time," she grumbled. "Give it one more day to set."

On the third day after they camped, the boy Kinel appeared a little past midday. Gemeti was already busy packing their few belongings, as if she knew what was coming.

"You are to meet with Mushezibti-Lila tonight," he told them. He stood farther away than he had the last time, his eyes lingering on their hair. They had not seen the leader of this caravan since the first day, and Kisare suspected she rarely left her wagon.

After a dinner of vegetable and rabbit stew, with fresh baked bread, Kinel led them to the large wagon. It was tied to the ground, the top expanded into a pavilion covering not only the wagon, but several body lengths on each side.

Inside, Mushezibti-Lila sat, back stiff, with her elders surrounding her. There was a breeze of whispers, and several pairs of eyes on their hair. The leader of the caravan did not rise, and Kisare saw now her legs were folded beneath her oddly, strange turns visible beneath the fabric of her pants. The rest of her seemed strong and able.

"We prepare to free Ishkun-Dim-Hbelu," the woman said after they sat. "We have had word of his intentions. He desires to drive the fourcolors out of Karduniash. The other caravans are in similar positions surrounding our old capital." She looked to Kisare, then to Bel. "You have the seed of the fifth godfruit?" Bel held forth the little box filled with earth.

"The elders of Hbe—of Ishkun-Dim-Hbelu's village inspected it with juice of the malus, and saw it was marked by the gods," Kisare told her.

Mushezibti-Lila raised one eyebrow. "So are all godfruit seeds."

"You saw it glow when I touched it. It is magical, and not like other seeds." This woman was making her sweat without even moving. It was something about the way she sat straight-backed, or maybe the tilt of her head.

An elder, hair nearly white, protested. "What proof do we have these former slaves speak the truth? They could—"

Mushezibti-Lila cut the elder off with one raised hand. "This will not be as the massacre of previous centuries. I have no reason to doubt them, and word from Ishkun-Dim-Hbelu's caravan says they are trustworthy. We have all seen the fifth godfruit and have no reason to doubt it. We prepare the might of our people."

"Where is Ishkun-Dim-Hbelu now?" Bel asked. Her face showed none of the doubt Kisare felt.

"He is still traveling with the fourcolor known as Aricaba-Ata, along with many soldiers and fourcolor nobility. They have left Neharda for Karduniash, paralleling our travel."

"And with Ilzi," Bel muttered beside her.

Kisare noticed the caravan leader's words: "traveling with," not "prisoner of." There was pride and poise, and then there was posturing. When the nobles wanted something, they committed to it. None of this waiting around for years. She could almost admire Aricaba-Ata for seizing the chance to capture an important prisoner. It was a strong move against these nomadic people.

Her lip twisted as Kisare realized what she was thinking. She had been listening to Gemeti lecture for too long.

"The fourcolor has a strong band and several magic users of unknown colors," Mushezibti-Lila continued. "We must act before they become stronger. I have heard disturbing reports of violence against traveling Asha-Urmana. This cannot spread." She looked at Kisare, who looked back, trying to keep her face blank. It was as if the woman could tell what she was thinking.

"We are three weeks travel by wagon from Karduniash," the caravan leader said. "It is closer than we usually camp, and we have taken the resting spot of one of the nearer caravans. Even without the advantage of the fifth godfruit, we have numbers to overthrow the fourcolors. With the favor of the gods, we cannot lose. Now is the time we have waited for." Her eyes flashed, and the elders murmured in low tones. Kisare had seen soldiers training with spears and square shields, and a group of women with curved swords. A smith had set up a workplace, hammering day and night.

"I have been told your plan is to infiltrate the city," Mushezibti-Lila said. "Is this correct?" She continued staring at Kisare.

"Ah. Yes." Kisare had to swallow before she could speak. The woman's gaze was intense.

"Then I would ask you one more favor."

Kisare frowned. What else would they have to do for these people? The Asha-Urmana provided much help, but they asked for heavy payment.

"How can we aid you?" Bel asked.

"There are rumors of a captured Asha-Urmana child in the capital," Mushezibti-Lila told them. "She is supposed to be of an age with my daughter, but none know where she comes from." Her face closed, her mouth pinching. "I have spies acting as clothing merchants in the city, but they have never gotten close enough to see her firsthand. Even the court regards her as something of a legend. They tell me she is a prisoner of the Dyad, kept as a curiosity for the powerful fourcolors in their court, but it is also said the prisoner is graced with a large amount of purple—enough to become the leader of a caravan, or even to take Ishkun-Dim-Hbelu's place."

Mushezibti-Lila sat forward. Kisare got the feeling this woman was not used to asking for anything. "I would have her freed. This captive could be a powerful ally to overthrow the Dyad and the court of the fourcolor nobility from the inside. Search for her while you are in the capital. My spies tell me she yet lives. Even if Ishkun-Dim-Hbelu's plans fall to dust, this captive may aid you. In return for your service to the Asha-Urmana, I offer you this."

She gestured and an elder left through the back of the cabin, returning with a small, covered basket and a bundle of cloth. A fresh, sweet smell rose from the basket, strong in the wagon.

"This is the first harvest of our morus tree. I pray to Dumzi that you may make use of it in entering the city. His mental gifts are as powerful as shoots of new growth in the spring."

Kisare blinked once. The basket was not tiny, and she had expected nothing like this. Gemeti's mouth was open and even Bel looked nonplussed.

"In addition—" Mushezibti-Lila motioned for the bundle to be unwrapped. "There are clothes for you, made as fine as any we sell to the fourcolors. They are the new design of this year, not yet sold. You will be the fashionable first in Karduniash."

Another handsome gift. Even if the elders were suspicious of two former slaves, it seemed Hbelu's word counted for much among his people.

"Thank you," Kisare said. "We will try our best to find this girl and free her."

Mushezibti-Lila bowed, still seated. Kisare, Bel, and Gemeti took their gifts with them.

CHAPTER SIXTEEN

Friends and Enemies

Pleased at the might of their creations, the gods looked down on the world to see which godfruit was more favored, and who would triumph in battle. All they saw were the magical nations, fat with power, which in their pride had enslaved the god's first creations, the blonds. Not content to merely dominate them, they bred with their slaves, then enslaved those with little or no magic.

Belili, Kisa, and Gemeti departed the caravan the next morning, heading south. It was two and a half weeks to Karduniash, walking. The caravan had given them provisions, along with their gifts from the elders. Oxen could carry heavy loads, but they were nearly as slow as walking, and the Asha-Urmana did not have an extra wagon.

Her new hairstyle made Belili stand taller, her head high. She was prepared to face Ilzi and make him pay.

"I have friends in Karduniash," Gemeti told them. "Others who fight for the blonds, like me. One of them lives along our path." At Kisa's expression, she explained. "We help slaves become free, through escape or legitimate means. Some accept the truth about our society. We may have been like the Asha-Urmana once, separate people with different magical colored hair, but we are now one, blond and noble alike. We must act like it. The practice of slavery must end."

"How many of you are there?" Belili asked.

"More than the nobles would expect," Gemeti said. "Khanni—my friend outside the walls of the capital—has been making papers for former slaves for years. He may not be the best forger I have met, but he is decent. One day he will pass his business on to his daughter, a lovely, kind thing. I have not seen him in several years, though I have passed him other...candidates."

Gemeti's words touched Belili. The old woman hadn't stated the nature of her work in such clear terms before, though Belili had suspected. If the Asha-Urmana thought this way, they could be better rulers than the nobles.

They wore the same clothes the first several days, not wanting to get their new gifts from the caravan dirty. Then Kisa unfolded hers to look at it, naturally. She didn't do well with surprises. So Belili had to follow her example.

"Oh now, that is pretty," Gemeti said, when the clothes were unfurled. These were not simple cotton clothes, but dresses, unlike any Belili had seen. She had never worn a true dress, though she had seen old Mistress Tiamai and Ubala wearing them. Slaves wore old wool castoffs—torn pants and ratty, ill-fitting shirts—when they had anything more than rags.

These were dyed different colors, with slashes of brown and silver at the bottom and on the shoulders. They were cut strangely at the neck, though it was impossible to see the true extent of the dress without wearing it.

"No dress for you, Gemeti?" Kisa asked.

"Of course not," the woman responded. "I will be your servant at the capital—a freed slave if you wish, or a freewoman, or a noble with no magical color. I have no need for fancy dresses." She swished her own mass of clothes, bundled around her like a maze to fend off anyone from getting too close. There was at least one dress in there, of simpler material, though Gemeti also was wearing pants beneath them. Belili still hadn't figured out what Gemeti looked like underneath all the makeup, dye, and clothes. The woman was a mystery, despite traveling with them for several weeks now.

"You won't show your color?" she asked. "Us with brown and silver and you with black would be more impressive, don't you think?"

Gemeti waved a bony hand. "No, no. I have little enough color. No need to bring attention to my deficiencies." She patted her white hair, smoothing an errant bit into place.

Belili could only judge what Gemeti said by Ilzi's past examples, and the slimy man always hid his power's true extent. Gemeti had healed them, but it took several slices of citron apiece, and their wounds were already closing by that point. With her completely white hair, there was no way to know how big the woman's lock of black was.

"Where do you think she's from?" Kisa asked one night after they laid out their sleeping mats.

Belili shrugged. "I'm sure we will find out eventually." For now, it was enough to know she was an ally.

* * *

On the sixth day after leaving the caravan, they followed a well-worn dirt road. Gemeti told them it was the main highway from Neharda to Karduniash. Kisa was acting like a squirrel caught away from her tree, though Belili didn't feel much better about being so vulnerable.

"Are you sure you don't see anyone?" Kisa asked for perhaps the hundredth time. She clutched the basket of mori as if they would protect her. They sounded like the most powerful of the godfruits. Belili's only experience, again, was with Ilzi, directing his thoughts into her mind, influencing her to...no. She had her own power. She would show *him* what she could do. If she'd had access to godfruit when she was captured, she could have defended herself and Ligish. She prayed the woman was unharmed in Ilzi's care. Perhaps Hbelu would be able to protect her, in some small way.

"Even if there was someone on the road, Kisa, who would recognize the slaves from the Aricaba orchard?" Belili thought her question was reasonable, but Kisa only swiveled her head like she would twist it off.

They had good clothes, well-cut hair, obvious locks of magical color. They even had their own servant. Anyone would only think they were what they appeared: minor nobles traveling into Karduniash. Belili ignored the itch between her shoulder blades. The capital city was still more than a week away. Instead, she watched the new species of trees, wondering how to prune them. The pomegranate was a simple vase shape, while the mango grew much like a malus. The guava was spare, often growing low to the ground. While they traveled, they had fresh fruit—the non-magical kind.

Day and night, Gemeti told them the ways of the capital. She talked while they walked along the road, and before sleep. The woman was a font of information, on every topic but herself. Where had she come from? She deflected all questions about her past. She said she had lived in Neharda most of her life, but she was obviously trained by a high noble family, from her information on Karduniash society. Belili shook her head, watching the sides of the road for disturbances. She checked her pack again. The box was nestled halfway down and padded on all sides. Now she knew more about the four godfruits, she wondered what the gods intended with the fifth one. How could it balance the others without making the nobles even more powerful?

Belili also watched Kisa as they walked. Her sister was becoming bolder. Freer, like a noble.

Along the way, Gemeti told them of Khanni and his daughter. She had known the man for years, and they had helped each other move slaves from Neharda to the capital.

"So, we left later that night, with the slave dressed as a guard, Khanni as the guard's mother, and me as his doting grandfather! By all the gods!" She wiped at an eye, laughing, then turned serious. "We would be lost without Khanni's papers and forging equipment. Getting into Karduniash is not like passing through the gates of Neharda." Gemeti looked thoughtful for a moment. "With the Prunus Festival coming up, there will be even more security." She counted on fingers. "Yes, if we hurry, we should make it. That will be a grand entrance for you girls to show off your 'noble heritage' from the Blasted Lands. It is probably when Aricaba-Ata intends to offer his prisoner to the Dyad."

Eight days after intersecting the road, they stopped in the morning at Khanni's small, thatched cottage. It was set back a few hundred paces from the main thoroughfare, and vegetables and herbs grew in neat rows to one side of the yard. A spindly prunus tree had a place of honor in front of the house. Belili eyed the pruning job on the tree, but it was far too late to fix it. The prunae were nearly ready to turn. Khanni might have already picked some.

"Why doesn't he have any other godfruit trees?" Kisa asked as they walked up the path.

"You are used to the orchards, and the Asha-Urmana caravans," Gemeti replied. "They are like small towns, so they have at least one of all the godfruit trees." She pointed at the prunus. "Single families do not have the resources or money to take care of every godfruit tree. I'm sure you know the investment of fertilizer that takes. They are lucky to have one. We will pass more houses on the way to Karduniash. Mark them. You will see the family has picked their favorite trees to grow. Of course, if the houses are close, they could not have multiples of the same godfruit tree. Neighbors will buy or trade with each other for different varieties of godfruit."

At the house, Gemeti fell silent, giving a polite tap at the door. A few moments later it creaked open a couple inches and a middle-aged man with the whitish hair of a natural blond poked his face out.

"Who're yo—" His eyes widened at the sight of Gemeti. "Oh, come in, quickly."

Gemeti hustled them inside and Belili looked around the room. It was small, but well furnished with old, comfortable furniture. On the mantle above the fireplace was a very expensive-looking clock. She had seen one before, in the Aricaba house, the pride of Aricaba-Ata, but this one was even fancier. She glanced around again, looking for other signs of wealth, but she saw none. Their guide had noted the clock too and frowned.

"My friend," Gemeti began, "I have two more strays who came knocking on my door. I am helping them get on their feet as minor nobles. They wish to travel to Karduniash."

Belili watched her sister tense as Gemeti spilled out the half-true story. The man's eyes flicked to Kisa as well. He was observant.

"So, you're well on your way, aren't you?" he said, standing back from them. He still hadn't offered them seats, or refreshments. His speech was informal. A former slave, or one used to dealing with slaves? Belili resolved to adopt the formal-sounding language Gemeti used. They would need it in the capital.

"We are," Gemeti said slowly, "but we will need a pass to get into Karduniash. Unless I remember incorrectly, you are the best forger this side of the capital. Can you help us?"

Khanni swelled a little at her words, standing straighter. "Of course. I just, ah, need my things, and we can begin. I'll fetch them. Wait there a moment."

He disappeared into a back room of the house, and they heard whispered conversation. Minutes passed. Belili looked a question to Gemeti, whose eyes were narrowed.

"What is taking him so long?" Kisa asked after a moment. "He's going to draw us up papers, not an entire book."

Gemeti made a shushing noise, which only made Kisa puff up. Belili crossed over to her sister. "Let's hold for another minute. He sounds like he hasn't done this in a while."

"Indeed," Gemeti said. "I wonder if—"

"Ah, here we are," Khanni said, returning around a corner. His smile was false. Belili had seen that smile on guards, on Ilzi, before they asked her to come see a wonder behind the barn. She took Kisa's hand, tugging, but Kisa resisted.

Something shut quietly in the back of the house, suspiciously like a door. Khanni started a little but tried to pretend he had heard nothing.

"Where is your lovely daughter, might I ask?" Gemeti questioned, craning her neck to peer into the back rooms.

Khanni moved to block her view. "Ah, I'm sure she must be out visiting one of her little friends. You know how girls play."

"I do." Gemeti took a step back, pressing Belili and Kisa toward the door. "I feel we have taken up enough of your time," she said.

"You don't have your papers," Khanni pleaded, holding sheets out toward them. "It will only take a short time. I have the forms here."

"No, I feel we have intruded too long already," Gemeti said. "Move!" she whispered back over her shoulder. Belili pulled Kisa toward the door.

"Please—they'll take her," Khanni said. "She's all I have left." He walked after them, papers dangling in one hand, as if he would catch them in a big hug.

"You should have thought of that before you sent her to the guard," Gemeti shot back. Belili, reaching back, found the door, then the doorknob. She pushed the door outward.

"Run!" she commanded Kisa, and for once, her sister didn't argue. They shot out of the cottage, Gemeti close behind, puffing and blowing. Khanni followed, but hesitated on his doorstep, head turning in both directions. Belili felt exposed in the low rows of vegetables and herbs.

They kept running until the cottage was out of sight and Gemeti lagged far behind. Belili stopped, but she waved them on.

"Go on, keep moving," the old woman shouted. "The Karduniash guard must have...gotten to Khanni...since the last time...I was here," she panted. "I always told...the scoundrel...his work was shoddy."

Belili saw Gemeti's eyes widen in fear and turned. A squad of guards was mounting the next rise in the road. One of them pointed.

"Flee!" Gemeti told them, closing the distance. She had her pack open, pressing handfuls of godfruit at them. "Use the mori to escape! Remember their mental powers. We will meet in the capital. Find me at The Blossoming Prunus."

One of the guards raised a hand to his mouth.

"They have godfruit!" Gemeti shouted. "Go!"

Belili shared a glance with Kisa as they both popped one of the small berries in their mouth.

Kisa disappeared as a guard burst into existence, reaching, touching Belili's arm. He was the one who had eaten something, and she saw a lock of brown poking from under his leather helmet as panic flooded though her. *He'll take me. I'll be a slave again.* Pushing hands away from her legs on the cold ground. *Never again.*

The electricity of the godfruit washed over her and she shivered as the possibilities of the morus spread before her.

Belili existed in limbo for a moment, a range of locations opening in her mind. *The morus gives those of the brown hair the ability to move from location to location.* Gemeti had told her, but she hadn't truly understood.

The guard wobbled back as if pushed, releasing her. *No. Use the brown.* She had power, and picked a location twenty paces away, beside a tree. Suddenly the two places were one, and she exhaled. The godfruit juice in her mouth was devoid of any flavor, or magic. She stepped behind the trunk, hiding from the guard.

Where was Kisa? She couldn't have traveled like Belili—she had a silver lock. The thought left her mind when another guard on the rise pointed toward her, and her heart raced. She was hidden from the guard who tried to catch her, but not from the rest of his squad. She would not be caught, would not be held again. She stuffed another four berries in her mouth, trying not to lose focus as the electric shuddering took her.

Belili felt a larger range in her mind, as if she could touch each bit of ground in a wide circle. This time it reached past where the guards were standing—away from their grasping hands. She picked another tree off the side of the road and made the places become one. Out of sight, she swallowed the now bland godfruit in her mouth and held her breath, her chest hammering. She should fight them, stay with her sister, but her limbs wouldn't go in that direction. *Never again.*

If she moved, the guards would hear her. Slowly, she raised four more berries to her mouth. She risked a peek around the tree as she chewed, the thrill running through her, jolts of lightning running down her body. Kisa was gone, hidden by another mental trick of the morus. Belili tried to convince herself Kisa would be fine on her own. Kisa didn't have the same fear she did, buried deep down. Every instinct told her to run. If this was how she reacted, what would she do when she met Ilzi?

Gemeti was standing in the middle of the road, hand at her mouth. The lone guard wasn't trying to capture her. Gemeti pointed at the guard, and he shook his head. What was she doing?

Belili pulled her head back as one of the nearby group looked around. She couldn't help them. She had to get away. Kisa had Gemeti to help her, protect her. She had to use the magic, would meet them at the inn Gemeti had named—The Blossoming Prunus. Kisa would be fine. Belili shut away the voice yelling to go to her sister. She couldn't. She chose a point as far along the road as she could manage and was there in the blink of an eye.

For good measure she ate two more mori and skipped again, at the extreme range of the area in her mind. Was this far enough from the guards? She had to hope. Only six more mori left, and she might need them to get inside the gates of Karduniash without a pass.

Belili straightened her dress, arranged her lock of brown over her shoulder, took a deep breath, and walked toward the capital. If she hurried, she might make it there by the next morning. She pushed away the guilt, the self-disgust. She would not be held again. There was time to meet Kisa and Gemeti in Karduniash.

CHAPTER SEVENTEEN

Shadows in the Trees

Four capitals warred with each other, using blond slaves as fodder for the swords of their enemies. Each land had their specialty in magic: reds with physical power and fire magic, browns with earth and the ability to move from place to place, black with healing powers and their knowledge of the thoughts of others, and silver with the ability to slip through dangerous places unseen.

It had been a week since Ata and Ilzi's hunting party left Neharda, swollen in numbers and in bravado. Hbelu watched the rolling prison cage, filled with prisoners, from his newest vantage: chained to a mango tree away from the fire. Twilight cast the figures in shadows, and his manacles made noise with the slightest change in position. The heavy chains had hollow sections that chimed with every movement— specifically for prisoners who attempted escape.

Two of the female Asha-Urmana in the cage were from Mushezibti-Lila's caravan. There were also three men, but one's head lolled against the bars, either unconscious, or dead. The fourcolor's soldiers had not been gentle when capturing the scouts. The two females they chased down and manacled four days out from Neharda, when the fourcolors still talked of searching the surrounding woods as they traveled. Now they only went after those who crossed their paths as they walked, day by day, closer to Karduniash.

Hbelu did not recognize some of the trees here—many giant and covered with moss, small ferns growing beneath them. Every so often they had passed a towering mango, its fruit like small rocks, prone to dropping on soldier's heads if they stopped too long beneath. The fourcolor's base humor soon led to them chaining him to one every night. He slept poorly, though he had plenty to eat.

Nor was he in the cage. Aricaba-Ata still had that much control over the train of soldiers, prisoners, and fourcolor nobility. The group was half the size of a caravan, though with far fewer wagons. But the big orchard owner had taken a bigger bite of godfruit than he could chew. Every day, he rode with a different fourcolor, appeasing or lording over them.

Hbelu learned that as long as he did nothing to provoke the fourcolors, they did not beat him. He should have protested his treatment, but was starting to wonder what simple speech would accomplish. The last two times he had spoken, a fourcolor noble directed a soldier to whip Hbelu for "his insolence." Hbelu was persistent, but not stupid. His back stung from the welts, and his feet from lashes they had given him to keep him from running.

He was glad Ligish had escaped when she could. She might have been able to warn Mushezibti-Lila's caravan, but if she did, it hadn't mattered much. Hopefully she was on to a new life somewhere. Ilzi had raged for three straight days, but could never quite lay the blame at Hbelu's feet. Ata's protection had kept the oily black-hair from killing him immediately on discovering his prisoner had escaped.

The next morning, a soldier jerked him to his feet.

"Get moving." There was no animosity in her tone—she was merely dealing with a recalcitrant prisoner. She unhooked his manacles from around the mango tree—with haste—and tethered them to the rear of the rolling cage, with just enough rope to walk as two oxen pulled the whole contraption along the road. Hbelu walked gingerly, limping when he stepped wrong on the wounds on his feet.

Enti-Ilzi hurried by, giving Hbelu a satisfied smirk. The oily man always had a jingling pocket nowadays, which had improved his attitude considerably after losing Ligish. That and there were plenty of prisoners to serve his tastes in this group. The cousins earned enough between wagering, begging, and patronage to pay for their expensive inn rooms and soldiers. Ilzi acted as a kind of grease, keeping the fourcolors from killing each other.

Ilzi stopped by another fourcolor noble with a streak of black hair and a bushy blond beard. Several bleached-blond prisoners in metal collars trailed the Nehardan noble at all times, one visibly with child. "Ziggurmas-Su, I have heard the other nobles speaking in awe of you, when they think I am not listening. We are so fortunate to have one of your status with us."

The man puffed his chest. His coat was still white somehow, his buttons shined, though they had been traveling for over a week. "I have spent many years building my holdings and am only happy to lend resources to your cause. How is the camp running? Are we still on schedule for Karduniash? It has been too long since I checked in on my houses, where my wife is certainly spending all my earnings."

They both laughed, falsely and long. Ziggurmas-Su acted as if the journey to Karduniash was his idea, ignoring Ata most of the time. Hbelu ducked his head, making sure he didn't trip as the rolling cage with its prisoners started forward. And so they couldn't see his sneer.

"Everything is running well, now we have your support." Ilzi waved a hand back toward Hbelu. "I am certain the Dyad will be pleased with access to the caravanner's magic." He leaned closer, looking back at the procession of soldiers. "We sorts have to stick together, yes?" He indicated his own stripe of black. "I heard yesterday Sutur-Cit had a source for some newly ripened mori. I thought it only fair to share the news."

Su ran a finger across his carefully trimmed mustache. "Does he now? Old Cit always had an eye for those things." Something clinked, changing hands. "Be a good lad, see if you can intercept some for me. No sense letting that red-hair get the better of us, hey?"

The two exchanged pleasantries, then Ilzi stopped and let Su and the procession move past. As Hbelu walked past, he could see the circles under Ilzi's eyes.

Definitely more godfruit than the two of them can chew.

* * *

Three days later, Hbelu began to see further signs of his people. His feet had healed enough for him to walk without wincing, and they had not secured him to a mango tree again, but his stomach protested the lack of food. His wrists were chafed from the constant movement of the metal manacles. He could scoop water from puddles and leaves as he passed, but those in the cage could not reach so far, even if they had the energy. The fourcolors had fed them, a few times, but not enough.

Hbelu was certain the caravans were on the move. Three times that morning, he had seen a flash of purple, keeping a watch on him and the cage. The scouts hidden around them were traveling parallel.

A woman fell over in the cage and Hbelu's manacles clanked as he tried to reach for the bars. The other scout looked to her compatriot, but made no move to help.

"That one will be no good for later in the day," a nearby soldier—a natural blond—remarked to his companion. "The nobles are already placing bets. We'll have to capture some new caravanners."

"I don't want to get one of their spears through my gut. Can't we give her food and water instead? She'll perk up."

The first soldier shook his head. "Ziggurmas-Su's orders. No food for the new slaves. He says they're too feisty. Got to break them in."

His colleague looked thoughtful. "I'd like to break her in."

Hbelu gritted his teeth. Such a man would be stripped of responsibilities in his caravan, ostracized. Yet all the fourcolors were like this, men and women. His manacles jingled as he stretched his hands to their limits. He didn't need them off to strangle the soldier. If he got a little closer—

"Caravanners! In the woods!" The call came from one of the Neharda soldiers. The two near Hbelu broke off, pulling swords from scabbards. One checked the straps on his leather armor.

"A hunt!" one of the fourcolors called, a brown-hair. The call was taken up by others. There had been too many hunts in the last few days. "We need contestants for this afternoon!"

A group of twenty men broke away, trailed by the brown-hair, and disappeared into the woods. As clashes and shouts floated from the line of moss and tree trunks, Hbelu realized he was alone with the prisoners.

"Quickly," he called, his voice harsh. "What caravans are you from? What are your names?" The woman who was still conscious only stared at him for a moment, as if trying to remember how to speak.

"I am Damma, from Ziral-Barital's caravan," one of the two living men said. The fourcolors had not removed the corpse, and the stink was something almost physical in the humid air.

The woman finally roused herself. "We are from Mushezibti-Lila. I am Belatsu."

"The caravans are traveling to Karduniash?" Hbelu would withstand all his mistreatment if only his people rose against the fourcolors. He could erase their barbaric ways after he retook the capital.

"They are," Damma said, his voice raw and hoarse. "Though I will not see my sons again."

"There is still hope," Hbelu returned. "I have seen more of our people, gathering. The caravans must be close. They will send combined forces to free us."

"You hope for much." Belatsu pushed herself up against the bars. "Your caravan lived high in the mountains, Ishkun-Dim-Hbelu. We know of your idealism, but not all Asha-Urmana agree. Those closer to the larger fourcolor cities see horrors you never have."

"Asha-Urmana cities," Hbelu corrected. "The fourcolors took them from us."

"Centuries ago," Damma said. He coughed once, a wet sound. The other man was watching with vacant eyes and had not contributed to the conversation. "You are our prince, and I will follow your word and the elders, but some of us think there is a reason we never regained our cities. We do not have the strength of the fourcolors, with their magic and their slaves."

"Their slaves will desert them, given a chance," Hbelu argued. "Their magic is limited by their wastefulness."

The woman laughed weakly. "Look around. They have held blonds as slaves for more than a thousand years. Why stop now?"

Hbelu thought of Belili, and Kisare, hoping they still had the box and its precious seed. With no knowledge of what the fifth godfruit did, save a promise of balance from the silent gods, he could offer no refutation to his imprisoned people. He hung his head.

The fourcolors brought back three new prisoners, two women and a man, all wounded. One woman was missing her right hand, her arm tightly bound in red-soaked rags. They were all thrust into the rolling cage, forcing Damma and Belatsu to stand, holding up their injured companions. None of the prisoners could stand straight, but at least the fourcolors disposed of the rotting corpse, thrown in another wagon to fertilize some fourcolor's tree in Karduniash.

Belatsu watched him, and Hbelu felt judged by her gaze. He would have called the caravans to act even if he knew this outcome. Even if it cost them many of their people's lives, it was time the Asha-Urmana regained their place and favor in the gods' eyes.

When the procession stopped for the night, the fourcolors made a circle next to the firepit, clearing brush, ferns, and moss. Soldiers set lit torches around it, and the fourcolor nobility, laughing and talking, filed around. Hbelu watched warily.

Aricaba-Ata, still laughing at some joke, unhooked Hbelu's manacles from the rope lead.

"Well, caravanner, you will have a place of honor over your people tonight. Like old times, hey? How are your feet? Feeling tender, yes? No matter."

Hbelu did not respond as the red-hair brought him, limping, to one side of the lighted circle. What was this new torment? Would he have to fight for them now? Give him a piece of godfruit, and he would show these inbred fourcolors what a fight was like.

Ata attached his manacles to a loop of steel on a pole driven into the ground. "The prince is ready to receive his subjects," Ata called, to much cheering from the soldiers and nobility seated on logs, and stools. "Who is the first to pay their respects?"

Only a familiar squeak of wheels answered. Hbelu's head whipped up, his heart thumping. That sound accompanied his every step. They could not...

Four soldiers rolled the cage to the opposite side of the circle. Harsh light from the firepit threw shadows of the bars into the forest.

"Come now," Ilzi took up Ata's question. "Who is the first to meet their prince face to face? We wish to know."

Damma stumbled down from the cage, holding on to a bar for balance. His clothes were soiled, his hair filthy, from days in the cage without even a bucket. A soldier shoved him from behind and he fell into the middle of the open circle. Damma pushed himself to his hands and knees. There was a round of whispers and curses. Hbelu saw money change hands between nobility and soldiers alike.

"Yes, bow to your lord," the arrogant black-hair—Ziggurmas-Su—said, with a cruel smile.

"We do not bow to our elected leaders," Damma said. His voice was hoarse from lack of water.

Hbelu wanted to agree with him, say something, but his mouth felt as dry as if it were he traveling in the cage instead.

Ata ignored him. "Who is the second supplicant? Come forward."

One of the newer prisoners, also male, was the second out of the cage. A similar round of payments passed through the fourcolors.

"No," Hbelu said. It was almost a whisper, but Ata must have heard him.

"Yes indeed." The orchard owner leaned close. "You have done everything in your power to lose me two of my workers. I suspect you enabled Ilzi's new slave's escape as well, though we have no proof. These two are not even from your little village. They cannot be worth as much as Belili and Kisare." He looked back up and waved a hand.

Soldiers pressed in from both sides, pushing the two prisoners closer. Damma and the other exchanged glances, confused.

"Well, fight it out," Ziggurmas-Su called. "We don't have all night, and I'm down three mori already. You better make it up." He pointed to the newer prisoner.

"We will not fight for your amusement," Damma called out.

The other man nodded his agreement. "We are not like the blonds you enslave."

"A pity," Ziggurmas-Su called. "Shall we have a vote? My godfruit is on the new one."

There was a quick show of hands, while Hbelu looked around the circle. It had the semblance of a ritual, but not one he had seen. He should have traveled south more often, out of his village near the Blasted Lands.

The vote concluded, but Hbelu had not seen the outcome. A soldier stepped behind Damma, drew his knife, and slit the man's neck. Hbelu jerked uselessly at his chains, but it was over before he could call out. The soldier tossed the bleeding body to the edge of the circle, where Damma flopped, then lay still. Hbelu swallowed.

"Another for the trees. Who is next to pay their respects?" Ata called out. Hbelu turned to him, hands clenched convulsively. The wounds on his feet and back faded to an annoyance. Yes, there would be bloodshed to retake Karduniash, but this was senseless death, merely to torture him.

Belatsu was next out, looking grim. Though exhausted, she held her stance as if sneaking up on a wild boar. Her hands were empty, but her fingers were held tight, out to each side, ready.

"Give greeting to your sovereig—oh!" Ziggurmas-Su did not finish his ridicule before the woman pounced on the newly captured scout, pinning him before he scooted from under her, and she rose to one knee, punching at kidney and face.

Handshakes, coins, and pieces of godfruit changed hands around the circle. Several soldiers cheered.

"No," Hbelu called. "This is not our way! The Asha-Urmana do not fight each other!"

Ata only laughed and slapped him on the back.

Belatsu proved a skilled fighter, weakened as she was. She blocked almost all of the larger man's punches, returning with quick strikes to his eyes, which he diverted, and one to his throat, which he did not. He choked and retched, rolling away.

On his feet again, the man towered over her and Belatsu struggled to rise. Hbelu knew how little food and water the woman had had in the last week. It was a blessing from the gods she had lasted this long. Gods. Hah. The gods had nothing to do with this.

The man rushed Belatsu and she readied herself, though the other Asha-Urmana was half again heavier than she.

Then a red-hair, Sutur-Cit, Hbelu thought, flicked a hand out. He was chewing something. The prisoner stumbled, just as Belatsu struck. The thrust of her palm, meant only to fend him off, snapped his head back with an audible crack, and the man crumpled to the ground.

Belatsu fell back.

"No fair pushing him, Cit," Ata called out. Still, money and godfruit changed hands around the circle.

"It was an unfair fight," the fourcolor called back. "I only evened it up. Another portion of food tomorrow for my champion!"

Hbelu watched Belatsu, gasping, hands pressed to the ground. To kill prisoners for sport. To *waste* godfruit—gifts from the gods—on such a pursuit. This rotting empire of barely civilized inbred killers must be torn down, fifth godfruit or not. Hbelu struggled impotently against his bonds, but his eyes were locked on Cit. The fourcolor held a handful of glistening mori. There must be a way for him to get some. With it, he could escape as easily as Ligish had, and bring all the prisoners with him.

CHAPTER EIGHTEEN

Karduniash

The four nations surrounded the people of the purple hair, who lived under the gods' protection. The Asha-Urmana, as they called themselves, fended off other nations' forays into their lands with mechanical constructs that threw great stones. They bolstered their technological prowess with sweet speech, communion with spirits of the dead, and giant soldiers riding giant oxen.

Kisare watched Bel disappear as the guard touched her sister. She gasped, and the guard turned her way at the sound. His eyes went through her, searching.

Kisare looked down, and almost gasped again. She couldn't see herself! She felt the juice of the morus draining away. The magic was working, doing something to her.

Dumzi the trickster put his guile in the morus. Our minds gain unearthly powers to serve us.

She was hidden from the sight of others. How long would it last?

She turned to Gemeti, wanting to ask, though the guard was standing not two paces away.

The guard focused on the woman. "Where did they go?"

Gemeti was chewing. "I know what you are thinking," she said, "but you will never catch them. Both are powerfully endowed with brown. They have moved farther from here than you can." Kisare frowned. That wasn't right.

"One of them had silver—" the guard began.

"A lie." Gemeti popped two mori in her mouth, twitching slightly as she did. "Dyed hair. Both are powerful nobles."

The guard shook his head, as if trying to clear it. "That is not..." He shook his head again as Gemeti's hands clenched at her sides. "Why...why did they run from us?"

Gemeti looked him over, and Kisare saw her take in the finely detailed leather, the polished silver spear he carried, the bright red plume on his leather helmet. "What would you do if a squad of Karduniash guard gave chase?"

Something glinted from the corner of Kisare's eye—a hazy outline, as if a shape in water. Her hand! She chewed two more mori. Her hand disappeared again.

Should she walk away? Stay with Gemeti? Find Bel? If her sister had moved across great distances, as Gemeti said, it would be almost impossible to catch up. She'd have to find Bel in Karduniash.

Kisare looked down to count her remaining mori, but her hand containing them was invisible. She tried to count by touch, careful not to damage the rubbery skin of the godfruits. Maybe another eight berries? How long would that last?

"I will go with you," Gemeti said to the guard. The others were coming down the hill to join their fellow. She put a whole handful of berries in her mouth, chewing fast. She spoke, words muffled, trying to keep juice from spilling. Bel's vague words about Ilzi came back to her. Gemeti, with black hair, weak as she was, could affect the guard's thoughts, though she had to use a lot of godfruit to keep the guard from suspicion. What had Ilzi done to Bel over the years? Bel had gone missing for hours when Ilzi visited, but never longer than one night. Just one night—Kisare's stomach turned, her vision blurring. Ilzi had held Bel for several days, and with how Bel had been acting... How could she have been so *blind*?

"You will not notice I leave these here for *anyone* to find," Gemeti was saying. She put the basket of mori, now less than a third full, on the ground, swallowed, and stood up again.

"What was that?" The guard shook his head again. "Come with us. We will sort this out back at the gates." Gemeti could not have much black in her hair, for how she struggled to make the guard believe her lies. The woman ate more berries while the guard spoke. "You will tell us where the others went. The report said they are escaped slaves. Fortunate we were stationed at the far outskirts, investigating a forgery. We will take you to talk with the commander."

"A misunderstanding, I am sure." Gemeti stepped over the basket. "Once we enter Karduniash, your superiors will clear this all up."

Kisare darted forward and snagged the basket. It became invisible as she touched it, and she put the berries she held back in with the rest.

The juice lost flavor in her mouth, and Kisare ate another morus. The tingling shock made her pause, then she walked after the retreating guard. Gemeti was leading her to the city. She just had to stay silent and avoid notice by the guards along the way. Like a slave.

* * *

Kisare watched the capital's countryside. She could pass as a noble, or maybe a freewoman, but the road was lined with houses, and she traveled in back yards as much as possible, occasionally sneaking out to see the troop of guards leading Gemeti. Here and there they stopped to talk with freemen and freewomen. There were no nobles out this far, or at least not with fine clothes like Aricaba-Ata and Enti-Ilzi wore. The people here were planting and tending gardens and godfruit trees. They talked with each other and went about their business.

She saw many godfruit trees. Neighbors owned different types, often repeating the order of trees so they were spaced far enough apart to bear. The houses were similar to those in Neharda but lacked the whitewashed construction. Here they favored varnished oak or birch planks, polished so they glowed in the daylight. When the houses crowded together, there wasn't enough space for the trees to produce, and some shared a tree. Most were surrounded with name-rails, and there were stumps surrounded with their own rails, denoting generations of families who had taken care of them.

Though these houses were not inside Karduniash, they were part of it. Little wonder the guard patrolled so far out from the city. If this was merely the outskirts, then how big was the capital? People moved up and down the road, often forcing her to use a morus when a yard was closed off, or the brush was too thick.

Other people's clothes were not much cleaner than hers, dirty from long days of travel. She was tempted to let her invisibility drop and walk the streets, but Khanni had given them away, and he had been a friend of Gemeti. Who else might? What if others were using mori, looking for her? Were there unseen guards or nobles? Was it better to be visible, or not? The rest of the day passed in a paranoid haze, buzzing from the magic of the godfruit half the time, checking over her shoulder the other half—creeping from building to building, tiptoeing around freemen and freewomen working in their yards.

Karduniash was a day away. Kisare spent it huddled behind trees, squatting behind rocks, and trudging through scrub just out of sight of large two-story wood houses, praying to all the gods that no one bumped into her, or no servants took the night waste out, or no one asked what she was doing on their property. She ate mori when there was no other option, and by the time the great wall of the city came into view, her basket was noticeably lighter. She cringed at wasting so much godfruit, but it was that or lose track of Gemeti and the guards while she tried to explain her way out of invading someone's yard. An irate freewoman might *call* for the guard, and she would lose everything she had gained by eating the mori. She had to follow, and the guards could not catch sight of her.

At last, they were in front of the gate. The houses marched right up to it, getting larger and more extravagant the closer they got. Here, Kisare saw true nobles—slave-owners—mixed in with the free class. Their bleached-blond slaves appeared, and these were not carefree and joking as in Neharda. To distinguish from free, natural blonds, they wore metal collars around their necks. Aricaba-Ata had not done that to his slaves.

There was a ring road around the walls where no houses stood, and there were guards on top of the wall, which was six or seven times her height. It was not painted and stuccoed like the wall around Neharda, and she recognized Asha-Urmana construction of close-fitted stones. Strange that the capital advertised the work of those who had not lived there in nearly a thousand years.

Kisare held her place behind a stone cistern, watching the guards on the wall, the house she hid near, and Gemeti and the guards. They were almost at the gate, where guards checked every person and their papers before letting them through. She would have to enter when no one was blocking the way.

She ate six mori at once, hoping the few left in the basket would be enough, and ran forward on the balls of her feet, trying to make as little noise as possible. *If only I had a slice of citron.* She almost laughed at the thought—regretting she didn't have enough godfruit.

One guard, with a lock of black hair, was scouting the road, chewing on something. Another with a silver lock like hers was on the other side.

As she ran up behind the squad, the black-haired man stiffened, still chewing.

"There's another mind here," he said. "Scared. I can feel it." He raised another morus to his mouth, taking a step toward her.

Kisare froze. If the morus made those with black hair able to read and affect minds, then she was in danger. She danced forward, hoping to get past. Even a malus slice might have let her speed through on a gust of air.

The silver-haired guard stepped forward too. He had a deep red prunus on a stem, and bit off half. He shuddered, then inhaled deeply.

"I can smell her." He raised a hand, finger moving along Kisare's trail. It would intersect her in a moment.

Geshtna's passions are always intense. Her prunae increase all five of the senses.

"Give me a morus," he continued. "She must be hidden." He reached for the other guard.

Kisare threw herself forward. The guards at the gate were closing in, arms outstretched. She glimpsed Gemeti, brow furrowed, mouthing, "Run!"

Kisare ran, feeling fingers catch at her cotton shirt. One caught hold, but she jerked free, hearing a rip as she did.

"I see her," came a shout behind her, and she looked over one shoulder, bouncing off someone. The guards were all visible, but now one pointed at her. How could he see her?

Kisare turned the first corner she could, cutting off the guard's line of sight, knocking into people on the street, running wildly, pack bouncing on her back, and the basket clutched close to her chest. She tried to breathe through her nose, but it left her winded. If she opened her mouth, the morus juice would dribble out, and she would be seen.

The streets were filled with people, and she lost herself, hobbling along with a stitch forming in her side. She tried to remember the turns she took: was it a right, a left, two more rights, and another two lefts—or was it three lefts? The streets were a warren, and groups of buildings with signs hanging in front showed their service.

The lightning on her tongue drained away, and she saw shadows of her hands appear, pumping by her sides as she ran. She felt in the basket, feeling the weave of reeds at the bottom. One half-crushed berry left. She popped the godfruit in her mouth and ducked into a narrow alley. There was almost no juice in this one, and she saw lightning dancing down her arms. It wasn't worth it. She swallowed, then gasped for breath. Her hands gained weight and color as she put them on her knees, bending forward to inhale. She threw the basket to one side.

Some of the godfruit must have bounced out as she ran, rolling into the gutters on the side of the street. Some beggar might find an expensive snack.

When she caught her breath, Kisare stood and looked around the alley. Stone buildings rose to either side, three and four stories. The top three stories of the building across the street shone in the sunlight, made of bright polished wood. The bottom floor was even brighter, made of marble that caught the morning sun. Gold leaf decorated the windows and gutters, and the roof was slate. It looked like the houses in Hbelu's village.

What to do? The alley was clean, but there was nothing of interest except an old, pitted block of stone. It might have fallen off a building and been forgotten. She sat down on it and watched the mouth of the alley. People passed by on the street outside without even glancing her way.

What she needed was a plan. She and Bel—wherever her sister was now—had been running since they left the orchard. Always, someone else directed her actions. She'd never had a chance to sit down and plan, like she used to in the orchard. Plan out the chores heaped upon them each day, divide them into chunks, and finish each part before the next. She had always finished her work first in the orchard, mostly to scowls from the other slaves.

Kisare counted on her fingers. She needed to find Bel, who would be hopelessly lost in the city and terrified with all the people brushing past. Bel had the box with the seed of the fifth godfruit. There was also Gemeti. She should try to find the old woman and get her out of whatever trouble she was in.

She also needed to find Hbelu. They had failed to free him or rouse the caravans. She didn't know if Aricaba-Ata was in the city yet, but it was a good guess he was, given the slow pace of the Asha-Urmana caravan she'd traveled with. There were questions she needed to ask Hbelu, about what he had meant when he invited her to join his caravan.

Then what? Free the prince and somehow get near the Dyad with the seed and all their problems would be solved? Well, she didn't have the seed, and she didn't have Hbelu. She guessed the Asha-Urmana might be the one presented to the Dyad, as Aricaba-Ata's gift. He had spoken of the Dyad's jealousy of the Asha-Urmana magic.

That meant Gemeti would be the easiest to find. She was probably being taken to the local law office. How to get in? The guards with Gemeti would recognize Kisare, especially with her clothes all dirty and torn.

She could wander the city looking for Bel. She yearned to, but she knew there was little hope of finding her sister. Gemeti was the best option. The old woman would know her way around.

Kisare unslung her pack and opened the top tie. Would her new dress be enough to distract the guards from recognizing her?

She looked around once more, moved deeper into the alley, and started changing.

* * *

Belili eyed the wall of Karduniash, estimating. Using the mori to move across the countryside had taken her out of her way, and she'd used more than she anticipated. She spent the rest of the day avoiding both houses and patrols. Had Khanni or the brown-haired guard passed her description around? Better to steer clear of them altogether, lest the question of entry papers came up.

Arriving from the west, rather than the north where the main gate was, she was confronted with a high wall, dotted with guards. Belili hid behind a tree as another passed. There was an open patch of ground between the edge of the woods and the city wall, but no gate.

Belili considered the two mori she had left, both worse for wear. The guard passed by on his rounds. It was now or wait for the next opening. Belili was not a fan of waiting. She chewed both mori, shivering, and felt a sphere of space open in her mind, with solid objects as a kind of resistance. Little jolts of lightning traipsed up and down her body. She had found she needed to see her destination, or she couldn't move to a new location.

She couldn't see the top of the wall, high as it was, but she could see the air just above it. She used the morus juice, knees braced as she dropped a few feet onto the stone of the wall with a thump. Belili was careful not to swallow any left in her mouth. By the taste, she had used up about half of the magic.

Heavy footsteps rang behind her.

"What was that? Hey! You should not be—"

Belili panicked, her magic sending a stray rock flying behind her even as she turned to face the guard.

The guard's metal helmet rang as if struck with a hammer, and he staggered, falling against the railing.

Belili rubbed the top of her stump with her thumb. She hadn't meant to do that. Control. In everything. Now she didn't have enough magic to travel to the street level.

The guard was stumbling back to his feet, sword half out. He would see her soon—see her face. There was nowhere to run.

Belili vaulted over the crenellation, down into the city. If this didn't work...

As she fell, face down, she latched onto the first location she could see, waited one instant, and *twisted* as she used the rest of the magic in the juice and her brown hair, churning her legs.

She stumbled as she hit the ground, catching her balance before she tumbled head over heels. Her speed propelled her forward and she ran awkwardly as she spent the energy from her fall.

Belili wobbled to a stop, hand against the side of a marble building. She swallowed the bland juice in her mouth, risking a quick glance up to confirm she was out of sight of the guard, though he would likely raise an alarm. She walked into the city, head held high, face expressionless. Blend in, as a noble. She pushed her hair back, revealing the lock of brown Gemeti had dyed. Her fingers paused underneath that lock. The hair there was dyed brown as well, though that was not its natural color. Neither was it blond. Gemeti had figured it out, but she was smart enough not to mention it. Belili rubbed the stump of her little finger again.

She walked, aiming away from the wall and toward the bulk of what seemed to be a small mountain in the middle of the city. As she did so, the buildings became more opulent, with more gold leaf, more polished marble, and newer wood paneling. Hbelu's caravan must have modeled their town after Karduniash.

Belili tried to stand tall, to walk as the Asha-Urmana did. She still caught glances from nobles in the streets, eyeing her dirty clothes and face. Well-cut hair was a start, but it wouldn't help her if it was too unclean to tell.

She looked for somewhere to change her clothes and wash her face but saw no sign for an inn. Would Ata have taken Hbelu to one, or to the palace? Gemeti thought he would be presented to the Dyad. She kept walking.

Here, the ground was higher, and she could see Karduniash laid out. It was a big city. People—well dressed and not—watched her as they passed. She could tell the nobles from the freemen and women. The nobles had bleached blonds trailing behind them, metal collars around their necks. One noble lady, a silver streak running from the crown of her head to her cheek, was followed by three slaves, carrying wicker baskets filled with clothes, books, and stranger objects. A day of shopping in the capital. There were prosperous-looking shops, from tailors, to jewelers, two-storied bookstores and eclectic shops filled with nonsense like Ubala had collected, back in the orchard.

Belili had walked for several hours, and crossed less than half of the city, though she was much closer to the mountain. It drew her. Ata would certainly set his sights on this most impressive aspect of the city. The mountain was man-made—a pyramidal ziggurat, like Hbelu's home, though massive. How long had it taken to build? She could see windows, high up on the sides.

To her right, something glinted. There were hardly any clouds in the sky; a perfect, warm, mid-year day. She angled toward it, trusting her intuition.

Closer, she realized a glass structure had caught her eye. There were several, all shaped like giant tents, nearly as tall as the city walls. Each covered enough land to provide food for several people. The glass houses marched away in rows, at least twelve in total. A high wrought-iron fence surrounded them, separated by stone columns with ornamental lanterns on top. At the line of the fence, the packed cobblestone of Karduniash's streets gave way to lush, manicured grass. There were probably gates to the fence, though she couldn't see them.

Belili looked both ways. She was on a larger street of the city and attracting attention. She was dirtier than the freemen and women, and many of the slaves. She would have ducked into a shop, but from the ornamentation and number of doorways with burly men and women guarding them, they may have charged her merely for entering. She needed a way to earn money if she would survive more than a day or two.

Her gaze drew back to the fenced garden and glass houses. The glass was warped and hard to see inside, but she could recognize the outlines of a tree, and what looked like prunae hanging from it.

She walked along the fence, keeping her pace steady. A glassblower's shop butted up nearly to the edge of the fence. Belili headed that way, steering clear of the few people around. One prunus could bring her money or favors. If she had another morus, she could appear right next to the tree, with maybe enough juice to move back outside the fence. But she didn't. She'd have to do this the old-fashioned way.

She came near the glassblower's shop, walking as if she knew exactly where she was going, then headed down an alley to the back. The lower section of the shop was rough marble, easy to grip with her boots, and the fence was within reach. She looked both ways again, then shimmied up and over the top of the fence, landing with a thump inside the grassy area. Fortunate she still wore pants and not the cotton dress.

She ran her fingers over the grass, greener than anything in the sheep-chewed fields outside Aricaba-Ata's house. Far off, a pair of people in leather stood stiffly to attention outside one of the glass houses. Guards. This wasn't an area open to the city. They weren't looking in her direction. She could just make out their brightly colored tabards, with five colors swirled together into a spiral: brown, red, black, silver, and purple. Only the Dyad would advertise control over all the colors of magical hair, including the Asha-Urmana. She crept to the glass wall, years of avoiding male slaves and guards letting her move silently.

Belili made sure no one was watching, then pressed her face against the glass, cupping her hands beside her cheeks.

Inside was not only a prunus, but several godfruit trees, in full fruit.

Belili gasped, then covered her mouth. She didn't think anyone had heard. She looked again.

All four types of tree were in the glass houses, and there were glass dividers between each one, sectioning each one into its own sanctuary. Citrons hung full and bright to her right, and she could see ice blocks misting on the ground inside, making water run down the inside of the windows. She moved around the perimeter, the temperature of the glass dropping as she came closer. Malae were around the perimeter of the circular building, also with ice. Belili moved farther, seeing the morus's roof open, the glass removed. Near the intersection of the morus and prunus sections was a locked glass door, to a glass hallway between the two trees' rooms.

She longed to go in and gather enough godfruit to sell and to use. In addition, she saw places that could be improved by a little pruning, after they stopped bearing. However, if they were all fruiting together, then were they all dormant at the same time? It seemed a waste to have all the magical godfruit come in at once, only to have to wait a full year. Her mind raced. Maybe there were trees around the circumference of the city that bore normally. Karduniash was big enough to support several plantings of godfruit trees.

What did the other glass houses hold? They were too close for godfruit trees to bear, given her experience on the orchard, yet she saw branching shapes within. Maybe they were ornamental? Belili crept to the next house, keeping one eye on the backs of the guards, far down the line.

It was full of fruiting trees too.

Belili squashed her nose against the glass, wondering if she had gone crazy. There was no way the trees were far enough apart to produce. Full, dark prunae hung before her eyes.

In the house after that one, the trees were not producing—not even the morus and prunus, which should have godfruit this time of year. The glass in those partitions shone wet with condensation, ice next to the trees that should be fruiting. This far south, and this time of year, ice would not be easy to come by. The expense to trick the trees into giving godfruit when the owners desired was more than she could imagine. If there was an unlocked door, she could—

"You there, stop!"

Belili spun, wide-eyed. She had watched the guards ahead, but not those behind. That would have gotten her killed, or worse, in the orchard. Stupid. One was walking determinedly toward her, pike held at an angle. His metal helmet caught the sunlight, and Belili shrank back, her palms sweating. Her eyes darted to the fence, to the nearest morus tree. No time. Running would only make him chase her.

"Who are you? How did you get it in?" The guard looked her over once he got close, taking in her stained clothes, her dirty hair. His pike lowered more. "This area is reserved."

Belili made herself show calm. *I will not be a slave again.* She could not let this guard put her in a cell. She had to be in control. The thought burned away any last reservations, and she straightened.

"Is there a problem?" she said, enunciating every word, as Aricaba-Ata did. As Tiamai had. "Am I not a noble?" She pushed her hair back, showing the brown stripe.

"Of...course," the guard answered, taken by surprise. The pike drooped, then came back up. "There are many nobles in Karduniash. Only those with the Dyad's permission are allowed here. Do you have that?" She hesitated, too long. "I will have to ask you to leave." He moved forward, trying to force her back.

Belili stood her ground. "I will not be cowed by you, freeman," she said, silently thanking Gemeti and weeks of lessons drilled into her and Kisa. She could push the fear away.

The guard paused again, staring openly at her clothes. "I do not think—"

"Does the lack of a clean dress mean I am no longer a noble?" Belili questioned, holding her nose high as she had seen Ubala do back in the orchard. She picked at her stained clothes. "Obviously I was set on by bandits—probably escaped slaves—while traveling." Her mind whirled, putting together pieces of the story she and Kisa had assembled to tell.

"I have traveled many weeks from our orchard on the edge of the Blasted Lands, to be in time for the festival"—what *was* the name of it? Gemeti had mentioned it—"the Prunus Festival, only to be set upon by ruffians two days from Karduniash." Belili took a step forward. Now the guard stepped back. "I would think the roads would be better cared for this close to the center of our power. I have had to wander through the city, my money stolen, and only a few odds and ends left in this pack." She hefted her bag. "If this is the reception I get from the Dyad, maybe I shall return to the Blasted Lands without giving them my present. And it shall be on your head." She wondered if the last bit might be over the top, but the guard hunched in on himself. Belili saw he was a few years younger than her.

"Ah—if you would be so good as to come with me, my lady, I am certain Mistress Arahuna can sort out your problems." He would foist her off on someone more important. "She may be able to find you accommodations within the palace. The Dyad would not wish you to"—

he swallowed—"leave without attending them." He bowed and turned. "This way, please."

Belili followed the young guard, keeping the smile buried beneath her calm exterior.

CHAPTER NINETEEN

Heightened Senses

Angry at the slavers' wickedness, the gods cursed the lands of the red, black, brown, and silver-haired people, making their godfruit trees wither and fail. The magical peoples, once favorites of Dumzi, Geshtna, Kigal, and Enta, were as powerless as the blonds they enslaved. Only those of the purple hair, who had taken no slaves, thrived.

Kisare tried to walk as Gemeti had showed her, back straight, head high. It was how a noble would walk, and she was free now, wasn't she? She caught herself hunching as a noble with a large streak of black turned her way and straightened with an effort.

It's not Enti-Ilzi. Aricaba-Ata and Hbelu are probably in the Dyad's palace already.

After walking for more than an hour, she had to admit she was lost. A mountain or small hill loomed over the city. She'd thought it would be easy to find where the guards took Gemeti, but the city was so big. Hbelu's village could have fit ten times in Karduniash, and the orchard was even smaller. She was revising her estimation of Aricaba-Ata. Was he even important enough to see the Dyad?

Finally, she stopped at an inn, The Cut Branch. The thought nagged something in the back of her mind, but she couldn't place it. So much had happened in the last two days.

The inside was much as she expected, with rushes on the floor, and lighting only where necessary. It was little better than her slave house. She could see the shine of wood and marble, hidden behind years of filth, and empty wooden holders on the walls. She smiled grimly. They would have held mirrors like the ones in Hbelu's residence, if the Asha-Urmana still lived here. They had probably been scavenged for looking-glasses long ago.

The innkeep was a tired-looking natural blond. He turned to her and bobbed his head when she approached the bar.

"What'll you have today, my lady?" he asked.

"I have a question," she said. She had no money on her, though she was hungry. She had to hope he gave out directions for free.

The innkeep only looked at her expectantly, hands clinking glasses around out of sight.

"Ah. As you see, I'm...that is, I am new to the city. Bandits attacked me on the road. I'm—I am looking for the guard station in hopes they may have recovered my things." She winced every time she slipped into casual speech. She hoped the innkeep didn't notice.

If he did, he gave no sign.

"Another dispossessed noble, huh? We get about three a week." He eyed her dress for a minute, then her hair. Kisare resisted the urge to straighten it. She hadn't had a chance to clean up.

He sighed. "Out the door, to the right. Take the second left and walk to the front gate. Then a left and a right on Guard Row. Tell them Nabu sent you."

"Thank you." Kisare tried to nod in a noble way and walked out of the inn.

With the man's directions, she found the guard station. Bored-looking guards stood on either side of the entrance, but they only nodded to her as she entered.

There was a desk in the front hall, and Kisare froze as she came close. The guard behind had been with the group that captured Gemeti. She almost left, but the guard looked up, taking in her Asha-Urmana-made dress.

"Problem, my lady?" he asked.

Kisare swallowed and stood tall. He must not remember her face. Sometimes it was good to be plain.

"Yes." She spoke carefully. "My sister and I were set upon by bandits along the road to Karduniash. I was wondering if you caught them, so I might get my possessions and money back."

"When was this?" The guard looked bored.

"A few days ago." She wanted to bring up Gemeti, but that would be suspicious.

"We have caught no bandits recently. Just an old woman trying to enter without papers." His expression darkened.

Kisare didn't know what else to say that wouldn't incriminate her. Bel was the better one at saying the right thing at the right time.

"Nabu says hello," she said, more for something to say than anything.

The guard's head snapped up. "Nabu, eh? Did he send you here?"

Kisare took a step back at the guard's gaze. "He gave me directions when I told him I lost my possessions on the road."

"Did he?" The guard got up. "Stay right there. I think we have found some of your things after all."

Kisare thought of the house where Gemeti had tried to get papers. Was Nabu working for the guards? She took a step backward. Then another.

"Find what you need?" a guard asked when she exited the building.

"Hm? Oh yes. I'll—I will be going now." Kisare walked away, aiming toward the massive pyramid.

"Stop her!" came a shout, but she was already far down the street.

Kisare ran.

Another hour later, she was lost again, though she had evaded the guards. Gemeti would have to wait until she learned more about the city. Maybe she could find Bel. Her sister was no doubt even more lost.

Similar to Neharda, free natural blonds ran the lower-class shops and market stalls. Those with a small streak of color in their hair were above them, and the nobles were at the top. Kisare could tell them on sight, trailed by one or more collared, bleached blond slaves. It was hard not to look down on those who still labored as prisoners. She was free now, but it had been so...*easy*...for her not to resist when she was in the orchard. If enough of them threw off their chains at once, the nobles could not stop them, magic or no. Kisare turned her attention to the building so she wouldn't have to look at the slaves. The prisoners.

The city was brighter and cleaner here. The buildings reminded her even more of Hbelu's village. Her dirty hair would earn her more notice, especially with her fancy cotton dress.

Kisare spared a look down. The hem was grimy from dust and dirt kicked up along the road, but the rest was still clean. It was more intricate than anything she had seen before, the slashes in the front showing silver backing beneath. The color carried into the detail on the bust and the arms, matching her silver hair.

She wondered if it was too fancy. The others she passed had good clothes on, but nothing like this. Maybe that was where some of the looks came from. Well, she would not change back now. Mushezibti-Lila had said it was a new style. She would start a trend.

Signs caught Kisare's eye. This section of the town had prosperous merchants, better inns, and better-painted signs. The one above her had a prunus tree in full bloom, looking real enough to smell the flowers.

The Blossoming Prunus. The nagging voice came back, louder. Gemeti, telling her to run, that they would meet at The Blossoming Prunus. But Gemeti was locked in the guard station.

Kisare hesitated, until she realized she was drawing looks. *A noble never hesitates.* Gemeti's lessons came back. *A noble takes what she thinks is hers.*

She pushed open the door.

The interior was not as dark as the last inn, but it was a bright spring day. She squinted, looking for the counter. It was off to one side, with a heavy-set woman behind it, a small streak of red pinned to prominence.

Not a blond then, thank all the gods. Kisare stopped walking. *She* had been blond until a couple of months ago. Now she suspected her own people. Would she buy a slave when she got enough money?

She shook her head, disgusted.

A whistle to one side stopped her. Someone at a table was waving. To the innkeep? No. To her.

"Gemeti?" It couldn't be the old woman—she was imprisoned.

The woman waved again, and Kisare went to her.

"You will get yourself killed before the day is out, if you do not stop behaving as a slave," Gemeti whispered to her when she sat down. "Do not stare like a rabbit caught eating the master's lettuce. A noble *takes* what she wants."

Kisare almost grinned at the words. "How did you get here? I checked at the guard station—"

"You went there? And you came out in one piece?" Gemeti fingered her chin with one hand, and Kisare could just see the remains of some stubble, like older women grew, under her makeup. "Maybe you are not as stupid as you look."

"How did you get out?"

Gemeti looked up instead, and Kisare saw the innkeep coming to their table.

"Anything for you? Early for a meal, but we have kaba, and the Prunus Festival is coming up, so you know what that means." The innkeep smiled.

"Two kabas, please," Gemeti said. Kisare winced. Now she would have to drink the vile stuff again.

"Would the young lady not like a small glass of prunus juice? It is cheap this week—on special. You could enjoy the scents of the city," the woman said, taking in Kisare's hair.

Gemeti paused. "How much?"

"Two kabas for a ha'penny, and the prunus juice is five coppers."

Kisare had no idea if that was expensive. She hadn't needed money so far. She knew Mushezibti-Lila's caravan made money from their clothes, but not more than that.

Gemeti considered, then dug out a leather pouch from under her layers. "The mistress would like both the kaba and the juice. Only the kaba for me, thank you." She laid out five copper coins and one more, clipped in half. Kisare thought about objecting, but it would look strange.

The innkeep nodded, scooped up the money, and left.

"You're not a slave," Kisare told Gemeti. "Why did you call me 'mistress'?" Her earlier thoughts on slaves came back and she blushed.

Gemeti patted her white hair. "Even free women servants call their employers master and mistress. I might be one of noble blood, but with no color in my hair. It is best to be vague."

Kisare frowned but asked the next question on her mind. "Prunus juice? Is that what I think it is? Shouldn't that be expensive?" She tried to keep her voice low. None of the tables nearby were occupied.

"It is expensive," Gemeti said. "It cost more than a meal for both of us, but the caravan gave me some money when we left. Enough for a diversion, since we used none on papers." She frowned. "You need to see how the nobles in Karduniash live. The Prunus Festival will happen in a few days. This glass is nothing compared to that."

The innkeep came back, holding two mugs in one hand and a very small glass in the other. She plopped the mugs down on the table but set the glass down with care in front of Kisare. It was full to the top with dark red liquid.

"Drink up quick, my lady, if you want the full potential." The innkeep left again.

Kisare looked to Gemeti, who only motioned to drink. "Quickly now. It loses potency in minutes." She was smiling.

Hesitantly, Kisare raised the glass to her lips and took a tiny sip. Fire washed through her and she gasped, barely keeping the liquid in her mouth. She set the glass down before she spilled it and held her hands out. Lightning tickled her arms, lighting their corner of the room.

Even that couldn't hold her attention. With each breath came a bounty of scents. Prunus, in her mouth. Then grasses on the floor. Alcohol. Wood. Sweat. Stone, and dust, and feet and metal and a breath of air as the door opened, carrying the sunlight from outside and maybe a light rain later in the day with mud on boots and the cobbles paving the road and—

Kisare swallowed convulsively and the scents faded.

Gemeti was smiling at her. "Good, eh?"

"Would you...like some?" She made to push the tiny glass, now only two thirds full, toward her, but Gemeti made a quick negative gesture.

"Do not offer it. Would a noble do that?" Gemeti's light eyebrows drew in. She carried on, her voice softer. "Besides, child, I have been to my share of Prunus Festivals. For black hair, it improves the sense of taste. I do not much want to taste my own mouth, or this kaba, more than I do already." She took a swallow from her mug. "Go on, enjoy. If we can get you into the Dyad's court before the parties start, you will have all the prunus juice you can stand." She leaned back and frowned. "We must meet up with your sister. She has the box, after all."

And find Hbelu, Kisare added. She still had no idea how to do that. The prince was integral to their plans, plus she had unfinished business with the man, never mind the box. *Did he mean what he said?*

* * *

Belili followed the Dyad's guard, now joined by another, toward the pyramidal bulk. Obviously, it was the palace. Where else would the Dyad make their home? It was like Hbelu's house, but much greater. Little balconies dotted the slopes, and walkways spiraled around it. Terraces and stairs added green around the base of the structure.

The pyramid was all of marble, smoothed by hand and time. It must have taken decades to build. Around it, like little moons, were smaller ziggurats and attached houses.

The guard who found her stayed in front, the other behind her, making Belili nervous. Both walked stiffly, and she followed, keeping her eyes on everything around for clues as to what to do next. She must act by Gemeti's teaching, so much a noble that no one suspected. She thought of Ilzi, the disdain with which he'd spoken to her and Ligish. Hopefully Hbelu had found a way to free himself and Ligish by now.

The guard pushed a wooded door open in a side ziggurat, only a little smaller than Hbelu's house. The second guard stayed outside by the door. Inside was a matronly woman dressed in cotton, with the five-color spiral dyed into the front. Clerks bent over tables behind her. The woman was writing on a sheet of parchment, much thinner than what Belili had seen Aricaba-Ata use.

The guard stood at attention, coughed. "Mistress Arahuna, another noble. This one claims she was robbed on the road. I will leave it in your hands." He made a hasty retreat.

The woman was nearly as old as Gemeti, though impressively beautiful, and she had a silver stripe, as large as Ilzi's black. A little bigger than her sister's expanded lock, in fact. This was a servant?

"And who do you claim to be?" Mistress Arahuna asked, her voice low and scratchy.

Belili took in a breath, then let her words fall as they may. One must not pause when spinning a lie. She kept her back straight, her head high, and her words clear. "I am from near the Blasted Lands and have traveled far to see the Dyad. I have a gift."

"For their Naming Day at the end of the Prunus Festival, I presume?" Arahuna asked. Belili didn't even pause.

"Of course. I meant to arrive earlier, but with the bandits..." She plucked at her cotton traveling clothes, as if to demonstrate what happened. "I have one dress left in my pack, along with the gift—the only items I could save, after my carriage was taken."

The mistress eyed Belili, who kept her face carefully blank. Her thumb flicked the stump of her little finger, and she stilled it against her side.

"The Blasted Lands, eh? Few come so far to visit the royal twins. What house are you?"

"Anagmeshu," Belili answered immediately, thinking of the little Asha-Urmana elder with the spectacles. "Anagmeshu-Bel." She stopped short of giving her full name. If Aricaba-Ata was here, he might investigate someone named "Belili."

"Show me your gift for the Dyad," Mistress Arahuna said, digging into her pouch. She brought out a single prunus.

Belili's mind raced at what the woman would accomplish with the godfruit, but she couldn't pause after getting this far. She swung her pack around and untied the strings at the top. Prunae increased the senses. Aricaba-Ata used them to improve his sight in the summer.

Belili slowly brought out the wooden box, warm to the touch.

Mistress Arahuna chewed the prunus, shivering as the juice separated from the godfruit. Little flashes of light ran down the outside of her cotton shirt and pants legs. She peered at Belili, and her nostrils flared. Belili forced her face neutral.

"What do you plan to do with this gift?" Arahuna mumbled around the prunus.

Belili had already said that. "I will give it to the Dyad."

The woman sniffed. "Truth. You intend to give it freely?"

What could she smell? Fear? Lies? Sweat? Belili focused on the simple truth. "I do not hope for any reward." True enough. "I give a prized gift to my rulers—something from my homeland, far away."

"Hmmpf." The woman chewed again. "Your intent is not to give this freely. I think you deceive in hope of a reward, but that is no surprise. I believe your claims of travel." She eyed Belili's stained clothes.

Mistress Arahuna swallowed, then spit the pit into her palm and tucked it in a different pouch. "Your story seems to fit. Have you any money, Anagmeshu-Bel? Unlikely if you were robbed."

Belili kept her shoulders back, refusing to give in to relief. She'd passed this woman's test, and she guessed Mistress Arahuna was no mere servant. She wondered where her placement was under the Dyad. "I have no money, but I saved one of my dresses, so I will have a decent set of clothes." She put down the box and removed her dress from the pack. The slashes of brown opened under the body of the dress, showing off the complexity of the pattern.

Mistress Arahuna looked impressed for the first time. "This is Asha-Urmana make, and not a style I have seen. Maybe you do hail from the Blasted Lands. The Dyad always appreciates their subjects from the outskirts of the realm paying a visit." She rubbed her hands together. "Yes, I think you will be a welcome distraction for the royal twins."

"Ah. One more thing," Belili said. "I have a sister. She was traveling with me, but we were separated after the attack. She will find her way here as well."

The woman's eyes lit up. "Two from the Blasted Lands. The Dyad will be mighty pleased at that. Both Samsu-Iluna-Nur-Sibi and Samsu-Iluna-Nur-Ishta enjoy the presence of new flesh around the palace. This way they will not have to share." She turned around. "Well then. Follow me and we will find you a room here."

Belili followed the woman, wondering what her last words meant.

The room Mistress Arahuna found was large but faced an interior corridor. Another attendant, this one a true blond though with no slave collar, showed her the way, opened the door, then scurried off.

There were no windows to the outside, and Belili had to fight down a stab of claustrophobia every time she looked at the wall where she imagined a window should be. The room was comfortable, pleasantly warm though on the interior of the pyramid, and several levels up. There was no fireplace, as there was no place for the smoke to go, but there were several candle holders, and a slanted skylight in the ceiling far above that poured daylight into the chamber. The room must intersect an outside wall further up. Belili also saw a set of openings around the edge of the floor. She investigated, and found they blew a gentle breeze of warm air.

There was a large four-poster bed made of light wood to match the marble walls. One carved malus sat atop each post, covered with gold leaf. Belili eased onto the mattress, which felt as if stuffed with something soft. Feathers? How many birds were needed to fill a mattress? There were three carved chairs with padded seats, an end table, and a larger table near the door. On it was a silver plate, with a cover of beaten silver, embossed with outlines of godfruit. Belili lifted the cover, then nearly dropped it.

Underneath was a pile of godfruit. Belili's eyes widened. One malus, one citron, a handful of mori, and several large prunae. Her hand dove out. Nobles at the palace were *given* these things? What about servants? Surely slaves would steal the godfruit, either to sell or eat. The thought flashed through her mind before she thought better of it.

She took a prunus, the only one she had never tasted before. Would she have a choice when she used it? Her thumb absently rubbed the stump of her little finger. She put the prunus, still on its long stem, in her mouth, and pulled. The stem came off easily, and she bit down, thinking of her brown hair. Juice squirted, and she shivered, leaning back on the bed, her eyes half-closing. She opened them to see little arcs of lightning jumping down her body, small details much clearer than before.

A thump sounded in the hall and she started. Then another. There was a constant *whoosh* of air coming from the ducts in the room. The thumps were getting louder, and the bed creaked alarmingly every time she moved.

Hearing. It improved my hearing. Carefully, so as not to spill any juice, she spit the seed out into her hand.

The thumps got closer, on a beat. One, two, one two.

Then there was a tremendous pounding at the door, and Belili clutched at her chest, willing her heart to slow. They had figured it out! They were beating the door in!

No, her hearing was more acute. She got up, wincing at the dreadful creaking the bed made, and walked toward the door, her own heartbeat almost covering the sounds of her leather shoes hitting the floor.

Belili paused by the door. There was still magic in the juice. She couldn't *waste* it.

She opened the door with a full mouth, wincing at the creak of the hinges.

Outside was a large man, a noble, older than her and dressed in cotton pants and shirt, both dyed a rich brown. He had a coat on over top of his shirt, of a strange, shiny material. It was green, with a blue emblem embossed on it. The emblem was a...worm?

"GOOD DAY, MY LADY," said the man, and Belili stepped back, swallowing. The magic faded, as did the noises surrounding her.

The man looked down to her hand, which still held the stem and prunus pit, back up to her face, and then to her hair. "My apologies. I see you were preparing for the upcoming festival. Has the magic gone?"

Belili nodded slowly, wondering what he meant. What he intended. *Always show calm. Don't let them see.* Then she took in his hair. On one side was a large lock of red. On the other was an equally large lock of silver. Two colors! Belili's hand went to her lock of brown. She didn't think others—

"Forgive me," the man said. He must have taken her shock for something else. "I have you at a disadvantage. I am Isbi-Bar-Marut, master of the Dyad's silkworms." He made a small bow over one pale and manicured hand. "Gossip at the palace has you all the way from the

Blasted Lands, and I would be remiss if I were not the first to invite such an esteemed guest to the Prunus Festival." He looked expectant.

Belili's mind whirled, thinking of anything to give her more time. Gossip? Already? He had the air of many of Aricaba-Ata's noble friends. Insistent, gracious, determined.

"Please, come in." Belili held her face still with an effort but backed away from the door so he wouldn't be too close when he entered. She had to find out more about him. He was probably high up in the palace. Anyone with two colors in their hair, three names, and the Dyad's master of anything had to be powerful. Could she use this man as a shield, as she had the guard outside? The godfruit was near—she could take the time to determine his motives.

Sometime later, Belili laughed at Isbi-Bar-Marut's joke. It wasn't funny, but laughing kept him talking, rather than acting. The man was a complete bore. At least he spoke before attempting other, more physical activities.

She had learned Isbi-Bar-Marut was a Duke Minor, liked gardening and buying slaves, and his jacket was made from excretions of a worm which only lived in and ate morus trees. Belili barely kept the horror from her face at that.

He had invited her three more times to the Prunus Festival. Would he be an adequate way to deflect more...persistent...nobles? He was no Ilzi, for certain.

"You see," Isbi-Bar-Marut continued, "old Nesbet wasn't waiting for my mother, she was *hiding* my mother from my father. Oh!" He chuckled and wiped an eye watery from mirth. Belili smiled pleasantly. She itched to use the other godfruit on the tray.

"But really, my dear, you must come with me to the Prunus Festival. It starts tomorrow, and I find myself quite without a companion."

I wonder why. Belili did not roll her eyes. This man was not so cunning as he thought. She could manipulate him. Her heart raced at the prospect of fooling this noble. Controlling him.

"You would honor me with your presence. What say you?"

Another indirect refusal would lead to more direct actions. "I...believe that would be enjoyable, Isbi-Bar-Marut," she said, keeping tightness from her voice.

"Please, call me Marut."

"Marut then." She nodded to the silver tray. Change the subject, avoid stated expectations. "I have never been to the Prunus Festival. It seems strange to celebrate only one godfruit."

Marut waved a hand. The fringe of lace around the edge of his silk jacket wobbling. "It is only a name, as the prunus expands the senses and makes the party so much more enjoyable. All godfruits are represented. The servants have been working the royal gardens overtime for weeks to get ready."

"You mean the glass houses outside the palace?" Belili asked.

"Wondrous things, yes? You cannot imagine the pure decadence of the party." Marut clasped his hands. "We will have such fun. I have the fortune of enjoying both sight and smell by the prunus, of course," he said, gesturing first to his red lock and then the silver. "A few have three colors, though usually small locks. The Dyad themselves have four. Oh, to be Sibi or Ishta tomorrow. Well, everyone wishes that."

Belili broke in before the man could take a breath and continue. "I am not familiar with the Dyad," she said. "Would you be able to introduce me?"

"Ah, you are in for a treat." Marut waggled his eyebrows at her, reminding Belili of his morus-eating worms. He had made no move toward her after sitting, and she relaxed, just slightly. This buffoon would keep other, more predatory, nobles away. "I am familiar with both the royal twins. Their parents were good friends of my mother, and my grandmother, since she was their cousin, on her paternal side." He leaned across the table and placed his hand on hers. Belili's face went rigid, but she forced herself not to pull away. She *would* be the one in control. "Many eagerly watch the Dyad for indication of children. Sibi has always been vocal in her disgust of infants, though they both know the royal line must continue. It is not that they do not enjoy each other's company, you see." Marut wiggled his eyebrows again, and realization dawned on Belili as to the Dyad's relationship.

"There have been rumbles in the court of a child in the last year. We are all eagerly waiting for Sibi and Ishta to announce the young thing, so we can see what all the secrecy has been about. Oh, rumors are flying, from a secret pregnancy and a child raised in distant seclusion, to adoption from a favored noble, to another sibling, deformed and kept secret. I think the last has an element of romance. What about you?"

Belili dove into the brief pause, her mind churning with the information from Mushezibti-Lila. Could this be the captured Asha-Urmana child?

"It sounds fascinating," she said, consciously showing interest rather than disgust. She took her hand back, hesitating only a moment before patting his lightly. "Well, if I am to go with you tomorrow, I must get some rest. It sounds as if this festival goes late into the night, and I will not want to miss a bit." She stood up. Marut followed her motion, talking again.

"The whole night. It is two days long." He shook clasped hands at her again. "Ah, the others will be so jealous to see you with me."

"They will." Belili moved toward him, forcing him back a step. *Control.* "I shall need much sleep beforehand, as I doubt I will get *any* during the festival." She gave him the best smile she could, filling it with promises.

Marut's mouth went slack for a moment and his eyes widened. "Just so, Lady Bel," he said. "Perhaps we should—"

"I shall see you tomorrow. When does the festival start?" Belili kept her expression neutral, pushing him back another step.

"At sundown, but—"

"Then I will see you at sundown. I shall work to contain my excitement." She pivoted around him and opened the door. "My lord."

Marut looked like he might push back, then bowed deeply to her and stepped out of her room. "Until tomorrow."

Belili closed the door in his face, and then slumped against it, heart racing, palms and back soaked with sweat. She had survived, and she had a shield. She waited for several minutes and peeked out. He was gone. She closed the door, locked it, and contemplated the tray of godfruit. It was time to find out what other surprises the palace held.

CHAPTER TWENTY

Colors of Strength

All but the Asha-Urmana fled their lands, now devoid of godfruit. They went to the only other place with magic—the land where they had been created, and where their cousins of the purple hair lived. They came as beggars, as refugees, willing to learn all the purple-haired people could teach them, as they had taught the blonds.

The nobles chained Hbelu to the rolling cage the night after the prisoners fought to the death, to "better commune with his subjects."

Belatsu was awake as well, and Hbelu heard the clinking of the bars as she turned, trying to find a place less uncomfortable to sleep. With the death of two of the prisoners, there was now room—barely—for the rest to sit or curl into a ball. The others were, if not asleep, then silent.

"It is not your fault," Hbelu spoke to the stars above him. The sounds in the cage ceased.

"I killed one of my brothers, and I would do it again," Belatsu growled back. "If I did not, the fourcolors would have killed both of us. Now I can pass information to those who follow."

Hbelu let out a slow breath. "You have heard them too."

"A babe could hear them, though these fourcolors fight amongst themselves so much their scouts cannot help but miss things."

"Will it be tomorrow, or the next day?"

"That I do not know." The woman shifted again, and Hbelu heard her stifle a groan as some injury came in contact with a bar.

"Then we will wait and see."

* * *

The next day was another agony of walking, Hbelu's feet protesting even his slow pace. The land was changing, and he heard the difference in birdsong. With a malus, he could have lifted a local animal's spirit to show him the best game and foraging.

Ata passed him at midday, clapping one hand on his shoulder.

"Are you ready for tonight's show?"

Hbelu did not answer.

"Two of your caravanners will die every night, to keep my noble brethren amused until we get to Karduniash. I will not have them sabotaging my plans with petty bickering." So, the man admitted the base personalities of his compatriots, if not his own.

"And then?" Hbelu asked.

"Then what?" The large fourcolor looked confused.

"When we reach Karduniash, and you present me to your Dyad, what then? Will you have all the riches you need? Will your...noble brethren take their share? Even Ilzi is due compensation, yes?"

The red-hair threw out his chest. "That is not your concern, caravanner." But he did not sound sure. Ata walked on, and Hbelu let the moment cheer him.

Later in the day, Ziggurmas-Su passed, trailed by his captive blonds, the pregnant one stumbling. The red-hair Sutur-Cit was by him, sporting a full, trimmed, and curled beard. The black-hair complained loudly.

"Cit, we have all seen the mori. What is your source? Surely the trees are bearing? There will be enough for all in the capital."

Sutur-Cit shook his head, red lock bouncing with his shoulder-length hair. It was curled, like the beard, in some manner that forced the red lock to the top—likely the work of his prisoners. "I have my sources, Su. If I give them up, then what is left?" He picked up a stick, dragging it across the cage bars. The prisoners jerked upright at the noise. "Do not send that rat Ilzi again." He dropped the stick and held one hand up to stop Su from speaking, "I know it was you who sent him. I count my godfruit very carefully."

"Yet you waste it on wagers and frivolous pursuits," Hbelu interrupted. "You look down on my people, who supply you with your toys and rich clothes."

"Lo, the prince speaks," Su said, turning with a smile Hbelu did not like. The black-hair gestured his collared blonds forward, took a glass of wine one was holding, and wet his lips. "How would your people spend power, if not by showing *how* you are powerful?"

"To heal my people, if I were the one with black hair," Hbelu growled. "To make your daily camp a better place, to move piles of kindling, had I red hair and a morus."

Cit scoffed. "That is why we have slaves." He gestured to the collared blonds. "They do the work that keeps our civilization running, to leave nobles time to progress and solidify our hold on this land."

Hbelu felt his face heat. "The land blessed by the gods, when all others were cursed. This land is rightfully—"

"The gods may as well be a child's tale," Su broke in. "They may have given us godfruit, but they have not cared about their *children* in centuries."

"Yet the godfruit that fuels your power still grows."

"Which is how we know the gods love nobles more than caravanners," Cit said. "If they did not accept and support our efforts"— he pulled a blond prisoner forward by one arm; the women shook, her head down—"then why are we the might of this land?"

"This land," Hbelu said. "But not your original homes—those we call the Blasted Lands. You destroy all and create nothing but blight."

Su waved a hand. "This is the only part that matters," he said, pointing at his streak of black.

"You destroy that too, by breeding with those who had no magic, who you collar and subject to torture. Your children have less magic than you." Hbelu knew he had hit a nerve by the sour expressions on the two nobles faces, and by the prisoners' stance. He was sure there was no coincidence all Su's blond prisoners were female, and Ziggurmas-Su's wife had not accompanied them.

"Yet again," Sutur-Cit said, "we are the ones with the slaves, and you are tied to a cage." One hand massaged his beard.

Hbelu opened his mouth to deny the accusation, but a call rang out. "Be alert! Something moves in the trees."

Another call, on the other side: "Over here too!"

The fourcolor nobility looked around, nervous, and Su shooed his prisoners toward the center of the column.

Hbelu smiled. "I am correcting my situation. Are you?"

At that, a heavily armored Asha-Urmana burst from the woods to his side.

"A scout!" a soldier announced. She pressed her helmet on her head and unlimbered a sword from her side. The two fourcolor nobility froze only a moment, and Hbelu gave them a little credit for their speed. Su pulled a whip from his side, while Cit had mori to hand in a moment.

The Asha-Urmana rushed forward, engaging the soldier, who stepped in front of Su and Cit. She was no scout. These were full soldiers of the caravans, with breastplate, spears, and sword.

"To me!" Ata called, forming a group of soldiers around him. Purple-haired soldiers emerged from either side of the woods overhanging the main road—these were shock troops of Mushezibti-Lila's caravan, if he read their markings right. The one on the other side of the road was a different group. Their attacks were coordinated, but unpracticed. They did not know each other well. Hbelu limped close to the rolling cage as it sped up. The oxen pulling it were not happy about their change in situation. As he stumbled, a hand grasped the back of his tunic, shredded and stained from travel.

"We are here for you and the others, Ishkun-Dim-Hbelu," an alto voice said. He looked back in time to see olive skin and braids of purple hair hidden beneath a helmet. Then a sword sang and the pressure pulling him forward ceased. He shook the rope free of his chains.

"These manacles will take longer to remove," Hbelu said, reaching for the cage door. It was difficult with the metal surrounding his wrists, but he managed to bump the latch.

"Back, my Prince," the woman said, and she struck the lock with her spear, sending pieces flying. The fourcolors' metalsmithing was not equal to steel forged by Ziral-Barital's caravan.

The prisoners churned out of the cage, the strongest helping the others. They left another woman who had died that morning—not Belatsu. The dead woman's head lolled to the side and Hbelu promised to remember her in his next prayers to the gods.

Free for the moment, Hbelu took stock of the scene on the road. Soldiers penned the fourcolors from both sides, but Ata had rounded the nobility up in the center, surrounded by a ring of troops. Hbelu saw Cit moving between the others, handing out mori from his pouch, but also what looked like larger godfruit. So, the fourcolors would work together in times of need.

There were seven of the nobility in the center circle, counting Ata and Ilzi. The red-hairs—Ata and Cit—threw out their hands.

In response, the spears of one group of Asha-Urmana shock troops flew out of their hands, and the fourcolor soldiers stepped in, stabbing. Another fourcolor soldier saw Hbelu free and paused, but moved to an Asha-Urmana warrior. So Hbelu was not a target for the soldiers.

Even as he prayed for his injured people, he reached for a dropped spear. The manacles he wore restricted his movement and exhaustion made his grip shaky, but he grasped the center of the spear's shaft, wrapping the chain over the haft. It would have to do.

Another group of Asha-Urmana, this one all male, left the shadows of the forest behind him. It was standard practice for the lighter, faster women to lead attacks, followed by heavier men, who could bring crushing force to the fighting once the enemy was pinned.

Cit and Ata ate more godfruit. How much did they have left? There was a great crack and the limb of a great mango, far overhead, dropped on the male band of warriors. Hbelu leapt forward. His people could not lose their advantage.

He struck a slower soldier, turning the sword aside with a clumsy stab from his spear and splitting his breastplate. The soldier died with a surprised look, as if it was not fair for Hbelu to fight back so chained.

But Ilzi and Su, the black-hairs, had godfruit too. They stared in his direction and the pressure in his mind kept him from raising his weapon. An Asha-Urmana woman next to him stopped, shaking her head, and the fourcolor soldier she faced slashed at the intersection of neck and torso. The Asha-Urmana went down in a splash of red.

The nobility had few mori, and Hbelu knew they would not waste magic on their soldiers when their lives were in danger. Three more Asha-Urmana went down under combined mental attacks of the red and black hairs. Hbelu spun, stabbed, and dodged, nearly dropping the spear as his chains restricted his hand movements. He merged with the remains of the male warrior contingent, now at the front line.

He could no longer see the nobility, hidden behind the soldiers fighting, but his people pushed the fourcolors back. Hope rose in his chest. Hbelu slapped a sword aside, shifting left. At least they had left his feet unbound. Adrenaline made the pain in his feet fade, though he would regret moving so fast later. With this fight won, the caravans would gain confidence. He ducked, then stabbed again, blinking away a splash of arterial blood. They would support the plans he had pushed for years to remove the fourcolors from power. He rushed to the next fourcolor soldier.

A golden-skinned woman in fine cotton clothing appeared before him, a slash of silver hair reflecting the overhead sun as she pivoted impossibly through three spear strikes, and, almost delicately, inserted her fingers into the throat of the Asha-Urmana warrior next to him. The man crumpled as she threw a blast of air into another warrior's face, blinding him, and striking.

Hbelu sidestepped the fourcolor woman, his head pivoting. Three other warriors came with him unasked, a male and two of the shock troop women. The nobility had a few citron and malus pieces left. Fortunately, this was the only wily silver-hair among their number—likely why they had gifted her with such precious out-of-season fruit.

He aimed toward the ragged ring of soldiers surrounding the nobility. He could barely make out three, four, five of the nobility in the middle. The silver-hair had moved invisibly into combat, but where was the seventh—?

A blast of fire burst to his left, from the center of the circle. Hbelu tried to block out the cries of the burned. He shoved forward with his guardians.

There was a shout, and Hbelu turned. A warrior thrust his spear at an unprotected man—a brown-hair nobility. The warrior's spear broke with a screech against the skin of the brown-hair. More citron. How much godfruit did these fourcolors squirrel away? It must be rotten or dry with months of storage, unless they had a special shipment from the capital. The magic would work somewhat, even with rotten juice, if one could keep from vomiting.

The brown-hair—a stocky and arrogant man named Heabani-Danos—swiped the broken spear away from the warrior and punched her. There was a crack of bone. The woman who attacked him gasped, and fell, her chest hollowed.

Then Danos faded so Hbelu could see fighting behind him and stepped through the male Asha-Urmana. He grabbed Hbelu by the wrist, but even as Hbelu tried to jerk the man off balance with his manacled wrists, the man's hand became insubstantial again, and Hbelu stumbled. Danos followed him, pushing and fading away when Hbelu stabbed him. His arms became solid, and he plucked the spear from Hbelu's grasp.

"I have the prince," the fourcolor shouted, and the soldiers adjusted their lines, the fourcolor nobility in the middle ready to receive him.

"To Ishkun-Dim-Hbelu," came a high voice. Asha-Urmana converged on him, though Hbelu tried to shoo them away, his manacles restricting him. The objective was not only his safety, but the removal of the fourcolors. Danos pulled him forward.

"Save the prisoners!" Hbelu called out, but the Asha-Urmana soldiers did not listen. Too many purple-haired bodies were in the road. The two women's columns were decimated, and the male troops nearly as ragged. All were moving toward him. The fourcolors pivoted, ready. Godfruit changed hands among the nobility. With three types of godfruit and four hair colors, the nobility could control the battle even against an overwhelming force. It was the problem his people faced every time. The rank of soldiers shifted, and a hail of ice shards sought targets in his people's necks and faces. Fire bloomed from the other side, enveloping a woman of Mushezibti-Lila's caravan.

His people were losing, again, and Hbelu spun to Danos. The citron could not last so long—the man did not have that much color. Though they were close to the other nobility, he felt the man's grip solidify and Hbelu pushed. Danos snarled, trying to fade again, but Hbelu saw failure in his eyes. He shifted his grip, wrapping chains around the fourcolor's wrist, then spun to the side so the man went off balance. Hbelu thrust forward, and Danos toppled into three shock troops. The fourcolor died with Asha-Urmana spears in his heart.

But it was too little. The remaining nobility were protected. The silver-hair was unseen with a morus, but the other six were clustered together. The ring of soldiers around them broke, ranging out into the remaining warriors, fencing Hbelu off from his people. Three armored fourcolors flanked him and he tried to engage them, but he had no spear, no warrior guards, and the manacles restricted his movement. In moments, the three soldiers surrounded him and grasped his manacles. One drew back a fist and Hbelu winced as the blow hit his solar plexus. He gasped, fighting for breath as the three dragged him fully into the circle of fourcolor nobility.

Inside the circle of troops, Ata came forward, smiling, his umber face flushed with excitement. He stank of blood, metal, and overripe fruit.

"All the self-professed superiority of you *caravanners*," he sneered. "How can you say our position is weak?" He waved a hand and Hbelu turned, though he did not want to.

His people lay dead and dying. Three contingents of troops, from at least two caravans. He looked away as soldiers stabbed a prone figure, trying to struggle to her knees.

There were shapes in the woods, so some of his people survived. He thought the prisoners in the cage also escaped. Belatsu would return to her caravan. Hbelu shrunk in, shoulders sagging. The soldiers still clung to him, as if he would throw them off and run for freedom, but Hbelu could not have moved if he tried. If this was all warriors of his people achieved against the fourcolors, then it was little wonder the conquerors had pushed the Asha-Urmana from Karduniash, to the corners of their former realm. The fourcolors had weaker magic with every passing generation, yet they defeated trained warriors when ambushed. What of his plans for the capital? He should be free, heading back to a caravan to plan his assault, not listening to the ramblings of an overbearing fourcolor.

"We told him earlier, Ata," Su chimed in. "He would not believe the rightness of our methods."

"Though Danos is dead," Cit said, coming to their little group. His beard was not so neat now. Hbelu tried to feel joy for his one achievement, but he could not find the emotion. His head fell forward.

"Danos was overconfident and an ass," Ata said to the other red-hair. "If he had not risked his neck showing off and wasting our godfruit, then he would not have died."

"What of Ahati-Waqrat?" Su asked. "She also used our old citrons and malae, and I believe that pile is hers." He pointed to a mound of corpses in the near distance, male and female alike. A few soldiers were stripping equipment from the bodies. Hbelu wanted to strangle them. If only he did not have these manacles on. If only he had succeeded.

"Yes, Waqrat did well, but now we have *no* godfruit," Ata said. "What if the caravanners attack again? We have lost many soldiers." He gave Hbelu a searching glare.

Hbelu knew his people would not attack again, not soon. They would lick their wounds as they had every time they were defeated by the fourcolors, retreat and recoup for another hundred years until Hbelu was dead and gone and the box with the seed of the fifth godfruit was a treasure in the Dyad's museum. They had been beaten too many times.

"We will press on to Karduniash," Ata decided. Ilzi joined them, as did the golden-skinned silver-haired woman, Waqrat, and another red-haired woman, who had done little. She was the wife of a fourcolor who had declined to come, and Hbelu could tell she had never been in combat. She was pale and shaking, though none of the other fourcolors offered solace.

"My soldiers are tired and need rest," Waqrat said. She flicked blood from the ruined sleeve of her tunic, though there was little point.

"No, we need to move," Ata countered. "I will not stay here in case the caravanners attack again. If you had not used up our citrons, then Su and Ilzi could have refreshed the soldiers."

Waqrat turned up her nose. "Those rotten things? I was hard-pressed not to spit them out and could not even swallow the juice. Why were you saving such things? We will be to Karduniash soon."

"You would not be here to speak if you had not used them, but little point bickering about it now. They are gone." Ilzi slipped into the conversation like grease, turning the fourcolors away from fighting. If he had not been there, Hbelu might have fomented more division. "The real concern is him." Ilzi nodded to Hbelu, who raised his head, looking the black-hair in the eye. Ilzi had a self-satisfied smirk on his face. "Maybe we should put him in the cage, now his fellow caravanners have emptied it for us."

Cit and Waqrat both laughed, while Ata got a curious look on his face. The red-haired woman stared out at the piles of dead, shaking.

Any appeasement of these fourcolors' baser natures would only strengthen their abuse. He straightened, not letting his fatigue show, keeping the anger from his face.

"I believe you have a point, Cousin," Ata said. He turned to Cit and Su. "Get the soldiers ready. I care not if they are tired. We march until nightfall. We will be in Karduniash in the next few days, before the Prunus Festival begins. While that happens, I will...correct the problem with our prisoner."

"What of the dead?" Waqrat asked. "Will we leave them here for carrion?"

"We should bring them as gifts to the Dyad, to fertilize their godfruit trees, but we have no room," Ata said.

"The slave's cage is quite large," Ilzi suggested with a smile.

Su waved a hand. "I will handle it. My blonds need work to remind them this is not their vacation."

Ata nodded. "Find a new lock. We will not keep our prize in the open any longer."

* * *

The next four days were a blur for Hbelu, locked in the rolling cage, filled with the stinking corpses of his people. After the second, even he no longer thought of them as such, only objects he wished to be free of.

In some small compensation, the fourcolor nobility ceased taunting him, likely because they did not wish to be near the corpses. The entire line of soldiers—those left after the fight—was pressing hard for the capital. There would be no more opportunity for attack, especially once they began to see houses with regularity. His people did not come this close to Karduniash in numbers. Though that would change once all the caravans were in place.

Only once did he receive information, and only at a cost. It was the day before they passed through the great Asha-Urmana-built wall that surrounded the ancient city. Hbelu was tired, so tired, and filthy. His body ached from leaning against the metal bars, and he had picked up a nest of fleas. They had not let him out of the cage since the attack. Fortunately, they fed him little food or water, so he did not foul himself too much.

Hbelu's head was down, watching the road pass by. At least his injured feet had time to heal.

"Ishkun-Dim-Hbelu." The voice was sweet, coaxing. He wanted to listen to it.

"Ishkun-Dim-Hbelu." His head came up, watching the Asha-Urmana woman who trotted beside the cage, something held in one cheek. She held a large cotton bag, stained with dark juice on the bottom. Hbelu's head swung to the soldiers walking all around. A few looked in their direction, faint frowns on their faces. The woman—she had a full head of purple—put another morus into her mouth, chewed. "I bear a message from Ziral-Barital's caravan." She paused, then turned to the soldier who had hesitantly adjusted his course to intercept theirs.

"Ma'am," the soldier said, "I am afraid the nobles said you may only have three minutes with the prisoner." He gave a wide smile. "I hope that will be enough."

"Quite enough," the woman answered, smiling back. She ate another morus. "Thank you for the excellent job you are doing here. Please convey my appreciation for the security surrounding your troop. Are you certain I may not take this man?"

The soldier slumped, his eyes moistening with tears. "I must refuse, Davci. Aricaba-Ata apologizes, but he says he needs this prisoner for what is to come."

Davci smiled once more, though Hbelu saw her hands clench. "Perfectly acceptable. Please let the four—the nobles know I will come by to help them forget this diversion in a few minutes. Have them gather at the front of the line." Another morus. Her bag was already mostly empty—too risky for her to give him any. She would have to hurry before the influence of the godfruit wore off. If only their ability could command the fourcolors to do something opposite to their wishes, as a strong black-hair could do.

"Yes ma'am." The soldier trotted off, and Davci's attention was fully on Hbelu. He felt more lucid than in days.

"What is the message?" His voice was gravel. He strained to keep his head up.

"The sisters are traveling with a Nehardan woman who shelters escaped blonds. They left Mushezibti-Lila's caravan a few days ago, headed to Karduniash. All caravans will all be in place by the end of the Prunus Festival, our scouts and warriors ready at the gate. You need only signal when the fifth godfruit has been activated, and we will be your strong arm." She ate another godfruit. To keep up the charismatic influence of the morus on so many soldiers must have cost her caravan a good portion of their godfruit—ones that could have been used when they went against Karduniash.

"I will be ready." Though he did not know how, or what the seed would do once he and the Dyad had touched it. He sent another plea to all four gods that the sisters and their guide would find their way safely. How would he signal? Much would change when they reached Karduniash.

He showed none of his concern. He was so tired, mere expressions were an effort. He only had to get into the city. Once there, many factions could help him.

"Then I will cover my tracks, and report back to Ziral-Barital. Stay strong." Davci bowed her head and trotted to the front of the column.

Hbelu went back to watching his feet, and the road beneath the cage.

* * *

They entered Karduniash at the end of the fourth day of travel after the ambush, all weary, the soldiers grumbling. Ziggurmas-Su complained about not having any more citrons to heal the blisters on their feet.

Ata guided them to the massive ziggurat presiding over the city. Even after they passed the walls, it was another hour and a half of marching. Houses stretched out before it, relics of Hbelu's people, stolen centuries ago. All through Karduniash, fourcolors and their blond and collared prisoners walked, in all stages of finery. Servants ran errands. Those with small amounts of magical hair worked in service to those with more. Hbelu saw a caretaker corralling a small group of children in a park, each with a significant lock of color.

When they reached the garden surrounding the palace, the nobles were questioned, though with such a large group they were accepted easily as guests for the Prunus Festival. The soldiers unhitched the rolling cage of dead Asha-Urmana from the oxen, Hbelu taken from it. He staggered, until his legs remembered how to support him. A group of prisoners pulled his cage around the corner of the ziggurat, where he could just see the edge of the fabled glass houses. Ata watched it go, thoughtful.

Hbelu's fists clenched almost beyond his control. "You steal our city, and our godfruit trees," he said, and a soldier jerked him forward. Hbelu resisted, pulling the woman back toward him. Another two joined in, though the fourcolor nobility looked on disdainfully. Ata frowned at him, as if he should behave himself now they had reached the capital.

"Now you even take the bodies of my dead, with their greater magic, to fertilize the stolen trees—" Cit casually backhanded him, and Hbelu fell into the woman trying to hold him back.

"Control your caravanner, Ata," Su said. "He will be worth nothing to us if the Dyad thinks him too undisciplined to receive as gift."

"Yet he is *my* prize," Ata told the black-hair. Hbelu wiped at a split lip, bending his head to reach his manacled hands. There was an abundance of godfruit in the capital, the court of the Dyad lazy by years of peaceful rule. Surely he could acquire a morus or citron easier than when traveling between cities.

"We would be happy to take over his care," Waqrat said. She flashed her teeth at Hbelu. "I expect I could break him in for you."

"The idea is not without merit," Ilzi added. "He has caused enough trouble for us, including losing one of my slaves and two of yours including my potential—"

"Your potential nothing." Ata took a step toward his smaller cousin, who backed away. "Both sisters *and* this one are my property."

"I am not—" Hbelu began, but Ata rode over him.

"And they will continue to be my property. That is the end of this!" He swiped a hand through the air, cutting through whatever Cit and Ilzi were about to say. "Bring him." Ata stalked farther into the palace, and the woman jerked on the rope threaded through Hbelu's manacles, making him stumble forward. All the soldiers kept quiet, their heads down. They had seen Ata's anger in the past. Hbelu would have argued more, but it took all his concentration to trip up a flight of steps at the soldier's fast pace. The other fourcolor nobility took up the argument behind Ata's retreating form, walking fast to keep up.

The passages of the palace were familiar, in a way, though on a massive scale. At each turn and set of stairs, groups of soldiers split off, heading for their rooms. The fourcolor nobility kept climbing. There were six now the brown-hair, Danos, was dead. Ata, Cit, and the timid female—he had never learned her name—of the red. Ilzi and Su of the black. Waqrat of the silver.

Finally, all the soldiers were disbanded to their rooms for the night, depending on their status. Su's collared prisoners took Hbelu's lead, though the two females, one pregnant and both exhausted, could never have stopped him if he wished to escape. The fourcolor nobility would do that. He lifted his head to a window looking out over the lights of the city. One of the moons—Shir-Gal—was high and mostly full. He could see the Asha-Urmana construction laid out before him. He would bring his people back to this city. Their city.

Up more stairs, and the red-haired female broke off. Up another level and Cit, Su, and Waqrat turned back to Ata and Ilzi near a door much like all the others on the upper levels—wood, with ornamentation, and a symbol.

"This is your apartment," Su said, motioning his prisoners to come to him. The women obeyed meekly. "You and Ilzi have quarters here, Waqrat is on the next level, and Cit and I will share a room above her." Hbelu felt the black-hair's eyes on him and stared back. He was so close to his objective, and yet so much else must happen. He was not worried. Not yet.

"If you would give up the caravanner to us, I am certain we could find you a place in a more...prestigious location," Cit added, running a finger down the sides of his beard.

Ata shook his dark head. "I told you. The prince is my gift to give. You have helped, I admit, and will share in the favor of the Dyad, but he is *mine*." Ata tugged on Hbelu's lead.

"And partly mine, no matter what you say," Ilzi put in. He had been staring at one of his hands, but looked up, eyes determined. "You would not have captured him but for me. We have both lost in keeping him. You know I am always ready to relinquish my claim, if you wish to give the girl to me when we find her."

Hbelu heard the orchard owner's teeth grind. "We will discuss later, Cousin," he said. He turned back to the others. "Goodnight. We will convene at breakfast tomorrow, yes? We can go over our plans then. I for one look forward to sleeping in a bed again."

Su turned away, waving a hand, and the others followed him. Waqrat looked back over her shoulder. "Make sure not to lose him while we are gone. I would hate to spend my time watching you. There are plenty of mori in the capital." She gave a wicked grin and kept walking.

"I do dislike that woman," Ata murmured when they were out of sight. Then he straightened, looking both ways. "I have an idea, Cousin, about how to keep our 'friends' away from our prize. Stay here and I will settle things."

Ilzi's eyes widened, and Hbelu felt the hope of a good sleep leave him. "I think I will follow you, dear Cousin, if it is all the same," he said. "You will not fool me as easily as the Nehardan nobles."

"Fine then, follow." Ata pointed a finger at Ilzi. "If I learn your leaves have turned colors and they hear of this, you will share *none* of the rewards, no matter your part."

Ilzi shrugged, but his face was dark.

Ata pulled at the lead and Hbelu resisted. "Do I get a say now your friends are gone?" he asked. "Finding the sisters is a great priority, before they escape your reach." Ata aimed a swipe at his head, and as weak as Hbelu was, the large orchard owner must have been tired. It barely jarred one of his teeth.

"Come on, caravanner," Ata growled, pulling until Hbelu had no choice but to follow or fall over. He would have, but he did not think Ata was against coercing a group of prisoners to physically drag him, and he did not wish more injury to drain his energy.

The way back down the stairs was tortuous, especially at the pace Ata set. Hbelu was at the limits of his endurance, starved, and wounded. It was dark, and servants and slaves lit candles. Several seemed like they would stop the three to ask if they needed anything, but one look at Ata's face sent them scurrying away.

At the ground level, Ata finally stopped, looking around the entrance hall, and Hbelu slumped against a wall. Ilzi was only seconds behind, feet noisy, his face concerned.

"This way, I believe." The manacles bit into Hbelu's wrists and he grunted in pain. He pushed off the wall, and Ilzi followed, breathing hard.

Night had fallen outside, and though there were torches lit around the perimeter of the ziggurat, Ata guided them away, watching something on the ground. Only when they passed a corner of the massive palace did Hbelu realize the red-hair was following the ruts of the rolling cage filled with dead Asha-Urmana.

Away from the palace, stray lights from the city peeked over the hedges, and the light of Shir-Gal guided them. Hbelu could tell they were aiming toward the great glass buildings that housed godfruit trees. His people had devised the structures, long ago, but the ability to reproduce them had been lost in the Asha-Urmana's flight from Karduniash. Hbelu wondered if the rulers of Karduniash had ever built more, or like the city walls and the palace, simply used what they stole. He had wished to see the structures for many years, though not in this way.

They passed glass walls, and Hbelu strained to look closer, but the man pulled him ever onward, head bent to the ground.

There were other buildings around the palace grounds, pyramids much smaller than the edifice looming over them. The ruts of the cage led them to one in sight of the glass houses, reflecting Shir-Gals' light.

"What...are you doing...Ata?" Ilzi gasped. He finally caught up as the red-hair, almost invisible in the night, paused outside a door set into the angled side of the building.

"Protecting my assets," Ata replied. "Help me open this and watch him."

Ilzi took the lead from his cousin, and Hbelu tensed to run. Could he make it far enough to hide from the two? This might be his one chance to...

"Stop thinking what you are thinking," Ilzi whispered. There was the rasp of steel and something cold touched Hbelu's neck. "I am less predisposed than my cousin to keeping you in one piece." Hbelu leaned back, but the knife followed, and he felt it nick his flesh. No, Ilzi was not the kind to bluff.

A rattle, and a laugh of triumph from Ata. "Quickly, in here, before anyone sees." Ilzi pulled him after Ata, and darkness enveloped them. Hbelu thought to pull away again, but the knife stayed close to his throat.

"Not this time. I am no ignorant blond." Ilzi pushed him forward, so he was between the two fourcolors, as Ata struck a light with his tinderbox, illuminating a torch in a bracket.

With the torch, they went downstairs, far underground. Implements of harvest surrounded them, bags of dirt, and cans of bloodmeal and lime. The air was stuffy, with the acrid scent of fertilizer and an undercurrent of decay.

There were several rooms underneath the small outbuilding, and they came across the dead Asha-Urmana, stacked in piles. Hbelu felt Ilzi recoil at the stench, though the knife remained steady.

"Ah. Here." There was a click, and the torch illuminated a side door, half open. "This place will be unused, I think, during the Prunus Festival. The servants and slaves will be too busy keeping their masters happy." Ata stepped back from the entrance. "There is a small room, and a bar for the door."

Hbelu saw too late what the man intended, but Ilzi was already propelling him forward to slam into the opposite side of the chamber—more a closet than anything else. Hbelu hit the wall with a grunt, tripping over a pile of something on the floor. His head caught a shelf with a spike of pain, and he fell.

"Bar the door. Push those bags here and erase those footprints." Ata's voice was harder to hear, as the door closed with a thud. There were noises from the other side, scraping and shoving, and lowered voices discussing.

Then louder, nearer: "—and I will hold you to that, Cousin." Ata's voice again. "You keep your tongue still, and when we find the girls, I will consider your proposition. Gods know why you wish a slave girl for your mate."

"Status, Cousin," Ilzi replied. "And lineage, and title. You do not keep all your secrets as close as you think."

There was silence.

"Then you know of that." Ata again. "Even if you were to marry Bel, you have no claim over my land. She would not—could not—be recognized—"

"The orchard is far from the capital, Cousin," Ilzi interrupted. "It is easy to muddle whether one is a slave, a freeman, or even a noble, with distance and the right words."

Their footsteps moved away, though Hbelu could hear the two arguing. He wondered what they had meant about Belili, but such things would have to wait. The light shining around the edges of the door faded, then disappeared. Hbelu was left in darkness. He felt his way to the door, avoiding the bags and the shelves. The room was only two paces across. He pushed on the door, then rammed his shoulder into it, but it was solid. Though old, the wood was thick oak planks, set close enough so that even his little finger would not fit through. Hbelu sat down, in the dark.

CHAPTER TWENTY-ONE

Reunion

The gods were still angry at their errant creations, and they fashioned another godfruit tree to balance what the slavers had done. Yet this was done in secret, and no mortal knew what they did.

Kisare and Gemeti walked down a winding street of Karduniash, but all Kisare could see was opulence. There were more nobles here than freemen and freewomen, all dressed in cotton. Most had either true blond servants, slaves with bleached blond hair and metal collars, or both. Fortunately, Gemeti had paid the innkeeper to let Kisare wash up before they left the Blossoming Prunus, or she would have stood out.

It was hot in the capital, as if rain hung in the air, though the sky was cloudless. In the woods and on the road, the overhanging trees had reduced the intensity of the sun. In the city, all was wide cobblestone roads, and stone and wood houses. Occasionally a bush or garden dotted the side of the street, but they gave no shade.

Slaves with rags and brooms removed grime from the buildings. Another group was chained together at the feet. A blond guard watched from a street corner, arms crossed, and a whip and sword at his side. This whole city ran on slave labor. She hadn't seen so many slaves in Neharda, though that was a lenient city, from what Gemeti told her.

"How do we get into the palace?" Kisare asked.

"I know certain people," Gemeti answered enigmatically. "There are more every year, nobles included, who, ah, share my views." She spoke the last with a lowered voice.

"You mean the ones who want the blonds free," Kisare whispered, but Gemeti waved a hand at her to be silent.

"It is not spoken, especially in this atmosphere." She turned her head to the right and left, marking out strolling nobles. A woman with a slash of brown passed close, eyeing Kisare's dress enviously. She snapped for a collared slave, wrote something on a scrap of paper, and sent him running. Gemeti watched after the blond. "In any case, we should not have a problem."

Above them, the bulk of the mountainous building grew oppressive. Kisare had mistaken it for a natural formation at first. Now she could see it was an immense ziggurat.

"Is that the palace?" She nodded toward the edifice.

"It is. Look familiar?" Gemeti had a sly smile. "I have heard stories this is the Asha-Urmana building style, which the nobles stole, as they stole the palace itself."

Kisare nodded. "Hbelu's village had a much smaller one."

They came to the head of the street, which widened, buildings dropping away before the giant pyramid. Here there was lush grass instead of cobblestone streets. Winding paths split off from the main walkway, disappearing into wild hedges of broad-leaved vines and strange trees with scaly bark and a topping of pointed-fern-like leaves. Something sparkled in the bright sun far to her right, though Kisare could not see over the hedges.

Two guards stood where the city buildings ended and the palace began. There was no wall. Gemeti watched Kisare looking over the grounds and anticipated her question. "The Dyad say they do not need walls. Any noble could force their way in by magic if they are worthy, and no slaves would dare. They say it proves their power." She lowered her voice so the guards couldn't hear. "I think they know they cannot rival the brilliance of the Asha-Urmana buildings, and so they do not try."

She approached the guards. "My lady is here for the Prunus Festival. We would like rooms at the palace."

"Name?" the guard asked. These had steel helmets, breastplates, and pikes. They also wore tunics over their breastplates, showing a spiral of the five magical colors of hair.

Gemeti gave the name they had come up with in The Blossoming Prunus. It had to be something Bel would recognize if she found them first. Something both Bel and Kisare knew from back in the orchard.

"My lady is Mulagunna-Kis, hailing from the edge of the Blasted Lands to the north," Gemeti told him. "We have traveled many weeks." Kisare hoped Bel would recognize the name of the old slave who escaped every year. She wondered if Mulagun was still alive. Maybe he would escape for good without the old master watching.

The guard gestured. "Follow me. I will take you to Mistress Arahuna to find you a room."

Gemeti paused, and Kisare almost bumped into her. "Pretend you are asking me something," she whispered.

"What do you mean?" Kisare leaned in, and Gemeti rolled her eyes.

"Good enough." She turned to the guard. "My lady asks whether we might see Master Eriba. He was a friend to her family, many years ago."

"Master Eriba went to feed the godfruit two years ago," the guard answered. "Mistress Arahuna is the new head servant."

Gemeti's mouth twisted, but she hid it quickly. "Lead on, please."

They were taken to a smaller ziggurat near the entrance to the palace. Inside were cabinets and stacks of parchment. In the middle were a few harried-looking clerks, and one older woman in a simple cotton dress with the swirl of colors. She had a prominent stripe of silver and was reading another parchment. Kisare looked to Gemeti to introduce her as before, but Gemeti was taking a detailed interest in the woodwork. Strange.

Kisare focused on making her words clear and crisp, the way the nobles spoke. "I am Mulagunna-Kis, here for the festival. My...servant and I would like rooms at the palace."

Mistress Arahuna looked up. "Do you have special qualifications? The palace is very crowded for the festival and the Dyad are choosy about who shares their generosity."

Kisare spared another glance to Gemeti. The useless woman was looking anywhere but at them. "I hail from the Blasted Lands."

Mistress Arahuna narrowed her eyes. "From the Blasted Lands, eh? Few come from there. Are you traveling alone with your...servant?" She also spared an annoyed glance for Gemeti.

Should Kisare tell the truth? Bel might arrive here, and she should prepare the way. "I was traveling with my sister, but we were separated. Gemeti and I went one way and my sister another. She will be arriving with a gift for the Dyad."

"Yes, she has already arrived," the mistress said, almost offhand. Kisare took in a breath, and even Gemeti looked around. Mistress Arahuna took a prunus from a pouch by her side. "Something does not ring true between your story, your sister's, and your...servant's." She ate the prunus, shivering, and Kisare's eyes flashed to Arahuna's hair as jolts of light flashed down her arms. Silver, like hers.

"First, why is your name different from your sister?"

Kisare's heart raced. Of course Bel chose a different noble name. "It is a long story," she hedged. Mistress Arahuna inhaled, her eyes closing, and Kisare frowned but continued. "Suffice to say my sister was married and widowed. I am single."

Mistress Arahuna held her breath, then let it out, opened her eyes, and nodded as if that was what she expected. She pushed the mass of the prunus to one cheek. "You intend to deceive me. Are you planning harm to the palace?"

Kisare blinked. "No!" Was the woman *smelling* her lies? Could she do that? "I do not believe my sister and I could bring this whole palace down." She tried to smile, but the woman's face was grim.

"I smell sweat, fear, and a certain—ah, you wish to meet with your sister again. Fair. There is something more, but no danger to the palace, or the grounds, or the staff." The head servant gave her a strange look, her nostrils flaring as she chewed. Streaks of lightning flicked down her arms. "You have a strange scent of confidence, like your sister. I assume it is intent on the Dyad, but what noble does not wish for their place, eh?" Arahuna took another prunus, spitting out the pit of the last one. "I am not yet convinced, as I smell something far more interesting." Kisare's face went hot at how easily the woman uncovered her deception. Mistress Arahuna wasn't even a powerful noble. She didn't dare ask about Aricaba-Ata.

"What is *your* intention in coming, Gemeti?" Kisare blinked in surprise as her traveling companion wheeled around. "It took me a few moments to recognize you, in those dresses. Finally realized you would never make it as a man, did you?"

"Rot your godfruit," Gemeti spat. "I should have known you would pry as usual, Arahuna. My business is my own. As is my gender."

Kisare stared at Gemeti a moment. She hadn't always been a woman? Things were definitely different here in the capital.

The head servant sniffed the air. "A non-answer. But you are afraid. Are *you* intending harm to anyone? Or perhaps you will offend nobles with your talk of decimating our work force for no reason."

"For a very good reason!" Gemeti shook her head. "No, I will not start that argument. My only intent is to see these women get the recognition they deserve."

246 Fruits of the Gods

Arahuna scoffed. "Deserve. Likely they are backwoods nobles with barely a claim to the title." Kisare tensed, and Arahuna's head swung to her, sniffing. She had a nasty grin on her face.

"If it is references you want," Gemeti said, "I can still supply many. If only Eriba was not gone..."

"But he is."

"Amilanu, then, or perhaps—"

Arahuna waved the comment away. "Dig up patrons if you must, Gemeti, and blackmail whoever you want into supporting you. I have no time to play your games. At least old Eriba is not around to cover your tracks."

"So, you will let us in." Gemeti put hands on hips, or into the profusion of clothes she wore. Kisare wished she could fade into the wall.

"Yes, yes." Arahuna made a vicious mark on a sheet of parchment. "I am certain you will attempt to give the Dyad a piece of your mind about your precious Asha-Urmana, as usual. Well, they no longer have reason to listen to your ravings."

The head servant paused and chewed again. "There is something—" she swallowed and spit out the prunus pit. "Bah. You are as slippery as ever. Perfume and old clothes to disguise your scent." She half reached into her little pouch. "No. It is not worth wasting another prunus. Did your hair turn white when you bolted, or do you deceive those around you?"

"I see you clawed your way to the top when the old Master of Servants died," Gemeti answered, sweeping her multitudinous clothes close. "Did you hasten his demise, or sleep your way to the top?"

"Watch out for this one, Mulagunna-Kis," the mistress told Kisare, though staring daggers at Gemeti. "He—no, *she*—will undermine you for her own agenda. Did she supply your noble name?"

Kisare paused, then remembered the woman wasn't chewing a prunus. She held her head high. "My name is my own. Now can you find us quarters or not? Please alert my sister we are here."

"Oh, I will find you something fitting your station," Mistress Arahuna growled.

* * *

A guard dumped them off in an underground chamber of the palace. It looked as if this room hadn't been used in years. There was one cot and a dusty oak table, one leg shorter than the others. The place reeked of dust and disuse. Sunlight filtered in from an open hole in the ceiling. Probably another of the Asha-Urmana's mirror tricks.

"This will do for our purposes," Gemeti said, glancing around. "I am certain many rooms are already taken by other visiting nobles."

"Yes, a little dusting and new furniture, and we might be as well off as slaves," Kisare answered. She had been hoping for a room with a good bed.

"No matter. I know many nobles—a few good words will get us a much nicer room. What matters is that we are in the palace." Gemeti placed her pack against one wall. Kisare followed her action.

"Yes, in the palace, with no Bel, no box, and no Hbelu. I didn't know there would be an interrogation to get in." She looked at the older woman. As antagonistic as Arahuna had been, she was correct. Everything Gemeti did was a lie, from her clothes to her speech to her posture to her hair.

Gemeti waved a hand. "That woman has always been good with prunae. She's a sneaky one. I cannot say I am surprised she leads the house servants."

"You told us you spent most of your life in Neharda," Kisare said. "How long were you in Karduniash?"

Gemeti sighed. "I may have padded the years. I grew up here, and left when I was twenty, though I have been in contact since. I was still very naïve in those days and insufficiently circumspect."

"You must have been near the palace to know Arahuna and the old Master of Servants."

Gemeti nodded. "Master Eriba. He was a kindly man and taught me how the world worked. Why slaves were slaves and nobles were nobles. He was a secret supporter of my cause and did much for the slaves in Karduniash."

"Why did you leave?" Kisare paused. "And does that have to do with you not always being a woman?"

"I have *always* been a woman, though many refused to see until I left," Gemeti said. "It is a long story. Enough to say, I was trying to lead a group of slaves to freedom when a set of vicious nobles found us. I escaped, but at the cost of all the slaves." She sat on the cot, which creaked under her. "I was not caught, and no one knew I led the escape, though I had been careless about my views. Master Eriba encouraged me to find a new home lest I be found out. I decided it was as good a time as any to fully accept the gender I felt more comfortable with. I have kept one ear and eye on news from the capital ever since."

"What about Arahuna?" Kisare asked on.

Gemeti waggled a finger at her. "Indeed. As I was leaving, she was asking leading questions, ones that used prunae, when she could get them. Neharda is much more trusting of blonds, and I imagined I could do better there, even though I was no longer in the rot of Karduniash."

"Did you?"

Gemeti sagged. "I have freed my share, working with the Asha-Urmana. It could have been more. I could have been bolder, even in Neharda. Leaving Karduniash did something to me." She eyed Kisare. Then she shook her head and slapped her thighs with both hands, making dust jump up around her. "Still, no use sitting around. Who do we find first?"

"Now? It's evening."

"Best time for it," Gemeti said. "Less people in the hallways."

Kisare shrugged. "We find my sister, then see if Hbelu is here," she said. If Mistress Arahuna's dig about the Dyad and the Asha-Urmana meant Aricaba-Ata had arrived, then they would have to work fast to free Hbelu.

"Do not wander about the palace yet," Gemeti warned her. "You are nearly a noble, but I think it best if I accompany you. For now, I will find my friends. They should know about your sister and Ishkun-Dim-Hbelu, and hopefully take care of the state of our rooms." Gemeti swept a glare around the dusty cell. "We will have to sleep here for one night." She ducked back out of the door.

"Wait—" Kisare said, but the woman was gone. Who did she think she was anyway? Leaving Kisare alone. She frowned around the dusty room. There was no way she was sitting around. She waited a few minutes for Gemeti's footsteps to fade, then opened the door.

The hallway outside was deserted, long and sparsely decorated with art and chairs with little tables between. Candles burned in chandeliers, but light filtered from mirrors lining the top of the hallway.

Kisare saw a metal collar and bleached blond hair disappear around a far corner. She followed, and up flights of stairs until windows opened to an evening view of the gardens. Any direction was good. Surely Aricaba-Ata and Hbelu would not be this low in the palace, but Bel might.

Down another long hallway, Kisare passed collared blonds lugging baskets of wet clothes. Another following them—a strong-looking male a head taller than her—had a bucket of water in each hand, a cloth pad wrapped around the handles. Steam rose from the buckets.

Kisare shook her head. The palace surely had systems like those at Hbelu's village and in Mushezibti-Lila's caravan. Why didn't they use water from pipes leading to hot cisterns? The whole thing ran on slaves knowing their place and working hard.

Kisare's head tilted as she followed the group. It was another gear in the nobles' system. If they could free Hbelu and balance the Asha-Urmana's power with the fifth seed, maybe they could demolish the slavery system. But take it away now and there would be utter chaos. The nobles didn't know how to do anything themselves.

A hand moved in Kisare's vision and she nearly squeaked.

"Can I get you anything, Mistress?"

Kisare turned, one hand to her chest. The servant, a natural blond, but with no collar, was watching her, but Kisare could tell the girl hid a smile. She hadn't jumped that much.

"I...I simply like to watch the slaves at their work," Kisare said. "I'm...I am studying them for, ah, for the Dyad. They wish to know more about their habits."

"Of course, Mistress," the servant replied, with no hesitation. She must have been used to hearing nobles twist their way out of tight places. "May I get you anything? Food? Some godfruit?"

"Godfruit?" Kisare's mind raced. Did they hand the stuff out here? But the servant was already gesturing to someone else behind her. Another natural blond lifting the lid of a silver tray, revealing malae, citrons, prunae, and mori. Kisare attempted to keep her eyes in her head.

Carrying a whole malus or citron might look suspicious, and Kisare wanted to stay out of the eyes of the nobles. Her eyes fell on the mori, and she took several. She paused, then took several prunae. No point wasting an opportunity. A servant handed her a cloth bag.

"That will do adequately," she said, trying to look haughty. She made a wiping motion she had seen Aricaba-Ata use, and the servants bowed and backed away. Kisare watched them out of the corner of her eye, pretending to investigate the godfruit for defects.

When they were out of sight, Kisare turned the other way. Each hallway in the palace had a set of stairs up and down at the ends. At some point she would arrive where more powerful nobles lived.

As she climbed, a voice drifted down.

"I will not have you asking more. He is safe."

Kisare froze. She recognized that voice.

"Come now, Ata," another male voice replied. "The other men—"

"And women," said a third voice.

"And women, yes, thank you, Waqrat, are all wondering where you have stashed our prize. Certainly, it is no trouble to tell us?"

"The Prunus Festival is in two days," Aricaba-Ata said. Kisare looked both ways. They were getting closer and would see her before she got to the bottom of the steps. They must be around the next corner. "I have said I will not make our captive a focus until the time is right. The Dyad must see his true value."

Kisare looked down at the cloth bag she still held. Mori. She bit down on one, shivered.

Aricaba-Ata, another red-haired noble with a ridiculously curled beard, and a striking woman with almost golden skin and a splash of silver curled around one ear turned onto the staircase. None of them looked at her. Kisare let out a breath and looked down. She could no longer see her hands.

"You must have him in the palace," the other red-haired noble said.

Aricaba-Ata wagged a finger as they passed by. Kisare flattened herself against the wall, but the stairway was not so wide. Her old master brushed past. Kisare closed her eyes.

"What was that—someone else on the stair?" Her old master looked around, even as Kisare scooted upward, no longer trying to be silent. "Blighted spies, trying to get at my secrets." He waved a hand, reaching up the stairs, but she was already beyond his grasp.

The others turned at the same time, the woman raising a morus to her own lips. She shivered but stayed in view. The other nobles glanced around her, but not at her.

The woman's eyes fixed on Kisare, narrowing, and she spoke from one side of her mouth, holding the juice in.

"It is a girl—probably some noble's shadow in training." The others looked blindly toward the woman as she spoke. Waqrat made a shooing motion. "Run along, little shadow. Ata will not tell us where his prize is stowed, so you will certainly learn nothing. Report back to your betters."

Kisare took a step back, then another. Waqrat nodded at her again, swallowed. Her form shimmered, and Ata and the other noble looked at her again. Kisare retreated up the stairs.

"Now you see why I will not talk?" Aricaba-Ata said. "Spies, everywhere, I tell you."

Kisare started down a new hallway, the taste of the magic fading. It seemed the morus was not such an advantage as she thought. Others with silver hair could see each other even if no one else could. Fortunate her old master wasn't actively looking for her or he might have asked the woman for a description. Maybe Gemeti had been right. Kisare looked for another stairway back down to her level.

* * *

If Belili was lucky, she could find Hbelu, and by extension, Aricaba-Ata and Ilzi. She contemplated the malus in the silver bowl, envisioning earth covering the little weasel's face. From what Marut said, most nobles regarded the powers the godfruit bestowed as little more than party tricks.

In the end, she took the handful of mori, the other two prunae, and cut the malus and citron in half. She winced as drops of juice leaked on the floor, spattering lightning. She was certain the bowl would be full when she got back. Belili put the fruit in a leather pouch, the malus and citron wrapped together in cloth.

She unlocked the door, opened it a crack, and looked both ways. No one in the corridor. If any nobles saw her, there might be hard questions to answer, or more invitations to the festival. There was a number on her door, and she committed it to memory.

Belili walked down the hall, footsteps muffled by the deep wool carpet. The hall's domed ceiling reflected light from the late afternoon sun, bounced through the walls by an intricate set of mirrors. There were candelabras too, slaves just lighting them. Paintings hung on the walls of past nobles, battles, and other pictures favoring the might of the nobles and the Dyad.

Belili picked a direction at random and mentally refreshed what the godfruits in her pouch would do with her brown hair.

Morus for moving without moving. Prunus for hearing. Malus for earth. Citron to change the solidity of my body.

She nibbled a prunus, enough to let a little of the juice in her mouth. She held it in one cheek, focusing on the brown in her hair. Her hearing jumped a level, and her footsteps became louder. Her eyesight seemed sharper too, but she ignored it, flicking at the stump of her little finger. She strained for signs of conversation.

There. She ducked into an alcove behind a statue of a man killing a giant catlike beast as two nobles passed, one with a large streak of black, the other with silver.

"Have you heard the latest?" one said. "Another couple of country nobles—sisters—arrived, all the way from the Blasted Lands to the north."

"I wonder if they know that Ata? Was he the one from Neharda or was it someone with him? I can never remember."

"Whichever it is, I for one will be glad when the festival is over and all these upstarts with hopes higher than their egos remove themselves. We need no more of—" His words faded as they moved farther away. Belili stepped out of her hiding spot.

Over the next few hours, she explored five levels, moving downward whenever she hit a flight of stairs. The light from the mirrors dimmed as the sun sank. She could no longer see out past the gardens and over the city when she passed a window. Chandeliers and candelabras threw shadows across the hallways.

The halls held nobles, their servants, and slaves with metal collars. Many seemed confused by the layout. Several nobles had two and even three locks of different color. She could not hide from all, and the ones she didn't, she nodded to as equals. She used a morus to skip past a group of finely dressed women, all with multiple streaks of color. Another time, she ate half a slice of citron to fade into a wall, avoiding a black-haired noble's retinue. He looked vaguely familiar, and she didn't want to chance a meeting. Later, a man appeared not ten paces from her, looked around furtively, light illuminating his silver lock, then nibbled at something and disappeared.

The hallways became longer the lower she went. From conversations she overheard, many new arrivals had lower rooms than she. Had Arahuna taken a liking to her, or was she being bribed to present herself as the Dyad's plaything?

At random, she picked a door to her left—the interior of the palace—and walked through as if she knew where she was going.

"Do you need something, my lady?" a slave girl asked. Her hair was bleached blond, a collar around her neck. She was a few years younger than Belili—maybe Kisa's age, but older-looking than a free woman of her age. The girl was scrubbing a load of clothes in a bucket of water. Behind her, other collared blonds worked. The room stank of soap, bleach, and lye.

"Only directions." Belili smiled tightly at the girl, saying the first thing that came to mind. "Where is the festival to be held?"

"The top of the palace, my lady. Third from the top floor. You may enter through the large doors in the middle of each of the four hallways, when the festival begins." The girl ducked her head as if she would be beaten for not speaking fast enough.

She is where I was not long ago.

"Thank you," Belili said, and caught the girl's surprised expression as she turned. The slave—the prisoner—had likely never been thanked before.

Belili went downstairs again. She was below the ground floor, the light in the hallways still bright thanks to the mirrors. In the middle of this hall was a large set of double doors, bigger than others she had passed. It must be something important, so she made sure no servants were around, then peeked in.

The room was empty, but a deep musty, fruity scent and rows of casks on the wall told her this was a wine cellar. Aricaba-Ata had a similar one, though much smaller, under his house in the orchard.

She walked in, closing the door behind her. At least she could wander this room with no fear of discovery. The less the nobles saw of her before she found Kisa, and before the festival, the fewer answers she'd have to invent. Kisa had no skill with lying and for sisters from the same place near the Blasted Lands, their stories shouldn't be so different.

She ran a finger over the rough casks, savoring the smell of the old wood, and the wine beneath. It smelled cozy down here. It smelled—

Something thumped in the corner, and there was a little cry. Belili nibbled another prunus, getting just a drop of juice.

"Shh, now, they will be gone in a moment, and we can get back t—" The voice faded out as her hearing returned to normal, but Belili's lip drew up, even as her heart sped, her palms sweating. That voice had haunted her days and nights.

She sauntered through the wine cellar, hoping to spoil his fun for as long as possible as she planned. It was the least she could do for his prey. She pretended she had heard nothing, touching each cask as she walked, reading little plates telling when each was made. It gave her time to tamp down her fear. She was in control. She had magic. Her hand sorted through her cloth bag, the other pressed to her leg to keep it from shaking. One of them would not leave this room, if she had her way.

A few minutes later there was a grunt, the sound of clothes, and a man stuck his head around a corner. It was dim in the wine cellar, but there were enough mirrors to let Belili see the surprise on Ilzi's face as he recognized her. Trying to hide from him would be a joke. She was ready, though spikes of worry chewed her gut.

"You!" Ilzi pulled his pants up, and a mousy bleached blond slave ran out, heading for another exit. It wasn't Ligish, and Ilzi didn't even try to stop her. What did that mean for his former slave?

"What are you—did you follow us? How did you get here? Get new clothes? Dye in your hair?" Ilzi narrowed the distance, not even bothering to finish his questions. His hair was as greasy as ever, his sneer familiar.

Belili raised the malus to her lips, relishing the crisp snap of the flesh, the silver taste of lightning.

"Sit down, Ilzi," she said. A wine cellar tile ground into grasping hands, pulling him to the floor. So, her magic could affect things made of earth too. Belili regarded the man—the toad, struggling on the floor. The malus was losing its flavor. "What did you do with Ligish? Tired of your toy already?" It was another reason to end him.

"Let me explain, Bel—" Ilzi began, but she cut him off.

"*Never* call me that. Here, you may address me as Anagmeshu-Bel, if at all." She spoke around the juice. He was struggling, the tile hands crumbling, and Belili swallowed. She understood the nobles. Better to waste juice and make room for another type of magic. She reached into her bag, but Ilzi lurched up, hand inside his vest.

Instead of a piece of godfruit, he brought out a small glass vial, sealed with a metal cap. It held a dark juice, and Belili's eyes widened. Of course they would juice the godfruit here, with such an abundance. She grasped, but Ilzi was quicker, spinning away while pouring the vial into his mouth. Belili scrabbled at her pouch as the man convulsed from the juice. She threw another morus into her mouth, and as he threw one hand out, Belili disappeared, reappeared behind him. A cask of wine exploded next to where she had been standing, the contents instantly turning to shards of ice. If she hadn't moved, she would have been skewered, at his mercy to heal when and if he chose.

Belili ground the morus between her teeth, raising a malus to her lips, trying to hold off the shivering as she chewed frantically. Better to attack physically or with magic?

Too late—she had hesitated, and Ilzi spun, looking right at her. He tapped his temple and spoke around the juice in his mouth. "Morus. I can tell what you think, little minx. You cannot fight me."

He threw his hand forward again and another cask exploded. Belili hunkered down as she pulled floor tiles up on end, blocking the shards of frozen wine. The malus juice went tasteless, and Belili stood, fixing on a spot behind Ilzi. The rest of the morus lost its taste as she appeared there. She swallowed both as he followed her, too fast even for her to push him off balance.

"So, you'd prefer that little shrew over me, would you? I finished with that pitiful creature on the way and left her corpse by the side of the road."

He was still using the juice from the vial. Belili pushed down a well of grief. She'd known there was little chance Ligish would survive long without her help. They never did. *He's stronger than me. He can last longer.* She stepped backward. He could control her, like he always did.

Ilzi nodded, reading her thoughts. "That is correct. When you are suitably restrained, I'll take my satisfaction out on you." He crept closer, hands out to either side. "Ata will never know about his *special* slave. You need not hands, nor tongue, to bear me plenty of children. He never let me have you—I had to sneak our special meetings together." He grinned, matching her steps, and memories of the loft in the orchard's barn flashed through Belili's mind.

"Our special place. Such pleasant memories." He was ready for her, completely in charge, waiting.

Belili did to her mind what she did to her face. Only let them see the mask, not the truth. It had worked with him, before. She reached into her pouch and took the first thing she touched. Ilzi saw her move and grabbed. His hand brushed her hair as she dove to the left.

She stumbled as incredible fatigue hit her. Not again. A familiar pain in her joints. Her eyes were closing. *I can fight back, this time.* She stuffed the godfruit into her mouth and bit down. *Shafts of moonlight in the barn, too weak, too tired to resist Ilzi.* Prunus. Her hearing increased. *Eager hands rolling her barely resisting body over.* Why hadn't it been something useful?

"The wasting disease, so useful when you gave me trouble." Ilzi chuckled, his laugh sounding next to her ear. The noise made her come back from the edge of sleep. "They are so much more pliable when weak."

I. Will. Not. Let. Him. Again. She heard footsteps, like thunder, coming closer.

Belili raised one hand, her arm like a lead weight, and slapped it against her ear.

She screamed at the pain, and all noise disappeared from that side, but the pain overrode her fatigue. She rolled away from Ilzi. He hadn't been as close as she thought.

She pulled the malus from her pouch and stumbled behind a cask. Not much left. She stifled a cough. In the past, Ilzi had healed her when he was...finished. She would have to find someone else for that.

Ilzi was too strong, she too sick. She focused on the pain in her ear, something solid. A trickle of blood ran down her neck. She'd ruptured her eardrum. She shoved the rest of the malus into her mouth, keeping her mind blank.

"I can tell where you are," Ilzi called, his footsteps coming her way. "There is no sense hiding. If you submit, perhaps I will heal you. You were always my favorite."

Belili peeked out and saw him lowering a second vial. She chewed, a drop of juice rolling down her chin.

His eyes were locked on hers, and she desperately thought about the brown in her hair. The *brown*. She chewed the malus, letting Ilzi get a little closer. There.

She reached out and used all the magic at once to call, not earth, but *fire*.

Ilzi screamed and fell backward as the streams of flame engulfed his chest and face. Belili kept the fire going as long as she could, until the malus was tasteless mush. She aimed high, toward his head, so the wine on the floor wouldn't catch. Her left hand was clenched about her maimed finger, now she was using her red lock so openly.

Ilzi's face was a mass of burns, his hair almost gone, one eye milky. Little flames dotted his ruined tunic. She crawled to an arm's length, her joints a mass of pain. Her mouth fell open. It wasn't fair.

His wounds were knitting together, his hair regrowing, his eye brightening. There was citron juice in the second vial.

"You bitch!" His words were slurred, but his healing slowed. Maybe he had used all the citron.

Then his hand shot out, fingers dripping putrid pus, and Belili scrambled back on swollen knuckles and feet. Maybe not.

She didn't wait to see what else he had hidden. She couldn't touch him, even to hit him. Instead, she ate her last two mori, focusing on the lock underneath her brown one—the red one her father had given her. Aricaba-Ata. Even Ilzi didn't know about it.

Belili pushed away with all the mental strength the morus gave her, as when knocking the guard out on the wall, and Ilzi slipped across the floor, crashing through a wine cask stand. His head cracked on a leg and his body went limp.

Belili slumped and swallowed. Her right ear was ringing, her body a mass of pain. Could Gemeti heal her when they met? Would she have to crawl to another noble?

She pushed to her feet, wobbled to Ilzi, and pulled him out of the wreckage of the cask, whimpering at the pain. It felt like her fingers would pop off. His face was still half-healed from the fire, but now there was a gash in the top of his scalp, blood flowing down his neck, staining his shirt and pants. Bits of wood and bone dotted the scarlet wound, and he stank of wine. She needed information.

She smacked Ilzi's cheek, hard. He groaned but didn't wake. She smacked him again, and her joints ached at the effort. His head bobbed and he cried out, though still unconscious.

Belili frowned, then pushed one thumb into the wound in his skull.

Ilzi woke with a scream, his arms flailing. His eyes tried unsuccessfully to focus. He only had to last long enough to answer questions.

"Where is Aricaba-Ata?" she asked. "Where is Hbelu?" Ilzi struggled to sit up, but she pushed him down, a strange thrill of pleasure running through her. She could force *him* to do what she wanted.

"Wher— Who? I move thi—" His words were slurred, disjointed. His eyes were looking at different things. Something was broken, inside his head. Belili slapped him again.

"Focus. You have little time." One hand crept to his belt, and she pushed it away, opening the pouch he was aiming for. There was another tiny vial of juice, and she smiled as she took it.

"Where. Is. Aricaba-Ata?" She willed the understanding into his head.

"Top. Top of sh'palce. Eight floor fr'top."

She turned her head to hear out of her good ear. "Where is Ishkun-Dim-Hbelu?"

Ilzi grinned horribly, showing several missing teeth. "Nobles want't take 'way. Cousin dosn like. I do like."

"You were betraying him? So like you. Ata hid him from other nobles?"

Ilzi nodded his head, barely, his face curling in pain at the movement.

"W'never find 'im. Fr'you." His eyes were glazing. She didn't have much time.

"I have to find him before the festival. He knows what to do with the box!"

Ilzi took in a breath and struggled again. His eyes opened with a last clarity. "The Dyad've all magic. 'll rule the caravanners." He fell back. The blood oozing from his cracked skull slowed, then stopped. Belili didn't know what his words meant. Her molars grated together.

She put a hand on his chest. Silence. There should be satisfaction, instead of numbness. And pain. Gods, her body ached, but she would not have trusted Ilzi to heal her. Her thumb flicked at the stump of her little finger. Aricaba-Ata had both favored and cowed his seven-year-old daughter-slave when he cut off her finger. For anyone else, eating a slice of citron and breaking her chains would be death. In return, she had submitted to this rapist for years, as a teenager, without fighting back. She was free now. It had taken fifteen years, but she had used the red again. Why was she still numb?

She fought to her feet, hissing at the pain in her knees, and looked around the wine cellar. A shadow flashed in the corner of her eye, but when she looked, there was nothing. Just her nerves. Floor tiles were uprooted, several rafters were singed. Three of the giant casks had burst, and wine covered the floor. Belili's shoes pulled at the sticky floor as she walked, slowly. She held one aching hand in the other, massaging her wrists. They were swelling, and she swallowed, feeling nauseous.

The bottom of her dress—her fine dress—was stained purple. She would have to get another. Maybe Marut could get one.

Aricaba-Ata would be suspicious when his little toady didn't come crawling back. She had to look her best for the festival. Had to find her little sister. Had to get healed. They would act the part of nobles right up to when Aricaba-Ata presented Hbelu to the Dyad. Kisa would have the box, and Belili would be ready.

She opened the door of the wine cellar, not bothering to check if anyone was in the hall. A creak of wood sounded in the wine cellar, but she did not pause. She held herself erect, refusing to show the pain. A noble would not. Each step was a carefully planned torture.

CHAPTER TWENTY-TWO

Decisions

Yet the gods also saw how humbled the other four magical peoples became after their exodus, and it soothed their anger. They decided not to share the new godfruit with their creations, knowing the destruction it would cause. But Kigal of the autumn favored Darice-Ili-Aya, Princess of the Asha-Urmana, and whispered the secret. Darice-Ili-Aya promised to take it to her grave.

Kisare woke the next morning to Gemeti shaking her shoulder. She hadn't come back before Kisare fell asleep.

"Your Asha-Urmana prince is here," Gemeti said in greeting.

"I know," Kisare answered, rubbing the sleep out of her eyes. The bed wasn't big enough for two. Had the woman slept at all, or somewhere else?

"Did a little exploring of your own, eh?" Kisare stopped rubbing her eyes and looked up at Gemeti, who waved a hand. "You did not get into any trouble, I gather."

"No." Kisare stopped before saying any more. "Did you find where he is being kept?"

Gemeti shook her head. "No, though Aricaba-Ata and his followers are staying eight floors from the top of the ziggurat. Quite a feat for a lowly orchard owner from the middle of nowhere. He must be talking up Ishkun-Dim-Hbelu. Or perhaps the nobles with him have more influence."

Kisare hesitated a moment, then added her own information. "The others with him don't know where Aricaba-Ata is keeping Hbelu." Gemeti raised her eyebrows. "Surely Enti-Ilzi knows. Maybe we can find him and pry it out of him?" Kisare would relish confronting the unctuous noble, especially after what he had done to her sister.

Gemeti frowned. "Possible, but that is not a good idea. I presume Aricaba-Ata has hidden the prince from stronger nobles who wish to steal him away. Unless he trusts his cousin implicitly—" Kisare snorted. "Then no, I do not think we should track down Enti-Ilzi."

"How do we find him?"

Gemeti took in a long breath. "It is the custom to give gifts to the Dyad on the second day of the Prunus Festival. Aricaba-Ata will wait until then to produce him."

"So, we will have no time to plan." Kisare went to the chipped bowl of water on the room's sole table to wash her face.

"There is not always time to plan," Gemeti warned.

"Now you sound like my sister. We hope we can free Hbelu under the eyes of all the nobles of the capital, and convince the Dyad to activate a strange seed with the Asha-Urmana prisoner?" Kisare dried her face on a rag and reached for the cotton dress, hanging over a chair. At least she had one wool shift to sleep in.

"Not quite." Gemeti tapped her nose. "I have my sources. In fact, I will introduce you to one this morning. Not all nobles agree with how our nation is run. Get dressed and I'll take you now."

Kisare changed using a folding screen. When she came out, Gemeti passed a critical eye over her, tucking her hair just so, adding a few clips to make the color stand out, and adding a few touches of paint to Kisare's face from a little case of powders she had hidden in her clothes.

"There. Now you look more like a noble."

* * *

Gemeti moved in front of Kisare, acting the servant to her mistress. They passed other nobles. A few even had two colors. Kisare's mind raced through combinations of godfruits and abilities.

"Keep your head up," Gemeti whispered back, and Kisare straightened as two maids came around the corner. They were a few levels above ground, progressing higher. Most nobles glanced once at her hair and didn't give them another look. She was too low in the pecking order—powerful enough to be a noble, but low enough to ignore.

Higher up, Kisare froze as the woman who had seen her yesterday—Waqrat—came around a corner. The red-haired noble who had been with Ata followed her, as did another black-hair.

"Keep moving," Gemeti whispered. Kisare forced her feet to slide forward, waiting any second for Ata or Ilzi to come around the corner.

The nobles' conversation died away as she came nearer, and the silver-haired woman gave a condescending wink.

"Shadow," she said. "Lose your master somewhere?"

Kisare wanted to answer, wanted to ask if the woman had found Hbelu. Wanted to make a snappy comeback. She only stared, forcing herself to walk. The trio of nobles passed by.

Only after they had passed did Gemeti let out a breath. There was no one else in the hall, and Kisare moved close.

"Two of them were with Aricaba-Ata yesterday," she said.

"Ziggurmas-Su of the black, Sutur-Cit of the red, and Ahati-Waqrat of the silver," Gemeti recited. "Three of the worst Nehardan nobles. I wonder where Heabani-Danos is. He would not pass up a chance like this. Fortunately, I am beneath their notice, or they surely would have stopped us." She shivered. "Come."

Near the top of the palace, the square hallways around the perimeter were lined with windows, showing Karduniash stretched out beneath, partially obscured in a morning haze. Mirrors directed early sunlight inside, the marble shining like polished metal. Kisare peeked down and out of one window, and her stomach climbed up her throat. No one should be this high. She kept to the inside of the corridors, next to the row of doors lining the hall.

Gemeti knocked at a door sporting a sketched outline of three buildings.

A bleached and collared slave opened the door and bowed them in. Kisare tried not to stare at the metal collar. Another slave led them along a corridor to a sitting room, with comfortable and expensive-looking furniture. More slaves—men and women, all collared—lined the walls, waiting for instruction. Kisare's lip pulled up in disgust until Gemeti flashed her a look.

"The Master of Planning will be here soon, my lady," said a short male slave in a pure white suit of cotton. His collar was burnished to match, and he had the same emblem on his coat as on the door. "While you are waiting, would you care for a glass of chilled prunus and malus juice?"

Kisare carefully closed her mouth. Two godfruits mixed at one time? Where did they get malae this time of year, anyway? She held her chin high. "That would be acceptable."

The slaves seated her in a dark green stuffed chair. Gemeti got her own chair, though no one offered her juice.

Not a minute passed before a female slave brought a small vial to Kisare, placing it with a flourish on a small silver platter on an end table.

Carefully, Kisare lifted the glass, not daring to look around. She eyed the pale orange-red juice, then carefully raised it to her lips.

The taste of magic exploded in her mouth, her sight clouding over for an instant. Lightning ran down her arms and legs, grounding itself into the floor. The smells of the room multiplied—fabric and cloth, sweat and oil, wood polish, and a spicy scent she thought was the metal collars. She could sense the slaves and Gemeti by their odors.

Kisare experimentally created a small breeze to cool her, the taste of the juice fading. The air brought her more scents, and she followed them instinctively. One slave had been cleaning, another cooking a morning meal. All this from one sip.

A side door swept open, and a slave bowed in a large pink man smelling of fermented grapes, soap, and sweat. He had a humongous gray mustache, an elegant robe made of shiny blue material, and three magical colors in his short sandy hair—red, brown, and black. Each lock was nearly twice as big as hers.

"Gemeti, my boy!" he said, arms wide. His face was broad and red. Then he stopped. "Or, I see it is 'my girl,' now. Glad you finally went with your gut. This suits you." He gestured at her profusion of clothes. "It has been an age since I saw you last."

Gemeti pulled herself out of her chair with a grunt and gave the large man a hug. "Good to see you too, Ami." Between her abundance of skirts and coats and the man's rotund belly, Kisare was surprised they could get near each other. So Arahuna was not the only one who had known Gemeti as male.

Kisare stood as Gemeti turned back to her, a hand on the man's arm. "Allow me to introduce Hasis-Adra-Amilanu, Master of Planning for the Dyad." The man gave a tiny bow. "My lord, may I present Mulagunna-Kis, recently come from the edge of the Blasted Lands."

Kisare nodded back. "What does that title mean?" she asked. Whatever it was, she liked the sound of it.

Hasis-Adra-Amilanu waved a hand. "An elegant sounding thing for a common role. I oversee the city of Karduniash, dealing with new construction, restoration, and a myriad of complaints from ungrateful landowners."

"In other words, you keep the city from falling down around the Dyad's ears," Kisare translated.

The man glanced to Gemeti. "I like this one, Gem. Where did you find her?"

"A happy accident," Gemeti answered.

"Then your luck is better than mine. But come, sit. We have much to catch up on, and if I decode your cryptic message correctly, this Prunus Festival will be one to tell my little grandchildren about."

They made small talk for a few minutes, the Master of Planning asking pointed questions about their travels and Kisare's upbringing. She was reticent to reveal too much, but Gemeti related the story of their journey with the Asha-Urmana, and how Bel was separated from them.

Amilanu, as he insisted they call him, must have seen her watching the slaves lining the room. Kisare had been in that place before. Nobles forgot slaves had mouths too.

"Do not worry your head about them, my dear," the big man said. "My friends here are all loyal."

Kisare's head whipped back to him. "Friends?" If Ata had called her that she would have hit him.

Amilanu chuckled. "I buy many 'slaves' to keep up appearances. Many I free to make their own way in other cities. Those here have chosen to stay and act as my staff. Balu!" he addressed a middle-aged, thick woman, pale and pink like Amilanu, who came to his side and touched his arm affectionately.

"Balu here is my daughter, through an early love of my life. If I were to set her on her own in Karduniash, she would be classed as the daughter of a slave, her mother, and thus a slave herself. Here, she can live in the lap of luxury, and dote on her old father."

"He dotes on us even more," Balu said, her voice surprisingly deep for a woman. "We have bushels of fun pretending to be downtrodden collared slaves whenever other nobles come to visit."

"Where is my drink, woman!" Amilanu roared suddenly. Kisare jumped. "If I have to whip you again for your laziness, I shall take the very flesh from your bones!"

"Yes, Master!" Balu said, cowering. "The drink is coming! Please don't beat me again!"

They held the façade for another moment, then both burst into laughter. Kisare pried white knuckles from the arms of her chair as she heard several of those standing around the room chuckle.

"Would you care for anything in truth, Daddy?" Balu said, serious again.

Amilanu nodded toward Kisare's unfinished glass of juice. "I would not mind prunus juice, and get something for yourself, if you wish." Then to Kisare: "Finish that up quickly. It loses its edge if you leave it out."

Kisare took another sip, shivering, her nostrils flaring as she searched the room for anything out of place. It smelled...comfortable, relaxed.

"Can't...can the other nobles not find out about—" She swept a hand through the air.

"I am not completely defenseless," Amilanu said. He made a hand-opening gesture and three more slaves appeared, once again making Kisare jump. Silver hair, and mori. Why hadn't she smelled them?

"They keep watch for me," the noble said. "Malus keeps their scent from others. Expensive, but worth it, in my situation."

Balu delivered another glass, raised her eyebrows at Gemeti, who waved her off, and returned to a corner, where she sipped at her own tiny glass. Amilanu took a sip, shivering, and shifted his position, smacking his lips. "The prunae are more acidic this year." He turned sharp eyes to Kisare, who eyed his red, brown, and black locks. "Now this old man can hear and see you clearly, let us plan."

"We must find Mulagunna-Kis' sister," Gemeti said.

Amilanu sat back, thinking. "I know of her. She is going by 'Anagmeshu-Bel.'" He frowned for the first time since Kisare had met the jolly old man. "I would have gone to her sooner, had I known she was one of your protégés, Gem." He fingered his glass before setting it back down. "She was set up on the twelfth level from the top of the palace—quite an achievement for one bluffing her way in. Even some of the true nobles do not achieve so much."

"She has a knack for that," Kisare said. Of course Bel would wind up in the middle of things. She attracted favoritism, just as in the orchard.

"Risky," Amilanu said. "If you are playing an exotic noble from the Blasted Lands, you have no true pedigree. I have known a few who live there." He grimaced. "With no godfruit trees, they hardly classify as nobles to begin with, so lack of family is not a problem. However, if anyone searches too deeply, they may be able to find records of your ownership at the Aricaba orchard." He gestured to one of his "friends." "Request the slave records for—" He paused, looking to Kisare.

"Kisare and Belili, from the Aricaba orchard," she answered.

Amilanu nodded. "Bring them to me. I will make sure they are suitably 'lost.'"

"Thank you," Kisare said quietly. Gemeti was smiling, Amilanu serious.

"You already know my sensibilities." He gestured around the room. "I will help as I can. As to your sister, the Master of Silkworms has been spreading rumors in the last day that she accepted his invitation to the festival. I do not envy her listening to his riveting conversation."

"Silkworms?" Kisare questioned. In answer, Amilanu plucked at his shiny blue robe.

"An affectation of the highest of the nobles. Silk is made of the product of tiny worms that feast only on the leaves of morus."

Kisare gasped. Amilanu nodded, seeing her horror.

"A decadent practice. It robs the tree of much of its godfruit and can even cause its death if not checked. Such is the wealth of Karduniash." He spread his arms in mock awe.

Kisare knew nobles were arrogant and self-serving, but really! "What of this Worm Master? Do you know if he is actually with Bel?" Could she handle a male noble, or would she fall prey to the same abuse Ilzi put her through? Worry drew her brow down.

Amilanu sighed. "Isbi-Bar-Marut is jealous, perhaps due to his lack of admirers, though he has a following. He is not one to cross. Even if he is not with her at the moment, he likely has her shadowed by someone. Anything you discuss with her may be reported back to him. I would avoid your sister until the festival, but that is your choice." He drained the last of his vial of juice, shivering.

Bel had the box with the seed, under the sway of a noble again. Gemeti had mentioned Hbelu, and his plans to confront the Dyad, but even here, Gemeti didn't mention the box. Her face was as concerned as Kisare's felt.

Amilanu coughed gently, and they both looked back to him. He certainly suspected something but was polite enough not to pry. "I have information on the Asha-Urmana's request to retrieve their captive member from the Dyad."

"You've seen her?" Kisare asked.

Amilanu nodded. "She is certainly of the Asha-Urmana, and powerful, though none of the caravans I am in contact with claim her as missing. The rumor is that Sibi and Ishta—" He looked at Kisare. "That is, the Dyad, Samsu-Iluna-Nur-Sibi and Samsu-Iluna-Nur-Ishta, will present the girl at this Prunus Festival, though to what end, I am not certain."

"Is it true they have four colors in their hair?" Kisare asked.

He nodded. "They are the most powerful among us. Merely a small lock of blond hair to each, though they dye that, of course. Cannot have less than perfection."

"Except they only have four of the five colors," Kisare observed.

Amilanu's eyes widened, and he coughed. "I would not say that to them, if you value your life."

"Can you get us an audience with this mysterious girl?" Gemeti asked.

Amilanu frowned. "Gem, for you I would do anything, but even I have only seen her for a few moments. Eleven or twelve, perhaps, her hair a mass of purple with very little, if any, blond. I happened to be in the Dyad's personal chambers for a yearly council on the capital's housing budget. She is newly come to the capital, but the Dyad acted as if she were a loved child, or maybe a pet. Ishta has never had what you could call a maternal instinct."

"What are they doing with her?" Gemeti asked. She was sunk into her chair until it was hard to see her over the mass of her clothes. "Last I remember, the thought of the Asha-Urmana's power drove the Dyad crazy. Drove their parents crazy too."

Amilanu nodded again. "They obsess over having all five colors, but so far, the Asha-Urmana have stayed out of their reach. This girl brings them closer." He watched Gemeti for a moment. "I know that face, Gem. It is best not to look for trouble. The festival starts this evening, and I would suggest you stay close to your rooms until then, though I am fairly sure you will disregard that advice."

"Speaking of rooms." Gemeti held up a finger.

"Ah yes." Amilanu let himself be diverted from his warning. "We will get you a new room today, a few levels higher. I cannot promise more than that." The old man rubbed his hands together. "It has been thrilling to speak to you, Mulagunna-Kis. And of course, to you, Gem. It has been too long."

Kisare could tell a dismissal when she heard it. "Thank you for your time."

Amilanu stroked his bushy mustache. "I can offer you protection during the festival, and introduce you to like-minded nobles, but not before. As to your plan with the Asha-Urmana"—he held up his hands as Kisare opened her mouth—"I do not wish to know. Then I can claim true surprise when the Dyad's plans are interrupted."

Kisare sighed. "I'm not a very convincing noble, am I?"

He smiled, his eyes crinkling. "You have the air of someone far from home. It will give you an aura of intrigue. The Dyad love mystery."

Kisare left with Gemeti, after another round of goodbyes. Several others nodded to her, and Balu even gave her a warm hug. Amilanu promised one of his "friends" would be along soon to transfer them to a room above ground level.

* * *

Belili awoke early the next morning, only because light reflected from a mirror struck her in the face. She groaned, tried to roll over, and gasped as pain shot through her. It felt as if there was glass stuck in all her joints. She still couldn't hear out of her right ear, but that was a pittance compared to the rest.

She might have laid there for another hour if the nausea hadn't struck. Whimpering, and trying not to empty her guts at the same time, she half rolled, half fell off the bed and stumbled to the chamber pot.

Later, with an empty stomach, she glanced around the room. She had noticed nothing after coming back the night before, undressing in extreme pain, and collapsing into sleep. Someone had replaced the bowl of godfruit when she was out the day before. She struggled into her travel clothes.

There was a knock at her door, and Belili limped across the room, took a breath, and stood straight. She opened the door, wincing at the grinding in her wrist as she turned the doorknob.

"Yes?"

A servant—natural white-blond, but no collar—wordlessly handed her a tray with bread, jam, two covered pitchers, and a selection of non-magical fruit. Belili took it and closed the door on him, only then letting her face relax. She put the tray next to the bowl of godfruit by the door, mainly because her hands were too weak to hold it any longer.

Condensation beaded on one pitcher. The other steamed when she opened it, and she inhaled the rich scent of kaba greedily. That at least might help her pain.

She put together a meager breakfast, wanting to eat, but unsure of her stomach. The nausea had passed for the moment, but threatened in the back of her throat.

As she nibbled a bit of plain bread at a small table—the smell of the jam had made her gorge rise—she regarded the ruined dress, thrown over the changing screen in one corner. She would have to get a new one for the festival. This one held both wine and blood stains.

Belili regarded one shaking hand. Had it been worth it? She still felt nothing at Ilzi's death. Yes, she was free from him, but she had been before. As soon as Kisa had freed her, and given her godfruit, Ilzi had no more control. Had it been worth it to avenge Ligish? She searched inside, but had no strong feelings on that either. She would have preferred the other woman be alive, and here with her, over Ilzi being dead.

Now, someone was bound to find the mess in the wine cellar. She only hoped there was no way to trace it to her. Then she frowned. The prunus. Could a noble with silver hair track her, like Mistress Arahuna had smelled her lies?

Another knock at the door made her jump and sent a wave of pain down her back.

"Gods rot it," she cursed, then pursed her lips. Control. Surely not a slave to take the breakfast tray so soon?

When she finally dragged herself to the door, Marut was standing there, dressed in another of his blasphemous silk jackets, this one red, setting off his tanned skin. His hair was carefully combed to show off his locks of red and silver, and his angled face was set in a scowl as he pushed his way into the room. Belili didn't have time to resist, in her state, before she was swept backward. Had he decided now to take advantage of her? Why?

A pale, compact woman with a haughty face and a ramrod-straight back followed the Master of Silkworms. The woman must be a minor noble, as Belili's eyes went to the small lock of silver. Where the male nobles were overbearing and aggressive, often the women were just as bad, though they covered their cruelty with sweetness as they stabbed each other in the back. This one smiled as if she knew Belili.

She had escaped Ilzi. No one else would control her. She glanced at the bowl of godfruit, calculating her chances of getting there before them.

"I must speak with you," Marut began, adjusting his coat. Belili tilted her head to hear better from her left side. "My new shadow tells me you had an...altercation with another noble yesterday." His mouth tightened. He waved a hand backward to the woman. Belili took another quick glance. She was short and buxom—certainly attractive—with dark nondescript clothes. She seemed familiar, somehow. "Is this true?"

Belili kept her gaze on Marut, relaxing just a little. He wasn't here to force her. Her mind went to the vial of juice she'd taken from Ilzi, hidden under her pillow. Farther away than the bowl by the door. How much malus would she need to—what was she going to do? Kill them both? Then what? The Dyad's Master of Silkworms was an important man, not easily missed. Not a minor noble from near the Blasted Lands.

"Anagmeshu-Bel?" Marut was still looking at her. He seemed only now to notice her, his gaze passing up and down her body. "Are you well?" The woman was watching her warily, as if she might collapse at any moment. She was not far wrong. Something nagged her again about the woman's handsome face, her strong nose, but Marut occupied her attention.

"I...find myself less than healthy today, partly from the...incident yesterday." Belili's feet ached. She didn't know how long she could stand.

"Then it is true?" Marut was frowning, though he looked more concerned than stern.

"I am afraid so," she said. Her knees were shaking, hopefully hidden under her trousers. "It is a matter of long history, dating back to my days near the Blasted Lands." The lie unfolded from her tongue, taking a life of its own. Maybe the sickness guided her imagination. Even through the pain, her face leaped to obey her story, creating the right expression to go with her words.

"He was the son of a local noble living near me, a cousin of another I have history with—a noble named Aricaba-Ata." She grasped a chair, hoping it looked casual, not as if she needed the support. She put her other hand to her cheek as if she'd had a thought. "In fact, I would not be surprised if he spread spurious stories about me. You have not heard anything, have you?" Her eyes noted Marut's expression.

"No, my lady. But what has this to do with...with what happened yesterday?"

"You had best sit down," Belili told them. *Before I fall.* The shadow closed the door quietly, taking a crossed-arm stance in front of it. Her eyes flicked to Belili now and then, but Belili couldn't focus on her. Maybe later she would be able to speak to the shadow as another low-status noble. The Master of Silkworms took a chair near the breakfast table and Belili took the one she had been sitting in, idly picking at a strawberry from the tray. Could her stomach keep it down? Best not to chance it.

"It began when we were all young. That is, Aricaba-Ata was significantly older than my sister and I, of an age with my father. He took us both on as scions, of a sort, as our parents had become ill from too much exposure to the Blasted Lands." She looked to Marut as if waiting for his agreement. She had no idea if the Blasted Lands made people sick, but Marut nodded slowly, as if it made sense. Belili kept her face carefully neutral at a pulse of pain and continued. Her voice sounded strange in her own head, now her hearing was unbalanced.

"I was soon left alone with my sister, while Enti-Ilzi, the name of the man you...found, joined Aricaba-Ata at his estate. My sister is much better at running our house than I, so I was left to make connections with neighboring nobles. The obvious choice was Ilzi, and he...courted me for several years." That was not the word for what Ilzi had done to her. Her fists were tight, under the table. The grinding pain in her knuckles helped her focus. "Ilzi became worried when I, ah..." She looked down from Marut, embarrassed. "When I showed signs of our 'courting.'" She looked back up to catch an understanding look from the noble. The shadow's face and stance had softened as she listened. Belili would definitely have to speak with her later. What was it about her that seemed so familiar?

"He wanted to provide a way to...terminate my condition, but I refused. Why not show the world the results of our engagement? However, Ilzi went to Ata, and told him what had happened. They confronted me, and I was forced to use magic to defend myself." She stopped talking, looking down at the table. She waited, trying to control her face, to not think of the pain. Ilzi had left one last mark on her.

"What happened then?" Marut asked. He was well caught.

She pulled her left hand above the table, waggling her maimed little finger. "This, for fighting back." She laid a hand on her belly. "And this, emptied by Ilzi's word. Ata seemed to think more was due, for challenging his authority, and took possession of our house, turning my sister and me out. He had the force of numbers and coerced us into becoming little more than two more of his servants." She looked Marut in the eye. "So, you can well expect some of the stories Aricaba-Ata will tell." The noble nodded, and the shadow's eyes were soft, as if she wanted to comfort Belili. Such familiar eyes.

"My sister and I only recently came into means to rid ourselves of Aricaba-Ata and Enti-Ilzi's presence, so when they followed us here, claiming to have captured an important caravanner of some sort as a cover, you understand why I decided to fix matters myself." She didn't look at her pack, stored in a corner of her apartment, box safely wrapped within.

Marut frowned, thinking. "It is true he claims to have a present for the Dyad, though no one has seen his caravanner. Was all this truly necessary? Ligish managed to cover up most of the...mess, but word will still get out, eventually." He waved a hand back toward the silver-haired woman.

Belili's eyes flicked to the woman despite herself. It took every other ounce of her control to keep her face still as the connections sparked in her mind. *New* shadow. The familiar face, but cleaned up so much from the last time they had seen each other—weeks ago now—that Ligish was unrecognizable. The streak of silver in her hair. Ilzi had lied when he told her he killed Ligish! Belili let her gaze linger on the woman for a moment and Ligish gave her a slight smile in return. There was a story here and Belili *must* hear it, as soon as she could get rid of this boor. Joy welled in her for the first time in weeks.

However, she leaned in, putting on an expression of despair. "You know now what those two are capable of. If I had not done what I did, in days, I would be little more than a servant again."

Marut watched her for a long time, measuring with his eyes. Belili kept her face neutral, but hopeful, fighting the pain of Ilzi's sickness. Finally, he spoke.

"I can promise you this insignificant noble will not touch you as long as you have my protection."

Belili smiled on the inside. She let her eyes flash to her ruined dress, still hanging over the folding screen. Marut followed her gaze.

"I will have my tailor here within the hour to take your measurements. You will not want for proper clothing, by my side. You will be dressed, tonight, in the best silks at my disposal."

Belili put one hand on Marut's. "Thank you, my lord. You have no idea how much this will aid me."

Marut stood, a warm smile on his face. "You have had a trying night," he said. "I would begin your healing myself if I could. Instead Ligish will bring one of the palace black-hairs to you. Then you may rest, and my tailor will have your dress ready tonight." He looked her up and down as she stood. "You will be a gorgeous flower, by my side. The envy of all other nobles."

"For two entire days," Belili promised, letting her face show more of her pain. Inside, she was exultant.

After Marut and Ligish—with one backward glance—left, she let the smile fade from her face. She had an ally now, against her father's word, and the possibility of a renewed friendship with Ligish. Like Ata's silent protection, his condemnation of her rights, the best lies were crafted of kernels of truth, carefully placed in the lace of untruth. She let her hand rest on her stomach for just a moment.

* * *

Marut's tailor, A dumpy middle-aged blond, took Belili's measurements quickly and efficiently, which was good as Belili had vomited twice before she came, and once again the moment she left.

She crawled back to bed after, wanting to sleep, or perhaps just die and get it over with.

There was another rap at the door.

"Come in," she croaked. There was no way she could get to the door again, and she hadn't bothered to lock it when the woman left.

"I have Lord Marut's personal physician," came a familiar voice, deep but pleasantly female. Belili raised her head. It was Ligish, followed by an ancient, bronzed woman, older than Gemeti, most of her hair a shock of white, but holding a wide streak of black. Belili locked eyes with Ligish for a long moment, promising a long talk as soon as they were alone.

"Let us take a look at you, hmm?" The old woman squinted toward Belili on the bed, shuffling over. She had a large pouch at her side, bulky with spherical objects. In almost the same method as the tailor, she poked and prodded, getting Belili to roll over, feeling the swelling in her wrists, knuckles, and feet. She investigated the damaged ear, picking off a stray bit of dried blood. Belili wondered why she didn't merely use a citron and get on with it, but she was too tired to care.

Finally, the physician stepped back, the wrinkles around her mouth and under her flat nose propelling her mouth to a frown. "I can help," she said, "but it will likely take several applications, over many days, to completely heal you. Even after, you may have symptoms."

Her eyes roved over Belili, and her face softened, wrinkles settling into new positions. "Poor dear. You do not know how healing works, do you?" Belili shook her head.

"For natural sickness, the one healing must know which disease they are to heal. For sickness *given* by a black-hair"—she raised a hand at Belili's open mouth—"hush now, it is easy to see this was given to you. For such a disease, only the giver can truly heal it. But I will do what I can."

She peeled a citron, gave the rest to Ligish, and chewed a slice noisily, with a smack of gums. Lightning ran along her arms, and up to her white hair. Her eyes rolled upward, then she laid one thin hand on Belili's forehead. Her other hand motioned to Ligish, who gave her another slice, her eyes roving over Belili with obvious concern.

Belili closed her eyes. There was more wet smacking. The pain lessened. It was splinters in her knuckles, not glass. Another jolt ran through her body. The splinters shrank to sand. More eating sounds. How many citron slices did it take? The woman's streak of black was at least as large as Ilzi's.

When she finally opened her eyes, Ligish's hands were empty. A line of juice dripped down the physician's whiskery jaw. The woman swallowed.

"Feeling better?"

Belili rolled her shoulders, which turned into a gigantic stretch and yawn. "Much," she said, when she could. The ache was still there, threatening, but it was manageable for now. Her hearing was back to normal, but her eyelids drooped.

The physician nodded. "I will come again in a few days. This should keep you going during the festival, though if you overindulge, you are liable to get sick faster. Rest till then." She patted Belili's hand, then shuffled to the door, not looking back.

Belili waited several moments until she was sure the physician was gone before her eyes were pulled back to Ligish, now Marut's shadow, still holding the citron skin. "You're alive. What happened?" was all she asked.

Ligish smiled back and threw the peel into the fruit bowl. Belili was again struck by the softness of her eyes. "I am. Lord Marut thinks I will look imposing and keep the other nobles from knocking down your door. He's right, but not in the way he thinks." She gave Belili a knowing grin. "He was desperate for a shadow, and I found myself in a position to fulfill that role a few days ago. Unfortunately, Lord Marut can be..."

"Odious?" Belili suggested impulsively. She was rewarded with a quick laugh.

"In a word, though he's *fairly* harmless. May I sit?" Ligish gestured to the foot of the bed. Belili pulled her feet up to give her room. Was the sudden warmth in her body from the healing, or something else?

Ligish sighed as she sat. "I've been running errands for that man since before dawn. But to answer your question, I stole a mori in Neharda while Ishkun-Dim-Hbelu gave those nobles more trouble than they could handle. They had no other silver-hairs with them at that time, and I was able to sneak away."

"But look at you." Belili opened a hand—her joints moving freely again—and indicated Ligish's sturdy clothes, her hair and face. She must have had as much help as Belili and Kisa. "You're beautiful."

Ligish gave her a long look, her lids lowering. "And I've admired you since Ilzi first brought me to your orchard, though we couldn't talk when that stink bug of a man was alive. Now he's dead, thanks to you." Her face softened. "Truly. Thank you. You've blossomed into your true potential, like I knew you would." Belili thought that was stretching things, but her back straightened at the words. Even with the physician's healing, she must be a sight, three steps from death.

"I wanted to see you again," Ligish continued. "I still have a few connections from my family, and I contacted an old friend in Neharda, who helped me hire a wagon to Karduniash. I knew you were coming here, and now I've found you, at last." Ligish leaned forward and grasped Belili's hand. Belili squeezed back.

"Now, I want to hear the real story. I cleaned up what you left of Ilzi. Good riddance. But I had better get the juicy tidbits to make it worthwhile." Her eyes were hungry with vengeance.

Belili stared, almost despite herself, at Ligish's posture, protective, yet safe, welcoming. Had she ever felt this way before? She gave a brief, but complete, account of her fight with Ilzi, leaving nothing out, even her hair colors. More than anyone she had ever known—even Kisa—she knew she could trust Ligish. They were the same.

"I've told you my side," Belili said, suddenly nervous at asking. "What happened to you? How did Ilzi trap you? You didn't grow up a slave like me."

"I did not," Ligish said. She took in a long breath, her eyes far away. "I pray my mother and my little sister, Sige, are well. I believe they are, since I accepted Ilzi's bargain."

"I am very familiar with those," Belili frowned.

Ligish nodded. "My little sister is a headstrong one. She remembers some of this place, where my mother used to work as a shadow, as I do now. But when our father was killed in a fight between two powerful nobles, my mother finally had enough. She took us far away from the capital, past even where Ilzi had his lands."

She paused, but Belili only watched her face, rapt as she searched for words.

"That may be why Sige would range far afield of our small homestead. Our garden and morus tree were sickly, and unbeknownst to us, she came up with a plan to fix it. Unlike my mother and I, Sige has a small lock of black—a gift from our father. All was well until she found a nearby property with a citron tree."

"Oh no," Belili whispered. Ligish nodded. Ilzi had loved his citron more than anything else in the world, except himself.

"She would use its magic to help heal our dying plants. But he caught her after she had run all the way from our homestead to Ilzi's plantation, climbed the tree, picked a citron from the top branches, then slipped and let the citron drop, where it fell upon a sharp rock."

Belili had a hand over her mouth.

"He brought her all the way to our house at knifepoint to ask us how we would repay the debt—*who* would repay the debt. I was the obvious choice. My mother was too old, Sige too young."

"Have you heard from them since?" Belili asked.

Ligish shook her head. "I dispatched a message from Neharda once I was free, but between the travel time to the Blasted Lands and my own travel, I have heard nothing."

Belili found Ligish's hands and held both. "You *will* hear from them. I know it. As for Ilzi, he's finally gone. All these years and all the pain he's caused me—caused us. He's gone."

Ligish smiled again, and Belili felt something in her shoulders relax—a tension the physician couldn't have healed. *That* was the feeling she had been hoping for since yesterday. Ligish gently pulled Belili into an embrace. Closing her eyes, she let her mask fall away and be happy, for maybe the first time in her life.

CHAPTER TWENTY-THREE

Whispered Words

Dumzi, Geshtna, Kigal, and Enta saw their creations cooperating, and saw the harm they had done to the lands they had cursed, now called the Blasted Lands. They decided to withdraw from the world for a time, leaving their creations to work together.

A light grew. Had it been four days? Five? Six? He had been fed six times, maybe once a day, though the intervals were by no means even. Forced to inaction, Hbelu had spent much of the time thinking, when he did not sleep. At least he was well rested, if underfed.

He meant to speak on his own terms this time, and he didn't care whether with Ata or Ilzi. Hbelu struggled to his feet, squinting against the brightness, though he knew it was only stray light from a torch, coming through the top and bottom of the door. One hand to the shelf to lever him up, foot braced against the bags he had been resting on. The scant objects in the closet had become old friends, coming easily to his hands.

Hbelu kept his eyes mostly shut, letting them adapt. He brushed off as much as he could of the dirt and grime. There was an extra bucket in the room, though after the time he had been in here, it stank. Or it should. He could no longer smell it.

The light flared brighter, and Hbelu forced his eyes open. He wanted to be able to talk, to look cognizant and reasonable. It was the only way he could convince the fourcolors to let him out. They would have to, eventually, for the Prunus Festival. If it had been six days, the festival was still a day away.

He heard the bags in front of the gods-rotten door sliding across the floor. The bar rattled in its holders. Hbelu moved fingers over his left shoulder, swollen and tender to more than light pressure. He had bruised it against the door's solidity, to no avail. He was sure the area would be black and green in the light. He had begun forcing the door with his right side, but ceased after the third day, as that shoulder swelled and bruised too. Not one of the door's slats was out of place.

Finally, the door swung open a hand's breadth. Hbelu was ready, and from the back wall, he rammed his right shoulder, the better one, against the wood. There was a cry, high and female, from outside, but the door only moved the tiniest amount. The heavy bags were still on the other side.

"Who's there?" he called, his voice a croak. "You are neither Ata nor Ilzi." He leaned against the door, slowly pushing the bags away.

"Stay in there!" Not only female, but a girl. Shuffling of feet. Hbelu put one eye to the opening. He could see only half the underground fertilizer room. The person must be around the edge of the door. He pushed again.

"Please stop." The voice was calmer, rational. Why did he need to open the door? His muscles relaxed, almost of their own accord.

"I would like to come out of this room," Hbelu said. Some voice in the back of his head screamed to force his way out, but it would not be considerate to the person out there.

"You may come out, but please do so slowly. I wish you not to intimidate me."

Well, that was reasonable. Hbelu put his shoulder to the door, ignoring the pain shooting through the bruise. He did not want to bother the person outside with the inconvenience.

The bags shifted across the floor, the gap in the door widening. When it was large enough, Hbelu slipped through. He had lost mass, and muscle, while captured. Good for fitting through doors, bad for overthrowing the fourcolors. The light was brighter in the open, and Hbelu squinted again in its full glare.

"That is far enough. Stand away from me, if you do not mind, and make no attempt to escape, for I wish to talk to you."

That was what he wanted—to talk. Who *was* this person? As his eyes adjusted, the girl—not far into becoming a woman, if that, raised a morus to her lips. Hbelu's eyes widened at the mass of hair, all the same color. All purple.

"You—how did you get here? Which caravan are you from?"

The girl stood straighter, talking from one side of her mouth. "I will ask the questions, if you do not mind." Hbelu felt his curiosity abate. He was being influenced by the power of Dumzi's morus, though having that knowledge did not let him break the hold the girl had over him. "My father and mother have told me much of the caravanners," the girl continued, "but I have not had the chance to converse with one personally. Fortunately, I found the provincial noble's room, and asked him to tell me where he had hidden you." She raised another morus for emphasis.

"Tell me what you wish to know," Hbelu said. "And who are your parents?" The first statement he was not averse to making, and that let him sneak a question in. He was familiar with the morus's tricks.

The girl put the godfruit to her lips, and Hbelu felt the hold on his mind increase. "My parents are the Dyad," she said. "That will be common knowledge in a few days. I wish to know why you and your caravanners continue to resist the noble's rule."

"That is a long answer, child," Hbelu began.

"I am not a child!"

Hbelu nodded. The morus's control was lessening, but he let its influence guide his answer. "Then what may I address you as?"

The girl held her head high. "You may call me Erishti."

Hbelu smiled. Information was congealing in his mind, information from many sources over a score of years. "Erishti then. I am Hbelu." He could see, even in the light from her torch, those characteristics strong in his people were lessened in the girl—darker skin, straighter hair, taller than he would expect for one of her years. Her hair, though, was— he tilted his head—*entirely* purple? Was that even possible? Though in contrast, the simple white dress she wore was silk, a blasphemous fabric he heard the upper echelons of the fourcolors used to show their power.

"Our people, the Asha-Urmana, those with purple hair, used to live in this city." He rubbed a hand through his dirty and matted hair. It likely appeared more brown with filth than purple. "The blond folk, with no magic, helped us build strong cities and farm land. This was before those of the four other hair colors came here, seeking our help." He licked his lips. "Would you mind if I had a sip of water? I have spoken little lately."

Erishti's face crinkled, considering, but she nodded. Hbelu slipped back into his cell and retrieved his bucket of water, nearly empty.

"May I sit here?" he gestured to the bags in front of the door. Erishti had not tasted a morus in several minutes. "This story is long, but I will tell it if you wish to listen."

"I...do," Erishti answered. She sat down cross-legged on the floor, between him and the exit to the ziggurat, heedless of what it did to her dress. "I have not seen another with this color hair before." She touched her purple locks. "Will you tell me more?"

By the time Hbelu told all he knew of the history of his people, it must have been late into the night. There had been a sliver of light just visible beneath the door of the ziggurat when he started. He had resisted asking questions, past those to make sure Erishti understood the story. He had not wanted to remind her of the mori. Several times he had to drink from his rationed bucket of water, when his voice threatened to give out.

"Now, do you understand what my people have been through?" Not "our" people. Not yet.

"It differs from what my tutors taught." Erishti played with one unbound tress. Hbelu was used to seeing girl's hair in braids, especially ones this young.

"Which do you think is the truer version?" Hbelu tread carefully with his questions, praying to all the gods.

"You sound as if you have lived what you told me," Erishti said. "And my tutor was a very old woman, who read dusty books to me in the tower where I grew up." She screwed up her face. "There was another tutor, long ago, but I do not remember him well."

Tower? How had this girl been raised? If the court of the Dyad did not know of her, she must have been isolated. He knew of the machinations that went on in the capital.

The girl was not finished. She shifted, wiping at smudges in her dress. "Yet if I believed everything I was told, I would be very foolish. Likely the truth is somewhere between the two, and now I know both, I may make my decision."

Hbelu raised his eyebrows. He had not anticipated such logic from a child, though what was one to expect from the Dyad's...daughter? Adopted, or stolen?

"Yes, the truth may be somewhere between," he allowed. "Though you see where I am"—he spread his hands—"and where the Dyad is. Does that give you more information?"

"I do not believe it is right to think you and the other Asha-Urmana are less than the nobles," Erishti allowed.

"What if I were to tell you I was planning on bringing the relations between the Asha-Urmana and the fourcol—the nobles back into balance? That you could see more people with your hair color in Karduniash?"

"From a gardening shed?" The guttering torch—they'd had to light a new one—showed disbelief on Erishti's face.

Hbelu smiled. "I will admit this was not in my plan. Though I think with your help I could give my plea to the Dyad. I hope for everyone to be equal, rather than having a concentration of power in the fourcolors—pardon—the nobles. Surely you see that using the blonds as slaves is wrong?" He did not want to scare the girl off, but he had to decide now, whether he would stay or leave this night.

"The blonds?" Erishti looked genuinely confused. "They are powerless. My parents told me we must help them become better, and so we use them, and in doing so, show them by example."

Hbelu did not grit his teeth. "Do you think you would want to have a metal collar around your neck, forced to do whatever your master says?"

"Well, no, but..."

"What would you do, if that happened to you? Surely your parents have given you this situation as a puzzle, to help you learn to rule after them?" Did the fourcolors shield their youth so much?

Erishti was shaking her head. "I only see Sibi and Ishta once a year, when they visit my tower. This is my first visit to Karduniash. My tutor hardly mentions the blonds."

"Then after tonight, watch them," Hbelu told her. "See if you would want to be in their situation, or if you would rather our roles be balanced." He spread his hands. "This is your chance to see how the court of the Dyad works. You have heard my story. It is up to you to determine whether the current state should continue, or if the Asha-Urmana, the nobles, their servants, and their blond prisoners should all be free to pursue their own paths without impeding other people."

Hbelu had decided. Slowly, so as not to startle the girl, he got to his feet. She rose too, eyeing him, fingers near her remaining mori. Hbelu gave her a nod and backed toward his closet.

"Wait. Do you not wish to escape?" Erishti took a step after him.

"Very much," Hbelu answered, "but I am putting my faith in you, little one. We will meet again at the Prunus Festival." Even if he could not touch the fifth godfruit at the same time as the Dyad, he would wager this little girl could.

"May I...may I see you again?"

"The Prunus Festival runs for two days, correct?" Hbelu asked. The girl nodded. "The Dyad are traditionally given their gifts on the second day?" Another nod. "Then I should be here for another night, if you wish to come again."

He stepped backward, squeezed through the door, and pulled it to. "Goodnight, Erishti," he called. "You should get your rest before tomorrow night."

"Goodnight, Hbelu," the girl answered, her voice uncertain. He heard the bar shift, and bags pushed back across the floor. After a few minutes the faint light faded away.

Hbelu sighed in the dark. He hoped he was doing the right thing.

CHAPTER TWENTY-FOUR

The Prunus Festival

Thus, the gods did not see the red, black, brown, and silver-haired people push the purple-haired ones out of their homes and into the wilderness. They did not see the practice of slavery start again. They did not see the people of the four colors become fat and corrupt, holding sway over all other people.

Kisare picked an imaginary piece of dust from the bodice of her cotton dress as she climbed the last set of stairs. She resisted the urge to look out the windows, even higher than she had been this morning. At least now the sun had set. She could only see pinpricks of light—all of Karduniash lit up. The citizens of the city were celebrating the Prunus Festival below, slaves, servants, and those nobles not invited to the palace. Aricaba-Ata never celebrated the festival back in his orchard. She didn't know whether through lack of knowledge, or because the festival was not a tradition outside of the capital city.

She reached the high doorway; its marble lintel polished until it glowed, following on the heels of the set of nobles in front of her. Gemeti walked behind, at a respectful distance.

A man dressed in a servant's white and blacks and even paler than Kisare stood next to the entrance to the Dyad's quarters. His hair fell past his shoulders in a flow of natural white-blond and the Dyad's swirl of colors was on his chest. He announced the name of the couple before her, then looked her up and down, taking in Gemeti a step behind. Kisare was about to tell him her name when he spun and addressed the room, half-full of nobles.

"The Lady Mulagunna-Kis, hailing from the Blasted Lands to the north, and servant Gemeti, once of Karduniash."

Kisare resisted the urge to run as eyes turned to her, sure her face was turning red. Gemeti gave her a tap in the small of her back, and Kisare took a step into the room. It was bright, and the ubiquitous mirrors lined the walls and ceiling, reflecting several beehives' worth of lit candles. Most eyes left her, and she relaxed. Amilanu would be here somewhere, a bastion of safety. She also needed to find Aricaba-Ata, without being recognized, and Bel. Her old master might even have Hbelu with him, though unlikely. He would have that slime Enti-Ilzi trailing him, as usual. She was willing to use godfruit on them, if necessary, to get them to talk about Hbelu.

Her cotton boots made no noise on the marble floor. The crowd pulled her in, and suddenly she was surrounded by the festival. Loud conversation washed over her, too garbled to understand. The walls seemed far away, and the ceiling, decorated with frescos celebrating the godfruit trees between the mirrors, was taller than twice her height. A pair of silver-haired nobles with skin the color of maple wood danced, limbs twisting in impossible combinations too fast for the eye to follow, and lightning danced with them. Every few steps they would pause, showing off postures no body could stay in unaided by godfruit. A red-haired noble, moderately dressed, chewed godfruit. He held a bowl of mori, then floated it from his hands with his mind, passing the bowl around the group he was with. Each other noble took a handful, and he offered it to Kisare as she passed. Her first inclination was to decline, but then she straightened her back. *A noble takes what she wants.* She grabbed a couple with a nod of her head. The noble—quite attractive, really—winked back, but Kisare kept walking. She didn't need any distractions, and the godfruit would be useful if she wanted to move around unseen.

The room was immense. Even at the top of the ziggurat, the room was wider than a field of grain back at the orchard. In the middle of the room, leaves reflected light from the mirrors and Kisare strayed closer. She could just see...

"Trees," Kisare whispered to Gemeti. "There are godfruit trees surrounding—"

"Surrounding the Dyad's thrones. Of course there are," Gemeti answered. She was wearing voluminous clothes as usual, but the top layer was a simple white cotton dress. "Only the morus and prunus will bear at the festival."

"It's like the Asha-Urmana village. Hbelu's village," Kisare said. She eyed the surrounding nobles, eating godfruit and laughing. So much lightning lit the air that the massive room stank of ozone. None were paying attention to her.

Gemeti nodded. "The trees have been there for many years. Whenever one dies, it is pulled out entirely and replaced with another, rather than leaving the stump. Rumor says the tradition dates to when the palace was built."

"By the Asha-Urmana." Kisare completed the unspoken words.

"Keep walking," Gemeti said in a low voice. Kisare almost couldn't hear her over the murmur that ran through the room. "Make your rounds. Show off that pretty dress. Let the nobles see you, become familiar. You want everyone to accept you before you do anything...unconventional." Her voice dropped at the end, but Kisare nodded, walking farther into the crowd, her head held high.

Past the red-haired noble were two lanky young men, shirtless, lying across from each other on a low divan, head-to-head, propped up on elbows. Lightning ran down their arms and legs and...Kisare quickly averted her eyes. The young men were not wearing much clothing.

After a moment's hesitation, her eyes were drawn back. A blond servant stood by the pair with a bowl of prunae. Both had a streak of black in their white-blond hair, and the nobles shifted closer, sharing a long kiss. Then one broke off and traveled farther down to—

Kisare hastily looked the other direction again and heard Gemeti's deep chuckle behind her. "Ah, the black hairs. I may have taken part in a few 'tasting sessions' myself when I was younger. Prunae bring out the passionate this time of year. Of course, those without magic have to taste the more traditional kinds of 'fruit.'"

Kisare walked the other way, Gemeti still laughing at her embarrassment. No one had mentioned how...free...the festival would be. She headed for a table, hoping for a plate on which to put the mori she held. There was no point in eating them yet. Gemeti wanted her visible.

Tables stretched out along one whole side of the room, lit with many candles. There were fine porcelain plates, and scores of crystal vials, cups, and glasses. Beside them stretched the food and drink, and Kisare's eyes lit up. Godfruit was everywhere.

She pushed through the crowd to see punch bowls with dark liquid, wine bottles, and large jugs of water, condensation beading on their surfaces. Next to them were trays piled with all sorts of food imaginable, with towers of cheese, and elaborate constructions of vegetables imitating animals, and slabs of cooked meat molded in the shape of gardens. Fresh malae and citrons hung from papier-mâché branches. Piles of prunae and mori spilled onto the table. There was candied godfruit and regular fruit, prunae crystallized in ginger next to glazed strawberries, next to citrons in a jiggly mold. The cooking process would destroy most of the magic, but she imagined that wasn't the point.

There was a pop next to her, making her jump, and a noblewoman with a streak of brown and black appeared. "Trouble deciding?" she asked, and Kisare nodded. "Try the choca covered prunae." She took a quick glance at Kisare's hair. "You've never smelled anything so good." She dipped a vial into a bowl of dark liquid and disappeared.

Kisare hesitated, wondering what "choca" was, but took a prunus dipped in some dark brown goo from the tray the woman indicated. She thought about putting it on her plate, but then shrugged and popped it in her mouth.

As she bit down, her eyes rolled back in her head, and she shivered. The brown goo was rich, bitter, and sugary all at the same time. Her increased sense of smell made the prunus a mouthwatering tart confection in the middle of the choca. Juice filled her mouth. The pairing was something directly from the gods themselves. She heaped several more of the choca-prunae on her plate as she inhaled deeply. The aroma of the food made her mouth water. Even the scents and perfumes of the nobles around her smelled delicious. With wide eyes, she waved one of the choca-prunae to Gemeti, who was filling her plate with meats and cheeses, and the old woman smiled back, nodding. Kisare pulled a few of each godfruit, including some candied malus and citron slices, onto her plate. She swallowed, guilty at the wasted magic, the scents fading, but quickly bit into another dipped prunus. She couldn't help herself.

More confident, Kisare turned from the table to search for one of her targets. While she walked, she bent to Gemeti, who was munching on a bit of aged cheddar.

"Don't the slaves eat the godfruit?" She watched a collared and manacled blond shuffle forward with another tray of meats to restock the table.

"Watch your use of language," Gemeti answered quietly, and Kisare felt her back straighten automatically. "To answer your question, I am certain there are some who get the chance to indulge." She nodded her head toward a line of natural blonds, servants and waiters, unchained, standing at attention to serve the nobles. "There is a very well-defined hierarchy. Even if a slave were to show off they had color, they would be torn apart by those wishing to keep them in their place."

"But aren't—are there not more slaves than nobles?" Kisare still couldn't understand why a slave would stay such, in a place like this. She and Bel would have been free in minutes.

"There are many slaves," Gemeti said, "but the nobles pit them against one another so they will not think of working together. Now, stop asking questions liable to get us thrown in prison."

Kisare fell silent, and waded through the tide of nobles, hearing snatches of conversations.

"I am keeping my gift to the Dyad a secret this year. If my sister does not know what it is, she cannot show me up."

"Why do they keep those trees in here? They have so many more in the glass houses outside, and those stay in bloom the year round. These shed leaves on the—"

"—local guard is recruiting only black-hairs this summer. They anticipate a larger crop of mori than average."

"I had my shadow follow that upstart noble from up north to see if I could glimpse this present he has been talking up—"

Kisare spun, trying to find the source of the last voice. It had to be referring to Aricaba-Ata and Hbelu.

"Mulagunna-Kis! How are you enjoying yourself so far?"

Kisare spotted the bulk and thick mustache of the Master of Planning. He was wearing a full silk robe, tied at the top with a complicated knot and open underneath to show a cotton suit, cut with slashes of bright greens and reds. Balu was behind him, trailing as Gemeti did for Kisare. She wanted to search for the noble she had overheard but dared not offend her one ally.

"Quite well, Hasis-Adra-Amilanu. It has been...eye opening."

Amilanu chuckled. "Then if your eyes have been widened already, let me introduce you to the Dyad."

Kisare barely kept from glancing to Gemeti for confirmation. That would not look confident. "Is that a good idea, so early in the festival?"

"Absolutely," Amilanu said. "They have already asked for the sisters from the exotic and little-known Blasted Lands, and it is...not a good idea to keep the Dyad waiting. We will keep it short for now. If they approve, you may have another audience tomorrow to bestow your gift."

Her sister. Bel was around somewhere. Kisare longed to find her, find out if she was all right. But the Dyad—they might not even get another audience? What about their "present"?

"What do you say?" the Master of Planning asked, extending a hand. Gemeti tried to take the plate from her other hand, but Kisare pulled it back. She dared not go to see the rulers of this slave nation completely without defense, even though there was only...one choca prunus and two mori left. It would have to do.

"Fine. Let's...let us meet the Dyad."

The Master of Planning gave his own plate and cup to his daughter and led Kisare forward. The big man carved a path through the nobles like a tree falling through a forest of saplings. Soon the leaves of the four godfruit trees surrounding the dais came into view. The prunus and morus were fruiting, the citron and malus with only leaves and small buds. The dais was set slightly past the center of the room, and the ceiling above the trees was cut away to give a view into the upper floors. She could just see a skylight at the top of the pyramid, giving a glimpse of Shir-Gal peeking through, nearly full, though Nana-Ru was not up yet. The moon bathed the trees in a paler light than that reflected by the mirrors.

As the crowd parted and became more rarified, Kisare saw there was an uneven spot, directly in front of the dais.

The old man followed her gaze and leaned close to her ear. "Another tradition. There is a patch of bare dirt in front of the thrones, so the rulers must cross it when mounting to their seats. It is said to remind them that their power comes from the earth."

Or from the trees permitting them to enslave the blonds.

Amilanu moved the nobles aside with his bulk or a few words. All here had at least two colors in their hair, joking and laughing as if they knew each other well. They all moved aside at the Master of Planning's presence, and soon Kisare was standing before the dais, the buds of a malus tree to her left, and morus leaves and godfruit above her head to the right. She pushed a few fallen godfruit aside to avoid stepping on them, glancing down at the two more still on her plate. Gemeti had been right, as usual.

In the center of the trees was the raised platform holding two figures seated in chairs, each with a swirl of hair around their shoulders. The Dyad. Kisare's heart thudded, and without thinking, she popped the choca prunus in her mouth, shuddering. The scents of the trees and the perfumes of the nobles intruded, and then, the unmistakable scent of godfruit wood, and varnish. Her eyes climbed to the chair backs, rising high above the Dyad's heads. Kisare had seen similar smooth grain and whorls of color in the stumps of older trees in the orchard. Some were polished in respect for those buried beneath them. All four trees were represented in the thrones.

The two on the thrones broke off conversations as Amilanu approached, and both stared openly, faces expressionless, at Kisare. She swallowed.

"What new item have you for us this time, Hasis-Adra-Amilanu?" asked the one on the left. The voice was smooth and high, and Kisare wasn't sure whether they were the male or the female. They both shared long hair, hanging over their shoulders, down thin chests to their waists. The one on the left had red and brown on the left shoulder, black and silver on the other. The Dyad on the right was a mirror image. In both, there was not a single strand of blond hair. They wore white silk, with patterns of godfruit sewn in different colors.

"My lord and lady," Amilanu bowed, "allow me to present Mulagunna-Kis, a noble who hails, with her sister, from the very edge of the Blasted Lands to the north." He turned to Kisare. "These are Samsu-Iluna-Nur-Sibi and Samsu-Iluna-Nur-Ishta, the Dyad."

"And where is the sister? You have brought us only half the pair, Ami." The one on the right leaned forward, peering into Kisare's face. "Not much to look at." This one's voice matched the other in tone and lightness.

"Ah, I am told the other sister will be appearing shortly with the Master of Silkworms, Ishta." Even Amilanu sounded nervous.

Ishta—the woman?—snapped a finger and a collared blond brought a basket of godfruit to her. She gestured impatiently, and the blond, shaking, hesitantly picked a citron slice and held it out.

Ishta took it with a pleasant smile, locking the blond in her gaze. Slowly, she crushed the citron slice in her fist, juice squirting and running down her arm. Then, still with the pleasant smile, she threw the crushed remains back in the slave's face.

"A prunus, you idiot. Not a citron." Her voice did not rise. The slave picked out a prunus with a shaking hand, but Ishta reached past him to pluck her own from the basket. "This one. You should have known, dear."

Ishta ate the prunus noisily, slurping the juice as she looked back to Kisare. "Still not much to look at. Do they breed you ugly, out in the Blasted Lands, Kis?"

Kisare was breathing quickly. She tried to keep her face neutral, felt her skin flush. "No...my...my lady." She desperately hoped she was correct in the title. "My sister is quite beautiful. I am told—"

"I would still take this one," the other twin broke in. "She has spirit, and courage to speak with you, Sister. You can have the pretty one."

"You like your girls ugly and your boys pretty, Sibi," Ishta berated her brother.

"You know my eyes are only for you, dearest Sister," Sibi replied, taking a slow glance up and down his sister. Kisare took a small step backward. She wondered if the two had forgotten about her.

"Do not move, ugly sister," Ishta told her, not looking. "We have not finished with you." She started suddenly, standing to look over the heads of the nobles. "Ah. Here is the other now. You can compare, Sibi, and tell me which one you really want more."

Bel was here? Kisare was split between relief at seeing her sister again, and disgust at the Dyad, discussing her like a side of meat. The nobles put up with this? It was barely better than being a slave. Still, she stretched to see over the crowd of nobles and their servants.

She felt a touch at her elbow, which quickly became a hard claw, and Kisare hissed in a gasp of pain. Her eyes widened as she found Sibi, one foot down from the dais, clutching her arm.

"Come up here with me, my pet, and we will see how your sister reacts to seeing you on the arm of the Dyad!"

Kisare let herself be pulled, eyes glancing at Amilanu, then Gemeti, for any help. There were appreciative murmurs from the crowd around the dais, and even some scattered clapping. Gemeti gave her a tiny shrug, mouth tight.

"You will not need that here." Sibi took the crystal plate with its pair of mori and threw it to a waiting slave, who barely caught it, mori flying to the floor at her feet. Kisare saw the slave glance down, then resolutely back up at her rulers.

Sibi stroked her arm, a smile on his empty face, and Kisare shivered. Surely they wouldn't...try anything in the middle of the Prunus

Festival? Kisare remembered the black-haired couple she'd glimpsed near the entrance. It seemed many things were acceptable in public at the festival. She tried to relax and failed. Sibi's thin fingers were cold and bony on her arm. As much for a distraction as anything else, Kisare stood tall, looking over the heads of the crowd.

She saw a vision of beauty enter the hall, dressed all in a shimmering dress of silk, white with slashes of brown. It was the same design as her cotton one. Bel could never keep from showing her up, could she?

* * *

Belili kept her face neutral as the eyes of the crowd played over her. Marut was standing like a rooster after the first crow of the morning, his hand uncomfortably low on her waist. She barely kept from twitching away. Ligish was a step behind, and Belili took strength from the woman's presence. They had spent much of the day talking and touching, heads together, in her room, as Belili regained her health. They'd had little time to simply talk, when Ilzi had them both manacled. Belili wished she had found Ligish on the Aricaba orchard years ago. It would have helped to have someone she could relate to. She would make up for that lost time now.

Marut pulled her into the confusion of the festival, and all Belili saw were open mouths, bright hair colors, and toadying looks for the Master of Silkworms and his latest catch. At least the powders and paint Ligish had helped her apply hid her true face. Nobles displayed their power with magic tricks, abusing the power the godfruit gave them. Belili ran through the list in her head as they made a path through the attendees, matching hair colors to effects of the godfruit.

Marut made a stop by the refreshment table, and Belili made sure to give him an excuse to show her off. She filled a plate with unadulterated godfruit, then accepted a slice of malus in some sort of sugary coating from Marut. She smiled back.

Then they were off again, traveling through the crowds, always toward the back of the room where she could make out shapes of godfruit trees under a skylight. As if she needed more proof the nobles had stolen Karduniash from the Asha-Urmana. It was a similar pattern to the trees planted around Hbelu's ziggurat, back in the village. Unlike in the glass houses, these trees were free to grow according to the seasons. As Marut introduced her to a pair of noblemen, one with a streak of silver and red, the other with red and black, she wondered how they pollinated the trees in the hall. Probably slaves did it by hand.

All too soon, Marut made his way to the dais near the middle of the floor, leading her by one hand. Belili looked to Ligish for support, and the shorter woman smiled back. Belili turned forward at Marut's pull and ate a prunus, letting the hidden red in her hair increase her sense of sight. The Dyad were occupying the seats on the dais, looking very stern, and—Belili's eyes widened—was that Kisa standing next to one of them?

Marut saw the same thing and she felt him tense. "Your sister, I presume?" he said to her.

"Yes, my lord," Belili answered. She could feel Marut's disapproval radiate from him. He had not been first to present his prize. "I am certain the Dyad will be eager to meet the other half of the famed sisters from the Blasted Lands." Belili turned the sentence into a harmless giggle, but she noticed Marut pick up his step.

"Doubtless." The word dripped displeasure.

Both of the Dyad—a strange, matched pair, nearly identically thin and tall, but for mirrored hair colors—stared at them when Marut pulled Belili to the front of a crowd of two- and three-color nobles.

"So, this is the pretty one," the one on the right said. Belili used the last of the prunus juice, held under her tongue, to look at the person's throat. Female. Then the other was the male twin. "Come here, my child. Let me look at you." The female Dyad held out both arms, throwing one look to her brother, who held Kisa prisoner with one hand. Kisa looked like she was about to throw something, possibly the Dyad.

"My lady," Marut began with an overly formal bow. "Allow me to introduce Anagmeshu-Bel, one of an exquisite pair of ladies hailing all the way from the Blasted Lands, far to the north. I had the extreme pleasure of meeting Bel here—"

"Do shut up, Marut," the woman said, still holding her hands out. Bel's estimation of her went up a notch.

"Of course, my lady Ishta."

Belili felt the noble's hand drop away, took a step forward, watched the woman's eagerly beckoning long-nailed hands, and took another step onto the dais.

Ishta grabbed at her like Belili was a juicy citron and pulled her close, examining her with narrowed eyes. She smelled overly sweet.

"Much prettier than yours, Sibi," she chided, looking to her brother with an almost jealous glare. Belili locked eyes with Kisa, trying to greet her and calm her all at once. They would get out of this, somehow.

"Stand next to me," Ishta commanded, and Belili took up a place next to her, standing tall. "Oh, you make a splendid figure," she said, gently squeezing Belili's upper arm. "So strong, and with such a full body."

"You have restraint, both of you," Sibi commented. "Mulagunna-Kis was telling me you have been separated for days now, set upon by bandits. You must tell each other of your adventures for our enjoyment."

Belili heard the crowd of nobles murmur in approval, and Ishta clapped her hands. Belili shrank in at the attention of the crowd, then squared her shoulders. A noble would not hunch.

"Godfruit, for all," Ishta commanded, and five blond slaves, iron collars on their necks, came forward with baskets overflowing. Bel took a prunus and a few slices of citron since Marut had taken her plate when she climbed the dais. Maybe the increased senses would keep her alert to differences in their stories. Ishta took a citron slice, biting into it with relish and letting her eyes roll back. Her brother took several prunae, eating one after another, but Belili saw Kisa take only one prunus.

The Dyad let the little bursts of lightning play over their bodies, but there was no outward sign of magic. Both swallowed before reaching for more godfruit. They weren't even using the magic they were wasting?

Belili ate a slice of citron, feeling the magic of the juice fill her mouth. She let herself grow a little stronger from the red, reluctant to waste the godfruit, as Kisa told a tale of her first time in a big city, with her *servant* Gemeti, over-pronouncing the word every time as if trying to alert Belili to their cover. She resisted phasing out of Ishta's tight grip. The woman would just counter her.

Then it was Belili's turn, and she related a simple version of what had happened, turning the guards into bandits, chased for a day, with a desperate jump over the castle walls when she couldn't find the gate, and a glance at the wonderful glass houses. Kisa nibbled her prunus while she listened, nostrils flaring, narrowing her eyes every time Belili dissembled. So, she had been through Mistress Arahuna as well. She would give them away if she was any more blatant. Kisa watched her carefully when she edited parts to leave out her red hair, and she skipped completely over the incident with Ilzi, hoping Marut had stopped any rumors before they started.

As she came to the end, there was a rustling in the back of the nobles. Several grumbled, and one complained out loud for the new arrival to "find a place with his equals." Belili would have ignored it, but she saw Kisa tense, eyes widening and nostrils flaring. It wasn't because of Sibi at her arm this time. Kisa was watching the crowd.

Belili paused in telling how Marut escorted her to the party as she looked over the crowd. There was a flash of red hair, moving quickly. It couldn't be. Kisa was about to tear herself away from the Dyad. Belili made a quick motion toward her, and Kisa stopped, but her eyes held hatred. They couldn't offend the rulers of the nobles.

Aricaba-Ata pushed forward, his parted streak of red nestled in white-blond. It stood out against the two and three magical colors of all the other court attendees. He was wearing a dark cotton tunic, bland against the silk prevalent with the high nobles of Karduniash. The massive bulk of Shuma loomed behind, dressed as best as she had ever seen him in a robe of fine-spun wool. Two other nobles followed him, one with red hair and a beard, and another woman with silver. Aricaba-Ata stared at Belili, then at Kisa, wrinkling his nose as if he couldn't decide if what he saw was truth or a strange coincidence.

"My dear, you have forgotten the best part of your story," Ishta said into the sudden silence. "Especially now *he* is here." Belili stared at her, calm on the outside, breathless with horror within. "The violence. The blood. Such fitness in our young noble." Ishta sucked in a great breath of air, as if relishing a delicious scent. "Surely you will not keep us in suspense about your old lover? Jilted, was he? Did he find another woman? Another man? I have rarely heard of anyone pushed to such sweet revenge."

Belili kept silent, for once at a loss of what to say. Disgust flooded through her at the implication there was anything remotely consenting between her and—

"Speak!" Ishta was suddenly in her face, the woman's eyes wide. "Tell us how and why you murdered this little noble? What was his name?"

Don't say it. Please. Belili was breathing hard, her control gone. She searched out Ligish's eyes, then her sister's. Kisa was staring at her in shock, her half-eaten prunus forgotten.

"His name was Enti-Ilzi," came the hard voice of her former master. Aricaba-Ata was pale with rage, even under his umber complexion. "My cousin. My blood. And this...this *slave* killed him."

There were gasps from the nobles, but Sibi sat straight in his chair, still gripping Kisa's arm. "Speak when you are spoken to, little noble," he said, and Aricaba-Ata shrank back. "You throw a dangerous accusation carelessly. These women have magic, yet come from near the Blasted Lands, where our rule does not extend, where no godfruit grows. How can they be slaves?" The ruler's face was open, questioning, though he obviously knew the lie of his words.

Belili took a risk. "He calls us slaves in error. After all, he is very familiar with my pedigree." She locked eyes with her father, whose mouth worked silently. So, he would not spill that secret yet. "Further, he has another free man locked up unjustly, who he is planning to give you as a present."

Aricaba-Ata glared daggers at her. "A handsome present, I hope," said Ishta. "I dislike my toys ugly." She cast a significant glance at Kisa.

"Do you have a present for us as well, my pet?" Sibi asked.

Kisa nodded quickly. "My sister has carried it all the way here."

Aricaba-Ata shot her a strange look, probably wondering where they had gotten enough money to buy a gift worthy of the Dyad.

Ishta patted Belili's hand, running her thin fingers through Belili's. "Oooh. A contest then, to settle this little dispute. It will be the highlight of our festival. A suitable birthday present, don't you agree, Brother dearest?"

Sibi tilted his head once. "Acceptable. Better than listening to this crowd try to one-up each other." There was nervous laughter among the nobles.

Ishta let Belili go to wave her hand, encompassing the gathering, "Then you will all enjoy the Prunus Festival, until late into tomorrow night. These sisters will give us their present, as will this noble.

Whomever's present is deemed best will win our favor. And maybe another favor or two." Ishta smirked at Sibi.

Sibi winked back, then pinched Kisa's breast. He let go to tent his fingers, and Belili saw her sister slump. "There will be no telling. Such lovely anticipation. I will not have our excitement ruined early." Aricaba-Ata looked like he would say something more, but Sibi stared him down.

"Then I will be back tomorrow, with my present," her father said at last, and stalked away from the dais. Shuma and the other nobles followed.

Ishta cupped her hand and called after him. "He had better be handsome."

There was scattered laughter again. Belili stumbled from a slap to her backside, and she grunted in surprise before she could stop herself.

"Now go enjoy yourself, and your sister." Ishta cast her what was supposed to be a smoky look. "I may call on you later. Or maybe Sibi will." She waggled a finger. "No more killing. I can stand to lose a few backwoods farmers, but the capital nobles will eat you alive, pretty sister."

CHAPTER TWENTY-FIVE

The Court of the Dyad

Those of the purple hair tried to call on their gods, to ask why they had been forsaken. For the first time, the gods did not answer, and the Asha-Urmana despaired.

Kisare pulled Bel off the dais as soon as Ishta finished shaking her bony finger. She wanted to be as far away from the rulers as possible. Aricaba-Ata knew about them!

"You still have it?" she said in a low voice to Bel. Without the box, everything was lost. The Dyad would stick them back in service to Aricaba-Ata—or to the two of them. She shuddered at Sibi's claw of a hand.

"Yes," Bel told her. "Now hush. You will spoil everything. Stay calm."

Kisare raised her eyebrows at her sister. Bel was never so forceful. It had only been a couple of days—long ones—since they were separated. She pulled Bel toward the far edge of the huge room. The farther they got from the center, the less the nobles would have heard of their exchange with the Dyad.

"What happened to you? Did you really kill Ilzi? How did you get into the city? Did you have trouble with the—"

Bel raised a hand and Kisare stopped talking, frowning back. She wasn't sure she liked this new version of her sister. She took in the silk dress, trying not to think of all the mori that might have been grown instead.

"We must know more about the nobles here. We need to find Hbelu before Aricaba-Ata presents him."

Bel was still speaking like a noble. On consideration, that wasn't a bad idea. Kisare stopped near a wall. There was a high window, letting in Shir-Gal's moonlight. It was already getting late, and Kisare wondered how much sleep they would get before the end of the Prunus Festival.

She looked both ways. There were no nobles within hearing, at the moment. She had to take a chance on some brown-hair listening in with a prunus. At this end of the hall, there were fewer partygoers and more servants and slaves, bustling new trays of food and drink. Doors opened along the far wall to let them in and out.

She waited for a group of slaves to pass, chained together and carrying a gigantic platter with cooked vegetables arranged in the shape of a massive bear. "Some of the nobles here are sympathetic to us. Gemeti introduced me to one, the Master of Planning for the city. If we can get word to them, they may support us when Hbelu activates the seed with the Dyad."

"How will that happen?" Bel whispered back. "We do not have Hbelu."

"We need a plan." Kisare hoped he wasn't suffering under Aricaba-Ata's care. He was somewhere nearby. Even not counting the box and the seed, she wanted to see him free and the Asha-Urmana back in their rightful place. Truth be told, she just wanted to see him. "What about the other caravans? Mushezibti-Lila must have contacted them. Can we get to them?"

"Hardly. We have no idea where they are. But we will figure out something," Bel told her. Kisare fumed. She wondered how her loose leaf of a sister had even gotten into Karduniash with no plan. This was why Enti-Ilzi was dead, and why Aricaba-Ata knew they were here. She was ruining their chances.

"I think we should split up," Bel suggested, and Kisare felt her eyes widen.

"Now? I only just found you."

"We have to cover ground. One of us can talk to the nobles, the other can look for Hbelu."

"He's obviously with Aricaba-Ata, just hidden," Kisare told her. "Ata's the one we have to track down."

Before she could say more, Gemeti appeared, squeezing Bel's shoulder. "Good to see you again, girl," she said quietly. "I'm only now free of that bunch." She jerked her head toward the crowd around the dais.

Close behind her came another silver-haired noble, not Waqrat. This one was short, well built, and wearing a form-fitting black wool uniform of some sort. To Kisare's surprise, she also brushed Belili's shoulder, and her sister...leaned into the touch?

"I am 'clearing the way' for Marut, so we must speak quickly if you have any plans you do not wish overheard." Her hand groped, and

Belili's filled it, a strange expression coming over her face. It took a moment before Kisare realized she was seeing behind that mask dominating her sister's face. She looked between the two.

"Kisa, this is...Ligish," Bel told her.

Kisare's eyes were already wide, but she made sure not to gape. *This* was the subservient slave cowering behind Enti-Ilzi? How had she gotten here? How had Bel rescued her? She forced herself to act calm, as collected as Bel.

"I gather you are aiding us?" Kisare asked, trying for casual. She'd never directly asked about her sister's romantic inclinations, but this...made a lot of sense. Ligish nodded. "And you work for that...worm-master now?"

The silver-haired woman snorted laughter. "As appropriate a name as any, though you may not wish to use it in his presence."

Gemeti looked Ligish over, lifting a hand to her chin, but her fingers were twisted oddly, pinky back and over the next finger. Ligish rubbed her nose, but Kisare saw her pinky was crooked in the same way.

"I see Ligish is familiar with those who think as I do," Gemeti announced, then looked between the two holding hands. "I am glad you two find comfort in each other, but I knew Marut when he was a spoiled babe, and if he is anything like he was then, he will not look kindly on this."

Ligish reluctantly removed her hand from Belili's. "True. Fortunately, as his shadow, he notices me as little as possible."

"Shadow." Kisare focused on the woman. "Another noble called me that. Ata was terrified of them. Why?"

"Shadows are the spies of the nobles. They gather the choicest bits of gossip to keep their masters' and mistresses' epithets sharp."

Kisare pursed her lips, looked to Bel. "Fine. If you want to split up, then stay here with your worm-master. I must follow Ata."

Ligish shook her head. "You are untrained, and from what I heard when I was a captive of Ilzi, Ata is as paranoid as they come."

Kisare only smiled at her. "You can't have had much more training than me, and he's *my* paranoid noble. I have known him all my life."

She spun from the women, pushing through thicker crowds as she reached the food tables. She grazed, filling a large crystal cup with handfuls of mori as she found them. Enough to last her for several hours. Then seeing a plate of cheeses and meats, she took a cotton napkin, and wrapped up a selection. If she *did* reach Hbelu, he'd be hungry.

When she reached the end of the table, she popped one of the small godfruits into her mouth, shivering, as little bolts of lightning trailed down her body. When she looked down, she couldn't see herself. She slipped from the throne room, noting a few other shimmering outlines of silver-haired men and women along the way. Other shadows, on the lookout for their masters.

* * *

Kisare hurried down corridors, searching for Ata. He had a lead of several minutes. She had served the man her entire life, save these last few months. She knew how he worked. Kisare began planning as she ran.

Where would he put Hbelu? It was a good hiding place, if the other nobles hadn't sussed it out. She noticed her arms and legs becoming visible and ate another morus from her cup.

Why hadn't the nobles found Ata's hiding place? They knew the capital much better. It would be close to the palace, if not in it. Ata would not want to inconvenience himself.

Kisare scrambled down another flight of stairs, almost colliding with a red-haired noble whose skin was a deep shade of walnut. She skidded to one side, wishing she had thought to bring a citron. The man must have heard her movement and reached out blindly. Kisare avoided him, catching a better glimpse of his face as she passed. It was the noble who had been with Ata the previous night, and at the court. She would recognize that ridiculous blond beard anywhere.

"Where are you running to, shadow?" the man yelled into the air. "You can't hide from old Cit forever."

Maybe, but I can for now. Kisare slowed, tiptoeing down the rest of the stairs, leaving the man groping his way behind her. When she reached the bottom, she sped up again, turning down the next flight of stairs, and eating another morus.

She was going the right direction. Hbelu must be downstairs somewhere. A memory of Mulagun surfaced, strung up in punishment for one of his many escape attempts. Ata always preferred making examples of slaves near the godfruit trees, as if reminding them of the source of his power.

She ran down several more flights of stairs, half watching ahead of her, and half watching the stairs so she wouldn't break her neck. It was only by a quick glance up she saw a shimmering form in the next hallway entrance to the stairs. As the figure turned, Kisare backed up, out of sight, and peered around the corner. More godfruit, another shock of magic in her mouth. The person was similarly hidden from sight. Ah, it was the silver-haired noblewoman she had seen with Ata, and who had accompanied him tonight. Waqrat. Her form wavered, as if seen through a pane of glass or a sheet of water.

Kisare was definitely going the right way. Ata had left his compatriots in a string behind him. But why was the woman out in the hall? Did that mean Ata had gone across this hall, to a different set of stairs? Likely. There was no way Kisare would get past the woman, but she could go down another level and cross there, and hope she picked up Ata's trail again. She ducked down the stairs as the woman turned away.

Soon, Kisare was near ground level. Chewing again, releasing juice into her mouth. She had the timing down and knew how long before eating each piece of godfruit.

Hbelu wasn't hidden near the godfruit trees in the throne room, so if Ata was following his pattern, that left somewhere outside. She guessed the Dyad got all this godfruit—especially the malae and citrons somehow out of season—from somewhere in the grounds of the palace. The Dyad didn't strike her as the type to depend on other nobles for their supply of magic.

She stopped on the ground floor, eyes peeled for her former master. She slowed as she reached a servants' entrance, leading outside the massive ziggurat. The door was pulled to, but not shut, as if someone had passed through recently. Kisare ate another morus before opening it.

It was dark outside, but Kisare would keep her magic going as long as she could. Shir-Gal's light helped, as did that from the palace, glinting off a structure in the near distance. A gazebo maybe? Or a small outbuilding? She crept closer.

Something flared to her left, and Kisare turned toward it. It was gone now, but it had looked like torchlight, quickly hidden. She padded that way, reaching one of the small pyramids encircling the palace like goslings around a swan. There was light visible under the door.

Kisare settled down to wait at the edge of the building, letting the effects of the morus leave her. Either this was Ata, or some servant or slave on an innocent errand. If the latter, she didn't know what other path to follow. Her hand crept of its own volition to the few godfruits left in the crystal cup, but Kisare closed her fist and set it firmly in her lap. No wonder the nobles guarded their magic so fiercely.

Shir-Gal had not moved far across the sky when a noise alerted Kisare. She peeked around the corner, long enough to see a lock of red hair against brighter white-blond. The umber of Ata's skin faded into the night, his cotton tunic little brighter. Kisare flattened herself against the building as he paused, looked around, then crept back to the palace.

She waited for twenty long breaths after he was out of her sight, her heart thumping in her chest. She knew who had to be in the building. Kisare went to the door and pulled it open to reveal a dark hallway. Ata had made a light, so there had to be a torch somewhere, but she had no flint. Ata could as easily have used a malus to increase his eyesight. She felt along the wall, finding a torch still warm, and descended deeper into what smelled like a storage shed, though a very large rat must have died in here. Or maybe several.

Kisare felt blindly, letting her eyes adjust to the trickle of light coming from the entrance.

"Hbelu?" she called softly.

There was an answering thump from her left, and she groped forward, almost tripping over a pile of what felt like bags. Behind them, another door.

"Hbelu, are you in there?"

"Kisare? Is that you?" He was past the door. Kisare tugged bags away by feel, then ran fingers up the door. There was a bar. She struggled to pull it up, out of the sockets.

"Kisare, you found me." The voice was deep, but hoarse. He sounded tired.

"I found you," she repeated. "Bel's here too, with the box. We're all here, in Karduniash." She was babbling. She fumbled too long with the door, finally wrenching it back with a growl. The smell hit her first, of unwashed man and excrement. There was movement toward her, and she put hands up, found larger, callused hands.

"Hbelu," she repeated. Why was she crying?

"I would offer you a chair," Hbelu said, "but I fear my host has not left me one."

"Come on. I have to get you out." Kisare pulled at his hands. "We can talk after you get cleaned up." She felt rather than saw him shake his head.

"I cannot leave."

"Why?" Kisare felt down his arm. "Does Ata have you chained? I can find something to break the lock."

"That is not it."

"Then why not?" she laughed. "You wish for more nobles to come beat you? What about the plan? Activating the fifth godfruit? Overthrowing the nobles? You can't do that from here."

"You may be surprised." Hbelu let go of her hands, and she heard him brace against the wall. Her eyes were adjusting to the darkness, by the light trickling from the upper doorway. She could make out his shaggy head, hair dirty and matted.

"I cannot go with you now. If Ata finds me missing, it will only rouse his suspicions and those of the Dyad. The best way for me to get close is to wait one more day. The presentations to the Dyad are at the end of the Prunus Festival. I have waited this long."

"Then let me stay and talk with you a while." Kisare pushed the door open wider to let in more moonlight. "I have food for you." She pushed the table scraps into his hands.

"I would welcome your company," Hbelu said.

* * *

"So that was the sister you told me of," said a voice at Belili's ear. Marut had finally joined them. One hand rested possessively on her shoulder, and she fought not to shrug it off. Belili watched Kisa's back as she strode down the table, gathering godfruit and food. Her sister had grown older, more decisive, in the few days they had been separated.

"We must be seen, my dear," Marut continued, moving his hand down her arm. Ligish met her eyes, then dropped her head to follow. Bel watched the woman's strong biceps, the tailored waist of her uniform, before giving in to the noble's hand pulling her. Gemeti was behind them, but Marut took no notice of the old woman, probably assuming she was someone's servant.

The red and silver-haired noble began a story about some relation of his who, through a tedious set of circumstances, ended up missing the last Prunus Festival. Bel stopped listening and watched the party, looking for a way to talk to more nobles. Gemeti was the one with contacts, so she claimed. Belili thought of the hand sign she and Ligish traded. If she could only get Marut away from her for a few minutes, she could ask about it.

They slowed as they approached a group of men and women sitting at a table with a bowl of prunae in front of them, all four hair colors between them. Their skins ranged from rose-pale, to bright copper, to one beautiful woman with nearly onyx features. They had delicate and fragrant foods on the table, a trio of musicians nearby plucking chords on their sitars and zithers, and several intricate puzzles set up by the bowl of godfruit. A trio of collared slaves stood ready if they wanted anything. It was the purest expression of the Prunus Festival she had come across, simple yet decadent. How did the nobles stand two solid days of eating nothing but godfruit? She did not envy the slaves cleaning the latrines.

"Perhaps we can stay here a moment, and enjoy the festival?" Belili offered as a test. If she could get Marut to talk to, or at, another noble, perhaps she would have time to talk to Ligish and Gemeti.

The noble only sniffed. "I have no time for such hedonists," he said, but his eyes drifted to a raised platform set nearby, where a pair of dark-skinned nobles wrestled in their shirts and breeches, both with streaks of red in their hair. Belili guessed they augmented their strength with citrons.

"Then perhaps wagering on a contest of strength?" she offered. "Who do you think will win?"

"An interesting question," Marut observed the two. "I believe they are from the south, perhaps as far as Rammat. Unknown quantities." He thought, then gestured over a servant in black and white with the Dyad's swirl on her tunic and dropped a few coins in her hands with some words. One wrestler flipped the other and pinned an arm down, and Marut leaned in. He was caught, at least for a few minutes. Belili stepped back just slightly, enough so his hand dropped from her arm. He only shifted his position to better see the match.

Belili took another step back, leaning on years of experience removing herself from Ilzi's side, and found Gemeti and Ligish.

"You said you had allies here," she asked the old woman. "Are there any we might speak to now?"

Gemeti nodded, the lines around her mouth pursing as she thought. "A few. I have already introduced your sister to my greatest confederate, a high noble in charge of city planning named Hasis-Adra-Amilanu, but he will not risk his position in such a public atmosphere. There are others I know."

"How long will he be here?" Belili asked Ligish.

The shadow cocked her head, gauging her master's back. "A good thirty minutes, I would think. More if he discusses strategies with a noble he knows."

Belili stepped forward again. "My lord, I have had no chance to see the festival yet, as I was speaking with my sister."

"She is fiery, your sister." He looked back to the match, sucking in a breath as one of the combatants slipped out of a pin. "If she were to compete, I would place a heavy bet on her." The noble laughed at his own joke, and Belili pasted a smile on her face.

She trailed one hand down the sleeve of Marut's tunic. "I will be back soon, my lord. I wish to mingle, where I can tell the other women how I captured your favor for the festival."

Marut grunted appreciatively but was already turning back. Belili took the chance to escape.

It took at least ten minutes for Gemeti to lead them around the festival hall, tagging various nobles with her crooked-pinky gesture. A pale older woman with a flat nose and eyes made up to look wider, her head shaved but for a large brown lock hanging to one ear. Two men with black locks, copper skin, and high cheekbones, who walked close and touched each other frequently. Ligish traded a look with them and took Belili's hand again after that with a gentle squeeze. Another woman, dark and thin in a high-collared blue cotton gown, with a curled lock of red. A pale, heavyset man with nearly translucent skin, a full beard, and a wide section of silver. Last, a fully blond woman, evidently a prosperous merchant who had got an invitation to the festival by her reputation. None of the nobles had any servants or slaves with them.

They formed a small circle in a corner of the hall, out of easy hearing of others, and Gemeti took the center, looking to each individual in turn.

"You all know me, from letters if not by face." There was mumbled agreement. "We, and those who cannot be here tonight, all share like views regarding the current structure of power in the capital." More agreement.

Gemeti pulled Belili forward, but she was remiss to let go of Ligish's hand. Ligish came with her, gently rubbing the muscle between Belili's thumb and forefinger. Belili felt her shoulders relax at the touch. Only now she was out of Marut's influence did she realize she still felt weak from that morning. The healer had taken away most of her symptoms, but it had been a stressful day.

"This is the noble I told you of, from the Blasted Lands. She brings the approval of the Asha-Urmana caravans with her, and if you do not know how slaves and servants are treated in the orchards on the outskirts of the empire, she can give you first-hand experience. Please, allay any concerns you have. If you have been hesitant to act, the time is fast approaching where you will need to decide on who you support."

The red-haired woman with the high collar spoke first. "Is it true the blasted lands kill all who tread on them? That there is no ruler and no godfruit?"

Belili had no idea, but she also knew better than to hesitate. "A rumor propagated by the elite in Karduniash. They wish to keep their power centralized."

"The orchards—they do not hold the Prunus Festival, do they?" This was one of the black-haired men, who shared a look with his partner.

"I have never celebrated it," Belili answered truthfully. "They look down on anything that runs contrary to any of their traditions." She raised Ligish's hand. Ata had beaten a male guard whom he had found with a male slave. It was one reason she had never actively courted someone like her. That and Ilzi.

More questions came after, about her life, slavery, the Asha-Urmana, and her travels. She answered what she could, deflected what she couldn't or wouldn't.

Finally, the heavyset noble with the silver streak spoke. He had been silent the whole time. As he shifted, a geometric tattoo showed above his neckline. "What is this change Gemeti warns of? Why should be we be forced to choose now?"

Belili inhaled slowly. Kisa would kill her if she knew what she was about to say. "My sister and I found an...artifact blessed by all four gods. The Asha-Urmana believes it may rebalance our society. We will present it to the Dyad tomorrow." Vague, yet menacing. She was prepared to deflect more questions, but the silver-haired noble fell silent, frowning.

"I believe it will begin the changes we have hoped for," Gemeti added. "Especially concerning the rumors of a captive Asha-Urmana in the palace. Does anyone else have word on this?"

The blond merchant, surprisingly, was the one who spoke. Her voice was quiet, yet insistent. "Lady Ishta summoned me four days ago for a jewelry fitting. The piece was much too small for her, and I asked to see the recipient, for a proper fitting. The lady was...hesitant"—the merchant rubbed her wrist, as if massaging an injury—"but finally agreed. I was introduced to the girl they will present tomorrow, and told not to say anything, on pain of imprisonment." Her voice lowered even more, and she glanced around as if she could see any threats. "Her hair was entirely purple."

Belili let her surprise show. This must be the one Mushezibti-Lila requested they find.

"This is the second time I have heard this news," Gemeti said. She smoothed her layered skirts, then folded her hands together. "The Dyad are getting closer to their ambition of ruling all five hair colors, and if they do, it will go poorly for the rest of us. Munaw, you must give me more information later. I may need to go exploring."

"Why would this Asha-Urmana, and such a powerful one, stay with the Dyad?" Belili asked. "Even a girl could plan an escape." Her mind went back fifteen years, to stealing a single slice of citron from Tiamai's parlor. The old mistress was trusting of the slaves working in the house, raising Belili for the job. She knew of her husband's indiscretions. With the strength it gave her, Belili broke the lock on her cell, leaving Kisa asleep with the slave wet nurse who had replaced their mother. She only got as far as the edge of the orchard.

Belili flicked the stump of her little finger as the older woman with the shaved head and lock of brown spoke. "The rumor in the court is that she has been a captive of the Dyad all her life. No one knows where she came from. Some think they must have captured a pregnant Asha-Urmana."

Gemeti shook her head once. "They keep good account of their people. I would have heard if a pregnant woman went missing."

Why did that seem familiar? Belili remembered an aside, back at their first meeting with Hbelu's elders. It was weeks ago, but he was speaking of how he persuaded his caravan to settle in their village.

"It was twelve years ago," she broke in, over something the red-haired woman was saying. "And not a woman, a man."

"Ahiyaba." As Gemeti said the name, Belili nodded in agreement. That was it. "He was the last one of the Asha-Urmana captured by the nobles and unaccounted for, right around the time Ishkun-Dim-Hbelu came to power. Ahiyaba was powerful in his own right, and may have even rivaled Ishkun-Dim-Hbelu for rule." Gemeti looked thoughtful. "Let's see. Afterward, they removed themselves further from our society. He was never found or confirmed killed. No demands on the Asha-Urmana came from his capture, no requests for ransom. They could have forced the Asha-Urmana in much the way Ata hopes to tomorrow."

"What does this have to do with the girl?" the other black-haired man asked. "They may have tried to breed him, but if her hair is as pure as you say, it makes no sense."

"The Dyad have lusted after the Asha-Urmana's power for years," Gemeti said. "There is some other seed planted here, I know it. I must find its sproutling." She moved closer to the blond merchant, speaking low and urgently, and Belili thought to ask the brown-haired noble of more rumors in the court, but Ligish pulled her hand away. Belili looked up into a clean-shaven face, red and silver locks above.

"Anagmeshu-Bel," Marut said. "I have been looking the room over for you, asking among the influential nobles, but none have seen you."

"I have been keeping her safe, my lord," Ligish offered.

Marut looked over the group, one side of his mouth pulling up. "Fine, fine. I can find much better company for you, my dear." He put a hand on her back, pushing her to one side. Belili thought of resisting.

Only one more day. "I fear my lord has pressing business for us," she said to the gathered nobles. "You will excuse me, I am certain."

The group made their goodbyes, none looking at Marut, and Belili reluctantly went with him, Ligish trailing behind. Gemeti stayed with the group, and when Belili took one last look back, she was moving off with Munaw, the blond merchant, still in conversation.

CHAPTER TWENTY-SIX

Silent Words of a Spirit

Secrets are like new growth. Wherever there is space to grow, they send up new shoots, seeking the sunlight of rumor and intrigue. Always, hope was hidden away.

"Ilzi is dead." Hbelu felt Kisare shiver as she spoke. "Bel killed him." She had brought him up to the present on all that had happened to her and her sister.

"I do not envy those she hates. I have just learned this myself," Hbelu told her. "Ata told me." He felt a loose tooth with his tongue.

"Did he hurt you?" Kisare growled in the darkness. "I can't see anything. Let me—" She took a small step closer.

"No," Hbelu broke in. "The light will only hurt my eyes, and...you need not see what he has done." Kisare's hands left his in an instant, moving up his arms, to his face, feeling the week of new growth on his face, his matted beard and hair. Hbelu sucked in air as her fingers touched the open wound on his cheek.

"Sorry." She softened her touch, feeling the extent of the injury.

"The injuries he inflicts are merely to show his power," Hbelu answered.

"I can find someone to help. Gemeti could heal you. There's godfruit all over the palace."

"Gemeti?" The name sounded vaguely familiar to Hbelu. "Ah, the one who frees blonds, from Neharda."

"Yes, she helped us. Without her we wouldn't have contacted Mushezibti-Lila."

It might have taken longer, but the caravans would have eventually found the sisters—for the box they carried if nothing else. "And you have the seed of the fifth godfruit?"

Kisare nodded. "Bel has it safe, though I wish she would stay with me. We split up again, for her to learn more of Gemeti's friends in the capital. I came here. I followed Ata, using mori." She sighed, the air brushing his cheek, and Hbelu knew she felt the pull of the godfruit as all magic users did. "Has no one else found you? Ata has been paranoid over other nobles figuring out his secret, but it was easy for me."

Hbelu smiled in the darkness. Kisare had grown since they separated. She was strong, and smart, and capable, as he knew she would be, with time to become herself. "I have seen one other than Ata and Ilzi—when he was still among us. She is coming again later. It is another reason I cannot leave."

"Who? Waqrat?" Kisare demanded. "But no, she did not know, at least not yesterday." She finished running her hands over Hbelu's head, down his neck and chest, then came back to his hands, with his broken and chipped nails—souvenirs from attempting to wrestle manacles and cage bars.

"Not Waqrat, thank all the seasons," Hbelu said. "No, an Asha-Urmana girl visited me, a strange encounter."

"The girl Amilanu spoke of? She is a secret around the palace, and the Dyad will present her tomorrow, I'm told." He felt Kisare squat, and he followed, glad not to stand in the cramped closet. Her warmth, her gentleness, was comforting. One of his own people would have been standoffish, concerned with his status. Kisare had never cared, as far as he could tell.

"Amilanu?" Hbelu asked.

"He's a powerful noble, and an ally," Kisare said. "Gemeti introduced us."

"I see. This girl was raised by the Dyad, she tells me, uncertain of her heritage," Hbelu told her. "She promised to come back tonight, and I believe she may help us."

"Then I will wait with you." Kisare said. She fidgeted with his fingers, seeming unwilling to let them go, and he relaxed into the motion. Finally, she spoke again. "Hbelu, are you sure you are doing the right thing?" she asked. "We only have an old story to go on, and a single seed."

"A glowing seed, marked by the gods," Hbelu reminded her, squeezing her hand. "Is this not a bit late?"

"I've seen so much more since we left the village," Kisare told him. "I was naïve then, going on about being a free woman, and how Bel and I would make a new life under the nobles."

Hbelu wisely did not comment on that. "Then we will rely on the Asha-Urmana who encircle the city." He deftly changed the subject away from her incompetence. "Their shock troops and scouts are moving through the countryside. They only wait for me to raise a ghost to signal them."

A ghost? How would that happen? Kisare sounded dubious. "After getting godfruit somehow? What if they cannot break into the city? They have been defeated before. If the seed doesn't sprout, it will be the same this time."

"Your friend Gemeti has allies, and we have two former prisoners with us," Hbelu countered. "The Asha-Urmana united with the blonds far outnumber those who call themselves 'nobles.' Surely you can convince some of them to our side?"

"Not all blonds will join you, even if they know the nobles are powerless." Kisare told him. "Many give up under the life the nobles enforce. Others are only out for money or power. I've seen the court."

"Some will. We must have faith in Dumzi, Geshtna, Kigal, and Enta."

Kisare snorted. "The ones who don't speak to you anymore?" she asked. "The ones who told you to keep your magic separate from the 'fourcolors'?"

Hbelu's shoulders tightened. "Why would that be an issue?"

Kisare slumped against the closet wall. "Ugh, how can you live with that smell?"

"The smell is the bodies of twenty or more of my sister and brother Asha-Urmana, slowly decaying." Hbelu tried to keep the anger and pain from his voice, though Kisare recoiled. "Ata and his soldiers killed them when they tried to free me. The fourcolor brought their corpses as another present for the Dyad and their stock of godfruit trees."

"Your elders will never admit a 'fourcolor,' even a slave, after what happens tomorrow," Kisare said. "If there are even elders left."

"There will be," Hbelu said. "There have always been Asha-Urmana."

"Who hold themselves apart from the others—who want to keep their magic pure," Kisare sounded accusing now.

Hbelu tightened his hands on hers. He could hear Muze-Shi lecturing him on his duties as prince of the Asha-Urmana. "We must deny our power to the Dyad." Slowly, he pulled Kisare's hands closer. "Otherwise, we would have been overrun generations ago."

He heard Kisare shift forward at his pull. "Then if we overthrow the Dyad, if we balance the Asha-Urmana and nobles and servants and blonds...then...will your caravan accept someone who does not have purple hair?"

Hbelu pulled again, then grunted as her head lay against his chest. Blinking, Hbelu put one hand on Kisare's hair, stroking. "If all that happens, I think Muze-Shi might even find a place for a certain woman with a streak of silver."

"I would like that," Kisare said.

* * *

They must have fallen asleep, Hbelu lying against the bags of dirt. Kisare was a weight at his side, one hand on his chest. What had awakened him?

Light, coming around the door. "Kisare, wake up," he whispered. She responded to his urgency, if nothing else.

"Hm." She pushed away, and her hands rose to rub her eyes.

"Ishkun-Dim-Hbelu?" It was not Erishti's voice, and he stiffened. He had not told her that much of his name. Bags were shifting, outside the door. One of Kisare's hands squeezed his upper arm. She pushed away and up, light flooding the room as she looked at him. Her face pulled into an expression of pain, and he wondered at his appearance. She shook her head, but had no more time for words. He and Kisare would face whoever was coming together.

"The girl is not able to come tonight. I found her as she snuck out of her parents' apartments. However, she told me of your hiding place before the guards brought her back to the Dyad's suite." The voice was an old woman's, and Hbelu heard shuffling feet accompanying the increasing light.

"Gemeti?" Kisare asked.

Hbelu had time for one startled look before the door to his closet opened. He squinted in the light.

The woman with the torch was dressed in layers of clothes, her hair entirely white with age. Though as Hbelu looked closer, it did not seem she was as old as the elders of his caravan.

"I came as soon as I could," Gemeti said. "The girl did not leave until her parents were senseless from an overdose of godfruit alcohol." She sneered. "Still, they must have discovered her nighttime wanderings and posted more competent guards."

"This is the Nehardan woman who works with the blonds?" Hbelu asked. He was trying to keep up with how many people other than Ata knew of his hiding place.

Kisare nodded and turned to Gemeti. "You saw her? The one Mushezibti-Lila asked us to find?"

"I did, and talked to her briefly, under cover of helping the guards round her up. We led them a little chase, but they were too close. They would have followed her down." Gemeti faced Hbelu. "She asked me to bring her condolences to you, Ishkun-Dim-Hbelu. She said she would have liked to talk to you again before the end of the Prunus Festival."

"I feel the same," Hbelu said, frowning. This woman knew much about his business. He had heard of Mushezibti-Lila's contact with the fourcolors in Neharda, knew she acted as a guide to escaping prisoners, but... He leaned over to Kisare. "What does she know of you and your sister's involvement?"

"Everything," Kisare answered, not bothering to drop her voice. Hbelu grimaced. "I didn't trust her at first either, but Bel liked her, and told her about the box and our plans." Gemeti was watching them both with a funny little smile, one eyebrow up. "Honestly, we would never have made it to Karduniash if she hadn't helped us."

Kisare spread a hand toward Gemeti. "I don't think I ever really thanked you for that."

"No matter." Gemeti waved the hand not holding the torch. "It was time for me to get up to my old tricks in the capital."

"What time is it?" Hbelu asked.

"Well past midnight," Gemeti answered, "but not yet morning. We have time, and I wish to know more of what you plan, Prince. I have allies who can help."

Hbelu shifted his shoulders. Another who insisted on titles and lengthy names, even when he was covered in injury and filth. Kisare was so...practical. "This was not how I intended to arrive in the capital, but as I am here now, I think this can be used to our advantage." He held a hand out. The other he left on Kisare's shoulder. "Please. Welcome to my parlor. I have many visitors lately."

Gemeti made herself comfortable on the bags outside the door, wrinkling her nose at the smell. He and Kisare dragged more bags out of his closet. The decomposing corpses were at the other end of the large room, and he had not been able to smell them, or himself, for a few days. Kisare at least was willing to stay near him.

"Did you bring godfruit?" Kisare asked. "Ata was here before me, and you can see what he did." She waved a hand at Hbelu's face. With all the minor cuts and scrapes he had suffered over the last several weeks, he was becoming numb to more. He could tell one eye was swollen by his reduced vision.

"I did." Gemeti adjusted her position to dig into her voluminous clothing. She pulled out a small bag, then a citron slice. Hbelu narrowed his eyes at Gemeti's white hair. What did the woman have hidden? She shrugged in return. "Easier for me to pass with little notice, but I have a streak of black." She leaned forward, one hand out. "May I?"

Hbelu nodded once. "A little healing. Ata will remember the next time he comes. I can feign that his blows were not as strong as he thought, but not that the blows did not land."

"Why stay here at all?" Gemeti still had one hand raised. "We could have you out of here easily." She chewed the citron slice, shivering, then traced fingers down the side of Hbelu's face. He could feel the swelling decrease and a small sigh escaped him.

After she finished, he shook his head. "I have already told Kisare. I will not leave yet. If we charge in, the Dyad and their guards will cut us down with little effort. It is why my people have not attacked the capital in centuries. The fourcolors are petty and divisive, but they are strong."

"We can plan." Kisare, of course. "Can we use the girl to get closer to the Dyad? Or maybe she could activate the seed—"

Hbelu cut her off with one hand. "I have already thought of this. I planned to talk to the girl this night, but we will have to wait until the festival."

"Do you think she is trustworthy?" Kisare asked. "How long has she been under the Dyad's control?"

"Her entire life," Gemeti said, and Hbelu tilted his head to her point.

"Yes, but where did she *come* from?" Kisare pressed. "I mean, a girl with purple hair can't be the Dyad's child, can she?" She would always get to the heart of the matter.

"Ahiyaba," Gemeti said. "I learned this a few hours ago."

Hbelu was instantly alert. "Where did you hear that name?"

Gemeti pointed to Kisare. "Her sister. Or rather, Bel triggered my memory. Said you mentioned it to them once."

"Yes, a member of my caravan. But why—" He cut off, thinking.

Gemeti waggled a finger. "Yes. The timing is interesting, isn't it? How old would you say the girl is?"

"Eleven? Twelve?" Gemeti nodded at his answer.

"What are you going on about?" Kisare had her hands on her hips.

Hbelu let out a breath he hadn't realized he was holding. "The last Asha-Urmana captured by the fourcolors, before recent days." He gestured to the other end of the large room, where the corpses festered. "It was a little over twelve years ago."

Kisare's mouth made an "O." Then she turned to Gemeti. "Do you have malus slices? If Hbelu could raise Ahiyaba's spirit, we can ask him ourselves."

Stupid. Hbelu had not even contemplated the idea, so concerned he was with playing out Ata's drama until he was presented to the Dyad. He raised Kisare's hand to his lips and kissed it. "Another reason Muze-Shi might accept you. Your insight." Kisare hid her smile.

Hbelu looked into Gemeti's confused glare, to Kisare's hand in his. "A long story. I promise to explain, if we live through the next day. Do you have malus?"

He could tell Gemeti wasn't satisfied, but she nodded. "Almost half a godfruit." She dug around, then handed him a piece.

Hbelu bit down in relief. How many days since he had tasted godfruit? He let the shiver run down his spine, felt little lightning strikes play down his face and chest. He closed his eyes and let his sense of the dead expand outward. The recently deceased across the chamber were the biggest pull, but he refused their quiet pleas to avenge. Later.

"I am sorry, brothers and sisters. Your pleas of vengeance must wait a little longer," he said.

There were a multitude of little dead animals on the grounds of the palace, but he was looking for humans, and ones dead many years. He extended his search, straining the limits of his senses. Though he was one of the most powerful Asha-Urmana, he could reach no farther than the palace and the crypts underneath. It was a vain hope that Ahiyaba's corpse lay nearby. It was possible the man was even still alive, somewhere.

"If Ahiyaba's corpse is farther than the palace and crypts underneath, or if he is somehow still alive—ah!" A familiar presence tugged at him.

"You found him?" Kisare clasped her hands together, fingers feeling the opposite knuckles.

Then he saw Ilzi's torn and burned face. But he refused that man too. "Hm. No—it is Ilzi." He peeked an eye at Kisare. "Your sister truly took her revenge."

The magic was fading, and he held out a hand. Gemeti placed another slice into it, and he chewed, replenishing the magic. Searching this large an area took much power.

He dug, rooting through faces whole and mutilated. Rich fourcolors, traitors to the Dyad, servants and blond prisoners by the score, worked to death before their time—

Wait.

A flash of purple hair, hidden. Cut, then bleached, like one of their prisoners. Yes, the face was right. Hbelu pulled the shade to him, opening his eyes and standing. Kisare and Gemeti rose with him.

He gestured again and Gemeti put the rest of her malus in his hand. Three more small slices. He ate one. They would have to work quickly, based on the distance of the ghost from his death, and his age. With both hands out, he used his legs to lever himself to his feet.

A shape floated through the far wall, walking without feet touching the ground. Kisare sucked in a breath as the shape came closer, and Gemeti grunted in sympathy.

There was a flash of short hair, cut and bleached. Ahiyaba's shade was missing all but one finger on his right hand, the ones on his left bent and twisted. Open wounds were visible through rent clothing, and he stared at them with only one eye.

"Are you...Ahiyaba?" Kisare asked. The shade nodded.

"Do you know of the girl Erishti?" This from Gemeti. Again, a nod.

Hbelu shifted malus juice to one side of his mouth, the taste already becoming bland. He had a guess what happened. "Did you tutor the girl before the Dyad grew tired of you?" Vigorous nodding at that. Hbelu took the chance to chew another slice.

"Then you are the girl's father?" Kisare asked. Now the shade paused, before tilting his head to one side. "What does that mean?" Kisare looked at Hbelu. Back to the ghost. "Can you talk?"

In reply, Ahiyaba opened his mouth, displaying only a mass of blood and missing teeth. He uttered a wet croak, then closed his mouth and growled. Kisare shivered.

"The Dyad took precautions," Gemeti said.

Hbelu tried again, sucking juice back. "Is Ishta, the female Dyad, Erishti's mother by blood?" Again, the spirit nodded.

"So, she's the mother and Ahiyaba was—not quite the father?" Kisare spread her hands. "Can you tell us anything else?"

Ahiyaba made a complicated gesture, opening his mangled hands wide, then holding up one crooked finger, then two.

Hbelu put the last slice in his mouth, making sure both women saw. Not much time.

"Can Erishti be trusted to help the Asha-Urmana?" Kisare again. In answer, the shade nodded, then beat his twisted right hand against his heart, then at his temple.

"I think he means he taught her some of her history," Gemeti offered. Ahiyaba pointed his one finger at her.

"Was this why you were killed?" Hbelu asked. The strain of keeping the form coherent and answering questions took a great toll. He couldn't hold much longer.

One last nod, and Ahiyaba began to drift backward, pulled away as the magic lessened.

"Wait! We have more questions," Kisare called after him. "What about Sibi? How does he fit into this? How does..." She trailed off as the ghost gave one final nod and disappeared into the stone wall.

Hbelu swallowed. "That is all we will learn. If nothing else, the girl has a chance of aiding us, both from Ahiyaba's assessment, and from my discussion with her yesterday. But we cannot depend on her. I say we go with what we originally planned." He pointed to Kisare. "You and your sister bring the box. Ata will bring me. The Dyad will accept both gifts, and once I am close enough, I hope to convince them to activate the fifth godfruit with me."

"And hope the Dyad does not kill us all before you can do so." Gemeti sighed. "It is getting late, and we should fix this place up. No telling when Ata may come back."

Indeed, Hbelu saw a sliver of light spilling down the stairs. Outside, dawn was coming. "Agreed. Help me shift the bags."

They worked in silence, making sure all was as it had been before, the door to the closet only open enough for Hbelu to fit through. Afterward, Gemeti offered her bag to him.

"You used all the malus, but the other three godfruits are in there. They may help you tomorrow, if you can hide them on your person."

"Thank you." Hbelu accepted the bag.

"Come on, girl," Gemeti said.

"One minute. Make sure no one is out there," Kisare said, scowling toward Hbelu where the old woman couldn't see. Gemeti humpfed, but went up the stairs, shaking her head and muttering.

"Stay safe until tonight," Kisare told Hbelu.

"I do not plan to go anywhere." He held a hand out, and she put hers in his. He raised her hand to his lips, but Kisare pulled, and he stumbled forward. She hugged him fiercely.

"Ugh, you stink," she said into his ear. "This had better work, so we can clean you up. You'll have to reintroduce me to Muze-Shi."

Hbelu smiled at her, and Kisare pulled his head closer, brushing her lips against his. Then she pushed him back. "Go on. I'll lock you in."

Hbelu squeezed into his room, and heard the bar fall into place. Pale light filtered under the door as her footsteps faded. Then he was again left in the dark.

CHAPTER TWENTY-SEVEN

Daughter of Two Nations

Whispers of the secret Kigal told Darice-Ili-Aya still survive. One day, those of the purple hair and the gods' first children, the blonds, will regain their original status.

Kisare felt dozens of eyes on her when the servant at the door announced her entrance to the great hall. Thoughts of Hbelu raced through her mind. Many had seen her with the Dyad the day before. What would they think of her tonight?

Gemeti followed behind her, eyes touching every person they passed.

"Look forward," Gemeti whispered. She poked Kisare in the small of the back. "You must ignore me. I am your servant, barely worth your notice. This night is for you and your sister." Kisare frowned at her but raised her head and focused forward. Time for things to change.

"Just worried about Bel. I would rather have the box with me," Kisare whispered over her shoulder.

She made the rounds of the banquet tables, gathering dinner and a selection of godfruits, but she paid little attention to what she ate.

An attractive noble with a splash of brown falling into his eyes motioned her over with a smile. He held up a prunus for her. He was no older than she was. If she had been born in Karduniash instead of in the orchard, or born to a mother who didn't have her hair bleached, would she be sitting there, waving a pretty boy over to nuzzle? She would never have met the Asha-Urmana prince. She shook her head at the young man, though she felt the smile grow as she did. The youth shrugged and went back to his friends. He was soft, raised in luxury. He had nothing on Hbelu.

With a sigh, she cast around for a way to appear occupied, to keep other nobles away from her. More food? Maybe she could find a corner to hide in.

She was about to head for a table piled high with cheeses and sliced meats when the servant at the door announced, "Lord Isbi-Bar-Marut, and Lady Anagmeshu-Bel." Kisare spun to see their entrance.

Bel was hanging on the Master of Silkworms again. The worm-noble had another silk jacket on, yellow this time. His streaks of red and silver meant he was not as powerful as Amilanu. Ligish, the woman Bel favored, stood behind them, dressed all in black again.

Bel had on what looked like a *second* silk dress, in silver with the same brown slashes. Kisare pulled out a fold of her cotton dress. She had cleaned it today, at least to get the worst grass and mud stains out. She had thought it an incredible gift when she first received it, but now knew it was only a serviceable garment, in the capital.

Kisare shivered. Bel had killed Ilzi. She had good reason to hate the man, but her sister had also left an impressive line of bodies after their escape from the orchard. Bel sought revenge ferociously for all that had happened to her.

Kisare made her way to Bel, draped over the arm of her noble. Gemeti followed. Bel nodded to her, a rare smile gracing her face. Kisare's eyes went to her other hand, holding a bundle wrapped in oiled paper. The box. They were finally here.

Kisare smiled back at her.

"Marut, would you be a dear and get us all vials of juice? I want to experience the last day of the festival as fully as I can." Bel turned a radiant smile on her escort.

"Of course," the worm-master answered. "Did I ever tell you of the time my great aunt came dressed only in—"

"The vials." Bel lifted her eyebrows at him.

"I shall be back in a moment," he said, and hurried off. Kisare watched her sister's face relax as much as it ever did. She pinched the bridge of her nose with her free hand. Ligish came up beside her, rubbing her shoulder.

"That bad?" Kisare asked.

"I only have to put up with him until we give the Dyad their present. Do you think if I killed him to shut him up, they would let us stay the rest of the festival?" Bel asked. Kisare laughed nervously. She was not entirely sure Bel was joking.

"Does the man not notice you two? Has no one told him?" she asked.

Ligish answered, her voice low and soft. "Marut sees what he wants to see. I have had several days to observe him."

"Did you observe what my sister did to Enti-Ilzi?" Kisare blinked. She hadn't meant to say that.

"I found the scene shortly after," Ligish said. Still she gripped Bel's hand. "It is not as unusual as you would think. You know not what the nobles are capable of."

"I was a sl—" Kisare felt Gemeti's presence behind her, remembered where they were. She hissed the word. "Slave. I know very well what they do."

"Not all." Bel's eyebrows were drawn down, eyes burning into her. "Not nearly all."

"I have learned—"

"Maybe this is a good time to discuss what we found with Hbelu," Gemeti interrupted Kisare.

Bel's expression vanished in an instant. "You found Hbelu?" Kisare nodded, trying to order her thoughts at the quick change in topic.

"How is he?"

"He is whole," Kisare said, and detailed what they had discovered, how the girl Erishti found Hbelu, how they found Ahiyaba's spirit, and the confusing question of parentage.

"So this girl has agreed to help us?" Bel cocked her head.

"Not necessarily," Gemeti answered. "She knows the Asha-Urmana's status, and believes they should be equal to the nobles, at least according to Ishkun-Dim-Hbelu."

"This could end up being more harmful than helpful," Ligish said. Bel nodded agreement.

"But she *agrees* with us. She's in a position of power." Kisare opened both hands. Didn't they see how that improved their chances? Bel had her arms folded, Ligish hanging on her as much as Bel had hung on Marut. Kisare thought seriously about dragging Hbelu off whether he wanted to leave or not.

A shrill whistle came from the center of the room, and nobles drifted that direction, trailed by servants and slaves. Kisare rubbed gooseflesh on her arms. They had no more time.

The four made their way through nobles with small streaks of color, then larger ones. As they passed to the concentrated ring of two- and three-color nobles surrounding the dais, the ranks parted for the sisters. A few even greeted them.

The Dyad once again sat in their respective seats, each dressed in white silk gowns, decorated with designs of godfruit. Maybe they were the ones they'd worn the first night, or maybe they were new ones. As

Kisare and her sister approached, Sibi was in whispered conversation with a slave. The nobles around her were talking, obviously as curious as she was.

"Now go," Sibi straightened, and the slave bowed deeply, the iron collar around his neck clanking as he moved. He was well dressed in a cotton tunic, emblazoned with the swirl of colors signifying the Dyad. Was he proud of his position? Did he feel superior to other slaves?

The slave ran off, and Ishta addressed the collected nobles.

Ishta rubbed her hands like a little girl expecting a stick of candy. "In anticipation of the presents you will later bring us this evening, we have our own surprise." She scanned the crowd, pointing out a slight noble with a shock of silver and black coiffured above her face. "You. You like surprises, do you not?"

The noble hastily nodded, glancing around for support. Several others edged away.

"I think we should ask Gallamta," Sibi put in. "He hates surprises."

Ishta grinned and addressed a large man near the front of the crowd. Kisare could see a silk vest covering his sizeable paunch. He had at least two hair colors, if not more. Ishta straightened from her slouch, putting on a petulant face. "Master of Arms Sar-Abu-Gallamta, please relate exactly how much you despise our little surprises."

The man stiffened in anger or embarrassment. "Forgive me, my lady, but I would much rather relate the positions of the caravanners who are surrounding Karduniash. We fear they are planning—"

Ishta waved a hand. "We have been tracking the Asha-Urmana for weeks. They were beaten back before and will be again."

Sibi leaned forward. "In fact, you provide us a magnificent segue. You are a true master of strategy." Gallamta set his shoulders and crossed his arms. "These caravanners, who insist on using the outdated name for their people, these Asha-Urmana will soon have reason to acknowledge the might and power of the nobles. It is fortunate they choose this time to creep closer to our capital. Soon they will see we have accomplished what has never before been done in the history of our people!"

He waved one arm out to his side, where the slave was returning with four tall, strong, bleached blonds, wearing their ever-present iron collars. Each pair held a long pole between their shoulders. A wooden base connected the rods, with a box on top of it, but masked in hanging purple curtains. The slaves moved solemnly, never letting the poles or their burden waver, approaching through the limbs of the malus and citron trees. They mounted the dais, setting down their burden between the godfruitwood thrones, then faded away.

The Dyad stood, each with one hand on the top of the curtains. In unison, they pulled, and the purple fabric fell to each side.

Gasps rose from the assembled nobles, and Kisare's head swiveled to Gemeti. Gemeti's mouth hung open, eyes wide.

"I thought you said her hair was all purple."

In a chair smaller than those of the Dyad, but similarly carved from wood of godfruit trees, sat Erishti. Then the girl stood, looking both left and right as if to make eye contact with every noble present, showing off her full head of long hair. Though the lock in front, stretching from temple to temple, was as purple as Hbelu's hair, Kisare saw black and red on one side, and silver and brown on the other. All five magical hair colors.

"Stupid," Gemeti hissed. "If she is Ishta and Ahiyaba's daughter, then she has all five colors, not just one. The Dyad must have dyed it all purple to encourage false rumors."

Sibi spread one hand to encompass the assembled nobles. "For all of you worryknots so obsessed with the movements of the Asha-Urmana, here is your panacea. The might of the nobles will conquer all, now we control every shade of the gods' magic." He closed his fist and Kisare snuck a glance over her shoulder to see hundreds of nobles, all shocked to silence.

"Tonight, we announce for the first time, our daughter by blood." Ishta waggled a finger at the nobles. She took Sibi's hand behind the girl's head. "Yes, we have heard your whispers and little plots. Asking for interviews, visits to our sanctuary—" She pointed the same finger at the skylight above the dais. "Now, the time for secrecy is over. Now, you know." In a moment, Ishta's face shaded to one of fury. "Poking around at all hours, ferreting out what is hidden. You all are—"

"Tonight is a special occasion," Sibi broke in over his sister's words. Kisare shot Bel a glance at the paranoia in Ishta's voice, which her sister returned, one eyebrow raised. Ligish sucked in a slow breath behind them.

"Gods blast it all," Gemeti muttered. "I should have realized." She didn't seem to have heard the pronouncement.

Sibi turned to the girl. "Introduce yourself."

The girl spoke in a loud, clear voice, carrying over the hushed whispers of the nobles. "I am Samsu-Iluna-Aya-Erishti, full blood daughter of Samsu-Iluna-Nur-Sibi and Samsu-Iluna-Nur-Ishta," she said. "I serve the nobles of Karduniash, waiting for when I inherit the throne of my parents." She looked at Sibi, and then at Ishta. The Dyad let each other's hand go as Erishti reached up, clasping her parents' forearms.

"The gods have blessed us," Ishta called out. "The caravanners will fall because the gods no longer speak to them. Instead, they pass the power on to us, through the conception of our *lovely* daughter." Rather than full of love, the expression she turned to Erishti could better be described as...hungry.

So, this was their ally. Kisare closed her eyes for a moment, swallowing the sick feeling in her throat. Had the girl told everything to her parents?

"My children shall have hair in all the colors of the gods, and the caravanners shall bow before us. I shall be the mother of a new reign of stronger nobles." Erishti held her head high, looking out on her future subjects. "My parents have given me leave to choose my own, most capable consorts. Finally, we will be at peace, as prophesied by the gods before they departed." She sat down, followed by the Dyad.

"We have given you our own present this year," Sibi said. "One of peace and strength."

"Go and celebrate." Ishta waved a hand outward, as if to shoo the mass of nobles away from her. "We look forward to the end of the evening." She smiled wickedly. "I wait to see if anyone has a gift grander than this—but I doubt it." She settled back in her chair.

Kisare resisted the movement of the crowd, letting silk clothes slide past her cotton dress with a hiss of fabric on fabric. Her feet seemed fastened to the floor. "We don't know how much Erishti told them," she said to her sister. "What if they already know about Hbelu? About us?" Bel shushed her, and Kisare glared back. The nobles around them were talking so loudly they couldn't possibly hear what she said.

"We cannot do anything about it," Bel answered, and Ligish nodded behind her. "If we try to leave now and the Dyad know, we will only draw them like a fox to a lame chicken." On the dais, Erishti beamed at Ishta, who had a hand over her arm, clutching it possessively.

At that moment Amilanu slid through the crowd to their right, locking eyes with her, then giving a brief nod to Gemeti behind them. Gemeti had finally looked up, her brows knitted together. She scanned the crowd for something.

"This is not what I expected," the Master of Planning said, his pale face red with anger. "I was as much a fool as the rest. I will have to discuss with the others. This changes how—"

Marut appeared on Bel's other side. "You nearly made me miss the announcement," he said, thrusting a vial at Bel. He hadn't gotten one for Kisare. "I had to stand in the back with the singles," he sneered. "Imagine, finally giving the caravanners what they deserve. Soon, they shall be a part of the empire, rather than annoying our cities and attempting to bribe us." He glared at Amilanu, who straightened, thick mustache bristling.

Kisare needed to get rid of the worm-wrangler. Amilanu might be an ally to their cause, but Marut certainly was not. "I think we need to talk, sister to sister," she told Bel, trying to give the right import to her words. Bel's face did not change expression.

"Maybe we should discuss this impending domination over the caravanners," Amilanu said to Marut, "one member of the court to another."

"Come now, in the middle of the festival? Even you are not that stuffy, Amilanu," Marut said.

"The ladies want to be alone for a minute, Marut," Amilanu countered.

"I am certain they do not mind my presence. Do you mind, my dear?" he asked Bel. Kisare folded her arms.

"Certainly, I do not," Bel answered him sweetly. She gestured to Kisare. "But as you can see, my sister is a little more private with matters of our family. You recall what I told you."

Marut's face blanched a little. "I see. Then I shall give you a moment to address your...issues." He turned to the big man opposite him. "Come, Amilanu. Shall we see if Zar and Bani are free for some wagering on the nature of gifts tonight?"

"Nothing would please me further." The Master of Planning gave Kisare a long-suffering look when Marut couldn't see and followed.

"What did you tell Marut?" Kisare asked.

"Not important," Bel answered, waving a hand. "What do we need to discuss?"

"Where that child came from," Gemeti said behind them. She stood on tiptoes, fixed on one point like a dog after a bird.

"The girl must be loyal to them," Kisare said, only remembering to lower her voice at the last second. "What's to stop them from taking the seed and using it for their own means?"

"We were supposed to have Hbelu with us, not captured by Aricaba-Ata," Bel answered. "That part of your plan is already changed."

"Is Abala-Ninsun still in charge of the Dyad's well-being?" Gemeti asked Ligish.

The shadow looked startled. "The Dyad? No. But she is Lord Marut's personal physician."

Kisare ignored them. "*My* plan?" she asked her sister. "I suppose you will just make it up as you go along?"

Bel shrugged.

"Oh, you're useless!" Kisare threw her hands into the air.

"Those two grafted saplings probably got tired of her and cast her off," Gemeti said. "Back when I was around, Ninsun knew more secrets than she let on."

"I still have the box," Bel said. "This is all we truly need. Neither the nobles' strategies nor the Asha-Urmana's need interfere with us. It is ours by right." There was a strange gleam in Bel's eye.

"If you two are done dawdling..." Gemeti broke in.

"What?" Kisare asked, annoyed.

"I would like your sister to take us to the edge of the crowd, right there." Gemeti pointed over the heads of the nobles and past the dais. "See that old crone with the streak of black?"

Bel craned her neck and surprise played over her face for a second. "I think so. Hold steady," she said, then raised the vial Marut gave her to her lips, sipped, and grabbed Kisare's and Ligish's arms. Gemeti took Bel's shoulder. Before Kisare could even gasp, they were in the rear of the hall.

Kisare exhaled. "Never do that to me again," she said. Bel swallowed.

They were next to an ancient woman, even older than Gemeti, her face a mass of wrinkles, especially around her mouth and under her flattened nose. If she was surprised by the sudden appearance of four women, she didn't show it. Her eyes took in all of them, resting longest on Gemeti, and Bel, for some reason.

"Ninsun, you old witch—" Gemeti began.

"Ha. I would not think they would let you back in, Gem," the woman answered, taking Gemeti's hands in hers. "I see you have finally joined us old crones rather than the clueless lords. It suits your devious mind much better." Then she addressed Bel. "Still holding up? Not too much stress today? Or last night?" One side of her colorless lips lifted in a knowing smirk.

Bel inclined her head. "Still feeling quite well, thanks to you." Kisare stared between them. Bel *knew* this woman? How many people had she met in the capital?

"Did you see that prunus flower show?" Gemeti sounded like she was talking through her teeth, and Kisare realized she had juice in her mouth.

The wrinkled woman nodded. "Bet it was a blow to you and your...friends."

Gemeti shrugged, taking her hands back. "You do not seem as surprised by the announcement as other nobles. Should I guess you know something of the child's conception?"

Ninsun raised both eyebrows and scratched her whiskered chin. "You tell me. How many of my memories have you sifted through with that morus juice in your mouth?"

Kisare was lost. "What? What does she know?"

Ninsun waved a gnarled hand. "Bah. It will come out soon enough. Take what you need. One more caravanner corpse the Dyad has buried under their trees."

"Ahiyaba was not lying," Gemeti said, incredulous. "Both he *and* Sibi are fathers to Erishti. Ishta birthed the child herself."

"How do you know?" Bel asked.

Gemeti pointed. "Abala-Ninsun was there. She assisted with the conception. A complex..." She shook her head.

Ninsun sighed. "You never had enough black to make training you worthwhile. If you had a bit more, I could have made you the next physician to the Dyad." She waved a finger in their direction. "None of this goes farther than you, hear?" Her finger settled on Gemeti. "It has been nice to be free of your schemes, these years."

She addressed them all. "Yes, the caravanner is the girl's father. The process had many steps but was rather simple in its genius. One of my better plans, I thought. Ishta merely had to lie with both men, one after the other—a simple request, for her. The work came after that. I had perfected the procedure on pigs bought from a local farm. I and three others planted the two seeds in the same pot, so to speak. Just needed a steady supply of godfruit, and all four colors. A red moved the father's seeds together in Ishti's womb with a malus, then a brown-hair merged the two together with a citron. A little air from a silver and water from me, some healing, and the red with a prunus to see whether our scheme was working." She shrugged. "Nine months later, Erishti was born healthy. Unfortunately, those two were not sufficiently stable to keep their captive whole enough to make a second child." The woman shook her head.

Kisare tried to keep everything together in her head, but she still couldn't quite follow the woman. Maybe if she wrote it down...

"Ingenious," Gemeti said. "Then the girl is legitimate."

"Oh yes," Ninsun answered. "She can use all five colors." She gave Gemeti a wicked smile. "As I said, a blow to your friends. Try getting your caravanners around this."

"Our way of life *will* change," Gemeti said, but Ninsun only laughed. Gemeti grimaced and took a step back. "I think we have used up enough of your time."

Kisare agreed. She moved away with the women, trying to keep up with Bel and Ligish.

"Remember to come for another treatment," Ninsun called from behind them. Bel stiffened in front of Kisare.

"What does that mean?" Kisare asked.

"Not important," Bel said.

"No." Kisare half ran to get in front of her sister, blocking her way. Gemeti was in front, grumbling. Ligish looked like she might rush to Bel's aid, but Kisare locked eyes with her, daring her to do something. She was Bel's *sister*. She deserved an explanation. Finally, the black-clad shadow looked away.

"Now—what happened?" Kisare asked her sister.

"Ilzi happened." Bel said shortly. "You saw how he can—could—create disease."

"That woman healed you of it?"

Bel tilted her head. "Not completely. I...don't know fully." Her shoulders slumped.

"And what of Marut?" Kisare put her hands on her hips. They needed to free themselves from the nobles.

Bel's eyes blazed. "You mean does he take advantage?" She spat on the floor. "No. He's a bore, but he's not that vile." She hefted the oil-paper package under her arm. "We can change that, with this."

Kisare swallowed. "If I never protected you from Ilzi, did I at least keep Aricaba-Ata from you?"

Bel's face showed something then, guilt or embarrassment. "Kisa, I want to tell you something—" She got no farther. A great cry went up from the nobles, almost a cheer, a battle cry. Kisare's head whipped around, scouting for signs of danger.

"He is here," Bel said.

* * *

Belili could just see the top of Aricaba-Ata's head from their vantage point. She knew that separated lock of red, combed down on both sides of his head. A mass of purple followed him.

Kisa was already moving toward the dais, and Belili felt a pang of guilt in not telling her about Aricaba-Ata, or the red she had inherited.

The nobles were cheering Aricaba-Ata, and once they got closer, Belili could see why. He was followed by his toadying collection of nobles and Shuma, who led Hbelu, naked, by an iron chain attached to the collar around his neck. He looked clean, though they had shaved his goatee down to stubble.

"Look at him!" Kisa growled to her. "They didn't need to strip him!" Then she gasped. "The godfruit Gemeti left him—it's gone."

"He was planning to do what with it?" Belili asked.

"I don't know," Kisa answered, pounding one fist into her thigh. "I should have argued harder for him to escape with me. We could have been long gone by now. At least they gave him a bath."

"This way," Belili said, drawing Kisa to one side. She crossed behind the mass of the crowd, the other two women following. They ended near the dais.

Ishta's arms were crossed, and Belili eyed the full bowl of godfruit near her. The Dyad were more powerful than anyone else in the hall, with the possible exceptions of Hbelu and their daughter, though Hbelu only had access to one set of abilities. Each godfruit the girl ate would give her five different powers. Was she then more powerful than her parents? Or did control count for more? If only Belili had learned more of her magic. She reached for Ligish's hand, felt the comforting presence of the other woman.

"What is it?" Ligish asked quietly. Belili only shook her head. The girl between the Dyad was staring at Hbelu, eyes bright. The next few minutes could go very right, or very wrong.

"This is not going as I expected," Ishta said from the dais. "He is early. I dislike when things do not go as I expect."

Belili felt in her pouch, loaded with godfruit from several tables. Her fingers touched a candied citron slice. Overwhelming strength with red hair, passing through other objects with brown. She could move through anyone who tried to stop her and pull down the Dyad. Malus. Fire to rend them and earth to bury them.

Sibi ate a morus as she watched, his eyes glancing around the room. Then they snapped to her. Instantly her mind felt pressed, like another was trying to share her head. Sibi mouthed something, but she heard it like tolling bells inside her head.

Far stronger have tried against us. Do not make me crush you, little one. My sister has a fondness for you.

Belili staggered back as the presence left her. She hadn't thought to hide anything. Had he seen their true origins? Their plans? Did he care? Belili let Ligish's hand go, felt her nails dig into the palms of her hands. She took one step toward the dais, but Sibi had a malus slice to his mouth. The very air of the room resisted her. Sweat broke out on her brow as she struggled, and her fingers buzzed as if she held them too near a flame.

I can char you from the inside out before you lift a finger. Be glad my sister is enraptured in her approaching present. She is not as gentle with over-ambitious noblings as I am.

Belili sagged again as Sibi left her, breathing hard. So much power. How could any of them fight the Dyad? A finger touched her shoulder and she nearly shouted.

"He's coming, Bel," Kisa said. While she had struggled against the Dyad's hold, the crowd let Ata and his retinue come close. She spared one last look for Sibi, but he paid her no attention. Could even Hbelu make the Dyad do anything against their will?

Aricaba-Ata stopped a respectful distance away from the dais, though his umber complexion was mottled with rage. The other nobles, one with red and a bushy beard, another with black and a snide smile, and a tall and attractive woman with silver, stood behind him. Shuma pulled Hbelu to a stumbling halt on his chain. Whispers went through the crowd, and nobles gestured. Hbelu kept his eyes down.

"I said I would return on the morrow and I have, with my present for you, my lord and lady." Aricaba-Ata straightened his broad shoulders, his chin high, trying and failing to smile.

"You are too early," Ishta said. "You spoil our festival, though the prize you bring is pretty." She considered Hbelu.

Aricaba-Ata's face fell further, but he pressed on. Belili saw his eyes dart to Erishti, glancing over her hair. "My gift is worth a great amount, and I have suffered the loss of much wealth to bring him before you—"

"Yes, yes, you have an Asha-Urmana. We have done better. You should have come to our announcement before wasting our time." Sibi waved Ata's claim away, but Hbelu's head came up, taking in the girl sitting between the Dyad. His brows drew down, then climbed. His mouth worked, and his eyes quested for Belili's and Kisa's, then down to the oil-paper-covered box Belili held.

"This man is free," Kisa spoke into the silence. "It is Aricaba-Ata who should be in chains."

Belili's eyes widened and ripples of gasps and muttering passed through the gathered nobles. Why now, of all times, had Kisa spoken her mind?

Belili saw Ishta's eyes flick toward them and settle on Kisa. "Hold your tongue," she said. "If Sibi did not like you so much, you would be dead." Her face was calm, as if saying she was hungry, or tired.

"But Aricaba-Ata took this free man captive and made him a slave." Kisa was ignoring Belili shaking her shoulder. "If nobles can make slaves of others, how does your government even stand?"

Belili watched Ishta's face grow dark as her sister spoke, but Sibi only laughed. "Little nobles of the Blasted Lands. You are all slaves of the Dyad," he said. There was muttering in the crowd of nobles, but less than Belili expected. "We are the only free ones in this land, my sister and I. And now our daughter. The rest of you are more or less a slave, depending on your station." Sibi gestured to Aricaba-Ata. "This man claims you two were slaves and escaped him. The details bore me, and I care not whether it is true"—she saw her former master stiffen at this—"but it proves my point. If slaves can be nobles, then obviously nobles can become slaves."

Hbelu spoke up for the first time. His voice was gravelly from disuse, but still strong enough to carry over the crowd. "I am no slave. Currently I may be held prisoner, but I am free." He rattled his manacles. "These chains, the lack of clothes—these do not change my self-regard."

He might have said more, but Aricaba-Ata backhanded Hbelu across the mouth. Belili saw a spray of red. "You have no say here, caravanner." He raised his hand again, but Sibi motioned, and he stopped.

"I have not had a good philosophical discussion in ages," he said. His sister rolled her eyes but said nothing. She reached for a malus slice. "The rest of these nobles are mere bootlickers." Sibi gestured to Hbelu, motioned to his side. "I expect you have questions about our daughter. Approach, and we can discuss how she changes the relationship between Asha-Urmana and the noble class. Finally, our peoples can be united."

Aricaba-Ata spluttered and stepped forward but rocked back as if he had hit a brick wall. He tried to speak, but no sound came out. Belili saw Ishta frowning at the man, meditatively chewing the malus slice.

Sibi snapped his fingers. "Someone get the man a covering. Fine a specimen as he is, I wish to separate when I am discussing politics and when I am planning to take another man from the rear."

There was a smattering of laughter at the joke and a slave ran forward with a rough spun tunic, long enough to make Hbelu decent. The slave held it out for him, forcing Shuma to orbit around them, still holding the chain.

When Hbelu was dressed he walked to the step of the dais, and Ata's guard captain gave up keeping him back. The chain clanked on the floor as Hbelu bent to Erishti. She shrank back into Ishta's embrace, and Kisa tensed, as if she would go to them. Belili stopped her.

"Well, Erishti, you are full of surprises." Hbelu spoke loud enough for all to hear. "If you had a choice, would you rather live where you will be a target for assassins, sold out to the best potential mate, or would you rather be free to explore your own path, learning what you will and going where you may better yourself? I can offer you that choice, among my people."

"Come now," Sibi said, "what of your edict excluding those without purple hair from your caravans? You claim the gods told you this, though I have never heard it. Do you still have their ear? I yearn to talk with them—to discuss what they think of our fair civilization."

"I am afraid we no longer speak with the gods," Hbelu answered.

"Then for what reason do you consider yourself so holy, so much above the rest of us?" Ishta asked. She was holding Erishti close, like a stuffed toy. "Why did you ever rule here? You have but one of the five hair colors. We have all. We are more powerful, more fit to rule."

"A fair point, but you could let the girl answer for herself," Hbelu said.

Ata and his crowd, forced to the side, were dour. Something would break there, soon. Belili would be ready.

"I...I stand with my parents, naturally," Erishti said. Her voice was not as strong as earlier.

"I could show you true freedom," Hbelu told her, still ignoring her parents. "I know not how you came by all five colors, but you can be a bridge between our peoples, as your father says, though not in the way he intends." Belili darted a glance at her sister. Hbelu had been eager to jump to that conclusion.

"Our daughter's birth was only possible by the combined might of the nobles," Sibi said. "What do you have that we cannot take?"

"You have only this one girl." Hbelu finally looked away from Erishti and to Sibi. "We may not speak directly with the gods," Hbelu answered, "but we still commune with the supernatural." Ishta snorted at this, and even Sibi looked unbelieving.

"It is true," Hbelu insisted. "Give me a slice of malus and I will show you the ghosts and spirits with whom I can speak."

Sibi idly picked through his bowl of godfruit, but Ata made a strangled noise and pushed forward. This time Ishta did not hold him back.

"Do not do it, my lord," he cried. He held up a wrist, crisscrossed with angry scars fading to white. "Their ghosts inflict terrible pain on those they touch." Sibi slowly raised his hand from the bowl, and Hbelu continued as if there were no interruption.

"While we see the spirits of those passed on, we also see the marks left by the gods themselves." He gestured with both hands, chains clinking, at the godfruit trees around them. "Did you know each magical tree bears the mark of the god who created it? The malus, that of Kigal. The prunus, that of Geshtna." He looked back to the Dyad, then out over the crowd. Belili was struck by his bearing, even chained and ragged as he was. "True, we do not mix our blood with that of other magical peoples. Though you may gain a greater breadth of power"—he motioned to the Dyad and their daughter—"the power held therein is lessened. Your color is not as strong in your children as the blond is. Whenever there is a mixture, there is always more of the blond."

The crowd was muttering, but Belili observed, with so many two and three-colors present, that those with a single color often had a lock bigger than those with two colors, combined.

"If you did not dye your hair, you would have less color than I do," he addressed the Dyad. "Your daughter may have all five colors, but as you dyed her hair purple, how much have you accentuated the colors she has?" There were gasps from the crowd, and Ishta did not look happy, but Sibi waved them off.

"I concede your point," he told Hbelu, "but is it not worth more to access many powers than be stronger with such limits?"

"You will lose that power eventually," Hbelu answered. "And with it any hope of ever speaking to the gods again."

Kisa leaned toward the dais as if she might run to join them. Belili knew this was the time, and Hbelu had given her an opening. She transferred the box to both hands and unwrapped it. She nudged Kisa, who looked her way, then saw what she was doing and nodded.

"We have a present for you as well, my lord and lady," Belili said, holding the warm box forward. "In light of what you discuss, I think it may be pertinent. It holds the marks of the gods, I am told. Perhaps the Asha-Urmana can help us decipher it."

Sibi blinked and Belili thought he would strike her down for interrupting, but Ishta gestured with both hands. "Bring it here, pretty sister," she said. "Anything to stop this tedious discussion."

Belili stepped forward, her sister next to her. She was gambling their freedom and likely their life on this, but with Erishti, there was no real hope for the Asha-Urmana. Only the fifth godfruit could change the path of events.

CHAPTER TWENTY-EIGHT

Fruit of the Gods

At the end of everything, magic is the right of the gods. It can be given, and it can be taken away.

Kisare held her head high, shoulders back. "The Asha-Urmana can answer your wager between my sister and me, and Aricaba-Ata." She doubted the two would give a malus slice to Hbelu after Ata's warning, but it was worth a try.

Instead, her former master pushed close enough she could smell his sharp scent, so familiar from years of working under him.

"May we know where this extravagant gift came from?" he asked. "Surely two minor *nobles* from the Blasted Lands cannot have such a store of great wealth." He sneered at the title.

"It is no matter," Kisare answered, taking care to speak like a noble.

"It matters," Ishta said. She was leaning out, across the dais, the child held too close. Erishti did not squirm, but looked uncomfortable. Kisare's mind raced to think of details.

"It is a family heirloom," Bel said, and Kisare let out a breath. How was she always so quick with an explanation?

"An heirloom?" Ata scoffed. "You have no family. How could it be passed to you?"

"It once belonged to my father, and my father's father," Bel answered him. She seemed smug, and Kisare saw rage on the man's face.

"This I can verify," came a voice from the crowd of nobles, and Kisare was surprised to see the worm-master step forward. He brushed past Ligish to put a hand on Bel's arm. "Anagmeshu-Bel told me of her history with this black-hearted noble, and how he attempted to subsume the sisters' right to their own lands." He glared at Ata.

"I think we are starting not to like the sound of you, little noble," Ishta said to Ata. She folded her arms, releasing the girl, and Ata shrank back, his eyes darting to Waqrat and the other nobles with him. The black-haired one took a step away. "Well, let us have it then." Ishta nodded to the front of the dais with her chin. "Put it there, where I can see your gift."

Kisare shared a look with Bel. She avoided glancing to Hbelu, standing beside Sibi. She hoped he was ready. She hoped he knew what he was doing.

Bel placed the little box on the dais. "We give this to you both freely," she said. "Once an heirloom of our family, now it is yours."

Ishta nodded to a collared slave, who ran forward to pick up the box. The slave raised it above his head, so all the assembled nobles could see the Dyad's present. The low noise of the room grew. It was obviously old, and its travels gave it an aura of mystery, in Kisare's opinion.

Ishta received the box from the slave, her eyes large as she looked it over. She dismissed the slave with a curt nod, and the collared blond, hair long and untidy, darted behind the godfruitwood thrones. She opened the lid, and Sibi popped up from his seat, craning his neck.

"Dirt? Made from ashes of the most powerful nobles in the Blasted Lands, if your sister had anything to do with it." Ishta frowned. "A fine gift, but not one with bearing on what we discuss."

"Not the dirt, my lady, though it is very good," Kisare said. "The treasure is beneath the soil." She saw Hbelu shift, positioning himself closer.

"What treasure?" Ishta asked slowly. She was not convinced yet.

"A seed, my lady," Bel said.

"We have seeds," Sibi answered. He gestured with a prunus for emphasis.

"This one is different—" Kisare began, but she stumbled forward at a shove from behind, hands out to meet the ground.

"I know that box!" Aricaba-Ata roared. "My grandfather told me of *his* grandfather finding it and burying it again. It is danger! It is death!"

"What he speaks is nonsense, as always," Hbelu cut in. He reached toward the box, clutched in Ishta's hands. "I can show you the marks of the gods on it."

Kisare scrambled up from the floor just in time to miss the gout of flame erupting from Aricaba-Ata's hand. "Get the caravanner away from it!" he roared.

Neither Sibi nor Ishta were prepared for the outburst. Both leaned back, but the fire washed over them and Hbelu, wilting the leaves and mori on the right of the dais and charring the budding malus branches to the left.

By the time Kisare was up, Bel was standing in front of the dais, blocking further attacks. She had a malus to her mouth, biting down. Two large nobles restrained Ata's hands, and he struggled against them.

"It will kill us all!" he screamed, then breathed fire.

Kisare ducked, and saw the fire head straight to her sister. *Block it with a spike of earth!*

Bel raised her hand, and the blast of flame curled up and away, scorching the ceiling above them.

How had Bel done that? More nobles, and even chained slaves, grabbed at Aricaba-Ata. One struck him across the face. He struggled, speaking of death and destruction, but did not call more fire. Guards ran from the edges of the room, arriving too late to help, and several nobles attended to the burnt trees.

Behind Bel, the Dyad rose to their feet, unharmed. Sibi waved the guards down, but they stayed close. Ishta moved an arm, sheathed in a long sleeve of the shiny white fabric. It revealed Erishti, also unharmed, hidden behind the silk. The box was in her other hand.

Hbelu did not rise, and Kisare craned her neck. Marut pushed forward, bowing to the Dyad. "I am so thankful you wear the robes my silkworms made. Now we have proof of their safety. Only the best silkworms, fed on godfruit, spun your robes. They are able to stop any magic."

"We thank you for your protection," Sibi told him. Even Ishta gave him a serious nod.

"Where is he?" Kisare asked. She tried to push Bel aside—she couldn't see the floor of the dais. "What happened?" Bel shook her head, but Kisare pushed her aside.

"It will destroy the order of things," Aricaba-Ata raved behind her. His voice sounded hoarse and parched. "The box will let the caravanners rule!" There was another slap and his voice died away.

Kisare climbed up next to Hbelu, ignoring the Dyad. Hbelu's face was blackened, his loaned coat nearly burnt away. Most of his hair was gone, his scalp charred. Kisare crawled around to cradle his burned head. His eyes were closed. She watched his chest. No movement.

"Help him!" she demanded of the Dyad, but they paid no attention, listening to Aricaba-Ata's protestations about the box.

"Go!" she yelled at a slave standing behind the thrones. "Get bandages, and water." The slave didn't move. She gritted her teeth. "Do you want the Dyad's present to die?"

The slave looked at her for a long moment, then sprinted away.

Kisare reached for Sibi's bowl of godfruit, above her head. It was too far away, and she had no black hair anyway.

"Here, girl." Gemeti's voice came between the citron and malus trees. She had a citron already peeled. "Move off. You cannot help. I will treat him as I may."

Kisare let Hbelu's head down gently to the stone of the dais. Gemeti was already reaching for him with hands ringed in lightning, her mouth full. Kisare stood, reaching into the bowl of godfruit. Sibi was focused on Ata. She picked up citron slices, malus, and morus. She left the prunus, not wanting to smell Hbelu's burned flesh any clearer.

Kisare chewed as she walked forward, stuffing all the godfruit she could in her mouth, letting the juice and lightning fill her, shaking with the power. Hands reached as she walked, but she danced out of their way with the citron. She became hidden to the eyes of others with the morus, and the hands fell short. Winds of the malus blew around her. She felt a pressure in her mind, and slowed, the air resisting her. Both were unfocused. The Dyad would have to see her to stop her. She only needed two more steps...

She became visible in front of Ata, who was still raging, spittle decorating his chin. Others held him and her fist came up at the perfect angle to close his teeth with a clack. Ata staggered back as she hit him again and again.

Someone yelled at her to stop. She thought it was one of the Dyad. They would use godfruit next.

She slammed a fist down and felt his collar bone crack. Ata collapsed with a cry. Even then she kicked out at his knees, his groin, his—

"Stop, Kisare!"

Her fist paused, and her breath came in gasps. It had been Bel's voice this time. Her lungs felt as if they couldn't get enough air. She swallowed, and the magic drained from her. Kisare spit the pulp out on Ata's bloody face. She had broken his nose and a few teeth.

"Kisa, I tried to tell you before..." Bel was right behind her.

Kisare spun to her. "What? What were you going to—" Then it clicked. Bel, standing, holding off Ata's flame.

"Gods of the seasons," she said. "You have red. You're his daughter." She had never known her father. Thought neither of them had. Her eyes flicked to the amputated pinky on Bel's left hand. So many things made sense. She was shaking. Nobles jabbered at her, plucked at her clothes, but she couldn't understand the words they said.

Bel nodded once. "While the old bastard deserves death, I do not think this is the time or the place. Take it from me." Hbelu's description of Ilzi's battered body floated through Kisare's mind.

"Everyone, please calm," said a high voice into the clamor, and Kisare looked up at that. Unbidden, the tension left her.

"We need not have violence here." The voice was Erishti's. "We must instead integrate our peoples." The sentiment suddenly made sense. Kisare shook droplets of Ata's blood from her hands, peering past Bel. All the nobles were looking to the dais. The Dyad watched their daughter, and even Ata had stopped groaning. As she watched, the girl ate a morus, holding the juice in her cheek.

"We must all work together. These sisters have given us a great gift, and it is a shame not to let Ishkun-Dim-Hbelu tell us of its worth," Erishti said. Kisare felt a spike of pride. They had brought a magnificent gift. The girl pulled at her father's hand, revealing Gemeti hunched over Hbelu. He stirred weakly beneath her arms and Kisare shuffled forward.

"If you are healed enough, Prince of the Asha-Urmana, then we should see what this precious seed does," Erishti said, and some of the nobles nodded. Ishta looked thoughtful. "I believe the sisters may know what to do. Shall we ask?"

"Yes, we shall ask," Sibi said, as if the idea was his.

Erishti was looking at her and Bel. She ate another berry and the compulsion to please the girl grew stronger. They went to the dais, and Kisare helped Gemeti bring Hbelu wincing and gasping to his feet. Gemeti had not been able to heal him completely.

Hbelu's lips curled upward, breaking a forming scab. A drop of blood squeezed out, and Kisare longed to wipe it away. It would only hurt him more.

"Charisma," Hbelu whispered to her, then jerked his head toward Erishti.

Kisare realized the entire hall was silent, staring at her and her sister. "We need the seed." Ishta already had a malus slice, and at Kisare's words, the little pip bobbed to the top of the dirt. Hbelu's eyes closed for a moment, then opened again and he drew in a shuddering breath.

"We believe this seed is a new kind of godfruit," Bel said. Suddenly nobles were talking again.

"Another godfruit?" Sibi asked. "From where?"

"What should we do next?" Erishti broke in and put another morus in her mouth. She looked between her parents.

"This seed requires the touch of all five colors to make it grow," Kisare said. "It is why we had to bring it as a gift."

"So the gods *did* intend cooperation between us and the Asha-Urmana," Sibi said. Hbelu raised what remained of his eyebrows and gave a tilt of his head to the Dyad. A valid point.

"Then shall we give them their wish?" Erishti asked, and Sibi was nodding even before she finished the question. The girl was eating godfruits every few moments, and Kisare wondered at the effort to keep this entire group of nobles agreeing to these suggestions. Were even the Dyad familiar with all the powers of purple hair?

"All three of you must touch the seed," Kisare said, and the Dyad leaned in to do as she said, each laying a finger on the edge of the tiny seed. It glowed, brighter than she had seen it before, and as Hbelu leaned forward with a grunt of pain and added his own finger, the seed's shine grew almost blinding. Then it diminished.

They all waited a moment.

"Is that it?" Ishta asked.

Kisare looked to Bel. Was it?

"Even the godfruit trees blessed by the gods take time to grow, do they not?" Bel said. "Perhaps we must wait for this to sprout."

Ishta crossed her arms. "This is not nearly as exciting. Maybe at next year's Prunus Festival we can see what this thing does. I will have to amuse myself with you in the meantime, pretty sister."

She started to turn away from the box. Kisare was very aware of what would happen when the Dyad lost interest in them.

"May I, Mother?" Erishti asked. "Might it be the gods meant to see all five colors in one person, not simply cooperating?"

Hbelu's eyes were wide. "Has anyone told you that you are far wiser than your years?" His voice was a croak, nearly as burned as Ata.

Erishti smiled, lowering her head, then looked up at her parents. Sibi shrugged.

Almost before her small finger contacted the seed, the whole box in Ishta's hands began to glow. This time it was too bright even to look at.

"It is the god-glow," Hbelu breathed beside her.

The box trembled in Ishta's hand. A fragile green stem emerged, not nearly as bright as the seed had been.

"Mulagunna-Kis. Take the box." Kisare felt the full weight of Erishti's attention on her, and stepped forward before she knew she was agreeing. Ishta offered her the box.

The soil writhed inside, little roots pushing through the black earth. The shoot was half as tall as her hand now, growing, the glow diminishing.

"Water!" she shouted and jumped down from the dais. Someone pushed a glass of liquid into her hand, and she splashed it on the box. The plant only grew faster. Kisare turned her head from side to side, wondering what to do, then stopped. Her shoe brushed a different texture in the floor, and Amilanu's words sprang into her head.

There is a patch of bare dirt in front of the thrones, so that the rulers must cross it when mounting to their seats. It is said to remind them their power comes from the earth.

Kisare looked from tree to tree. The dirt made a pentagon with the other four around the dais. She knew what to do.

"Bel," she called as she knelt. "Malus." She looked up to the crowd of nobles. "More water."

At Bel's command, the hard, packed dirt, crossed by countless nobles and rulers, nearly as hard as the stone that surrounded it, roiled and churned to become freshly tilled. Someone brought a bowl of water, and Kisare pointed to the new planting bed. The water splashed her cotton dress, but she paid it no mind. The little plant strained against the sides of the box. She turned it over and shook the container, dislodging it.

The stalk lay on the earth, twisting like a snake. Kisare parted the now pliable dirt, making a hole. She placed the writhing, glowing tree in the cavity, pouring the good dirt from the box in after. Bel was beside her, guiding the stem straight and true.

Kisare stepped back, brushing dirt from her fingers. The box, blessed by all four gods, lay discarded to the side. Its contents had been buried properly.

Limbs grew off the main trunk, sprouting large and flat green leaves. Bel snapped off interior branches as she could reach them, evening out the canopy. The tree sprouted up like seconds were years.

"Stand back," a voice commanded, and Ishta stepped down from the dais. Kisare looked to Erishti, no longer chewing. Hbelu closed on the girl, speaking softly. Erishti nodded.

Sibi stepped down beside Bel, watching as the tree caught up in height and breadth to the other four trees around the dais. Buds grew, plumped, and burst into shining white five-petaled flowers, each bristling with stamens.

Sibi reached up, his hand receiving the first godfruit grown from the new tree. It was fleshy, changing from dark green to light green, to a pale yellow. It looked almost like the pears Ata grew in his orchard, and triggered a memory in Kisare.

The godfruit separated from the branch with a little *pop* and fell into Sibi's hand. As it did, its glow faded.

He twisted the godfruit and it broke, revealing a light red center, filled with seeds. He gave half to his sister and as one, they bit down, shivering. Little bands of lightning ran down the outside of their silk robes. The great festival hall was silent, but for the sounds of chewing.

"I feel...nothing," Sibi said. "What is this godfruit supposed to do? What is it called?"

Kisare could only shake her head. "I do not know."

"Then what use is this gift?" Ishta hissed. She threw the rest of the godfruit to the floor and stepped toward Kisare, who shrank back from her eyes. "Your presence here has caused enough disruption to our festival—"

"It is a guava," Bel said, and Ishta stopped her advance. "We saw them while traveling here."

Amilanu stepped out of the crowd of nobles. "The girl is correct," he said, holding up a finger. "It is not common, but the tree is—was—not magical. It grows in the southern climes, mainly near the coast. If we keep to the ancient names of the gods, we should call it a"—he cocked his head to the side, thinking—"a *psidium*."

* * *

Belili noticed the nobles holding Ata down were staring at the tree, their captive forgotten. Ata was conscious and glaring at them, slowly crawling backward. There was a table behind him with a large bowl of godfruit juice on it, filled almost to the brim.

"Watch him!" she yelled, but Ata pulled the bowl closer with his good hand, half-falling into the table. One of his knees seemed not to be working correctly after Kisa's beating and his other hand was clutched close, protecting his shoulder and collar.

"It will kill us all!" With a shout, her father dumped the bowl forward, juice drenching him, Ata holding his mouth open. Lightning ran down his skin, reacting with the juice dripping from him. He had always been a powerful man, and was now driven wild by hate and fear.

He reached toward the tree and it bent toward him. Plates, cups, and chairs rose in a storm around him, and then Ata himself rose, lifting his body with the mental power of the morus. Other nobles scrambled out of the way.

"You've done enough, nobling," Ishta snapped. Her eyes were cold and Belili could see the bulge in her cheek. Ishta raised a hand, but nothing happened. Her face paled, and her arm dropped.

"This abomination must be destroyed." Fire sprouted from Ata's fingers. He half floated, half limped toward the tree. Lightning crackled around him, throwing shadows in the glossy green leaves. With the strength of the citron, he could pull the freshly planted tree out by the roots. It had godfruit hanging in great clumps, more than it could realistically bear, as if the tree produced its entire crop at once.

Sibi was frowning too, and a servant stepped toward Ata with a candlestick held high, but Ata merely glanced in his direction and the man flew to the side. Belili stepped in front of the listing tree, guarding it. The trunk creaked, leaning toward him, and bumped into her back. As it did a single ripe godfruit fell. Belili caught it, and without thinking, she raised it to her lips and bit down.

The juice was fresh and sweet, and her eyes rolled back as she felt the lightning in her mouth. Then Aricaba-Ata was upon her, fire leaping toward her face. If only she had a few more seconds to discover what the psidium did.

The fire died, and her former master—her father—slowed, stumbling, pushing her into the rough bark of the tree as he fell. Belili saw the strength leech out of his hands, muscles relaxing. The plates and chairs whirling through the air clattered to the floor, and the new tree straightened. Ata landed on the floor with a crash.

"What—?" He looked at her in horror. "The magic is gone!" The juice of the new godfruit in Belili's mouth had turned bland at the same time. Ata drew a dagger from his belt with one hand and raised it to throw. "Get out of the way, Belili," he said. "I will not stop with a finger this time." Then his face went pale with rage...Belili frowned. No. He was afraid, of something behind her. Belili turned, and gasped, one hand coming to her throat.

Ilzi—alive. It can't be.

"Don't touch my sister!" It was Kisa, swinging the candlestick the servant had brandished. It cracked against Ata's head and he fell limp, blood pooling by his head. She panted and threw the candlestick to the side.

Belili pulled her mind back from the gibbering fear, making herself look at—*through*—Ilzi's body—his shade. Hbelu was on the dais, chewing, one hand outstretched. Ilzi's mangled form floated near the guava tree, shaking his head. The Dyad turned back, as Hbelu gestured sharply with one hand. The spirit flew off, still struggling, scattering the crowd. It disappeared through the wall of the ziggurat.

Ishta was staring at her hands as if they belonged to someone else.

"Guards!" Sibi called. His face was closed, eyebrows pulled down. Belili half thought he would strike her down on the spot, but his hands only flexed spasmodically.

The guava had stopped Ata's magic—negated it. Both of the Dyad had tried to use the juice, then used other godfruits. Could it be...?

"What have you done?" Sibi whispered. He put something in his mouth, and this time Belili felt a pressure on her mind. She still held the guava—the psidium—and took another bite. The pressure faded and Sibi's eyes widened.

The godfruit had negated their power for a few seconds. Which hair color triggered it? All of them? Or one in particular? She formed a guess.

"Tear that tree out!" Sibi commanded. "And bring me her head!" Ishta wobbled back, her gaze distant. On the stage, Hbelu gathered Erishti to him, and the girl did not resist.

Belili shared a look with Kisa, and they ran.

Hands grasped at her, tearing her silk dress, but the smooth fabric slipped away from them. Then a hand clamped on her biceps and swung her around. A brown-haired noble held her arm behind her back and marched her forward.

They had caught Kisa too, holding her before the dais, and Hbelu, Erishti and Gemeti were nearby, surrounded by guards. Even Amilanu had a noble holding his arm. Belili's eye sought Marut, still free, and searched the empty space behind him. She hoped Ligish had removed herself from view.

"This must be the precursor to the caravanners invading our city again," Ishta said, her face crumpling into an ugly grimace. She had recovered while they ran, fleeing prey focusing the predator's senses. "These *slaves* are obviously in league with them." She turned to her brother. "I told you. I told you they were trouble. Can we kill them? This once?" She brushed Sibi's face with a finger, tenderly, as if she had forgotten about anyone else.

Sibi took his sister's hand, kissed her finger, then took an entire citron from the bowl next to him. "We will pass sentence on these criminals, but first, there is a larger problem." The noble holding Belili pulled her back as Sibi headed for the tree.

"My lord." It was Marut, and Belili stared at him. He was the last person she expected to come to their defense. "Is it not at least worth studying the tree, to find out what its magic does with all hair colors? Maybe you did not..." He fell silent at Sibi's cold gaze.

"Do you believe I have made an error? That I am not competent to know what magic a godfruit contains within it?" He held Marut's gaze until the Master of Silkworms looked away.

"No. I deeply apologize, my lord." Belili gave the coward some credit for trying. It would not help his standing with the rest of the nobles. She tried not to look for his shadow, hoping help would come from that quarter.

Sibi walked slowly to the new tree, peeling the citron, taking the time to show he still held power.

Belili gave an experimental tug, but her captor held her fast. She could kick a foot back and up, but someone else would take his place.

Sibi left a trail of peel in his wake. All eyes were on him. He peeled off two sections of citron, let the rest of the godfruit fall to the ground, and chewed the slices. His chin lifted and his eyes closed briefly, lightning playing around him.

He stepped to the new tree, planting his feet on either side, hands on the trunk. He lifted, arms visibly straining. Belili stepped into the man behind her as she heard a deep crack. It went to the bottom of her stomach, twisting.

The crack became a ripping, tearing sound, and Belili looked away, to her sister. Kisa looked forward while a black-haired noble held her arms back. Belili saw tears on her cheeks.

There was a final crack and a massive thump that shook the floor, raising a cloud of dust and leaves. The beautiful tree lay on its side, past the morus on the right of the dais, godfruit spread across the floor. Leaves drifted down like feathers around the stump left in the square of dirt. All their effort, to this, so easily. The court was silent.

"*This* is what happens to those who rebel," Ishta spat. "*This* is why we rule. We have the power to do so. We control the blonds, by the will of the gods." She stepped to a collared slave and pulled him down by her side, shaking the chain attached to the collar. His head wobbled as she shook him, and his eyes were wide.

"You will be put to death," Sibi said, returning to his sister. Kisa struggled at the pronouncement, but her captors held her fast. Belili didn't bother. "So will the caravanner prince, and I see we must educate our daughter further." Sibi's frown at Erishti was almost concerned, almost sorry. "I believe we may have underestimated her power and loyalty."

"No matter," Ishta said. "We can make another, now." She walked to Hbelu and took his stubbly chin with one hand. "Maybe with this one, if I can convince my brother to keep you alive. Though perhaps without tongue and hands. You will not need those for what I intend." Hbelu pulled back, but Ishta crooked her finger, digging long nails into his skin. "Worry not about your little army," she said. "We have plenty of soldiers. There is nothing they can do. They will be beaten back, like last time, and the time before that. We will capture plenty of candidates to cement our claim over the caravanners."

Belili saw something from the edge of her vision. A mass of whitish hair; a ring of iron. The shape darted behind the fallen tree. She looked back to the Dyad, but several of the nobles had noticed too, heads turning.

"How will you murder us?" she asked. "I request you do it yourself." Ishta rubbed her hands together. She would probably enjoy it.

"No," Sibi said. "You are not worth my time."

"You will not even use your magic on us?" Belili let her contempt show on her face. "That is the only thing you hold over your slaves, is it not?"

Kisa stepped forward. "This tree would have changed that. This is why you are so scared!" Another shape darted, and Belili heard clinking chains. Briefly, she thought she saw the black-clad form of Ligish.

"At least have the decency to use your power for this," Hbelu added. "I am a prince of my people. I *deserve* this." Belili smiled as she saw another shape move behind the fallen tree. Some of the nobles were backing away, muttering, but the Dyad weren't paying attention. With all the guards in the room clustered close around the dais, the slaves would be momentarily free of observation.

"So what if we *are* slaves?" she said. There were gasps from the crowd, and she turned to them, spreading her hands. "That's right. We were raised in an orchard. Nothing to our names. We were property. We fooled you all."

"And you hadn't a clue," Kisa joined in. "You control them with magic." She pointed a finger to the crowd of nobles. "Anything you don't agree with, you smash." She looked at the tree.

There were no slaves left behind the thrones. Shadows moved in the rear of the room, where the canopy of the tree lay crushed, godfruit spread far. Some of the slaves must have guessed as she did.

"Silence!" Sibi stalked toward them, his face dark. "You dare to belittle us, in the seat of our power?"

"We do," Hbelu said. "So do they." He pointed to the back of the room. Many slaves held one of the dropped godfruits. Ligish and a few nobles were with them, mostly ones with little color. "After you kill us, you will have to kill them. Can you prevent all word leaving this room? People will talk of what happened here. It will give your prisoners hope. There are more of them than of you." He smiled, slowly. "If you knew more of the gods, you would realize that if this godfruit is like the other four, *all* guavas are now *psidia.*"

"We are the ones with the magic!" Ishta screamed.

"Are you?" Belili asked. A few of the nobles in the crowd around them were taking out weapons, but not many. This was supposed to be a festival. More went for the bowls of godfruit and juice. "Go ahead. Test it out against them."

"You little bitch!" Ishta snatched a malus from the bowl near her and turned, biting into it. Fire blossomed from her hands, not toward the slaves, but toward Belili. She threw an arm up over her face.

There was no heat.

When she peered through her fingers, Ishta's face was dumbfounded. There was a slave beside her—the girl who had picked the wrong godfruit for Ishta the day before—a true blond. She held one of the new godfruits, and there was a bite out of it.

"We have magic," she said into the stillness of the festival hall. "Godfruit that gives power only to blond hair. The gods did not forget us!"

The slaves and nobles in the back of the room crept closer, many of them holding psidia. A few picked up chairs and bottles.

"Guards!" Sibi roared, and the soldiers surrounding the dais pivoted outward, unsheathing swords and maces. This would not be a battle won with godfruit. The guards had swords, but there were many more slaves. Nobles were slipping from the festival hall, and Belili saw chained slaves slipping in. Servants with the spiral on their chest joined them. How many were there in the palace? Hundreds? Thousands?

"As for you..." Ishta was still facing them, and her brother turned back.

"Go." It was Amilanu. He was surrounded by slaves and servants, all holding weapons. He had a spiked mace. "They are under my protection," he stated to the room. He advanced on the dais, and the nobles holding Belili and Kisa thought better of their choices. Hbelu, Erishti, and Gemeti came to join them.

Belili watched the slaves and guards as she backed away from the dais. The nobles around them were becoming scarce, either fleeing or joining the slaves. Ata lay unconscious, by the felled tree. Belili didn't care whether he survived the night or was dead already. The Dyad looked furious, both with godfruit in their hands.

"Here." Kisa thrust something into her hand. It was half a psidium. Belili took a bite, shivering as the juice washed through her mouth. She held it ready, tasting the sweet flavor, her eyes constantly moving.

The guards engaged the slaves and nobles, and a clatter of metal and flesh rang through the hall. The sharp tang of oiled metal—or maybe blood—reached Belili. Many slaves would die today. A scream of pain tore through the air.

"You will not leave. I forbid it." Ishta had a vial of liquid in her hand and drank. Belili stepped in front of the others and felt *something* splash against her, then dissipate. Kisa was beside her, chewing, her eyes wide. Amilanu, across from them, raised a hand and rocked back, but held his ground. Ishta's eyes widened.

"No! We are the Dyad! We are the strongest! Sweet Brother, tell them—" Her words were cut short with a gurgle. A length of metal protruded from her chest—a fireplace poker.

A slave stepped from behind Ishta as she slumped forward.

"Sister!" Sibi gestured, and the slave's head exploded. Belili backed up. There was still some taste to the juice in her mouth. Sibi ran to his sister's body.

As if Ishta's death was the real trigger, not the fighting in the back of the room, the rest of the nobles erupted around them, some joining the fight, some running away. No one touched them.

"That door will bring you down the back stairs," Amilanu said, pointing out an entrance on one wall. "Take the prince with you. He will need to tell his people what has happened." Belili nodded at Amilanu and turned away.

"Gemeti, are you coming?" Kisa asked.

Belili turned back to see the old woman shake her head. "My place is here, helping the slaves. This is where I should have stayed, years ago." She hefted a table leg.

"Erishti?" Belili's sister looked to the child.

"I will come with you." Erishti looked worried. "I do not believe my paren—my father—will be as forgiving as he once was."

"Quickly now," Amilanu said. He moved away as Sibi rose, face contorted, and Gemeti joined the crowd around him.

Belili pushed Kisa ahead of her, Hbelu and Erishti to her side. Together they ran. Belili felt something at her back, and the juice in her mouth lost its taste abruptly. Kisa stumbled, but kept going.

At the door, a shape shimmered and Belili caught her breath. Then Ligish appeared and took her hand. She had a glass bowl of godfruit clutched under one arm, all *five* kinds represented. Belili breathed out noisily, and they barged through the door.

"Marut?" Belili asked the woman beside her.

Ligish shook her head. "He will find a place to hide. He is a survivor."

The halls of the palace were in chaos, but Hbelu led them, with Erishti commanding slaves and nobles out of her way. Most obeyed, and any who didn't were swayed by the size of their group. As they descended, the hallways grew more deserted.

The night air was a shock to Belili as they exited the palace. The guards were gone from their posts, several clumps fighting with slaves. A few slaves brought psidia down, yellow-green skin barely visible in the torchlight.

Then Belili realized where the light was really coming from—a glow reflecting off the walls of the city.

"Fire!" yelled Kisa, pointing almost at the same moment as Belili saw it.

"It is my people," Hbelu told them. "Though he protested, I commanded Ilzi's ghost to tell them when to start the assault, and of the fifth godfruit growing. If we are lucky, they will have learned the effects already. I believe I saw psidium trees on the road outside the city."

"So the man was useful for something," Kisa said, and Belili snorted a laugh.

"Come. We need to navigate Karduniash," Ligish said. "I would rather not stay in one place."

"My people are at the walls, and the citizens will be unprepared from celebrating. It should be easy to cut across the city." Hbelu took Erishti's hand. For once, the girl looked small and lost. He bent to her. "Will you come with us? You can become to the Asha-Urmana what the Dyad could never truly recognize: a bridge between our peoples, and a sign that the gods have once again given us a path."

Erishti paused, then nodded. "I have no place here." She flipped her multicolored hair. "With the psidia, this will be less impressive than my parents think. If I can help my two peoples reunite, then I can at least be of use."

Epilogue

The gods removed themselves from mortal affairs. That did not mean they never again observed their creations.

"Take this to the scouts at the front," Hbelu said. He gave the parchment with the latest military movements to the soldier. The Asha-Urmana, not one he was familiar with, nodded and ran off, her boots thumping on the earth.

Around him, the camp was alive like a wasps' nest knocked from a limb. Their wagons, wheels chocked, made a massive circle around Karduniash. In the two weeks since the fighting had begun, almost all the caravans had joined, save his own. They were due in another ten days. Their blockade had no access to year-round godfruit like the nobles still fighting over the ziggurat, but there was enough traffic between former prisoners, servants, and fourcolors joining them to have a steady influx even of malae and citrons. Psidia were readily available.

Most of the fighting was with traditional weapons, as it had always been. Now, thanks to the blond former prisoners, the overwhelming magical advantage of the fourcolors was easy to counter. Most of the blonds were eager to join in, though there were still a baffling few who stayed with their former masters, and it was difficult at times to separate the spies from those genuinely wishing to join them.

Hbelu nodded to the two soldiers guarding the entrance to the large tent of waxed cotton. He brushed aside the flap, and strode in, interrupting an argument.

"So, you would have us mix with the nobles, and give up the only thing that has held our identity together these centuries?" Mushezibti-Lila sat as usual, her twisted legs folded beneath her on a raised platform. She addressed a slightly younger man, though both had white strands in their purple hair and were older than Hbelu, more experienced. He held to his title of prince as a shield.

"It only makes sense, Lila," the man said. "This girl has paved the way by her birth. We have survived longer than in any other assault.

The fourcolors' power is breaking." He spotted Hbelu. "You agree with me, do you not?"

"I do, Ziral-Barital," Hbelu said. "Though Mushezibti-Lila's point is valid. It will take many years to adjust our people's view on mixing with the fourcolors."

"Not that long," Barital answered. The older man pushed his spectacles up his nose. "I already see our soldiers fighting side by side with fourcolors and blonds. I cannot observe them all night."

"No self-respecting Asha-Urmana would do such a thing," Lila said, swiping one hand through the air.

"They have, Lila," Hbelu said, gently. His thoughts went to Kisare. "Erishti's activation of the fifth godfruit shows the gods wish us to work together. It is only a matter of time, no matter what you say."

"The gods indeed," Lila snorted. "From what you tell us, the godfruit may have been activated by you and the Dyad, not the girl. It may not be necessary to *breed* with them." Lila's brows drew down.

Hbelu tilted his head slightly, acknowledging the point. "Despite this matter, I have more news from inside Karduniash." Lila crossed her arms, but Barital looked interested.

"Do tell," he said.

"The latest prisoners who come to us speak of a coalition of fourcolors with three colors in their hair. There is still no sign of Sibi, but they may be hiding him. Amilanu holds half the lower levels, but the coalition has a way out to the city. Also, it seems the Dyad left some magical artifacts in their private chambers."

"It is only a matter of time until we take back Karduniash," Lila said. "One thing I will agree with you on, Hbelu, we would not have gotten any farther than the last time without the help of the blonds and the fifth godfruit."

Hbelu accepted the partial compromise. "Then we will see what else we agree on in the future."

* * *

Belili sighed as Ligish rolled away, letting cool air come between them.

"Stay with me," she said.

Ligish shook her head. "No time, greedy woman." She ran a hand down Belili's side. "My shift is due, and I am certain the one I replace wants to rest."

"You did not have to volunteer to act as shadow for the Asha-Urmana," Belili said. She tried to keep the grumble from her voice. After months of running and years of imprisonment, she was ready to take time at ease.

"I *wanted* to," Ligish said. "I like to work for others. It gives me purpose."

Belili tried to answer but a fit of coughing took her. When she finished, Ligish was back by her side.

"Have you been to the black-hairs yet?" she asked. Belili shook her head, one hand to her chest.

"Abala-Ninsun told you the sickness would need more attention. Go to them. You have plenty of time, while I am on patrol."

"Fine, fine," Belili said, rolling to a sitting position. "You will not stay to help me recover?"

Ligish sent her a wry glance before she pulled on her tunic. "I will be back in a few hours."

"I know," Belili answered. "Go on. The more information you can gather on the nobles, the sooner Hbelu can break their hold on the capital."

Ligish gave her a smile and left. Belili watched her hips as she left their small tent. Even if the fighting never stopped, she was free to make her own choices, and that was all that mattered.

* * *

Kisare returned to her tent at the same time as Hbelu. "You're early. Has Mushezibti-Lila changed her ways at last?"

Hbelu shook his head. "No, and I cannot stay long. The elders have a conference later this night, and I must keep them aware of all sides, not just that of the Asha-Urmana."

"You would think they could make an exception for one who helped break the rule of the nobles."

They entered Kisare's tent, but Hbelu only took her hand once they were inside. "Our ways are changing," he said, "but slowly. Give it time." He looked around the small tent. "Where is Erishti?"

Kisare gestured with her free hand. "Out somewhere," she said. "She's been helping with the planting schedule I've made up. By all the gods, I don't think those nobles know a carrot from an onion. If we're staying for a siege, we need to have seeds and crops ready to plant. At least it's warmer this far south."

"Give them time," Hbelu repeated. It was his mantra lately.

"Ah," Kisare took her hand back. "I saw Nidintu today. She's just come in ahead of your caravan. Charming as ever." She frowned.

Hbelu let out a sigh. "Finally."

"But that's not the news," Kisare said. Hbelu looked down at her. His hair was filling in after being burned off, and he had opted for a full beard this time, rather than the braided goatee. She wasn't sure how much she liked it.

"She says word came through the caravan from their farthest ranging scouts. There was a story of a giant woman seen on the very edge of the Blasted Lands. The rumor has already made it through Neharda and caught up with the caravan yesterday."

Hbelu cocked his head. "Could it be?"

Kisare shrugged. "No one knows for certain. It is Geshtna's season. She hasn't been seen in living memory, but who else could it be?" She shrugged, negating her own question. "Kigal, I suppose, but autumn is still far away."

Hbelu shook his head. "If the gods have returned with the activation of their godfruit, then all things are possible. Truly it is a time of change."

Appendix

According to studies done through a set of magnifying glass lenses, the color of what is termed "magical" hair is all one solid shade, with no variation between individuals. Nor does it have any of the gradation of normal blond hair pigment, but acts as a permanent dye, albeit one that cannot be washed out, and grows out as normal hair does.

—From the journal of Anagmeshu-Ea, Elder to the Asha-Urmana, caravan located in the Ashur mountains north of Karduniash

From the writings of Hillalum-Shum, court philosopher to the dyad:

There are five known colors of hair that grant the owner abilities, the four "noble" colors: Red, Brown, Black, and Silver, and the "caravanner" color: Purple, only seen on the nomadic individuals that come to trade in our cities.

There are, also, four fruit tree species blessed by the gods:

Morus, Genus Morus, producing in spring and associated with the god Dumzi

Prunus, Genus Prunus, producing in summer and associated with the goddess Geshtna

Malus, Genus Malus, producing in autumn and associated with the goddess Kigal

Citron, Genus Citrus, producing in the winter and associated with the god Enta

It is notable that the godfruits are all from different genera, and thus have resisted any attempts to cross-breed them. Indeed, these trees always breed true and new ones may be grown by seed from the parent tree. A new tree will refuse to produce when within a certain radius of another godfruit tree of the same type, so care must be taken to place the trees at appropriate distances.

New godfruit trees cannot be grown by normal methods of plant propagation. Because of their magical nature, the seeds must be "activated" by the touch of one with magical ability along with the juice of a godfruit distilled from that same type of tree. For obvious reasons, this method is not shared with the blond slaves.

Godfruit tree yields tend to be greater than that of non-magical flora, and the godfruit stays fresh much longer. This must be assumed to be part of the blessing bestowed by the gods. Yields, in general, on a good year and a mature tree, can be approximated as such:

Morus: 7,000 godfruits per tree

Prunus: 2,000 godfruits per tree

Malus: 500 godfruits per tree

Citron: 500 godfruits per tree

However, because the trees can only be planted a certain distance apart, this limits the number of possible godfruits grown per year.

Now, combining the magical hair colors and magical godfruit types, it is easy to create a chart of all the combinations allowed. The challenge is then to fill the table with the abilities given to us by the gods. There is a common children's rhyme which gives some insight:

> *Dumzi, the trickster, put his guile in the morus. Our minds gain unearthly powers to serve us.*

> *Geshtna's passions are always intense. Her prunae increase all five of the senses.*

> *Kigal can call all the elements to her. The malus' juice gives them out to the user.*

> *Enta, old man winter, is hard as leather. His citrons make our bodies fitter, stronger, deadlier.*

Though of course this verse does not give enough specifics to be very useful. However, through my travels and studies, I have, for your perusal, filled the aforementioned chart with my best simple descriptions of the abilities granted.

Godfruit	Morus	Prunus	Malus	Citron
God	Dumzi	Geshtna	Kigal	Enta
Season	Spring	Summer	Autumn	Winter
Category	Mental	Senses	Elemental	Body
Hair Color	**Power**	**Power**	**Power**	**Power**
Blond	None	None	None	None
Red	Telekinesis	Sight	Fire	Strength
Brown	Teleportation	Hearing	Earth	Phasing
Black	Telepathy	Taste	Water	Healing/ Disease
Silver	Invisibility	Smell	Air	Balance
Purple	Charisma	Touch	Contact spirits	Growth

ACKNOWLEDGEMENTS

I can say with certainty that this was the hardest book I've written so far. It started with the gardening skills I've developed over the years, passed to me from my mother, also an avid gardener. What if seasonal fruit gave magical powers? How would it affect society?

Then, a trip to the Charleston Museum with my sister and my spouse gave me more fuel in the form of artifacts from the antebellum South and how that slave-owning culture developed. It also gave me the idea of a "name-rail" marking where a person has died. It used to be the practice to plant the headboard of the bed in which the person died. Go look it up!

With a dash of Babylonian mythology and a pair of spunky sisters, this book emerged. It's changed quite a bit in its iterations and many thanks go to the crew of Reading Excuses for critiquing and feedback, especially Robinksi. Also, special thanks to J.S. Fields and Reese Hogan for in-depth critique and beta reading.

Update for the 2023 Edition:

I'm so happy to finally re-publish the edition of this book I really wanted to see out in the world. The original published version did not include chapters eight, eleven, fourteen, seventeen, twenty, and twenty-three. Chapter twenty-six was told from Kisare's point of view. Re-introducing Hbelu's part of the story, once hidden (much like Psidia) gives a depth to the world, and a larger peek into how the nobles see themselves and vie for power. In addition, the fantastic cover art from Moorbooks finally gives the vision I want for this book, an epic tale of gods, plants, sisters, seasons, and a changing society. Thanks for reading!

William C. Tracy

ABOUT THE AUTHOR

William C. Tracy writes and publishes queer science fiction and fantasy through his indie press Space Wizard Science Fantasy (spacewizardsciencefantasy.com).

His largest work is the Dissolutionverse: a space opera with music-based magic, including ten books and an RPG. He also has a standalone epic fantasy with seasonal fruit-based magic, a nonfiction book about body mechanics and correct posture, and a hard sci-fi trilogy, The Biomass Conflux, about generational colony ships and a planet covered by a sentient fungal entity.

William is an NC native and a lifelong fan of science fiction and fantasy. He has a master's in mechanical engineering, and has both designed and operated heavy construction machinery. He has also trained in Wado-Ryu karate since 2003 and runs his own dojo in Raleigh NC. He is an avid video and board gamer, a beekeeper, a reader, and of course, a writer.

You can get a free Dissolutionverse novelette by signing up for William's mailing list at spacewizardsciencefantasy.com

Follow him on Bluesky (wctracy.bsky.social) and Twitter (@wctracy) for writing updates, cat and bee pictures, and thoughts on martial arts.

Please take a moment to review this book at your favorite retailer's website, Goodreads, or simply tell your friends!

Printed in the USA
CPSIA information can be obtained
at www.ICGtesting.com
LVHW051916210224
772491LV00007B/26